Hope Returns

D1522638

Carolyn Digh Griffin

PRESS

Acknowledgments

Thanks to my husband, Hoyle. You have been a constant source of knowledge and support during this writing adventure. You're the best!

Lori, Mark, Leah, and Andrew Edgerton—Julie, Brian, Brian, Jr., and Seth Hunter—thanks for your constant support during this writing project. A special thanks to Leah for the lovely art work.

George, Mary, and Walter Digh, thanks for believing in me.

Thanks to the friend who critiqued my writing and encouraged me to press on.

Ruth and David Winn, Susan and Keith Wagoner, and the Empty Nesters at Calvary Church, thanks for your encouragement and prayer support, especially Leslie Christian, Eleanor Henderson, Beth Hargett, and Diane and Wyn Harter for your writing suggestions.

Dave Thomas, thank you for keeping my computer running.

Drs. Ed Davis, Mary Ellis, Roger Ashford, and Mr. Johnathan Moultrie—those endless hours working with you prepared me for this life-changing adventure. Thanks!

This book is dedicated to the memory of my parents,
Julius and Pauline Digh
By their example they taught me the true meaning of
forgiveness, faith in God, and the power of prayer.

Chapter 1

T he world was dark outside, and soft moonbeams filtered through the windows in the hospital room that night. I watched as my dear sweet mama struggled to hang onto life, knowing I was witnessing something that would be etched in my memory forever. She was so frail from the ravaging cancer that had invaded her beautiful body, and I had been at her bedside day and night for a week.

While I rested my head on the side of her bed, I carefully took her hand in mine. I tried to remain awake, but I was so exhausted, I slowly succumbed to sleep.

I dreamed I was walking through a meadow of beautiful spring flowers when I heard someone calling my name.

"Hope, Hope, where are you?"

Suddenly, my dreamland became muddled with reality. In a few moments, I recognized my surroundings and realized I was at my mama's bedside in her hospital room.

With only the moonlight shining on Mama's helpless body, she placed her hand on my head and continued to call out to me. I stood up and leaned closer to reassure her that I was there by her side. She became very agitated and frantically attempted to sit up in bed.

Where did that burst of energy come from? I asked myself. She had not spoken in several days and had hardly moved in the last two days. I gently tried to push Mama back down in the bed when she grabbed the front of my blouse in desperation and drew me closer to her.

As she desperately gripped my blouse, she looked into my eyes and whispered, "Hope, please promise me you will go back to Grandpa and Grandma Martin's and find the journal."

"Mama, what are you talking about? What journal? Please try to relax. Just calm down and tell me what you're talking about," I replied anxiously.

At first I thought she might be hallucinating, but I soon realized, for the first time in several days, Mama was completely alert and aware of her surroundings. *Why was she so disturbed and agitated?* I knew from her appearance she was absolutely coherent. She was holding onto me as if she were holding onto a lifeline in the middle of a raging sea.

Face to face with Mama, she began to explain her frantic state of mind. "Hope, your grandma kept a journal throughout her entire married life, and she wanted you to have it. You know Ma's mind was almost gone before she died, and she couldn't remember where she put the journal. I'm sure it's in the old farmhouse where I grew up.

"Honey, you must have realized by now that the old home place will be yours when I'm gone. I know my time is drawing to a close, and you will be the only Martin left. I know you have your music and your teaching, but you must go to Martinsville. You must preserve our heritage, and, most importantly, find your grandma's journal. She always kept the journal in her bedroom. She showed it to me one time as a child, but I never saw it again."

Mama stopped talking for a moment and began gasping for breath. As she continued to cough and struggle to breathe, she released her grip on my blouse. I immediately readjusted her oxygen to make sure the tubes were in place.

Between coughs and labored breathing, she attempted to finish telling me about the journal. "Hope, I have t-t-t-to finish telling you this. Please let me finish. You have to listen. When your g-g-g-grandma was dying, she told me to find her j-j-j-journal and keep it for you. She kept saying something about a family secret that must be u-u-u-uncovered."

Mama again began coughing, and as I adjusted her pillows, she attempted to speak between coughing spasms. "Your grandma would not tell me what the secret was, but you know that her mind had g-g-g-gotten bad before she died. She couldn't remember where she and Pa h-h-h-hid the journal. Your daddy and I practically tore the house apart looking for it, but it was nowhere to be found. Hope, I have no idea what mystery surrounds our family, but she did say the journal would change our lives forever. Please try to find it. I know you c-c-c-can.

"Your grandma became confused and started rambling on about someone named Prissy. She said something about snow being deep and Amos being gone. Just before she died, she kept mumbling, 'My child, my child, my child.' And then she was gone. Hope, there is something hidden in that old house, and you must find it for your grandma's sake. Please promise me you will go there f-f-f-for her sake and mine. You must fix up the old house and farm and start a new life there. Please!"

I squeezed my mama's hand and assured her I would carry out her wishes. In my heart I was feeling so much grief and anger. She was making me promise to do something I did not want to do.

Mama began to relax somewhat and fell into a deep sleep. A few moments later, I noticed that her breathing began to change. She seemed to be struggling more, so I readjusted her oxygen tubes and took her hand in mine. As I stood there beside her bed watching her struggle to breathe, I began to hear a definite change in her breathing pattern. I dropped my head as tears began to flow from my eyes. I looked up as she tried to speak.

Then I heard her feebly utter, "Find…Ma's….j-j-journal. Please!"

A few moments later I heard that same terrible "death rattle" that I had heard coming from Daddy's throat when he died six months earlier. There was no mistaking that horrific sound. It was a sound that would echo in my mind forever and could only originate in a place of torment. Cancer had stripped her of everything in life and racked her body with so much intense pain and suffering. I could not understand why any human being had experience such agony.

I stood there all alone that night and watched my beautiful mama slowly succumb to death. Standing beside her bed and watching her lifeless body, I knew I had no choice but to go back to the old home place and honor my mama's request.

The day my mama slipped into eternity and left me all alone, I experienced feelings I had never felt before. As I left her hospital room that day, I walked down that long corridor leading out of the hospital knowing that my life had changed forever. Mama had asked me to sacrifice my hopes and dreams to satisfy her own desires. Could I really do what she had asked me to do just before she died? I had no desire to move to Martinsville and pick up the pieces of my grandparents' legacy and start a new life.

I felt not only sorrow but anger. No, it was more than just sorrow and anger, I was furious. It didn't seem fair or reasonable for me to do what she had requested. I asked myself, *can I really leave my career behind and move to that God forsaken place in the foothills of the mountains of North Carolina? And why did she wait until she was dying to spring this on me? How could she do this to me?*

Two weeks after Mama's death, I found myself en route to Martinsville as she had requested. The grief had somehow overshadowed the anger, and I was coming to terms with what I had to do. I knew I had to get control of my depressing thoughts and anger; so I put in my favorite CD of classical music and directed my thoughts to the beautiful scenery along the roadside.

Early spring had always been my favorite time of year, and the countryside along the interstate from the Charlotte area was breathtaking that particular April Sunday morning. The trees and flowers along the road were bursting forth with vibrant shades of pink, red, and yellow. Monet could never have painted a picture as lovely as the scenes that lined the busy highway that day. As the cars and trucks whizzed by me on I-85, I occasionally managed to catch a glimpse of the lovely scenery. The deep rich color of the evergreens served as a backdrop for the other beautiful budding trees that were beginning to come alive in varied shades of green.

North Carolina had to be the loveliest place on earth in the springtime. Traveling with the top down on my car, my mid-length blonde hair was blowing in the breeze. My fair skin was turning beet red from the blazing sunshine, and I was sure I would have a million freckles by the end of the day. Even though my thoughts were consumed with Mama's death and her dying request, I managed somehow to enjoy the beautiful spring morning and was in the outskirts of Martinsville before I knew it.

Chapter 2

As I approached the circle drive of my grandparents' old farm house, I was overcome with an overwhelming sense of nostalgia. I pulled my little red sports car to the edge of the narrow dirt road at the entrance of the property and felt a fragrant gentle breeze on my face that smelled of honeysuckle vines and pine trees. The sweet-smelling breeze seemed to have a note of mystery and sadness about it as it filtered through the trees, and, for just a moment, I thought I could smell wood-smoke in the air.

It was a beautiful April morning, and the country air and sunshine gave me a tremendous sense of peace and serenity. It definitely was a sharp contrast to where I lived in Charlotte. There were no sounds of traffic or horns blowing, only the gentle breeze and the beautiful melody of birds singing in the trees. I could hear the soft sound of leaves and pine needles rustling as the fragrant breeze filtered through them. I could remember the joy I felt as a child when I was with my grandparents surrounded by country air and sunshine. Their old clapboard house, that stood facing me, was definitely in need of repair and several coats of paint. The circle drive in front of the house was overgrown with wild onions, Johnson grass, and other tall weeds.

I turned and spied some wild blackberry bushes blooming in the field beside of the house, and their tiny white flowers dotted the landscape as if an artist had painted them there. I was reminded, right away, of berry picking days with my grandma.

The direction of the wind changed, and I got an overpowering whiff of Grandma's old juniper bush. I couldn't believe it! There it was at the corner of the yard still alive and doing well. It was enormous! As I approached it, I realized it still reeked of that strong stench it always had. While standing there looking at the smelly old bush, a smile crossed my face. As a child, I thought it smelled like a cat's litter box. It definitely had a rancid catty smell. Grandpa would prune the old shrub back, but the pruning would only make it grow larger the next year. I never understood why anyone would want a juniper bush anywhere around their house.

The towering white pine trees in Grandma's front yard seemed to be weeping with a note of sadness. The lovely pinecones under the trees reminded me of huge teardrops, and the pungent fragrance of the pines, themselves, reminded me of the times I played beneath those majestic trees.

My cousins and I loved to rake the fragrant pine needles back and form walls for make-believe playhouses. We would carefully arrange the walls in the playhouse with narrow rows of pine needles, and Grandma would give us old cans and buckets to sit on for furniture. We even raided Grandpa's woodshed for scrap boards to prop on top of cans to make benches and tables. I could almost see myself under those aromatic trees as a little girl playing with my cousins and our baby dolls. We would play for hours in our fantasy home, and our imaginations would run wild as we pretended to sweep our floors and feed our dolls.

No one had lived in Grandma and Grandpa's farm house for years. In fact, no one had lived in the old house since Grandma died. The old home place had been in my family for four generations.

My ancestors left Tennessee in 1855 and forged their way through the valleys of the Appalachian Mountains by wagons and sleds. They settled in Rutherford County, North Carolina, in the foothills of the mountains. I recalled hearing Grandpa tell the story of his ancestors in his southern Appalachian brogue, as he held me on his lap. He was so proud of his heritage and was determined to keep it alive in my heart.

Grandpa was a tall stately man with beautiful gray hair and bright blue eyes. His handsome face had been weather beaten by years of hard work outdoors, but those wrinkles only added character to his appearance.

My heart began to swell with pride as I recalled many stories he used to tell me about my ancestors and family genealogy. There was one thing for sure, Grandpa was proud of his German-Scots-Irish ancestry, and he was equally proud of his country.

Grandpa and Grandma never lost their Appalachian dialect, which was a carryover from their German-Scots-Irish ancestry. Most of the people in Rutherford County, especially the old-timers, never lost the influence of those European countries in their speech. I smiled to myself as I recalled the way the people in that area pronounced Rutherford. They all seemed to pronounce it as Rullerford, and I never understood that pronunciation.

Grandpa loved to tell me stories about his ancestors and the old country, as he called it. He was especially proud of his German ancestry and the fact that Grandma was of German decent, also. Because of that, he often called me his little fraulein. He wanted to be sure I knew everything there was to know about my pedigree and my bloodline. I could still recollect the many times Grandpa told the story of the first Martin to arrive in America.

As he would begin the story, Grandpa would always say, *"Now, Hope, you pay close attention, 'cause this here is very*

*important. You need to know all about our people and where
we come from.*

*"On August 29, 1730, our first ancestor in America,
Johannes Ludwig Martin, on my pa's side of the family, come
to the new world from Europe on a sailin' ship called "The
Thistle of Glasgow." That boat wuz from Scotland and left
from Rotterdam by way of Dover and come to rest on the
coast of Pennsylvania. Johannes, his wife, Magdalena Koch,
and their fifteen chil'ren come to the new world not under-
standin' what they was a gittin' into.*

*"Now, Johannes and Magdalena just wanted to live in
a country where they could worship the Lord the way they
wanted to. Now, Johannes wuz a hard-shelled Baptist and
wuz a bein' persecuted in Germany 'cause of his religion.
It took 'em pirt'near six months to get to America. On their
long journey across the ocean, six of their chil'ren died from
pneumonia, and two died from the bloody flux. That's what
they called the dysentery back in 'em days. With all of his
chil'ren pirt'near gone, they put down roots in Pennsylvania
in a hamlet called Germantown, since they wuz from
Germany. Since the first settlers in Germantown were from
Germany, they decided to name their little town after the
country they come from. Germantown became a thriving
little town and more folks come there to settle.*

*"Hope, yore great-great-great-great-great-grandpa wuz
one of them chil'ren that didn't die on the journey across the
ocean. He wuz the baby in the family. His name was Benjamin
Martin, and his wife's name was Safronia Chapman. They
reared their ten chil'ren in Germantown. Now Safronia's
ancestors wuz from Ireland. Benjamin and Safronia had
one son who's name was Reuben Martin and his wife was
Rebecca Jones. Hope, now, that wuz yore great-great-great-
great-grandpa and grandma. They wuz like many of them
people who had settled in Germantown; they commenced to
scatter out everywhere in the new world a huntin' a place to*

live. It seemed near 'bout every last one of them wanted land to farm.

"So, Reuben and Rebecca left Pennsylvania with their eight chil'ren and come to Tennessee. They traveled the "The Great Wagon Road" that might near spread from Pennsylvania to Geo'gia, and they settled for a short spell in Tennessee. They later come on down across the mountains to Rullerford County with their son David and his family.
"Now, David was the only one of their eight chil'ren who put down roots in Rullerford County. The rest of the chil'ren went out west. David was yore great-great-great-grandpa, and his wife's name was Carrie Parkinson and her ancestors wuz from Scotland. Their only young'un was yore great-great grandpa, Henry Martin, and he was just a sprout when his pa and ma made that long hard journey through the valleys of the Appalachian Mountains in 1855.

"W'y, they had to cut their way through the mountains and ford many a stream to get to Rullerford County. They wuz faced with Indians and wild animals while they come across the mountains. I hear'd many a tale about them fightin' bears and wildcats. Them mountains wuz rough and rugged. W'y, David Martin even had a bear skin coat, and I'm sure they ate bear meat along the trail.

"The Indians wuz bitter toward the white man, and they had a right to be. W'y, our people just come in and took their land away from 'em. Many of the Indians wuz sent out west. President Andrew Jackson signed the Indian Removal Act of 1830, and just simply took their land away from them. He ordered the United States Army to round up the Indians like a herd of cows and they wuz sent out west. Might near four-thousand Indians died on that terrible journey. What didn't starve to death, died from many a disease and the cold mountain air. That trail they traveled is called the Trail of Tears.

"Yore great-great-grandpa, Henry, married Hester Philbeck from over near Rullerfordton. Back when he come here, there wasn't a lot of folks in this here neck of the woods. Land sakes, you could ride yore buggy or wagon for might near a hour or two and not see nary a soul. They settled ri'chear on this very land and raised yore great-grandpa. His name wuz William, and he wuz my pa.

"My Grandpa Henry lived in a little log cabin jist 'cross the road from where my house sits today. The only thing left of that log cabin is an old rock chimney.

"Yore great-great-grandpa, Henry, wuz a cotton farmer and a hard workin' man. He planted his cotton on every inch of this here land. Near 'bout everybody grew cotton 'round here back then, and that's why I always have a good size cotton patch. I followed every footstep my grandpa made until he died. My, how I loved that kind old man, and he taught me ever'thang I know'd 'bout farmin'.

"My pa married a fine-looking young lady from over near Bostic, and her name was Mary Elizabeth Gooding, yore great-grandma. Ma and Pa built a one room log cabin with a little kitchen at the back and settled ri'chear. That little cabin is part of this house that me and yore grandma live in. I built the front part of the house and connected it to the log cabin that my pa built. I turned the log cabin's sittin' room into the dining room and left the kitchen like it wuz."

Jolted back to reality by an old crow cawing in the pine trees behind me, I surveyed the old farm house that Grandpa was so proud of. The log portion of the house was located at the rear of the house, and the addition of the front portion occurred after my great-grandparents' deaths. Grandpa's remodeling of the log cabin was truly a labor of love, and Grandma often told me how Grandpa painstakingly made sure every board fitted correctly.

Grandpa was consumed with family history and genealogy; therefore, he felt the need to preserve the log portion of the farmhouse. He had the ingenious idea of turning the log cabin into the dining room and kitchen. He then added the front part of the house covering it with clapboards. It was architecturally different from most houses, but it was representative of two generations of North Carolina history.

As I stood there looking at the house, my mother's dying words again flooded my thoughts. Her death had been so recent, and it felt like a knife piercing my heart every time I thought of her.

Feeling like an abandoned orphan, I left immediately after Mama's funeral and began to make arrangements to do what she had requested. I turned in my resignation as a chorus teacher in Union County, North Carolina, and began to make preparations for coming to Rutherford County.

When I met with my principal, Dr. David Benson, he of course did not want me to resign. I informed him that I would take a few days and come to Martinsville to start the renovation process at the farm, but I would come back and finish out the school year.

I was finally doing what I had wanted to do all of my life, and resigning my teaching position was the most difficult thing I had ever done. In my heart I could not shake the devastating feeling that life had somehow thrown me a curve. I couldn't help but wonder why things had happened as they had.

I had inherited quite a bit of money as well as the farm. Financially, I had no worries. However, I felt cheated, because I was giving up my dreams.

Since Grandpa was an only child and my mother's only sibling, Uncle Cletus and his wife, Aunt Mary Lou, and their two children were killed in a car accident several years earlier, everything was left to me. I was the only surviving member of the family, and I had absolutely no one to turn to.

That nostalgic feeling returned as I remembered Grandpa and Grandma and how they had loved that old farmhouse. The seventy-five acre farm was located on a little dirt road leading off of the main highway going to Martinsville. Grandpa had farmed his land with love and care and took great pride in every clod of dirt, every stalk of corn, and every boll of cotton his land produced.

Mama often talked about the times she and Uncle Cletus helped Grandpa pick cotton and shuck corn. I heard her tell how Grandpa and his neighbors would work together at harvest time. When the corn was harvested, the community would gather around the old crib for a corn shucking. Grandma and the women would cook for days getting ready for the event. Oh, how their hearts would break if they could see what had become of their beloved home place.

As I stood there transfixed under the towering white pines, my thoughts went back to a happier time. I could still see my sweet grandpa coming out on the front piazza, which was what Grandpa always called the front porch, to greet us when my parents and I went for visits. That big piazza stretched across the entire width of the house. Grandpa never pronounced piazza correctly, but that was okay with me. He pronounced it "piazer."

As soon as his eyes fell on me, his wrinkled suntanned face would light up, and I would run into his arms. I always screamed with delight as he lifted me into the air. He and I shared the same birthday, and I think that strengthened our bond. He called me his "little birthday present from heaven." Oh, how I loved that dear old man. Just being in the presence of Grandpa gave me a feeling of security. He died from heart disease when I was sixteen years old, and Grandma followed him six months later. Nothing was ever the same after they were gone.

I closed my eyes and remembered the smells of the old farm. In the spring and summer, there was always the smell of honeysuckle vines, smoke from the wood-burning cook-stove, and Grandma's beautiful rosebushes.

Every time I entered their home, I could smell distinct odors that would enfold me and give me a sense of security and love. There was the sweet smell of lemon oil that Grandma always used to polish her furniture, and there was always the smell of Grandpa's Prince Albert pipe tobacco or Grandma's Society snuff. I tried to stay away from Grandma's spittoon as much as possible. I never forgot the time I tipped it over on its side. It was so-o-o disgusting, and I never understood how she could dip that nasty stuff.

I never forgot the day that Grandma caught my cousins and me trying to smoke Grandpa's pipe. That truly was a momentous day. We had taken the pipe and the Prince Albert tobacco tin to the woodshed that was connected to the crib for a little smoke. We even gathered some pine needles to chew on after we smoked, in hopes that the pine smell would remove the tobacco smell from our breath. We didn't use enough common sense to realize that someone might see or smell the smoke. Grandma evidently had gone to the outhouse, and she was on her way back to the kitchen when she smelled Prince Albert smoking tobacco rising from the woodshed.

She knew Grandpa was in the house, so she went in and told Grandpa what she suspected we were doing. When Grandpa arrived at the woodshed, we just knew he was going to tan our hides with the keen little hickory switch he held in his right hand. But when he saw all three of us lying prostrate on the ground, surrounded by pine needles and sick as we could be, he couldn't do anything but laugh.

He and Grandma gently picked each of us up and carried us into the house after we finished throwing up. They put all three of us to bed, and Grandma gave us sips of Coke to settle our stomachs. After that incident, I was never able to drink Cokes again. The smoking incident was never mentioned by

Grandma or Grandpa, and I always believed that they knew we had learned our lesson, and, as far as I knew, they never told our parents.

I remembered the mouth-watering aromas that emanated from Grandma's kitchen. The smell of sweet potatoes or biscuits baking and wood-smoke permeated the air. At any given time, one might find Grandma baking tea cakes or old fashioned ginger snaps, and she stored them in her old pie safe in the dining room.

Thanksgiving and Christmas were truly special occasions at the Martin household. Grandma never failed to cook a turkey with the traditional trimmings of homemade cornbread dressing, giblet gravy, and cranberry sauce. There was nothing like the smell of a turkey roasting in a woodstove.

A family tradition at Thanksgiving and Christmas in the Martin household was to have a fruit salad prepared from fresh fruit. It usually consisted of oranges, apples, bananas, grapes, and if Grandma could get them, plump juicy raisins. Grandpa would make a run into town to purchase the fresh fruit and raisins the day before the holiday meal. Grandma would cut up the fruit and mix it with a small amount of sugar, and, believe you me, that dish was fit for any king.

Grandma did all of the cooking on those special holidays. She would start several days in advance getting everything prepared for the big day by baking desserts. She usually had a fresh coconut cake, homemade apple pies, and pecan pies. The pecan pies were my favorite. They were thick, rich, and full of pecan halves. Holidays were not just holidays at my grandparents' home, they were major events.

Grandma always prepared an egg custard and a delicious lemon pound cake when she knew company was coming. Grandma's egg custards were cooked to perfection with tiny pats of melted butter on top. She would open a jar of her home canned peaches or strawberries to top off her pound cake. Everyone in the county agreed that she was the best cook in that neck of the woods. Her fried chicken and home-made apple pies were always winners at church socials and corn shuckings.

Every time we had a family meal, we would gather around the old claw-foot oak dining room table, and Grandpa would ask my daddy to give thanks for the food. It was only natural that Daddy do the honors, since he was a deacon in a little Baptist church in Raleigh where I grew up. No one could pray like my daddy. When he prayed, I thought he would never finish his prayers.

In those days, the adults always ate first. I never understood that. My cousins and I had to stay on the piazza or in the sitting room until the adults finished. I remember thinking to myself, *if they eat as long as Daddy prayed, we'll never get to eat!* Before the meal was over, we were starving to death. Our only hope was that something would be left for us to eat.

If Grandma had prepared fried chicken for the meal, Grandpa would always get the pulley bone from the platter, but he would never eat it. He knew it was my favorite piece of chicken.

When it came time for the children to eat, he would carefully place the pulley bone on my plate saying, "I ate might near all my food, but I jist couldn't eat this here last piece of chicken. Do you want it, Hope?"

What a sweet man he was! He was the best grandpa in the world.

I went to every grocery store in the Charlotte area looking for pulley bones, and no one knew what I was talking about. I had to explain to them that the pulley bone was the wish-bone connected to the breast of the chicken. They informed me that they would not cut up a chicken like that.

As a child, I loved to go in the backyard to play, and I distinctly remembered the smells behind the house. You could smell the aroma of hay and farm animals. Grandpa had two mules and several cows, and he had a name for every one of them. He would hitch his mules, Minnie and Jake, to the plow, and that's how he worked his farm. Bessie, his favorite milk cow, produced delicious milk for the farm.

Then there was the pungent, overpowering aroma of the old outhouse. It was a known fact, throughout the surrounding area, that Grandpa had the grandest outhouse in Martinsville. It was a "two-seater." Not many people had a "two-seater" outhouse in that day! As times began to change, they never installed indoor plumbing. They loved their life just as it was.

While I stood gazing at the house, I recalled the various sounds of the farm from years gone by. I could still hear that lonesome sound of the old train that ran below Grandpa's property. What a forlorn sound it made as it wound its way from the foothills of North Carolina toward the Blue Ridge Mountains. I remembered the many times I spent the night with my grandparents, and I could hear the train as it rumbled up the tracks that led to the mountains. It reminded me of distant drums. I often spent weeks with them in the summer, and at night my imagination would run wild as the train went by. I fully expected the entire Cherokee nation to come down from the mountains and get me. Even though I knew in my heart that the rumbling sound was only the train, I always imagined someone was coming after me. A smile crossed my face as I remembered how afraid I was. I would pull Grandma's homemade crazy quilt over my head until I fell asleep.

As I drew closer to the house, I heard the sound of rushing water. I thought about the many times Grandpa had taken me to the river below the barn to fish and throw rocks across the water. We would sometimes wander down the riverbank to the old train trestle that crossed over the river. I was terrified of that train and gigantic trestle. My grandparents never had to worry about me slipping off and getting on the railroad tracks.

My mama often told me the story of her calf, Maude, and how she wandered away one day and found herself on the train trestle. Needless to say, Maude never made it back, and I sure didn't want that to happen to me. Tears would fill Mama's eyes as she told me the story of Maude's demise on that old train trestle. She blamed herself, because she left the gate open in the pasture. After hearing that heart wrenching story of Grandpa finding Maude's body on the trestle, I never had a desire to go anywhere near the train tracks.

The sounds of the farm had been indelibly etched in my memory. The crowing of the roosters at dawn never bothered me at all, and the mooing of the cows and neighing of the mules were wonderful sounds to a little girl's ears.

I can still remember the chickens roosting in the trees in the backyard behind the "two-seater" outhouse. I never went barefooted at Grandpa's for fear of stepping in their "business," at least, that is what I called it as a child. It only took one time for me to step in their "business" and feel it squish between my toes for me to decide to never go barefooted at the farm again.

Grandpa had an old rooster that had the personality of a mad rattlesnake. That hateful old bird decided to chase me one day, and I barely made it to the back door. That old screen door slammed just as that mean old rooster flew toward it. He hit the door with such a bang; it knocked him flat on his back in the backyard. He staggered to a standing position, tucked his tail feathers between his legs, and hobbled toward the barn. I vividly remember how angry Grandpa was when he saw how upset I was. I don't think I ever saw him as mad as he was that day. By the way, we had chicken and dumplings for supper that night. It didn't dawn on me until I was much older that we had eaten that hateful old bird.

Most of those wonderful sights, smells, and sounds were gone and had become precious memories. The old train no longer went by the farm. Minnie and Jake were long gone, and Grandpa and Grandma were in heaven. My eyes filled with tears as I drew closer to the old house. I had never felt such loneliness. Truthfully, I had no one to turn to.

As I looked at the huge albatross that stood before me, I questioned why everything happened the way it had. I thought to myself, *what in the world will I do with seventy-five acres of farm land, dilapidated old out-buildings, and a run-down old farmhouse?*

I was a successful teacher, had my own life, and did not want it to change in any way. So that I could pursue my dreams, I had purposely chosen to remain single and focus on my career. Oh, I had dated some, but never was serious about anyone. I wanted to leave my mark on the world in the hearts of young people, but it seemed that would never happen. I knew I was financially secure and did not need to work at all, but teaching music had been my passion for years. That passion had been my reason for living.

I again recalled my mother's dying words, and I knew she didn't want me to sell the property. She left me with an assignment, and she fully expected me to carry it out, like it or not. My thoughts were like a whirlwind inside my head as I asked myself, *can I really leave the Charlotte area and move to this God forsaken place?*

I began to panic as I thought about what I would have to do. Not being from the area, I did not know a soul who could possibly help me. As I stood looking at the old house, tears began to stream down my cheeks. I was overcome with all kinds of emotions. Sadness overwhelmed me, and I felt as if my heart would break into a million pieces.

When I left Charlotte that morning, I had no idea I would be affected in such a profound way. I guess I assumed everything would look the same as it did when I was a child.

Disappointment and sadness besieged me, and I suddenly realized I had not been back to Martinsville since my grandma died. That had been sixteen years ago.

Consumed with grief and anger, I knew I had to face the problem head on. There was devastating grief for what I had lost and intense anger for what had been dumped in my lap by my family. Finally, I decided to "bite the bullet" and go in the house. Fear gripped my heart as I began to ascend those old front steps that Grandpa had constructed from river rocks he had gathered from the river below the farm.

Chapter 3

While stepping onto the piazza, I looked up and saw the rusty hooks on the ceiling from which the old piazza swing once hung. That lovely old bench swing had been Grandma's thinking place. She would sit in that swing, read her Bible, and pray.

I remembered the many times she and I sat together in that old swing, and I listened with anticipation as she told story after story from the Bible. No one could tell a story like Grandma. She had a unique gift of making every character come alive. I could see Moses parting the Red Sea and David killing Goliath with his little sling as she dramatically told the stories. She told the story of Daniel in the lions' den with so much fervor and passion; I could almost hear the lions roar. Grandma knew everything there was to know about the Bible.

I knew I must enter the house, so I made my way to the front door on the left. I never understood why my grandparents' house had two front doors, but I later found out that many houses that were built in the early 1900s had two front doors. The door on the right led into a hall that divided the house. The door on the left went directly into the sitting room which led to the dining room and kitchen. *Those two front doors sure would have been handy when I was a teenager,* I lightheartedly thought to myself.

Standing there gazing at what was left of my grandparents' lives, I began to sob uncontrollably. There were no words adequate to express my feelings as I looked at my surroundings. I thought I had experienced all of the shock I could bear when I drove up, but what awaited me on the inside of the house blew me away. Everything was in shambles. The necked light bulb that hung from the ceiling by a single cord in the sitting room had been yanked down. The old woodstove from the kitchen had been pulled into the sitting room. Cobwebs shrouded the entire room, and I was reminded of a haunted house I had seen in a horror film.

It was evident that vandals had ransacked the house. Trash and beer cans were everywhere. I looked on one of the walls of the sitting room, and the shadow of where a picture once hung was still there. It had been a picture of a guardian angel behind two children crossing a narrow little bridge. I remembered how Grandma would hold me on her lap and explain to me how God always protected us, especially little children.

As I stood there gazing at the wall where the picture once hung, a strange sense of peace overwhelmed me. The longer I stood there, the more I wept. No wonder the huge pine trees in the front yard seemed to be weeping when I drove up. They were trying to prepare me for what was in store for me inside the house. Where had that strange feeling of peace come from? Could it have been from just being in the room where Grandma and Grandpa had spent so much time or was it something else?

I could almost sense my grandparents' presence as I stood there. I slowly stepped over the piles of trash and junk and made my way to the dining room. It no longer had the smell of Grandma's wonderful cooking mixed with the aroma of wood-smoke and tobacco. The air was heavy with a dank, musty smell.

There was only one window in the dining room, and it was so dirty you could not see the outside. An old pair of dirty ecru curtains still hung on the window. They were the only tangible reminder of my sweet Grandma and days gone by. She took so much pride in her home, and she always kept her curtains clean and starched. She would have been devastated if she had seen how filthy they were.

I stepped to the window and pulled the filthy curtains aside and was immediately engulfed with a cloud of dust. As I took my fingers and wiped the dirt from the window so I could look out, I started coughing and sneezing.

I could see where Grandma's old "yellow bell" bush had once been. That bush had been her pride and joy in early spring. Surprisingly, her gorgeous dogwood trees still graced the yard of the farmhouse and were in full bloom.

I slowly made my way to the little kitchen where Grandma did all of her cooking. It was totally empty except for the mass of cobwebs hanging from the ceiling. I walked over to where the old cast-iron woodstove had once sat, and I closed my eyes and imagined the smell of homemade biscuits baking.

As I turned around, I peered out the dirty, little window at the back of the kitchen. After wiping it with my fingers, I could still see what remained of the old barn and outhouse.

I looked to the center of the room and pictured in my mind the handmade round table she had used to prepare her food. That little table had found a home in my apartment in Charlotte. My mother had given it to me after I moved out on my own. Grandma's father made her the little table from poplar wood that came out of the mountains of North Carolina. Since the kitchens in Grandma's day had no counter space, she used that little table as a surface to prepare her biscuits and pies.

Furnishings for her kitchen had been sparse, to say the least. She had her woodstove, her little table, and a small cabinet that Grandpa built for her. She brought water from the well on the back porch, and she kept her wood for the cast-iron cook stove in a wood-box under the window. In the summer months, her little kitchen would get so hot you could hardly breathe, and there was always the lingering smell of wood-smoke coming from Grandma's kitchen.

Overcome with a deluge of memories, I regained my composure and returned to the sitting room. I needed to get some fresh air, and I knew I needed to find a motel room before dark. Therefore, I decided to come back the next day and explore the remainder of the house. I retraced my steps to the front door, closed it behind me, and descended the old rock steps to the jungle of weeds in the front yard.

I turned to look back at the house one last time. I had never felt so alone. I proceeded to my car with an overwhelming sense of insecurity and despair. Bitterness consumed me as I drove away from the farm, and I felt deep within my heart that life had been unfair to me.

Chapter 4

The bumpy ride back to the main highway seemed to take an eternity. The narrow dirt road was lined with blackberry bushes just beginning to bloom. As I approached a curve in the road, I saw a gigantic tractor plowing. The driver was sitting in a glass enclosed cage. My, how times had changed since I was a little girl.

I remembered how Grandpa would follow behind his faithful mules, Minnie and Jake, as they pulled his old plow in the hot sun for hours. Grandpa finally broke down and bought a small tractor, but he never used that tractor in his vegetable garden.

Following him in the garden one day, he turned to me, "Hope, there's a special touch to layin' off a garden and plantin' with a mule. I jist don't trust that tractor machine around my green beans and "oakree." Ain't no way I'd get 'round my d'mater vines with a tractor! W'y, I'd be a jumpin' off and on that contraption all the live long time to knock the clods of dirt off my plants. A feller could slap dab ruin a garden with a tractor! With my trusty old mules, I'm right behind 'em and I can just kick the clods away as I go along."

I'm very sure he would have said that monstrous machine with the glass enclosed cage had no place in real North Carolina farming.

By the time I reached the main road, I felt as if I had swallowed a gallon of dust. When I looked in the rearview mirror, my blonde hair was almost brown, and my face was several shades darker from the filth and dust in the old house.

My thoughts again returned to Mama and her death. For the life of me, I just couldn't understand why she waited until she was dying to tell me about the secret in Grandpa's house. She seemed especially anxious to tell me about the hidden journal, and I was beginning to feel that same sense of anxiety. I consoled myself by hoping that someone in Martinsville could help me.

I was only a couple of miles from the town of Martinsville when I decided to stop beside of the road and put the top back on my car. I could hear thunder in the distance, and the sky was as black as indigo ink over the Blue Ridge Mountains. Surely, there would be a motel in town somewhere. I pulled my hairbrush from my purse and attempted to brush the dirt from my hair. I wiped my face with tissues, as best I could, and heading toward Martinsville.

I spotted a quaint little restaurant on the main street of town and realized I had not eaten since eight o'clock that morning. The carton of yogurt and handful of granola I had eaten for breakfast were long gone. I had been so consumed with the condition of the farmhouse; I didn't even realize I was famished.

The little town of Martinsville only had street parking, and there just happened to be a parking place directly in front of the little cafe. I pulled my vehicle into the angled parking space, and, as I was getting out of the car, I noticed an older gentleman sitting on a bench in front of the eating establishment. I could tell he had a pinch of snuff in his lower lip by the way he was pursing his lips. I smiled as I looked at him in his bib overalls and tattered straw hat. He was propped on a homemade walking stick, and his spittoon was beside him. His tattered straw hat did not keep me from seeing his face.

He obviously had spent many days in the sunshine, because his face was weather beaten and furrowed. Even though his skin was the worse for wear, he had a sparkle in his eyes and a smile that radiated like sunbeams in the early morning sunshine.

As I approached the Red Bird Cafe, I spoke, "Hello. How are you today?"

He replied, "Tal'ably well, Tal'ably well."

After greeting me, the wrinkled little man proceeded to spit in his spittoon. I noticed that his spittoon was an old, rusty pork-and-bean can that still had the label on it. I immediately recognized his distinct southern Appalachian brogue that I remembered being so common among most of the older folks in the foothills of North Carolina. A lump arose in my throat, because he sounded like my grandpa.

I saw him look toward the western sky with a look of concern. "Little lady, you better git inside. It's a gittin' late. There's a storm a makin' over da Blue Ridge. Why don'cha go inside and git'cha a bite to eat? My young'un does the cookin' in 'is here eatin' place. It's purdy dawg gone good iffin I hafta say so myself. Her cookin' is mighty fine."

"Thank you, sir. I think I will. I haven't eaten since early this morning, but don't you think you should come in also?" I replied as I looked toward the ominous looking gunmetal gray sky that was hanging over the mountains.

"I'll be in t'rectly, you jist go on in," he said.

As I entered the cafe, I had the feeling that I had stepped back to a simpler, less-complicated moment in time. Norman Rockwell could not have painted a more realistic picture of hometown USA. The front door had an old screen door with a spring closure that slammed with a bang as I entered, and the furnishings actually appeared to date back to the 1950s. Chrome bar stools with red Naugahyde seats lined the counter, and on the opposite side of the cafe, wooden booths lined the wall with those same red Naugahyde seats. It was quite a large eating establishment, and in the center of the large room were several vintage looking tables and chairs in that same chrome and red Naugahyde. I could definitely tell that the furnishings of that place had most likely been there since the 1950s. It truly was a step back in time, a time before I was born.

As I made my way to the counter and claimed a red bar stool, I looked across the bar and saw myself in an antique looking mirror. It covered the entire wall behind the bar, and was turning gray and dark around the edges. Below the mirror was an old-fashioned soda machine, and to the right of it, was a vintage milkshake machine. If I had closed my eyes and opened them quickly, a soda jerk might have appeared before me dressed in a white hat and apron.

Local people were sitting around the bar and in the booths looking like they didn't have a care in the world. Everyone was dressed in simple clothes, and most of the men were in overalls. They all seemed to be happy and enjoying themselves, and I knew right away that I was looking at true Americana at its best.

I looked to my right and saw an old jukebox filled with records. I could hear Elvis Presley singing "Love Me Tender" in the background. You could barely hear the music above the talking and laughter of the patrons and the clanging of the dishes in the kitchen at the rear of the cafe.

There were two large ceiling fans going at full speed. I automatically assumed there was no air conditioning in the eating establishment. When I looked to my left, I saw the older gentleman with the wizened face come through the front door carrying his walking cane and his pork-and-bean spittoon.

As he slowly limped toward the counter, he asked me, "Is you new in 'is here neck of da woods?"

"Well, I guess you could say that," I replied. "My mother grew up here back in the 1940s and 1950s. She just recently passed away, and I have inherited my grandparents' farm."

His face perked up immediately. "Who wuz yore grandpa?"

"His name was Amos Martin. My grandma was Lillie Mae Martin."

I realized the older gentleman had no teeth when his face broke into the widest grin I had ever seen. "W'y, little lady, I know'd yore grandpa and grandma. 'Em was fine folks and always a willin' to help a body. They wuz a mite older 'an me, but I remember 'em. And I know'd yore ma when she was jist a young'un. She was a purdy little thing. Sure wuz sorry to hear 'bout yore Uncle Cletus and Aunt Mary Lou and 'eir young'uns a gittin' kil't da way 'ey did. Yea, it wuz a mighty bad thang. 'At wreck and all, da whole family a gittin' kil't all at one time. 'At 'ere had to be mighty hard on yore ma."

"Yes, it was hard on Mama. It took her a long time to recover from their deaths, and I don't think she ever recovered. I'm just glad Grandpa and Grandma weren't around to know about their tragic deaths."

Sitting beside me, he asked, "What's yore name, little lady?"

"My name is Hope, Hope Logan. My daddy's name was Whitley Logan. He was from here, also."

"They law me, I know'd him, too. I recollect 'at he wuz from further up towards da Blue Ridge. Yore grandpa and grandma wuz so proud of you when you wuz born. W'y, Mr. Amos had yore birthin' announced da very nex' Sunday at church. Mite near everybody 'roun'chear went to da Martinsville Baptist Church down da road from Mr. Amos' place back 'en. It wuz da only church close 'roun'chear. We got a heap of churches now. They is Baptist, Methodist, Presbyterian, and Catholic. You name it we got it. You know 'ey even named our church atter yore great-grandpa. I never know'd him, but I hear'd he wuz a fine feller.

"When we got ready to build our new church, ever'body got in a big ol' rookus. Some of 'em church members wanted to move da church to town and call it da First Baptist Church of Martinville and da rest of da members wanted it to stay right where it wuz. I ain't ever seen such squabblin' in my life. Since da church wuz on a dirt road, not many people wuz a comin' to church services. We needed to move.

"'Em church folks wuz a carryin' on some'um awful. One Sunday, a bunch of 'em so called Christians got in a big ol' fuss durin' preachin'. It wuz da worse thang I ever seen. God's heart had to be mighty grieved. Mr. Amos, he must'a took all he could stand, and when he stood up an' cleared his throat you could'a hear'd a pin drop.

"Mr. Amos, he told 'em good. He said he wanted what was best fer da church and I never will ferget what he said 'at day. He purdy much tol' 'em people that wuz squabblin' and a fussin' 'at if Martinsville Baptist Church stayed out 'ere in da country on 'at dirt road, it wouldn't grow nary a speck bigger 'an it wuz. Mr. Amos' eyes commenced to waterin' and his voice started a quiverin', and he told 'em fussin' Christians 'at God wanted it moved and da name changed to da First Baptist Church of Martinsville. And 'at little girl, wuz all it took. Nex' thang we know'd, we had a new church right on main street in Martinsville. When da church building wuz done, 'ey even hung yore grandpa's picture in it right nex' to yore great-grandpa.

"Yea, Mr. Amos Martin, he wuz a God fearin' man. Yea, he wuz. Now weren't yore ma's name Amelia? I b'lieve I recollect 'at folks called her Amy for short."

"That's right, everyone called her Amy. I think Grandpa started that, because it had a similar beginning as his name. But I never heard that story about the move of the church. That's really a surprise to me. It must have been built before I was born. I remember Grandpa's picture hanging in a hallway in the church beside of my great-grandpa's picture.

The people in the church must have respected him a lot, and I never knew he had that much influence. He truly was a great man."

"You is mighty right, little girl, you is mighty right."

I decided to question the kind old gentleman. He had given me my first ray of hope since I had arrived in Rutherford County. He seemed quite knowledgeable about my family and the Martinsville area. I watched him as he eased upon one of the bar stools beside me.

I turned to him and asked, "What's your name, sir?"

"Snuffy Dobbins, jist call me plain Snuffy. My pa called me 'at cause I commenced to dippin' snuff when I wuz jist a chap. My real birthin' name is Foy Hershell Dobbins, but ain't nary a soul ever call't me Foy Hershall. I ain't a havin' nobody a callin' me 'at. I ain't a answerin' to nuttin' but Snuffy. Da very idea of my ma and pa a nam'in' me Foy Hershell? W'y, I wouldn't name my ol' hawg 'at."

I started laughing at him in spite of all I could do. He was so delightful, and I could tell that he was going to be my friend.

"My pa and ma wuz good friends with yore grandpa and grandma. W'y, we lived down the road jist a short piece from 'em. I hear'd my ma and pa a talkin' 'bout the Martin's a heap."

I was intrigued by this wrinkled little man. He had to know something about the history of my family, so I decided to question him in more detail.

"What exactly do you remember about my grandparents and my mother?"

"To da best I can recollect, 'em wuz jist like all da rest of us foothill folk. 'Em wuz God fearin' folk. But I do recollect 'at 'ere was a time when yore grandma and grandpa both seemed to be a might sorrowful. I think it wuz about da time yore ma was born," he replied.

"All of a sudden yore grandma and grandpa seemed to change. Yore grandma would commence ta cryin' in church, and she'd hafta get up and leave. W'y, she'd leave right in da middle of preachin'. Yore grandpa would get up and commence to followin' her right out da church door. Then you'd see his old 1937 Chiverlay truck a rollin' out of da church yard in a cloud of dust. I don't thank nary a soul ever found out what wuz da matter. Yore grandma, she perked up atter a little bit. I do recollect 'at atter you wuz born, 'ey wuz both happy as "two pigs in slop." Yea, Mr. Amos and Mrs. Lillie Mae wuz right proud of you."

"You don't have any idea what caused the change in my grandparents after my mother was born, do you, Snuffy?" I inquired.

"Nope, but'cha know how nosey some ol' women can be. 'Ere wuz several tales a goin' 'roun'chear. 'At 'ere hateful Pearly Mae Ledbetter started a tale 'at yore Grandma didn't want her young'un. 'At 'ere ol' nosey Lou Phipps had the galled nerve to say 'at yore Grandpa probably had his self a girlfriend on da side. Weren't nary a soul believed 'at lie, 'specially me! I know'd what a good man yore grandpa wuz. W'y, he'd a kilt hisself afore he'd upset yore grandma by "jumpin' da fence" fer some ol' loose woman. Nex' thang I know'd, some of 'em old hens wuz a whispering 'at yore grandma had gone slap crazy. I know'd weren't nary a word of 'at so. Lillie Mae's thinkin' always wuz as sound as a dollar. Not nary a one of 'em old hens know'd what 'ey wuz a talkin' 'bout. Good folk. 'Em Martins wuz mighty fine folk. Yea, Mr. Amos and Mrs. Lillie Mae wuz salt of da earth kinda folk!"

I thought to myself, *what an intriguing old man, and even though he walks with a cane, he still has a lot of spunk. There's certainly nothing wrong with his mind.*

I could have listened to him talk all day. His Appalachian dialect had such a distinctive lilt, and I loved to hear it. I knew it went back to the early settlers of Rutherford County who came from England, Germany, Scotland, and Ireland. The Appalachian people even used derivatives of words and phrases from the Elizabethan era.

"Snuffy, thank you so much for giving me all of this information. I was so young when Grandma and Grandpa died, I have forgotten so much about them. I just know that they loved me with all of their heart. When my mama died, she was very insistent that I come back to Martinsville and fix up their old home place. I plan to stay here for a week and see what needs to be done. I'll be going back and forth to Charlotte on the weekends. I teach school in Union County, and I have to finish the school year there. Then I plan to move here."

"Laws-a-mercy, you is one of 'em 'ere school teachers. I ain't had nary a bit of schoolin', 'cause I had to stay home with my ma and keep up da farm. My pa died when I wuz jist seven year ol'. 'At 'ere Emmer Ledbetter teaches old folks like me how to read, but I reckon I jist to old to read. I ain't ever been to her teachin' school. My ma, she taught me how to cipher. An' I can do a purdy good job of cipherin'."

"Snuffy, a person is never too old to read. You should enroll in the reading class. If you can cipher, I know you can learn to read. I call ciphering, arithmetic. You know, Snuffy, I always had a hard time with arithmetic. It just didn't come easy for me. A person never gets too old to learn."

"I know. I know. Maybe I might jist do it," he replied.

"Snuffy, do you know where I could get a room for the night?"

"I shore do," he replied, as he pointed his walking stick toward the main street that went through the town,

He began to give me directions, as he pointed with his walking stick. He even took time out to spit in his pork-and-bean can.

"Go down 'at 'ere street in front of 'is here cafe, and when you come on an ol' house, you'll see a sign a hangin' out in da front yard an' it'll say Martinsville Inn. It's across from da First Baptist Church. Ain't no way you can miss it. 'At 'ere Emmer Ledbetter runs a boardin'house, and she stays 'ere too. She's da teacher I wuz a tellin' you about. Shouldn't cost you a whole heap to stay 'ere. Miss Emmer is Ms. Pearly Mae Ledbetter's young'un, but she ain't nuttin' a tall like her ma wuz. She's a fine woman, she is. Atter Henry Ledbetter and 'at hateful ol' Pearly Mae died, Emmer bought 'at 'ere old house at da end of Main Street and fixed it up. It's a might biggity fer da likes of me, but you'll take a likin' to Miss Emmer. She's a ol' maid school teacher, and all da young'uns in Martinsville jist love her. 'Course she don't teach young'uns no more. She jist runs 'at 'ere inn and teaches ol' folk like me to read. She calls it a inn, but it ain't nuttin' more than a boardin' house."

As I picked up a menu, a delightful looking lady walked in from the back of the cafe. Her face was beaming like sunshine, and she had on a cute pink waitress uniform with a white apron. She had a chubby little face and stood about five feet tall and had short, curly, fire-engine-red hair.

Snuffy yelled to her, "Sissy, get over 'ere. You need to talk to 'is 'ere lady. Her grandpa wuz Amos Martin and she is Hope Logan. She ain't et nary a thang all day. She's got to be a perishin' to death. Tell Lucy to fix 'is chap some'um' to eat."

As the lady approached, she said, "Nice to meet'cha, Miss Logan. What can I get' cha? Ye must be starvin' to death!"

"You can just call me Hope, and I am very hungry. Did I hear Snuffy say that your name is Sissy?"

"My real name is Esther Louise, but everybody calls me Sissy. Why don'cha try our famous cheeseburger all the way wid the best french-fries in the county?" she replied.

"That sounds great. You can fix it with all of the trimmings except the onion."

"What can I get cha to drink?" she asked.

"Do you have iced tea?" I answered with a question.

"Sure thang. It's nice and sweet. How 'bout some lemon?"

"That would be great. I haven't had any good sweet tea since my mama died."

Sissy yelled to someone in the back of the cafe, "One cheeseburger all the way, hold the onions, and one order of fries." You would have thought she was yelling to someone in the next town.

She then proceeded to pour the iced tea from a tea-stained plastic pitcher. As she poured the amber colored liquid, my mouth began to water. She plopped a plastic amber colored glass on the counter filled with iced tea in front of me, and I couldn't resist the temptation to taste the drink. When I took the first sip, my mind was instantly flooded with memories of Mama's delicious iced tea. Before I knew it, I had drunk the entire contents of the glass.

"Wow, ye must'a been mighty thirsty," Sissy said. "Here, let me get cha a refill."

As she refilled my glass, I saw another lady come from the kitchen in the back of the cafe. She was carrying a huge platter with a large cheeseburger surrounded by an enormous mound of homemade french-fries.

"Come 'ere, Lucy. 'Is here's my young'un, Lucy, and 'is is Amos and Lillie Mae Martin's gran'young'un," Snuffy said as he introduced us.

"It's so nice to meet cha. I've heard so much about yore family and what good folks they wuz. Welcome to Martinsville. I have some fresh apple pie in the kitchen. If ye decide you want some, jist let me know," she said.

Lucy had a pleasant smile on her face and looked to be about forty years old. Her long brown hair was pulled up in a bun which gave her a, somewhat, matronly look. She could have been a beautiful lady with a little fixing up here and there.

I looked at her as she spoke to me, "Has Papa been a burnin' yore ears? Don't let him, 'cause he'll talk ye to death! By the way, sweets come with the meal, and that apple pie is fresh out of the oven. I'll be glad to fetch ye some with vaniller ice cream, iffin ye want me to."

I didn't know how I was going to eat all of the food that was before me, so I gracefully declined the pie. There were no words to describe how delicious the burger was. It was dripping with homemade chili and slaw, good old southern style slaw made with Duke's Mayonnaise. The food melted in my mouth, and I closed my eyes to savor every delicious morsel.

After finishing the meal, I looked at Snuffy and Lucy and said, "Wow, I can't remember when I have eaten so much. Thanks for your hospitality and the delicious meal. I've never had such a tasty hamburger, and the fries were out of this world! How much will that be?"

Lucy replied, "That'll be two dollars and ninety-nine cent."

When she told me how much the meal was I was shocked. I stood there a moment before either of us spoke.

She looked at me apologetically. "Is that too much?"

"No, No, No. I don't think it's enough. Where I come from, it would have cost an arm and a leg." After paying Lucy and leaving a tip for Sissy, I started toward the door.

"We commence to servin' breakfas' 'roun'chear at seven in da mornin' iffin you want to come by," Lucy informed me.

"I'm not much of a breakfast eater, but thanks for the invitation," I replied as I prepared to leave. "I'll be working out at the farm tomorrow, and maybe I can get away long enough to come into town and grab a bite of lunch."

"Why don'cha jist come on by in da mornin', and I'll have ye a poke lunch packed and ye can take it wid ye. That way ye won't have to stop a workin' to come into town to eat,"

"Thank you, Lucy, I really appreciate that. I'll see you in the morning," I replied as the screened door slammed behind me. I smiled on the way to my car and asked myself, *what in the world is a poke lunch?*

Chapter 5

As I approached my car, I spotted the Martinsville Funeral Home across the street from the Red Bird Cafe. It was in a lovely Victorian house that dated back to the 1890s. It gleamed of white paint, and the lovely eighteenth century style turret on the right side of the house was barely visible because of a huge magnolia tree in front of the house. The entire mansion was trimmed in ornate Victorian gingerbread millwork and molding. Each gable was decorated with that same lovely trim. The elaborate mansion was surrounded by several huge magnolia trees and gardenia bushes mixed with spring flowers. A stone walkway led to the front door of the funeral home. It was lined with yellow and white daffodils and tulips of every color.

Grandma passed away in the hot summer time, and the smell of magnolia blossoms and gardenia bushes was over-powering as we approached the funeral home the day she was buried. The inside of the mansion was unbelievable and was filled with gilded mirrors, heavy ornate draperies and wall hangings, and lovely Victorian furniture. The ornate framework around the fireplace in the main parlor was made of mahogany and extended up to the ceiling where the mahogany crown molding began. The ceiling in the main reception area had a lovely pastoral mural painted on it.

As a child I had been overwhelmed with the beauty of that place, but the chandelier in the foyer captured my attention more than anything else in the house. To my young eyes it looked like a million diamonds dazzling in morning sunshine.

Even though the funeral home was surrounded by beauty, the place still horrified me. I had never experienced a death in my family until my grandparents' deaths, and the memory of that place was etched in my memory forever. I had no desire to go back there anytime soon.

While standing there looking at the old mansion, many painful memories resurfaced. I could almost sense Grandpa and Grandma beside me. I recalled Grandpa Martin's funeral and a few months later, Grandma's. As a child, I didn't understand the finality of their deaths. I felt a huge lump rise in my throat, and again tears began to fill my eyes.

I stood looking at the little town and sadly thought to myself, *this little town was once a big part of my life. Why have I let this part of my life slip away from me?*

Just the short time I had been in Martinsville, I had experienced a sense of peace and security I hadn't felt in a long time. I had been so consumed with my career, and I had forgotten some of the important things in life. I didn't even realize I had missed them. I can't say I missed the funeral home, but it created a stirring in my heart that I had not felt in years. Just hearing the lilt of Snuffy's Appalachian accent gave me a feeling of comfort and peace.

I fastened my seatbelt and made my way up Main Street. Nothing had changed. I noticed the little stores along the way. There were no huge malls or department stores like the ones I frequented so often in Charlotte. I had always been a faithful customer at the South Park Mall in Charlotte, as well as Carolina Place Mall in Pineville. It did not surprise me that there wasn't even a Wal-Mart or Target in Martinsville!

Where in this world will I buy the necessary items I need? I thought to myself. Then I remembered my grandma, she never had those items I felt were so necessary. If Grandma survived, I knew I could survive, also. Grandma made her own soap and shampoo, used a chamber pot instead of a bathroom, and had no hairdryer. I could still see her as she bent her head over the old wash pan on the back porch and shampooed her long white hair. She drew water from the open well that was located at the end of the back porch and heated it on her woodstove in the kitchen. After she combed her hair dry in the sunshine, she would twist it up in a bun at the nape of her neck. When she shampooed it in the winter, she would sit by the stove until her hair was dry. Sometimes she would even let me comb it for her. I always looked forward to that same ritual of getting my hair shampooed at Grandma's, but everything I did at Grandma's house was a special event.

Continuing down Main Street, I spotted a little drug store. Beside of it was a shoe store, and across the street was Mildred's Dress Shoppe and the theater. Grandma and Grandpa called it the picture show. They believed the picture show was the devil's workshop. I never understood why they felt movies were so bad. They never had a television either, and they held that same view about television, devil's workshop.

I spotted the post office. Because of the huge American flag that was waving in the front yard, you could not miss it. Beside of the post office was a small florist, and sitting off to itself was an old service station. I smiled as I remembered Grandpa calling it the fillin' station."

He would drive up to the gasoline pumps and say, "Fill 'er up, Rupert." Mr. Rupert Bedford owned the service station back then.

I spotted the Martinsville Inn across from the First Baptist Church of Martinsville. I made a right turn into the parking lot and got out of my car. The sight before me was awesome. It, too, was a lovely Victorian home that had been restored to pristine condition. It had the traditional Victorian Gingerbread millwork and trim. The turrets and widow's walk were also trimmed in that same exquisite millwork and trim. It had lovely ornate corbels and brackets supporting the roof.

As I approached the front door, I could hear beautiful piano music coming from inside the house. When I rang the doorbell, I was surprised to hear chimes playing a short rendition of Ludwig van Beethoven's "Hymn to Joy." I knew right away that a musician lived in that old mansion. *Ummm, I thought to myself, kindred spirits.* The piano music stopped abruptly, and I could hear someone coming to the door.

When the door opened, I was greeted by a very kind looking lady. She appeared to be in her sixties. In fact, she looked about the age my mama was when she died. She was perfectly dressed in a tailored lavender shirtwaist dress which accented her lovely gray hair. She had the brightest blue eyes I think I had ever seen. Her fingernails were perfectly polished a soft color of pink. Her appearance was that of a prim and proper southern lady. Standing in her presence only reminded me how dirty and grungy I was. I knew I must look dreadful from the dust covering my body, but she did not seem to notice.

"Hello, what can I do for you?" she asked me in a soft southern drawl.

"I'm looking for a room for the night. Is that a possibility?"

"Certainly, please come on in? My name is Emma Ledbetter. We don't have very many guests. Rather than stay here, most folks who come through Martinsville want to stay in a motel over on the bypass. I'm so thrilled you decided to stay with us. What's your name?" she asked.

"My name is Hope, Hope Logan. I'm from Charlotte," I replied. "I just arrived here this afternoon."

"Please come in Miss Logan and welcome to the Martinsville Inn," she said. "I remodeled this old house many years ago so it could be used as an inn, but we have very little traffic through here. Sometimes I rent the formal area of the house out for weddings and receptions. Some brides still love to have Victorian weddings. The Martinsville Women's Club uses our inn for teas, and we have been known to have a soiree or two."

I realized she also had that lovely southern brogue so common to Rutherford County. Of course, her grammar was impeccable, as I expected, since she was a teacher.

I followed her to a small ornate desk in the foyer. It was at the base of a lovely winding staircase. I was overwhelmed by the interior of the inn. The lovely marble floor in the foyer was designed in a black and white checkerboard pattern, and I felt I had stepped back in time to the antebellum period of southern history.

The room to my left was the formal living room, while the room to my right appeared to be a library or drawing room. The furnishings were typical of most nineteenth century homes. There was an ornate marble fireplace in the formal living room, and the walls were tastefully adorned with lovely Victorian paintings. The furniture was upholstered in elegant crushed velvet in varied shades of mauve. Also, in the living room, I saw a magnificent Steinway piano and assumed that Miss Ledbetter had been the one playing the lovely music I heard when I approached the front door. On top of the piano was a gilded candelabrum that matched the chandelier that hung from the ceiling. *What a beautiful room. Just look at the light reflecting off the prisms on the chandelier and candelabrum,* I noted.

The room to my right was also filled with lovely nineteenth century furniture and old books. That room, too, was decorated in varied shades of mauve.

The floor in both rooms was constructed of a deep toned hardwood, and in the center of each room, there were luxurious Aubusson rugs, which carried out the same mauve color palette that was in both rooms.

Miss Ledbetter opened up a large ledger book to enter my name.

"You said your name is Hope Logan? Are you kin to the Logan's from here in Rullerford County?" she asked.

"I sure am. My parents were Whitley and Amelia Logan," I replied.

Miss Ledbetter suddenly had a peculiar look on her face. Her whole demeanor seemed to change, and I thought I detected tears in her eyes. She remained cordial, but somewhat remote. A red flag immediately went up in my mind. *What in the world could have caused her to change so quickly when I mentioned my parent's names?*

I gave her my credit card, and she took care of the paperwork. She then retrieved a key from the desk drawer and asked me to follow her.

As we started up the winding staircase, she turned to ask me a question. "Where are your parents now?"

"My daddy passed away about two years ago, and my mother died about a month ago."

I detected a note of grief in her eyes, and again I thought I saw them fill with tears. *Could she have known my parents, if so, why had they never spoken of her? Could Miss Ledbetter know about the secret in my grandparents' house?*

I didn't feel like it was the appropriate time to question her, so I followed her up the winding staircase. Each step seemed to creak as we ascended, as if they were trying to tell me something.

She took me to the room at the top of the stairs. When she opened the door, I felt once again I had been transported back to the nineteenth century. The room was breathtaking. I knew right away that I was definitely out of place in my jeans and soiled pink tee shirt. To fit into Miss Ledbetter's house, one needed to be dressed in a beautiful, long dress with a bustle and crinoline petticoats.

I made my way to the massive high-backed bed that had to date back to the 1800s. The bed was made from solid walnut and the headboard was inlayed with burl. I had never seen such a beautiful bed.

The walls in the room were painted a lovely shade of lavender, and that same color was tastefully used throughout the room. The curtains were lavender and white as was the hand-crocheted bedspread. Every vase and trinket in the room coordinated with the lovely lavender color scheme and the antique furniture. There were several pieces of hobnail milk glass throughout the room. I was overwhelmed by the elegant beauty surrounding me, and stood in awe as I surveyed every nook and cranny of the room.

I turned to look at Miss Ledbetter and thanked her for her assistance as she gave me the key to the room. She turned to leave the room, but before she left, she informed me that breakfast would be served at seven o'clock.

Miss Ledbetter hesitated a moment before she left the room, but she only smiled and said goodnight. *What a delightful lady,* I thought to myself.

After I closed the door, I realized just how tired I was. The surroundings in the bedroom were absolutely breath-taking, and I couldn't wait to crawl into the beautiful high-backed bed. Looking around the bedroom, I felt so out of place. I quickly decided that that vintage bed was only fit for royalty.

I put my small suitcase on the floor, retrieved my pajamas and toiletries, and entered the bathroom. I felt so dirty from the events of the day, and the old claw-foot tub seemed to beckon me. I proceeded to fill the tub with hot water and lavender bath salts, and I almost fell asleep as I soaked in the fragrant water.

As I lay there, I relived the events of the day. My mind seemed to be going in so many different directions. As I tried to pull my thoughts together, I realized that my head was pounding like a jackhammer.

After completing my bath and drying my hair, I reached for a soft fluffy towel and dried myself and put on my pajamas. I took an aspirin, brushed my teeth, and went directly to bed. The beautiful bed linens smelled of sunshine and lavender, and I immediately relaxed. I thought to myself, *Miss Ledbetter must like lavender as much as I do. Maybe we're kindred spirits.*

I surveyed the room one last time and pulled the cover up to my chin. Before I knew it, I had drifted off to sleep. I was awakened suddenly by a noise somewhere in the house. I assumed it was Miss Ledbetter going to her bedroom, but I was too tired to get up and see what it was. Within a few minutes, I forgot about the noise and was sound asleep.

I don't think I moved all night.

I awoke early the next morning to the smell of coffee and bacon cooking. Since I planned to go back to the farmhouse, I put on a pair of faded jeans and a purple Old Navy tee shirt. I knew Miss Ledbetter would be dressed to the nines, but what I had planned for the day required old shabby clothes.

When I entered the dining room, which was off of the living room, the large Queen Anne table was set for only two. A lovely silver coffee urn was on the buffet surrounded by other silver containers filled with the most delicious looking food I had ever seen. Not only did it look delicious, it smelled heavenly, and I immediately associated the smell with Mama and Grandma's home cooking.

I heard someone coming down the stairs, and Miss Ledbetter entered the dining room. She was dressed beautifully in a mauve pink dress with matching accessories. She greeted me with a radiant smile and invited me to serve myself from the buffet.

"No one else is staying here this week, so it's just you and me for breakfast. Let's take our breakfast out on the sun porch. It's so nice out there, and a little less intimidating," she said.

As I approached the buffet, I saw the most inviting layout of breakfast foods I had ever seen. Bacon, eggs, grits, fruit, muffins, and scones, it was fit for a king. I indulged and took a sample of everything. After I filled my coffee cup, I followed Miss Ledbetter through the house.

As we approached the rear of the house, I found myself in a very cozy informal sunroom with comfortable wicker furniture with plush cushions. The color palette of the sunroom was the same lovely shades of mauve that were used throughout the rest of the house. Miss Ledbetter sat on a chaise lounge, and I sat on the beautiful sofa. Because the sun porch had a lived in look, I had no qualms about putting my coffee cup and plate of food on the wicker coffee table. There were magazines and books everywhere, and it was obvious that someone did a lot of reading and needlework. She had her needlework basket beside of a recliner, and it looked as if she had been crocheting a lovely cream colored afghan. It was quite evident that that area of the house was the area she lived in.

Miss Ledbetter looked toward me kindly and said, "Hope, tell me about yourself."

"There's really not much to tell. You know who my parents were and that I live in Charlotte. I grew up in the Raleigh area and did my undergraduate work at the University of North Carolina at Chapel Hill. I always knew what I wanted in life, and that was to be a music teacher. Immediately after graduation, I went back to UNC and received a Master of Arts degree in music. From there I went to the Charlotte area to live, and I currently teach in a high school in Union County. I have been teaching about ten years. I truly love teaching, and music has become my life. I noticed you have a lovely piano."

Miss Ledbetter replied, "Yes, I love my piano. I, too, am a teacher and a musician. Your grandma taught me how to play piano as a child. She was the best piano teacher in these parts. I play piano for the church I attend. Do you play for a church anywhere?"

I replied to her timidly, "Uh-uh, I-I-I don't attend church anywhere, but I do play piano occasionally for an upscale nightclub in Charlotte. I also have played for weddings and special events. Teaching takes up most of my time. I work in conjunction with the drama department at my school, and we have produced several musicals. In fact, we have done several Broadway plays."

I immediately saw disapproval on Miss Ledbetter's face when she heard me say that I played piano in a nightclub, and I could sense she didn't approve of my lack of church attendance. However, when I mentioned the musicals, her face instantly lit up. We continued our conversation while we ate breakfast.

"I took a leave of absence from school when Mama got so sick. I was with her when she died. Almost to the point of desperation, she became frantic to tell me something prior to her death. She told me she wanted me to renovate Grandpa's old house, and she also left a surprising mystery for me to solve. I have to tell you, it is a seemingly impossible task.

"Her dying words instructed me to look for a journal that my grandma kept in the old house, but she didn't know where it was. According to Mama, Grandma hid the journal somewhere in the house, and she couldn't remember where she put it. Due to the fact that Grandma had been diagnosed with Alzheimer's, her mind became very unstable during the last year that she lived. It was so sad to see her in that condition. She didn't even know who Mama and I were most of the time. She seemed to dwell in the past every time I went for a visit. Grandma rarely had times when she was at herself, and it was during one of those lucid moments that she was coherent enough to tell Mama about the journal. She was never able to recall where she hid it.

"I really would appreciate any help you could give me. If you and Mama were friends, you probably know more about the old farmhouse than I do."

"I would be glad to help you, Hope," she replied with a sigh. "I knew both your mother and father. At one time many years ago, your mother was my best friend. I spent much of my childhood at that old house, and I might know about places there that you don't even know exist. In fact, I just lived across the river from your mama. My pa's farm joined your grandpa's."

Her revelation gave me a renewed sense of hope and led me to ask myself, *why had Mama never spoken of her? Could their relationship be a part of the secret journal? Maybe she will be able to help me find the journal and solve the mystery that surrounds my family. Could there be skeletons in my family closet?* For some reason I felt that when I did find the journal, I would probably expose many secrets and disturbing facts about my family.

"I'm delighted to know that you knew my parents. Please tell me all about your relationship with them! I can't tell you how much this means to me."

Miss Ledbetter looked at me with a sad faraway look in her eyes and said, "Yes, your mama was very dear to me at one time. And to be honest with you, Hope, I have missed her terribly. I didn't realize just how much until I saw your lovely face. You are so much like your mama. I hate to even tell you this, but Amy and I had an unfortunate misunderstanding about forty years ago, and we never spoke after that."

I was dumbstruck at her revelation and asked myself, *what in the world could have wrecked their friendship?*

When I was finally able to speak, I responded with just one word. "Why?"

She answered hesitantly. "I had rather go into that at a later time, but I just thank God that you have come into my life. I have wanted to make things right for so long. Maybe I can somehow make up for all of those wasted years with your mother. You are such a beautiful image of both your parents, and I hope you will allow me to be your special friend."

Tears filled my eyes as I replied to her, "It would be an honor to be your friend, Miss Ledbetter. I feel so alone at times, especially since Mama died. I feel like an orphan. I have buried myself in my work for all of these years, so I really have only a few friends. Here I am, thirty years old, and I have no one."

"Child, you are not alone now. I have been alone my entire life, myself. You know, I have found that sometimes relationships in this life are very unimportant and fleeting when you look at them in the grand scheme of things. Being alone has taught me not to depend on myself but on God. He has been my strength during my entire adult life, especially since I retired. I enjoyed a fulfilling career of teaching and had great students. I am now devoting my life to my church and its mission. I volunteer with adults who cannot read and mentally challenged children. Even though I'm not teaching in a classroom, it's such a satisfying feeling to contribute to society by simply helping older folks and handicapped children. My life is so full of wonderful memories and nothing can take that away."

As I listened to Miss Ledbetter, I was amazed at her strength of character and genteel manner. I couldn't understand how a God no one could see could take the place of family and friends. It sounded ludicrous to me. She was beginning to sound like my parents and grandparents, but I never really understood their faith either.

I deliberately changed the subject away from God and faith and said, "Miss Ledbetter, you are an amazing woman. I'm so glad you have come into my life."

"Please, don't call me Miss Ledbetter," she replied. "Everyone in this little town calls me Miss Emma, and you may call me that, too. If you will allow me to go with you, I would love to go out to the farm today."

"Oh, I couldn't let you do that! You can't imagine how filthy that place is. You might ruin your clothes and your beautiful hairdo."

"Not to worry, child. That's what soap and water are for!" she replied adamantly.

After completing our breakfast, Miss Emma shouted to someone in the kitchen and said, "Hattie, we are going out for the day. Just go about your business and fix what you want for supper."

I heard someone reply from the kitchen area, "Shore thang, Miss Emma."

She turned back to me and emphatically said, "Now don't you start worrying about me helping you! I assure you I am up to the task! Hattie helps me with cooking, and Samson, her husband, helps me with yard work. The Alexander's have been with me many years. In fact, I have known Hattie my entire life. They live in a cottage behind the inn, and they are my family. I guess you could say they are my only family. They take good care of me, and Hattie makes sure I eat properly. Hope, you just stay here and enjoy the view while I go change. I'll be back in a jiffy."

After Miss Emma retreated upstairs by way of the back staircase, I relaxed on the beautiful sofa and soaked up the warm sunshine that filtered through the windows. Her sun porch made me feel like I was being granted a "little piece of paradise." It was rainproof and had central heat and air so it could be used year round. She had beautiful African violets scatted throughout the room. I looked to my left, and there was a lovely fichus tree behind a wicker rocker and a huge Boston fern hanging from the ceiling. At the other end of the sun porch from where I was sitting, a large basket was hanging from the ceiling. It was filled with small ferns and other trailing plants.

The backyard looked like a scene from *Better Homes and Gardens.* Every shrub and flower was perfectly placed to form a lovely English garden, and it resembled a painting by Thomas Kincade. With a huge fountain at the center of the landscape, the garden was aglow with vibrant spring colors of pinks, yellows, and purples. The windows were open, and I felt a soft breeze coming from the direction of the mountains. There seemed to be hundreds of birds singing in the trees. Beautiful bird feeders were strategically placed throughout the entire landscape. I saw several blue birds feasting at one of the feeders, and several seemed to be singing in harmony from the huge magnolia tree at the edge of the yard. I even thought I heard a mockingbird singing with them. An old red-headed woodpecker seemed to be chiming in with the other birds as he added his "peck-peck-peck" in syncopated rhythm. As I sat there, I knew in my heart that everything would work out in my life with the help of my new friend.

I heard Miss Emma coming through the kitchen, and I stared in surprise as she entered the room. There she stood in faded overalls, brogans, a straw hat, and leather working gloves.

"Wow!" I exclaimed. "This is an unexpected change. You've transformed yourself from a genteel southern lady to a true southern farm girl."

"Yea, I guess this would be a surprise to a lot of folks in Martinsville. Most people have never seen me dressed like this. Only Hattie and her husband, Samson, and a very few people have seen me this way. A few boarders have caught a fleeting glimpse of me like this from time to time. They probably thought I was the gardener. I do believe it's time this little town sees another side of Miss Emma Ledbetter, the retired prim and proper schoolmarm. This little town needs a little jolt, and what could be better than to meet the real Miss Emma Ledbetter?

"I have a new friend that God has brought into my life and a chance to make up for so many wasted years. So let's get going and get some tools and cleaning supplies from the shed, and we'll be on our way," she exclaimed.

"Oh, I almost forgot one thing, Miss Emma. Lucy at the Red Bird Cafe is packing me a lunch. Let's call and get her to pack you one, also."

"Don't worry, I'll take care of that," she replied.

I listened as she telephoned the restaurant and instructed Lucy to prepare her a poke lunch, also. Then I heard Miss Emma tell her to be sure and send some sweet tea and chocolate cake.

She then said, "Put it on my tab, Lucy. We'll be by in a few minutes. Thanks. Goodbye."

Chapter 6

Miss Emma and I walked out the back door of the Martinsville Inn and proceeded toward the shed at the edge of the backyard. It was a charming little building that perfectly matched the Victorian inn. It reminded me of a quaint little dollhouse. It looked more like a carriage house than a garage and shed combination. I also spotted the cutest little Victorian style home next to the shed and decided it must be Samson and Hattie's home.

I was concerned that Miss Emma might fall, so I followed close behind her. My first impression of Miss Emma was that of a very fragile lady, but that assumption reminded me to never judge someone by a first impression.

She seemed quite at home in her overalls and blue gingham shirt. I could see little wisps of white hair peeping out from under her straw hat, and it wasn't just any straw hat, it was the hat of all hats. It was white and was adorned with a lovely blue ribbon and violet silk flowers, and I must say it made quite a show. Even in her overalls and straw hat, Miss Emma remained the picture of a genteel southern lady.

We gathered several yard tools, and Miss Emma picked up what looked like a rather large metal tool box and handed it to me. She then pulled out a sprayer and a bottle of weed killer.

She looked at me quizzically and asked, "What? You think I can't work, young lady? I'm used to hard work, and I love it. When we moved here, I supervised the entire renovations of this inn with a little bit of help from two local carpenters. And the yard work, I've done a lot of that, too. Of course I have some men who come once a week to work with Samson, and together we manage to keep up the yard work.

"Land sakes, I even drive the tractor if needs be. Just trust me, this is not going to hurt me or make me sick. I'm as strong as an ox. Women from this neck of the woods have always been hard workers.

"Here, hold this weed killer while I get the wheelbarrow. We will drive my old truck since we have so much to carry," she commanded as she handed me her tool box with a questioning look.

"What? You think I can't drive a truck either?" Miss Emma laughing asked.

"No, no, no," I replied. "I just hate for you to feel like you must help me."

"Now you just hush up, young lady. I'm doing this because I want to. It's about time I make up for the time I lost with Amy. I just wish she could be here so that I could really make things right. When you walked into my life yesterday, I realized something. I'm sixty-four years old, and I'm not a 'spring chicken' anymore. I don't want to meet my maker with anything left undone. And you, Hope, are going to help me fix the 'undone' part that I should have taken care of years ago. Now let's commence to gittin' it done!"

"Miss Emma, you are something else. I will never forget what you are doing for me. I've always been so self-sufficient. I guess I just don't know how to accept help from someone. C-C-Can you tell me what happened between you and my mother?"

"Hope, it will take a long time to tell you everything, but I will tell you. I promise I will explain everything on the way to the farm. Your mama and I were not only friends, we were like sisters."

I followed Miss Emma as she opened a side door leading into the garage and was surprised to see a shiny red truck. Parked beside of her car was the older-model Ford truck that looked to be in mint condition. We loaded the truck with the supplies, even the wheelbarrow, and Miss Emma got behind the wheel. Believe it or not, she looked right at home perched behind the wheel of the shiny red truck in her overalls and straw hat.

As we were leaving the inn, she looked at me and said, "Hope, now I want to tell you about your mama and why we had a disagreement. I have carried this heavy burden in my heart for far too many years. I'm not sure I even understand all that took place. I know you probably won't understand it, but I'm going to attempt to explain anyway."

She began the story. "Your mama and I grew up in the same church. In fact, my mama and daddy's farm joined your grandparent's farm. The two farms were divided by the river, and there was a small bridge on the dirt road that crossed the river where we would meet each other. We played together, went to school together, and were like sisters. We used to build playhouses under the beautiful pine trees in front of your grandma's home. I went home from church with your mama every Sunday. Amy didn't come to my house often because of my ma and pa. I think she was afraid of my pa, because he had a bad drinking problem. I never understood why my ma was so spiteful and mean to folks, but she was kind to me in her own way. She was a bitter unhappy soul and treated my pa like an outcast. To be honest with you, I think she had mental problems. And with Pa's drinking problem, I can look back on it now and understand why Amy was afraid of him. She wasn't used to being around an alcoholic.

"When I was twenty years old, I met a young fellow and fell madly in love with him. Your mama and I attended the same college, but I returned home before she did. It was during that time that I met the young fellow. When your mother finally came home; we didn't see much of each other. Because I spent so much time with him, your mama and I began to grow apart. He didn't live around here, and I wanted to spend every moment I could with him. We had even discussed marriage, and I even began to put items in my hope chest for our marriage.

"There was a town picnic in Martinsville, but I was unable to go with him to the event. An epidemic of influenza swept through the county that year, and I became very sick. I told my beau to go ahead to the picnic without me and have fun, and he did just that. He met someone there and fell madly in love with her. They later married.

"Hope, that other girl was your mama, and my beau was your daddy. Your mama had never met your daddy until that day, and I never recovered from the shock and disappointment. Amy had no idea that your daddy was my beau. I felt betrayed by both of them. Your mother made every attempt to mend our relationship, but I didn't want to hear anything she had to say.

"My hateful spirited ma got involved, and she raised a stink about it. That only added fuel to the fire of my jealousy. Ma was an expert when it came to causing problems. Because of all of the talk and hard feelings, Amy and Whitley moved away from here quickly after the wedding. They first moved to the Charlotte area and then to Raleigh where you grew up. I never saw either of them after that.

"I'm ashamed to say I didn't even attend your grandparents' funerals. Since that time, I have forgiven them and myself. I asked God to forgive me and begged him to somehow let me make everything right. He has sent you into my life, and that's why I want to help you and be there for you during this time."

I stared at Miss Emma in disbelief. "I just don't know what to say. I had no idea all of that happened. Mama never mentioned you to me."

"I don't blame her for not mentioning me. I was so hateful to her and to Whitley.

"Now that I have told you everything, I hope we can put all of this behind us. God has given me a second chance and the opportunity to deal with my bitterness. I know you are my second chance.

"Whitley loved your mama, and I should have accepted that. I let one incident shape my entire life. I didn't allow myself to fall in love again, and as a result I have lived a lonely, empty life. Look at me, I have absolutely no one. I see now that I was only hurting myself. Hope, if you never learn anything else in life, remember this, you just can't hold hate and bitterness in your heart. Unforgiveness only hurts you."

"Oh, Miss Emma," I replied. "I'm so sorry for what happened, and I'm sorry you and Mama were never reconciled. Daddy truly did love Mama, and they had a happy life. I only wish you could have been a part of our lives as a family."

"I could have been if I hadn't been so pigheaded and unforgiving," she exclaimed with regret. "I've learned one thing from all of this, I can't go back and change the past, but I sure can make the future different. So, please, let me continue to be a part of your life and help you fix up that old house and find that hidden journal. It's got to be there. For two dying women to request that it be found, it must have some mighty powerful words written in it."

As Miss Emma pulled into a parking space in front of the restaurant, I exclaimed, "Of course you can be a part of my life. I have no family either, and I really need a friend. You have been so helpful to me, and I will never be able to properly thank you for all you are doing, but I must say I am still in shock. Who would have ever dreamed our paths would cross at this particular time?"

"Hope, this has not been an accident, it was a divine appointment."

I gave Miss Emma a bewildered look and asked, "What do you mean? I'm not sure I understand what you're implying."

"You showing up on my doorstep was no accident. Someone greater than you and I orchestrated this entire meeting. I simply asked God for something, and he gave. It's as simple as that."

I knew that my parents and grandparents believed that God controlled everything in their lives, but it was hard for me to believe and trust someone I had never seen or heard. Discovering Miss Emma's deep faith shook me to the very core of my being. I immediately thought to myself, *maybe there is something to God and His control in our lives!*

We arrived at the cafe and Miss Emma was reaching to open her door when I spoke up, "Miss Emma, you just stay in the car; I'll go in and pick up the lunch."

"Absolutely not! It's about time this town sees me in another light. I don't want to always be remembered as the prim and proper schoolmarm of Martinsville. We'll both go in, but I'm payin'. So don't you even think about pullin' out any money."

I knew it was useless to argue with her; therefore, I followed her into the cafe. It was filled with local folks eating breakfast and talking when we entered. When Miss Emma entered the cafe, one would have thought we had walked into a funeral home. It became so quiet; you could have heard a pin drop.

Miss Emma scanned the cafe and finally spoke emphatically, "What's the matter? You folks never saw a lady in overalls before?"

She turned back to the counter and asked, "Sissy, are those lunches ready yet?"

"Shore thing, Miss Emma. I'll get 'em for you'uns. How you a doin', Hope?"

"Doing great, Sissy, and how about yourself?" I replied.

"Fair, I reckon. I fell last night in da dark. I tripped over my husband's ol' hound dawg on da front porch. I likened to a broke my neck." she replied.

"I'm sorry, Sissy, I hope you'll be okay," I replied.

"Yea, I'm okay, jist sore as a boil."

Sissy then looked at the both of us, and I could tell she was dying to find out what we were up to, but she never said a word.

I stood back as Miss Emma paid the bill. Even though she was wearing overalls and a straw hat, she carried an elegant black purse that must have cost at least two-hundred dollars into the cafe as if she were dressed to go to church. I had to smile as I watched her. Miss Emma was one classy lady.

As we were leaving, I approached the screened door and started to open it for Miss Emma. I realized she wasn't directly behind me, so I turned around just in time to see her bow to her audience in the cafe.

As the screened door slammed behind us with a loud bang, the talking resumed in the cafe, and I heard one old gentleman exclaim, "Who in 'is world is 'at 'ere young filly with Miss Emmer? And what's happened to Miss Emmer? Has she done gone slap dab crazy? I ain't 'ever in my life seen da likes of 'at. W'y, she had on britches. 'Em wasn't jist britches neither, 'em wuz overalls. What's 'is worl' a comin' to?"

When we got back in the car, she looked at me and burst into laughter. "By lunch time, word around town will be that

Miss Emma's gone plum' daft. There is no telling what will be said about me. They've never seen me dressed like this before and will probably try to have old Doc Henry come over and check me out. Old Doc Henry will probably want to send me to a mental hospital for a checkup."

I joined in the laughter, of course, and replied, "You look great to me. I wish you could have seen the faces of your captive audience as you were paying the bill. One old man had his eyes bugged out and his mouth hanging open, and it was full of food. It was gross!"

"Oh, that must have been that old nosey Lum Henry. W'y, he's somethin' else. He'll be down at the hardware store talkin' about me all day today. Some of these old folks around here don't cotton to a woman wearing britches."

We laughed so hard we had to stop and catch our breath before we could continue the trip to the farm.

After I caught my breath, I looked at Miss Emma and exclaimed, "We needed that laugh to get us ready for what we have ahead of us. I still can't believe you're helping me."

"Honey, I want to help you. You have not only given me a second chance to make up for what I did to your mama and daddy, but I can also try to make up for some of the things my ma did while she was on this earth. Ma was the meanest woman in this town when she was alive. She came from a very wealthy family and was an only child. She always had everything she wanted. When her parents died, she inherited all that they had, but she never shared her wealth with my father. You would never believe how she hurt the people in Martinsville, including your mama.

"I decided as a young girl that I never wanted to be like her. I promised the Lord if he would let me live, I'd try to make up for all the harm she had done to the folks in this town. She destroyed so many people with her mean spirit and gossiping tongue. "Don't get me wrong, I loved her. She was my ma. I can't help what she became, but I can control what I am. I almost became just like her when I treated your mama and daddy so awful."

"You are an amazing lady, Miss Emma. I really mean that. I don't think I have ever met anyone quite like you before. I think we will get along just fine," I replied.

"Yes, we will, Hope. Yes, we will," she replied. "Now tell me a little more about yourself. I know you are a music person, but let me hear more about your life in Charlotte."

"Well, I'm not a social climber, and I don't really date a lot. My students and school take up most of my time, but I do have a wonderful dog. His name is Leonardo, and I call him Leo. He is staying with a friend, and I know he wonders what has happened to me. I miss him so much! He's a large dog, but very gentle. Most people are afraid of large dogs, but Leo is an ideal pet. He is a three year old pit bull."

Miss Emma's mouth flew open, and she looked at me with excitement and said, "Hope, I had a blue pit bull for ten years, but he died last year. He was such a great companion to Samson and me when we were working in the yard, and he loved Hattie to death. He was a house dog most of the time, but since the backyard is fenced in, we let him out everyday to run and play. We miss him so much, especially Hattie. In fact, he slept at Hattie and Samson's house as much as he slept at mine."

"What was his name?"

"We named him Spike. We got him when he was eight weeks old, and he was just like family. When he died, all three of us cried for days."

As I looked at Miss Emma, I saw tears glistening in her eyes as I spoke. "I am so attached to my dog; I can't imagine not having him. I, too, got Leo when he was just a puppy, and he is such a loyal buddy. I live in an apartment complex, and I'm never afraid when he is with me. I usually walk him early in the morning before I go to school, and I never worry about attackers. I think pit bulls get a bad rap sometimes, but Leo is just a big baby."

"It's my belief that every family should have a dog, especially children and older folks. Spike really took care of us for ten years. Leo will love living in the country, and you will never have to worry about intruders with him around," replied Miss Emma.

We made our way to the turn off and found ourselves on the dirt road leading to the farmhouse. Within a few minutes we pulled off the road in front of the house.

The next thing I heard was a gasp from Miss Emma's direction, and I saw the stunned look of disbelief on her face. I realized at that moment that she was not prepared for the rundown condition of the farm.

She finally managed to speak, "Well, in this world! What's happened here? Looks like a war zone. W'y, you can hardly see the house. There's enough Johnson grass growing in this yard to bale. We may have to get old Sam Hicks to come in with his hay baler and cut these weeds. And look at the wild onions. W'y, I can't believe this, but the honeysuckle vines sure do smell good. Look over there in the field. It's loaded with blackberry bushes. I wonder if your grandma's blueberry bushes are still out there behind that field. I knew we should have brought the weed eater or a sling blade!"

I stood there for a few seconds and let her take in the scene before her, and then I spoke, "I guess we can start on the inside first. Oh, by the way, what is a sling blade?"

Miss Emma laughed and exclaimed, "Honey child, I sure can tell you're not a country girl, and you don't know the first thing about farm life. A sling blade is just what it says. It's a blade with a handle on it. You sling it back and forth in the weeds to mow them down. You might be a great teacher, but I can see I'm going to have to teach you a few things about country livin'. And that will be my pleasure!"

As we started toward the house, Miss Emma's eyes filled with tears as she commented, "I have so many unforgettable memories of this place, but I'll tell you about them later."

When we reached the front door, I felt I should prepare Miss Emma for what was on the other side of the door. If the condition outside had been a shock, I knew she would be upset by the interior of the house.

I gently touched her arm and said, "Miss Emma, I hope you are all set for what's inside."

"Don't worry about me, Hope, I am fine. Let's get this done!"

I gave the door a shove and we found ourselves in Grandma's sitting room. We stood there in the doorway in absolute silence. Everything was just as I had left it the day before.

She broke the silence by saying, "Honey, let's get busy, we have our work cut out for us. There's no time for crying or looking back, we've got a passel of work to do!"

I grinned at her expression and began the tour of the house.

As we assessed the situation, Miss Emma's first response was, "We can do it! We can do it! I'm going to call Sam Hicks to come and bush hog the yard first."

I looked at her quizzically and asked, "What in the world is a bush hog?"

That really brought a laugh from her as she replied, "Hope, a bush hog is a large mower behind a tractor. A bush hog would be more practical than a hay baler. You do know what a hay baler is, don't you?"

"Yea, yea, but I really don't know anything about farm equipment or remodeling an old house. I'm embarrassed that I don't know about these things."

"Not to worry, Honey, you'll understand everything when we finish," she replied.

We began wandering from room to room trying to decide where to start.

After we had explored every nook and cranny in the house, Miss Emma looked at me with a look of determination and said, "I say we spend the rest of this day trying to unravel the mystery your mama left for you to solve. We can get the rake and shovel out of the back of the truck and get some of this mess out of here. Until we get some help with the yard, there is really nothing we can accomplish outside today. This house is so deep in trash we need to call for a bulldozer to sweep it out," Miss Emma jokingly exclaimed.

"When your mama and I were children, we used to play in the room at the end of the hall. I think it once was a bedroom, but your grandparents used it for storage. We used that room for a playhouse, and we let our imaginations run wild. We made furniture out of old boxes and crates. I say we start in that room."

"Miss Emma, you know more about this house than I do. If you feel it is the best place to start, that's exactly what we'll do," I replied.

We went back to the truck and retrieved the tool box, a shovel, and a rake. I barely remembered the little room at the end of the hall, because Grandma never let me go in it. I guess she felt I might get hurt on all of the junk she kept in the room.

When we opened the door to the storage room, the stale air took our breath away, and I thought to myself, *I should have brought us a mask.*

We began to pull the trash and boxes out into the hallway. Most of the boxes were empty. After we pulled the contents from the storage room out into the hall, we began to explore every inch of the room. We searched it from top to bottom and found nothing.

The walls and ceiling of the entire house were covered with pine bead board that Grandpa had harvested from the trees on the farm. He had taken the timber to a saw mill near Bostic to have it milled. Miss Emma was fascinated with the woodwork throughout the entire house.

She kept talking about the beautiful wood and even made the statement, "I wish these walls could talk to us. It would be a sight what they could tell us! And just look at these lovely pine floors. Many a step has been made on these old boards."

Miss Emma suggested that we search Grandma and Grandpa's bedroom next. When we entered the room, I smiled as I recalled the scary old train and the hoot owls that terrified me at night.

Grandpa had built me a cot to sleep on and put it in their bedroom. He knew I was afraid of the dark, and he did everything he could to allay my fear.

I was immediately brought back to reality when Miss Emma said, "Hope, tell me again what Amy said just before she died."

"She just said for me to find Grandma's journal that is hidden in the house. She said she and Daddy searched everywhere they knew to look."

"Let's look at this logically," Miss Emma suggested. "If you were going to hide something in here, where would you put it?"

"Well, I've never had anything worth hiding, but if I did, I would probably put a safe somewhere. You know there was a little room off of their bedroom that Grandma never allowed me to go in. I figured that they didn't want me to go in there, because that was where they kept their chamber pots. They had a little chamber pot for me and kept it under my little bed in this room. Grandpa would always empty those smelly pots first thing in the morning. I hated using a chamber pot, but I would have done anything to stay with my grandparents. The fun I had at Grandma's far outweighed the dreaded chamber pot."

"You know, Hope, your grandma could have hidden a journal in that little room. Let's start there," she exclaimed while pointing to the small room.

After we entered the little room, Miss Emma used the hammer to tap around on the floor and walls and came up empty handed. Every board sounded the same.

"Hope, there are evidently no hollow places in this room to hide anything," Miss Emma exclaimed as she continued to tap on the walls.

I looked at Miss Emma with a defeated look.

We went back into the bedroom and checked every inch of the wooden floor. To our dismay, we found nothing.

"Now don't fret child, we'll find it. Try to think about everything your grandma had in this room. Just close your eyes, and try to remember where all of the furnishings were placed," Miss Emma suggested when she saw the gloom on my face.

I did just that and pictured the room as I remembered it. There had been a table between our beds and a large wardrobe on the wall facing the beds. Also, there had been a small chest of drawers under the window. The bead board in the room had been painted pale blue, and Grandma had made lovely lace curtains to cover the windows.

I began to look around the room again and noticed something. The two window ledges were made differently.

"Oh! Oh! Oh! I think I've got it Miss Emma! Come here, hurry! It's the windows. Look, the window ledges are different, and one seems to be loose!" I screamed excitedly.

We began to methodically check the wood under the window that faced the road, and I carefully ran my fingers over the wood. I had a gut feeling that we were very close to finding the journal, but nothing was there. I slid my hand up to the base of the window and rubbed both hands along the window ledge. I noticed that the window ledge seemed to protrude out from the wall farther than the other window in the bedroom. I was attempting to manipulate the wooden ledge when I heard something make a cracking noise. All at once, the ledge came loose, dropped to the floor, and banged as it landed at my feet. I knew I had either torn something up or found something.

I screamed to Miss Emma, "Oh, my goodness, I think I found it!"

Before I knew it, Miss Emma was on her knees beside me and exclaimed, "Well, in this world! Let me look! Here's a flashlight. Let's see what's behind this wall!"

I took the flashlight from Miss Emma and directed the beam into the hole the ledge had left. All I could see was rotted wood, dead bugs, and spider webs. The spiders had been busy over the years, and their webs filled the space between the interior wall and the exterior wall. I carefully put the hammer down in the hole and brushed away the cobwebs to get a better look.

"Miss Emma, there is nothing in here," I lamented.

"Now child, don't get discouraged. We're gonna keep on looking. It's got to be here somewhere," she replied.

We left Grandma and Grandpa's bedroom and went toward the dining room. After searching that area with no results, we moved to the kitchen.

Some of the bead boards in the kitchen were coming loose from the wall. We even pulled some of the boards off the wall in the kitchen with a crow bar and found only spider webs and bugs as a reward.

I sat down in the middle of the floor in defeat and cried, "Miss Emma, let's take a break and eat lunch. I don't think we are ever going to find anything in this house."

"Eatin' sounds mighty good to me. As the students in my adult reading group say, 'I'm might near starved to death. Let's get some vittles.' We can sit on the front steps to feast and enjoy Lucy's delicious poke lunch."

Smothering a laugh as I peered into my brown lunch bag, I asked, "Miss Emma, I hate to ask you this, but what in the world is a poke lunch?"

"They law me! You have never heard of a poke lunch. That's what folks around these parts call a brown paper bag with your lunch packed in it."

"I'm going to have to go back to college to learn all of the words and phrases you folks use around here. We could get you to teach the course at the Community College and call it Appalachian Foothill Dialect 101."

Miss Emma went into a fit of laughter. She was laughing so hard I was afraid she would have a stroke.

When she managed to catch her breath, she exclaimed, "You just wait, you'll be talkin' just like Rullerford County folks before long. It's like some of those childhood diseases. It's mighty contagious.

"I lost some of my accent when I went away to college but not all of it. I enjoyed my years at Queens College in Charlotte. Of course, your mama was there, too. After I graduated, I was more than ready to return to the foothills and the fresh air coming down from the mountains.

"You know, Hope, the dialect of this area of the country goes back to our earliest ancestors. When this area was first settled, most of the settlers were either from England, Scotland, Ireland, or Germany. They were pretty much isolated from the rest of the world because of the mountains; therefore, they have through the years continued to maintain the influence of those countries in their speech patterns.

"Some of the areas in Appalachia have a heavier Elizabethan English influence in their speech than others. Some areas are influenced more by Scottish, Irish, or German ancestry. To be honest with you, much of the beautiful Appalachian dialect in this area is a dying art form. You find it mainly in the old-timers that live here, like Snuffy, for instance.

"If you check Elizabethan literature, you will find variations of some of the words and phrases that are used in this area of No'th Ca'olina. I guess the Scots have had the strongest influence in this neck of the woods."

"I think I am a conglomeration of German, Irish, and Scottish, and I have always loved to hear folks from this area talk. Mama and Daddy lost a lot of their accent, but they still used a lot of phrases and colloquialisms that are only used in this area. One thing in particular that they never got away from was their pronunciation of Rutherford County. They always called it Rullerford County." I replied.

"Yea, if a person is born and reared here, they never 'get above their raisin,' as the old-timers say. We all say Rullerford County," Miss Emma responded.

We found a place to eat on the piazza and sat down for our lunch. Miss Emma quickly said a prayer of thanksgiving, and we opened our poke lunches and delved into the delicious food. The sun had slowly gone behind the clouds, and a soft fragrant breeze was blowing through the pine trees. The hypnotic smell of honeysuckles and pine engulfed us as we ate our lunch.

Miss Emma finally spoke. "Just smell that wonderful fragrance of honeysuckles and pine. There's nothing to compare with the fragrance of springtime in the country."

She continued to rattle on. "That Lucy really knows how to pack a lunch. Her ma died when she was twelve years old. She had to quit school to keep house and cook for Snuffy. You just wait until you taste her chocolate cake. It's to die for."

We attacked the lunches like two ravenous wolves. I couldn't imagine anything being better than the BLT's we were eating, but when I tasted the chocolate cake, I understood what Miss Emma meant when she said it was to die for.

After finishing the meal, I leaned back against the piazza railing and sighed, "If I keep eating like this, Miss Emma, I'm gonna gain so much weight I won't be able to get in my clothes."

"Oh, don't worry. We'll burn it off workin'," she replied. "But I must tell you, we may not be worth two cents the rest of the day. Lucy is a wonderful cook, but she doesn't have a clue about fat grams or calories. We'll just have to get busy workin' them off. Let's gather up our tools and get started at the rear of the house. We're gonna solve this mystery today."

Chapter 7

After overindulging ourselves on the poke lunch, we could hardly move. Miss Emma and I had to force ourselves back to work. We managed to make our way across the hall into the living room.

Once again my mind was flooded with memories of Grandma and how she loved her living room or "front room" as she called it. As I approached the spot where she always placed her cedar Christmas tree, I could almost sense her presence. The fragrance of cedar always permeated Grandma's house during the holidays.

I had so many memories of Christmases past. I kept many of the gifts and treasures Grandma and Grandpa had given me over the years. I had them safely tucked away in the "hope chest" Grandpa had made for me. It was a lovely trunk type chest made from a select group of cedar trees that Grandpa had harvested from the farm. The detailed carvings on the chest were exquisite, and he had even carved the Martin coat of arms on the lid of the chest.

As I turned around to face Miss Emma, I looked at the spot where Grandma's old upright piano used to stand. Grandma had always been my artistic inspiration. She was the reason I became a music teacher, and I had definitely inherited her deep love for music and poetry. I would sit behind her on her beautiful Duncan Phyfe sofa and listen to her play for hours on end. She played for her church and all of the weddings in the area. She loved the classical composers, especially Beethoven and Brahms. At Christmas she would play carols, and the entire family would gather around the old upright piano to sing. Grandpa had a beautiful bass voice and Grandma an angelic soprano voice. Mama would sing the alto and Uncle Cletus sang tenor. Their four-part harmony was amazing. Grandpa always read the Christmas story from the Bible at the end of the caroling, and then Grandma would sing her own rendition of *O Holy Night*. Grandpa always said listening to Grandma was like being transported to the portals of glory.

Grandma taught piano and voice lessons to individual students her entire adult life. Because of the influence of Lillie Mae Martin, music would remain alive in North Carolina and beyond for years to come.

I looked at Miss Emma with tears rolling down my cheeks. She reached out to me, and I fell into her warm embrace.

As she held me in her arms, she whispered, "Go ahead and cry, my child, get it all out. You've had more on you for the last while than any mortal soul ought to have to bear. Just be thankful for your memories and your wonderful legacy. You've been blessed with a Godly legacy, and don'cha ever forget it. Just let it all out child, just let it all out. Cryin' is good for the soul."

"Oh, Miss Emma, I feel so unworthy of that legacy. I don't deserve this house. I didn't even want to come here; now that I'm here, I am determined to forge ahead and reno-vate this place. I want to make it something that my grand-parents and my mama would be proud of. I will find that journal, and I know that its message will probably change my life forever. My original plans were to come here this week and find the journal, get started on the renovations, and possibly sell the farm. But, everything has changed now.

I have lived a self-absorbed life for far too long. Maybe, just maybe, I am supposed to fix this place up and live here instead of Charlotte. Let's get busy, Miss Emma, we have our work cut out for us."

"That's the spirit, Hope. Let's get on with it," she replied.

We took the rake and shovel and raked out the living room as best we could. You can't imagine the rubbish we pulled out of that room.

I looked at Miss Emma and exclaimed, "I sure wish I knew who trashed this house. I'd go get them and make them clean it up."

Miss Emma just laughed at me and said, "Yea, as my pa would have said, 'Somebody needs to tan their hides.'"

Discouragement set in as we searched every inch of the bead boarded living room, but we pressed on. We even pulled up some loose floorboards with no results. It seemed we were destined to find nothing but spider webs, dead bugs, and dust bunnies. We checked every inch of the rock fireplace with no results.

I asked myself, *where in this world would Grandma have hidden that journal, and why was there such a secret? If she wanted me to have it, why didn't she just give it to me or Mama when she was able to?*

I looked around the living room to the closet in the corner of the room. As I opened the door, I just knew in my heart we would find something there. Miss Emma and I pecked around on the walls of the closet with hammers and came up empty handed. One wall did sound a bit different, but after thorough investigation, we determined there was nothing there.

I turned to Miss Emma and said, "I can't believe this. I just knew we would find something in here. Well, we have one more room, and that's the back bedroom. Let's go down the hall and finish up for the day. I know you're exhausted, Miss Emma."

"Now, Hope, don't cha worry about me. I'm just fine. I'm strong, and I want to help you do this."

We made our way down the hall to the last room which had been my mama's bedroom when she was a child. As we entered the room, it was a delight to see that it wasn't filled with garbage and trash.

"Well, in this world! I can't believe my eyes. I believe some angels came in before us to make our day easier," Miss Emma exclaimed.

"I don't know why there's no trash in here, but whatever the reason, I'm grateful. I won't complain," I replied.

We began to check all of the boards throughout the back bedroom to no avail. On the wall backing up to the living room was an old rock fireplace. Mama frequently told me how Grandpa would make sure she had a cozy warm fire on cold winter nights. Grandpa built the fireplace from rocks he gathered from the river that ran below the farm. In fact, the house had four chimneys, and each one was constructed from rocks that came from that river. Grandpa had also used rocks from the river to lay the foundation of the house.

While staring at the mantle that Grandpa had made from a pine log, I suddenly remembered Mama telling me that she had a special hiding place for her treasures behind one of the rocks in the fireplace. When I was a child, I often tried to find which rock it was, but I never had success. I decided to check every single river rock and see if I could get any of them to move. I had just about completed my check when I came across a stone near the floor that seemed to be loose. I immediately took both hands and carefully began to move it back and forth. Suddenly, the rock moved forward and fell into my hands. I stood there dumbstruck. I saw a small box buried deep within the cavity.

"Miss Emma, look at this! I found something!" I shouted.

"What is it? What is it?" she exclaimed.

I carefully removed the box from the cavity where the rock had been and held it in my hands. I began to tremble as I opened the lid. As I peered inside of the ornate metal box, I was surprised to find some old jewelry. I carefully removed the items from the box. They appeared to be just some old necklaces and rings. I looked at Miss Emma with surprise and disappointment when I realized there was no journal in the box. We directed the beam of the flashlight back into the hole in the fireplace and saw nothing but dust and spider webs.

Miss Emma immediately spoke up, "Let me see what we have here. I remember these pieces; they were your mother's. She must have forgotten about them. We may not have found what we wanted, but it looks like we have found some priceless pieces of your mother's past."

I looked back in the cavity where the rock had been and saw nothing. Out of curiosity, I bravely stuck my arm all the way to the back of the open cavity. As I was pulling my arm out, my fingers brushed against something. Whatever it was appeared to be crammed back behind the other rocks. I grabbed the edge of what felt like a piece of paper and gently pulled it out.

In my hands I held a yellowed piece of paper that appeared to be a map. We started reviewing the document and discovered it truly was a map. The date on the map was not clear, but it looked like it was dated in the 1800s.

Excitedly I exclaimed, "Miss Emma, this is a map of what appears to be a gold mine. This is unbelievable." It had been pushed back so far that I could barely reach it.

Miss Emma commented, "Years ago Rullerfordton was known for producing gold. In fact, there was a time when it was the center for production of gold in the United States. There was even a mint in Rullerfordton. I can't remember all of the details, but the best I can recollect, the mint in Rullerfordton minted the first gold coin in the United States. As a matter of fact, Rullerford County had a flood of people moving here during that time hoping to strike it rich."

"That's interesting; no one ever talked about that in front of me. Let's see if we can figure out where this gold mine is located."

As I perused the document, I realized that it was so old and faded it was impossible to really determine the exact site of the old mine.

"Miss Emma, this just adds another twist and turn to the mystery. There are no markings on this map that can be used to find the mine," I exclaimed.

"Child, you have made quite a discovery. But we better finish looking for the hidden journal. We haven't checked the attic space yet. Do you know where the entrance to the attic space is located?"

"Oh, that's out in the hallway," I replied.

I looked at Miss Emma as she turned to leave the bedroom. She had a quizzical look on her face. I gathered our findings and followed her as she went into the hallway.

When we got into the hallway, I looked up at the scuttle hole in the ceiling that led to the attic and said, "Miss Emma, I saw a ladder on the back porch. I'll go get it and climb up and see if anything's in the attic."

"Make sure the ladder's safe," she replied.

I retrieved the ladder from the back porch, and after checking the sturdiness of the ladder, I stood it up under the scuttle hole. It was just tall enough for me to reach the opening, and I wasn't very trusting of the dilapidated old ladder. I was so anxious to see what was in the attic that I tossed caution to the wind, and climbed to the top of the ladder. I reached up to push the board aside that covered the scuttle hole, and Miss Emma handed me the flash light. I proceeded to shine the light throughout the attic area. To my disappointment, there seemed to be absolutely nothing there.

Putting the board back in place in the scuttle hole, I made my way back down the ladder and said, "They must not have used the attic space to store anything. There's absolutely nothing up there but bugs and spiders. Ugh, those critters make my skin crawl."

Miss Emma smiled and gave me that same curious look I had seen on her face a few minutes earlier. "I want us to go back in the living room and give that closet another once over. For some reason I have a gut feeling that we missed something when we were in the living room. Let's just check it out one more time.

"Around the turn of the century, homes often had a secret area or a hidden room in a portion of the house. They would disguise the entrance so that no one could find it. Maybe we can find something if we search the closet again. I noticed when we left the bedroom there seemed to be some lost space between the bedroom, hallway, and living room. I know the closet in the living room takes up a portion of that space, but according to the layout of the house, both rooms should be much larger than they are."

Miss Emma retrieved her tape measure from her toolbox and instructed me to hold it as we measured the wall in the hallway from the door of the bedroom to the door of the living room. It measured exactly fourteen feet. I watched her as she began to calculate how much wall space should be on the other side of the wall.

We first measured the living room and then the bedroom. The living room measured three feet from the door frame to the corner of the room, and the bedroom measured four feet from the door frame to the corner.

Miss Emma looked at me with excitement and said, "Hope, I think we've found something. We've got about six or seven feet of missing space between these two rooms.

Now we just have to figure out how to get into that space. It may be nothing, but then it may be just what we're looking for. I know one thing, there is some missing space somewhere between these two rooms, and we're gonna find it today. Let's get on the move, young lady."

"Oh, Miss Emma, I hope you're right. It'll be dark in a little while, and we'll have to leave. I just hope we find something soon."

We went back into the enormous closet that Grandma had used to store all of her music and Christmas decorations and started looking around. The dimensions of the closet were approximately seven feet by five feet. We began to tap the bead board walls and ceiling with no success.

I was getting ready to turn around when something caught my eye. There was a tiny crack in the center of the wall on the left side of the closet, and there was not one on the right side. All of the bead boards on the right wall were in one piece and were perfectly joined in both corners. The left side, however, was constructed of short pieces of bead boards that seemed to have been pieced together to form a hairline crack.

As I stood there in the semidarkness and stared at the almost undetectable slit, I realized that it went from the floor to the ceiling. It appeared that someone had cut the wall in half from top to bottom. *Could this possibly be an entrance to another room?* I asked myself.

When I tried to wedge my fingers into the small hairline crevice, I saw that it was impossible. I proceeded to lean against the wall and felt something move. Before I knew what was happening, a small opening appeared in the left corner.

My screaming startled Miss Emma, and she turned just in time to see a portion of the wall as it slowly moved to the right. My heart was racing as I pushed harder. I heard a cracking sound, and slowly a large opening appeared the size of a doorway. Miss Emma grabbed the flashlight and directed the beam into the small room that lay before us. We stood there speechless with our mouths hanging open.

"I do believe we've found what we we're looking for!" I shouted as I regained my composure.

"Yes, my child, I believe we have," Miss Emma emphatically agreed.

Chapter 8

M y heart was racing as we stepped slowly into the hidden room. The room was probably seven feet in width and fifteen feet in depth. I turned to my right and realized that there was a small niche backing up to the closet we had just come through. That small space probably added four or five more feet on the wall backing up to the bedroom and was filled with clothes and boxes. Everything smelled of dust and mildew, and the entire room was shrouded with cobwebs.

My first thought was, *what in this world possessed Grandpa to build a secret room.*

Neither Grandpa nor Grandma seemed to be the type of people to have secrets. It disturbed me to know that they had a secret aspect of their lives that Mama didn't even know about.

I looked up at Miss Emma and lamented, "I can't believe this. Evidently Mama and Daddy didn't know about this room, or she would have told me. Mama said they had searched the entire house looking for the journal. Miss Emma, what do you make of all of this?"

"Hope, I just don't know what to say. There never seemed to be anything secretive about your grandparents. I don't have a clue what they might have wanted to hide. I was here at their home many times and never suspected anything secretive about them. Your mama never said anything about this room to me, and I honestly don't think she knew about it. I think if she had known about it, she would have told me. We were like sisters. I just can't believe your daddy didn't figure this out, but he was not a builder or architecturally inclined."

"No, he couldn't even hang pictures. Mama had to do all of that."

As we stood looking into the room, a small desk came into my line of vision. It backed up to the hall that divided the house. To the right of the room was the wall of the back bedroom and the back side of the fireplace that we discovered in the back bedroom. On the left side of the secret room was an old trunk or hope chest similar to the one Grandpa made for me. There was a large map hanging on the wall over the desk. The room was really quite large for a secret hideaway.

We approached the map with a keen sense of anticipation, and Miss Emma commented, "You know, Hope, this is sort' a upsetting. Maybe we don't really want to know what's in this room."

"I feel the same way, Miss Emma. What if I do find something that I really would be better off not knowing?"

"But we need to press on, honey. Your dear mama and grandma wanted you to find that journal. You must find it, whether you want to or not," she said as she directed the beam of the flashlight on the map.

The map was only a map of Rutherford County with a few places marked in pencil, and it seemed of no importance.

My eyes fell on the desk. There was an old oil lamp on the corner of the desk that was still filled with kerosene. Several pieces of yellowed paper lay on the desk, but they seemed to be of no value. I opened the drawers and found nothing there.

I turned around to the small niche behind us to investi-gate some of the clothes that were hanging from a rod that was suspended from the ceiling. Grandpa had even gone to the trouble of finishing the walls and ceiling in the same bead board he used throughout the rest of the house. He had even painted the walls of the secret room. Surprisingly, they had not faded as much as the rest of the house.

I moved the clothes aside to see what was behind them, and to my surprise there was a portrait of a young couple that had to be over one-hundred years old.

"Who in this world is this couple, Miss Emma? It's not Grandma and Grandpa. This picture look like it dates back to the turn of the century. You know, this woman looks a lot like me. It has to be a relative."

I pushed the clothes back into place and exclaimed, "These are some of Grandma and Grandpa's old clothes. Look, Miss Emma, here's a pair of Grandpa's overalls and a dress Grandma wore. Here's her old blue coat she wore when she went outside in the winter to bring in firewood. She had this old coat on the day she caught me and my cousins trying to smoke Grandpa's pipe. I remember that like it was yesterday."

I turned my attention to four hat boxes in the small niche and discovered they only contained old hats and shoes. I pulled one of the hats out and put it on.

When I turned to show Miss Emma, she laughingly exclaimed, "You look just like a flapper from the 1920s. All you need is a flapper's dress to match. W'y, you could cut a rug and do the Charleston."

"Miss Emma, look here!"

I knelt down to the area that was the backside of the chimney that was located in the back bedroom and exclaimed, "Look at this opening. This must be where the old map came from!"

After closer investigation, we discovered that there was a rock missing on the back side of the chimney. Beside of the gaping hole at the base of the chimney, several other documents were rolled up in that area. Most of them appeared to be of no value. *Why in the world did Grandpa hide these documents near this little hole?* I asked myself.

"Miss Emma, I wonder if this hole goes all the way through the chimney to the other side?"

I picked up an old walking cane of Grandpa's from the corner of the room and pushed it through the small opening in the back of the chimney. When I did, we heard the loose rock on the other side of the chimney fall out of place.

"Ah, ha, this is how the map got in the secret place in the chimney. Maybe it got into the hole by accident or Grandpa could have put it there. I can't believe he was so secretive. Why in this world did he do some of the things he did?"

"Hope, we are probably going to find many unanswered questions on this quest, and we may never know the answers."

I turned to my left and approached the rustic old trunk. As I drew closer to it, I recognized the familiar Martin coat of arms on the lid of the trunk, and under the ornate carving was the word "MARTIN." Grandpa evidently had made the trunk for Grandma when they were first married, because it appeared to be very old.

I hesitated for a moment and slowly lifted the lid. I was engulfed with an overpowering smell of mustiness and cedar. It was then that I realized that the inside of the pine chest was lined with cedar. The trunk appeared to be only packed with clothes. Lying on top of the clothes was an exquisite white dress.

I held it up and exclaimed, "Look, Miss Emma, this must have been a dress that Grandma treasured. Could this have been her wedding dress? Look at the style! It's so typical of the 1920s. Look at the detailed needlework; wonder if it was handmade?"

"Most assuredly, that trim work is hand-done tatting. I recall that your grandmother was an expert when it came to tatting. She once told me she would teach me the art of tatting, but I never learned," Miss Emma answered.

"Miss Emma, look at the lines of this dress. It's has a beautiful dropped waistline and is accented by a pink ribbon. Just look at this hem line. I think it is called a handkerchief hemline. I don't know who made it, but the handwork is exquisite. This dress could be worn today. I have seen styles similar in magazines. This cedar lined trunk has, without a doubt, preserved this dress. I believe I could wear it."

I continued to remove the contents of the trunk and found a lovely cloche hat that was so reminiscent of the 1920s. It was trimmed in the same pink ribbon as the dress. I also found some ladies bloomers and a camisole trimmed in a lovely lacey design. Underneath all of that, I found a man's three piece suit. It was an elegant dove gray pinstripe, and beneath the suit, I found a red and blue necktie and a white shirt. I noticed two leather items that were gray in color with small black buttons.

I turned to Miss Emma and asked, "Do you know what these are?"

"Certainly," she replied. "Those, my dear, are spats. Men wore them over their shoes when they dressed formally in the 1920s. These outfits must have been your grandparents' wedding clothes. You just don't see spats this day and time."

While kneeling beside the trunk, I noticed a tiny baby dress in the bottom.

"Oh, Miss Emma, this must have been Mama's. And here is her baby blanket. I can't believe I am finding all of this. These are priceless treasures, but where is the journal?"

We continued to go through the items in the trunk. Underneath the clothes were books and more documents. There were old pictures and an old yearbook from Grandma's high school days.

It was when I picked up the yearbook that I noticed a charming, leather bound book with a lock on it. My heart felt like it was beating two hundred times a minute as I lifted the book from the trunk.

Panic-stricken, I looked at Miss Emma through tears and whispered, "Do you think this could be it?"

"It has to be. It just has to be. What else could it be?" she replied.

I carefully tried to release the latch on the lock. Surprisingly, it popped open on the first try. As I opened the book, I immediately recognized the handwriting. I began to sob as I turned the pages.

Miss Emma put her arms around me and said, "Hope, you have found what your mama wanted you to find, it seems. Now let's go out on the piazza and see what your grandma has to say to you."

Like a small child, I wiped away my tears with my tee shirt. We placed everything, except the journal and a few documents, back in the trunk. I rose to my feet and followed Miss Emma out of Grandpa's secret room. Our flashlight was getting dim, and it was difficult to find our way out of the little hideaway. We managed to get back to the opening of the room and stepped out into the closet area. Miss Emma and I carefully pulled the door of the room back into place and made our way out of the closet. As I closed the closet door, I realized that it was getting dark outside.

I looked at Miss Emma and said, "I guess we best go back to the inn to read the journal. It'll be dark in a few minutes. I didn't realize it was so late."

"Time flies when you're having fun. Hope, I picked up a pile of the documents that were on the desk as we were leaving the secret room. I thought you might like to mull over them tonight."

I suddenly felt a familiar strange sensation, and I realized that I was going to have a panic attack. I had a history of panic attacks, and I recognized the symptoms right away.

I grabbed Miss Emma's arm frantically and gasped, "Miss Emma, I don't feel so good. Could we sit down for a minute? I can't seem to catch my breath."

Everything began to turn dark and my chest began to hurt. I was gasping for air, my ears were ringing, and I began to slump over. Miss Emma realized what was happening, and she immediately went into action. She managed to get me to the front yard, and I bent over and hung my head between my legs. Miss Emma continued to encourage me to relax and control my breathing. I finally lay down on the ground for a few minutes.

As my feelings began to improve, I sat up and said, "I'm so-o-o sorry. This has happened to me before, when I have been under stress or have been upset. The last time it happened was the night Mama died. I'm feeling much better now. I think I'll be okay. It has helped so much just to get some fresh air."

Miss Emma offered me some cold water from a thermos she had brought with us. After drinking some of the refreshing liquid, I splashed some on my face.

"Thank you, Miss Emma, I feel so much better now. I think I'll be able to go back to the inn now."

I managed to drag myself to a standing position, and with Miss Emma's help, I climbed into the truck. After closing up the house, Miss Emma quickly loaded the truck with her tools and some of the items we had discovered, all the while, I continued to clutch the journal close to my heart.

As we were leaving the property, I turned to look back at the old house one last time. As I held the old journal, I thought to myself, *I just wish this house could talk to me, but since it can't, I guess I will have to depend on this little book from the past. It is my lifeline to my grandma's past.*

Leaving the yard that afternoon, I looked at the towering white pines that dominated the front yard, and the wind seemed to be whispering secrets through their branches. *Maybe they are trying to tell me something,* I thought to myself.

I turned to Miss Emma and remarked, "There are many hidden secrets on this old farm, and those majestic evergreen pine trees have witnessed every single one of them."

Chapter 9

Miss Emma instructed me to lie down in the seat of the truck, before she drove away from the house. While lying there, I continued to clutch the journal to my heart, and I relived every moment of the day. The panic attack had knocked the wind out of me, and I succumbed to sleep during our ride back into town. I awoke with a start as we pulled into the driveway of the inn.

Miss Emma helped me from the truck and yelled for Samson, Hattie's husband, and with their help, I managed to get into the house. Samson then began to unload the tools that were in the back of the truck. After getting me settled in the sun room, Miss Emma went back to get the box of items we brought back from the house.

As I lay back in the lovely chaise lounge, I continued to hold the journal near my heart. Miss Emma placed the box of treasures we had found at the farm on the coffee table and began giving me instructions.

"Now, Hope, you just lie there and rest and when you feel up to it, go on upstairs and get your bath and put your pajamas on. Hattie will have your supper ready when you come down, and then we'll start going through the journal. I'm going to buzz up these back stairs myself and get a quick bath. I'll meet you back down here in a few minutes. As soon as we eat, we'll delve into this mystery your mama and grandma left for you to unravel."

I listened as Miss Emma went up the back staircase that led from the kitchen to the second floor, and after a short rest, I quickly followed her. I held onto my grandma's journal and didn't even want to put it down to take my bath. After making my way to the bathroom, I gently placed it on the small vanity that was near the sink. I guess I was being paranoid about the journal, but I just couldn't seem to part with it or let it out of my sight.

The bathroom that was attached to my bedroom not only had a lovely white claw-foot tub, but it also had a walk-in shower stall. I decided to take a quick shower and let my hair dry naturally. The warm water felt refreshing as it cascaded down my body. I felt as if I had one-hundred years of grunge all over me. I reached for the fluffy white towel Hattie had put out for me and inhaled the fragrance of fresh linen. After towel drying my hair and combing it into place, I donned my pajamas and bedroom slippers and descended the back staircase to the kitchen.

I did not get to meet Hattie that morning before we left to go to the farm and was anxious to meet her. As I approached the kitchen from the back staircase, I could have followed the wonderful aroma coming from the kitchen with my eyes closed. Hattie had evidently cooked something out of this world. I could hear someone singing an old spiritual, so I stopped on the stairs just to listen. I figured it must be Hattie singing, so I just stood there and absorbed every beautiful word. In a lovely contralto voice, I heard her singing an old slave song, "Swing Low Sweet Chariot."

I entered the kitchen just as she started the second stanza. She had her back to me, so I listened intently as she continued to sing those beautiful words. She stopped singing the moment she realized she had an audience.

"They land sakes, you must be Miss Hope. I'm Hattie, Hattie Alexander. I'm married to Samson Alexander, and we live ri'chear wid Miss Emma. Honey chil', you jist sit you'self right down here and eat yore supper."

She began mothering me, and I immediately felt as if I had known her my entire life. She had on a lovely pink pantsuit and comfortable white tennis shoes. Her beautiful dark skin radiated like sunbeams bouncing off of amber glass, and her lovely smile was warm and infectious. Her hair was almost completely gray, and she had it pulled up in a little bun at the nape of her neck.

"Miss Emma tol' me what you'uns found, and 'at you had a sinkin' spell. You better get some'um' in yore stomick. You still look a might peaked. Miss Emma'll be down directly. Samson and me, we done et, so you go ahead and commence ta eatin'."

As Hattie handed the plate full of food to me, I said, "Thank you, Hattie, it's so nice to finally meet you, and thank you for having dinner ready for us. We had such a long day, and a good meal is just what we need to revive us.

"I have to ask you, where in the world did you learn to sing like that? You have one of the loveliest contralto voices I have ever heard. I teach music, and I don't think I've ever heard anything so beautiful."

"W'y, Miss Hope, I been a singin' my whole life. My mama she sung to me all da time and my grandma loved to sing. Sometimes when I can't pray and my heart gets so heavy I jist can't hardly bear it, I jist commence to singin'. It makes my soul glad. It shore do, Miss Hope, it shore do. You know da Good Book says, 'A merry heart does a body good like a dost of medicine: but a broken spirit it dries up da bones.' And 'at be true. I jist lift up my voice to da Lawd, and my soul, it gets so happy I can't stand it. 'Ere ain't nuttin like singin' to my won'erful Lawd. It do make a heart merry, and I shore don't want no dried up bones."

As I started to eat my meal, I asked Hattie, "How long have you and Samson been with Miss Emma?"

"Miss Emma, she took us in atter her mama died. I guess 'at wuz about thirty year ago. When she wuz a livin' out at her old home place, we stayed right behind her jist a short piece through the woods. When she moved here, we come wid her, and she built us a new house right behind hers. She's da best woman who ever walked in shoe leather.

"Me and Samson, we have one boy. Miss Emma paid fer his schoolin' at Duke University. He's a doctor, and we is so proud of him. He stays up around Asheville.

"When Miss Emma started a fixin' up 'is here house, like I tol' you, she had our house built right behind hers so she could look atter us. She takes good care of us, and it don't cost us a penny to live here. Miss Emma, she's like family to my Samson and me. We's been wid her a many a year. We look atter her and she looks atter us. I've know'd Miss Emma since she wuz a baby. She done told me who yore mama wuz, and I know'd her too."

Hattie had prepared a scrumptious meal of chicken and dumplings, green beans that were cooked southern style with ham hocks, and steamed carrots. I didn't realize how hungry I was until I began to eat. She had prepared a delicious lemon pound cake for dessert, and I savored every morsel. I had never tasted such good food. Even though I was anxious to read the journal, I knew I needed to eat to regain my strength. Panic attacks always left me weak and hungry. We had the journal, and that's what was important. Miss Emma and I had the entire night to review it.

I looked at Hattie and said, "Hattie, this food is out of this world. You must give me you recipes."

"Law me, Miss Hope, I ain't got no recipes. I jist cook like my ma did, and she jist cooked like her ma did. My grandma was da best cook in 'ese here parts, and she learn't from her ma. 'At bein' my great-grandma. She and my great-grandpa wuz slaves back in da olden days. When Mr. Lincoln stopped da war, and when my people wuz freed atter da war, 'ey come to No'th Ca'lina from Geo'gia. 'Ey wuz on a plantation somewheres pirt'near Atlanta. You know, Miss Hope, Mr. Lincoln wuz born ri'chear in Rullerford County up on Puzzle Creek right close to Bostic."

I looked at her in amazement. "No, I didn't know that. I thought he was born in Kentucky."

I could not believe what Hattie was telling me. All of the history classes I had taken had taught that he was born in Kentucky.

"No, chil', 'at be what 'em politicians wants you to believe, but I know better. W'y, Nancy Hanks, his ma, was a member of Concord Baptist Church up near Bostic.

"Da story goes 'at she didn't have nary a ma or pa to look atter her, so she went to stay wid a family up on Puzzle Creek. She was jist a young'un when she come to stay wid 'em folks. They left Rullerford County and moved up to da mountains or somewhere, and while 'ey wuz 'ere, I thank at' 'ere man 'at she wuz a livin' with grew to liken her in a sinful way. The next thang everybody know'd, Nancy Hanks was in a family way. The very idea, she wuz jist a chap when she birthed Abraham. Yep, that's da way it wuz. 'At 'ere wife of hisun pitched a hissy fit, so he sent Mr. Lincoln's ma back to Rullerford County to have da baby. She birthed little Abraham up 'ere on Puzzle Creek, ri'chear in 'is county. Ever'body in 'is neck of da woods knows all about Mr. Lincoln's birthin'."

"I've never heard that story. Are you sure that's correct?" I questioned her with hint of uncertainty in my voice.

"Yes'um, I's sure. 'Em politicians, 'ey don't want nary a soul to know 'bout it, but it really happened 'at a way. W'y, you otta see pictures of some of 'em folks that supposed to be his relations. 'Ey looks jist like Mr. Lincoln, sure as da worl'." And his ma, Nancy Hanks, her name wuz on da church roll at Concord Baptist Church over at Bostic for many a year, but it got burnt up in a far. 'At 'ere man who kept da church's roll, his house burnt to da ground. But I know'd folks 'at saw her name on da roll. You jist gotta believe me. Da pictures tell da tale."

As I was finishing my meal, Miss Emma entered the kitchen. She must have heard what we were talking about, and she proceeded to verified Hattie's story.

"Hope, I truly believe that story, myself," she said. "In fact, many people in this area believe it. We can go on the internet, and I can show you pictures of Honest Abe and some of his Rullerford County relatives, and you won't believe the resemblance. In fact, I have a couple of books here about Abe Lincoln's Rullerford County roots. I think they are both out of print and are collectors' items now."

I sat there in shock and replied, "I don't know how many more shocks I can take today. This is mind-boggling. Do you think we can go to Puzzle Creek sometime this week and see where he was supposedly born?"

"Sure," Miss Emma replied.

Hattie spoke up and said, "I'd like to go wid you'uns when ye go."

"That would be great, Hattie. I'm not sure where the exact spot is anyway, and you have kept up with the story more than I have," Miss Emma replied as she began to eat her dinner.

"Oh, Hattie, you've outdone yourself. This meal is scrumptious," Miss Emma said.

"Miss Emma, I don't rightly knows what scrumptious is, but a comin' from you it got to be good," she replied with a laugh.

I was anxious to get into the journal, but Hattie's account of Abraham Lincoln's birth had spurred my interest in the Rutherford County legend. I looked at Hattie as she poured me another glass of iced tea and asked, "Hattie, this story of

Abraham Lincoln has come as a shock to me. Please tell me more!"

"Well, Miss Hope, back afore da Civil War, my great-grandpa and grandma wuz slaves. I even got 'eir slave tags ou'chonder in my house. They wuz all freed atter da great war."

I spoke up at that point and asked, "Just what is a slave tag, Hattie?"

"When my people come to 'is country, might near all of 'em was sent to Charleston, South Ca'lina. When 'ey wuz sold at da slave market in Charleston, 'em slave traders put tags 'round ever' slaves' neck. My great-grandpa, he said he weren't to ever take it off. It had his number on it, and it had da name of da town he wuz bought from. Da man who made the tag had his name on da back of it. 'Em tags wuz made of real thin copper, and 'ey wuz all different. 'Em slave traders treated my people like cattle at a auction. My great-grandma, she told my ma all about it. My people wuz auctioned off jist like 'ey do at one of 'em sale barns for cows and hawgs. Like I done tol' you, I got my great-grandpa's slave tag out at da house, an' I'll show it to you sometime.

"When 'at great war wuz over and da slaves wuz freed, my great-grandpa brung his family from Geo'gia to No'th Ca'lina. He built a homestead ri'chear in Rullerford County jist across da river from yore grandpa's old farm, an' it wuz right back of Miss Emma's pa's farm.

"My great-grandpa and great-grandma had ten young'uns. Some of 'em moved away, and da rest stayed ri'chear in Rullerford County. My grandpa wuz da oldest young'un, and he got Great-Grandpa's homestead when he passed. It wuz jist a little piece of land.

"When my great-grandpa got here, ever'body wuz a talkin' about Mr. Lincoln a bein' born up on Puzzle Creek near Bostic. Mr. Lincoln had already been kilt by that time, and ever'body in Rullerford County wuz a speculatin'. Da rumors wuz a flyin'. When we go up 'ere, I'll show you ever'thing. You can see for you'self what I been a talkin' 'bout.

Chapter 10

I looked at Hattie and held up the journal, "Hattie, since you know so much about the area, I would like for you to come into the sunroom while we read my mama's journal. Mama left a mysterious secret for me to unravel, and maybe you can help. Apparently, a secret is revealed in this journal my grandma kept. I'll help you with the dishes so you can be with us as we read it."

"W'y, Miss Hope, that's kind of you. I done filled up the dishwashin' machine, and all I has to do is put da rest of 'em dishes in the da machine. Thank da Lawd for dish-washing machines. Shore has made my life easy. I be 'ere in two seconds, and I be happy to help anyway I can."

As soon as Miss Emma completed her meal, we proceeded to the sunroom to open the box of documents and papers that we had discovered in the secret room. We made ourselves comfortable on Miss Emma's lovely sofa and spread the contents of the box from the farmhouse on the sofa table. When Hattie entered the sunroom, she sat in the recliner across from Miss Emma and me.

I looked at the two of them and said, "Well, here goes."

I took the old journal, which was still in my grasp, and buried my face in the yellowed pages and began to read aloud. I didn't know where to begin; therefore, I started to read at the very beginning.

"Saturday, April 11, 1925

"Ma and Papa gave me this lovely leather bound journal for my college graduation, and what a perfect day to start recording my life. I just graduated from Queens College in Charlotte with a degree in music last year.

"It is a beautiful spring day, April 11, 1925. I am going to marry the man that I love this afternoon at three o'clock. He is everything I ever hoped for in a husband.

"I know it wasn't an accident that we met at the picnic in Martinsville. I can still see him now as he tried to impress me with his antics by participating in every event at the picnic. I was thrilled when Amos finally asked me to join him in the sack race. He was so comical trying to catch the greased pig, but the highlight of that day was when he asked me to join him for the picnic with his family. I shared lunch with his ma and pa and some of their friends. The entire picnic area was filled with families having fun and fellowship over deli- cious food. Mrs. Martin had prepared the most wonderful southern fried chicken and fried apple pies. She promised that she would cook some for our wedding supper after the wedding.

"My ma is preparing all kinds of food for the meal after the wedding. We are going to have a huge ham that Papa cured in the smokehouse during the winter months, potato salad with lots of Ma's homemade fourteen-day pickles, home-canned green beans with ham hocks, deviled eggs, and Ma's homemade pickled-beets. Our pastor's wife is making homemade bread and her famous tea cakes for the children. Miss Ludy Parker has made a beautiful wedding cake deco- rated in white icing and homemade candies.

"I am so excited and nervous. I know that God has brought Amos Martin and me together. I prayed as a child that God would send into my life the perfect man, and he did. I can't believe this day has finally arrived. Amos will belong to me today.

"I must go for now and get dressed for my wedding. I certainly don't want to keep my groom waiting for me. I want this day to be perfect in every way, and I want to look beautiful for Amos.

"Sunday, April 12, 1925
"The wedding was absolutely beautiful, and I have never been happier. Amos and I were married at his family's home place under the beautiful lofty pine trees in front of the Martin home. Their log house is small, and we had to have the wedding in the yard. Amos had decorated the yard beautifully. He had built a beautiful lattice arbor. The columns holding up the arbor were made from lovely cedar stained in a rustic raw umber color. He had gone into the woods and gathered tons of scuppernong vines and ivy. Amos and his pa had draped the ivy and vines all around the arbor and carefully placed an assortment of spring flowers among the greenery. It was the loveliest sight I had ever seen.

"We invited the small congregation from our church and some very close friends. We had a total of approximately forty people there, and one of Amos' friends, John Reynolds, played his fiddle. Mr. Reynolds did a lovely presentation of music. His selections were exactly what I requested. He played several selections before the service, but his rendition of 'O Love That Will Not Let Me Go' and 'Jesu, Joy of Man's Desiring' were my favorites. I could hear him from inside the Martin home, and my heart was overflowing with joy and happiness. When he started playing the 'Bridal Chorus,' I looked at Papa and saw tears forming in his eyes. I had never seen Papa cry before.

"The dress Ma made for me was breathtaking. It was made from a beautiful piece of soft flowing white cotton. She bought the fabric at The Lovelace Mercantile in Martinsville. She ordered a Butterick pattern out of a catalog to make the dress. It was designed with a fashionable dropped waistline

and had an elegant handkerchief style hemline that flowed when I walked. It had a beautiful two inch pink ribbon around the dropped waistline, and the neck of the dress was designed with pink and white tatting. Ma had used the same pink ribbon to make a lovely flower. She attached it to the dropped waist. I have seen pictures of famous ladies in dresses like mine, but I never dreamed I would have one. Ma also made me a lovely camisole and bloomers to go under the dress. I was so stylish for 1925. To top off the wedding dress, Ma found the most beautiful bell shaped cloche hat and a lovely pair of honey colored silk stockings at the mercantile in Martinsville. The hat was soft white, decorated with pink and white flowers made from ribbons that matched my dress perfectly. I never dreamed of having a store-bought hat. Ma and I always wore handmade hats, and I was definitely thrilled to have a hat that was not homemade.

"I styled my natural curly bobbed hair into finger waves that softly fell around the edges of the hat. Ma really outdid herself on my beautiful bridal bouquet of redbud and dogwood blooms. It was held together with the same pink satin ribbon she used on my dress. She also gave me a long strand of imitation pearls and lovely matching earrings. I have never felt as beautiful as when my papa presented me to Amos.

"When Papa gave me away, I began to cry. They were not tears of sadness, but tears of joy. I looked into Papa's big brown eyes and saw tears streaming down his cheeks, as well. I looked away from Papa's face and spotted Amos standing beside our preacher, and my heart melted. He looked so handsome in his three piece gray pinstriped suit, white shirt, and lovely black silk necktie. His black shoes were perfectly shined beneath his gray leather spats, but his shoes did not outshine the radiant glow on his face when he saw me in my wedding dress.

"The ceremony was absolutely perfect, and I felt as if I had been transported to the gates of heaven. The ceremony was completed when I sang 'O Perfect Love' as the closing prayer. Ma had ordered the sheet music of the song, and Mr. Reynolds followed me beautifully on his fiddle. The first time I heard Ma play and sing 'O Perfect Love,' I knew I would sing that song at my wedding. I think it was published around 1904. It was a perfect ending to a perfect ceremony.

"After the ceremony, Amos kept telling me how pretty I was, and he never took his eyes off of me.

"I feel extremely young to be a married lady, but I feel very mature for a twenty year old. Amos is six years older than I am and very settled. He loves me so much, and I feel so safe when I am with him. Even though his education is limited, he is an honest, hardworking man. Amos was not able to finish school, because he had to help on the farm after his father's health failed. Mind you, he is a smart man and reads and writes beautifully. You might say he is a self-educated man. His grammar is not always perfect, but he is a very wise and knowledgeable man. I would not change anything about him. In my eyes, he is perfect.

"We couldn't afford to go on a honeymoon trip, so we went to our little house that we have been remodeling across the road from Ma and Papa's. The little house is in terrible condition, but we're just glad to have somewhere to live and be together. Because of Amos' ma and pa's bad health, they want us to add on to their log house and live with them. We will probably do that within the next two years. But for now, I am so content just to be Mrs. Amos Martin. God definitely knew that it was not good for man to live alone. I know now what God meant when he spoke about becoming one flesh. Only God could design that for a man and a woman. We have become two lives joined together as one. Marriage is beautiful. I was afraid I would be embarrassed on our wedding

night, but Amos took the Bible and read to me from the book of Genesis. He knew how anxious I was.

"As I sat there on the side of the feather bed that Amos had made himself, he took the worn looking Bible and looked into my eyes with love and tenderness. 'Lillie, don't be afraid; this night was born in the heart of God a long time ago. He has given you to me, and I will always love and cherish you, because I know you are a gift sent from God. Let me read to you what God says about marriage from my Bible.'

"Amos opened his tattered looking black Bible and began to read. 'And the Lord God caused a deep sleep to fall upon Adam, and he slept: and he took one of his ribs, and closed up the flesh instead thereof; And the rib, which the Lord God had taken from man, made he woman, and brought her unto the man. And Adam said, 'this is now bone of my bones, and flesh of my flesh: she shall be called Woman, because she was taken out of Man. Therefore shall a man leave his father and his mother, and shall cleave unto his wife: and they shall be one flesh.'

"After reading from the Bible he looked into my eyes and said, 'You see Lillie, God planned all of this, and He tells us not to be afraid. From this act of love, God will give to us the gift of children. That will be the results of our becoming one in him. The wedding today was only the legal part of our becoming one, but this act of love will be our sacred union in him.'

"Amos is such a Godly man, and he did make my wedding night all it should be. I tried many times to talk to Ma about what would happen on my wedding night, but she was too embarrassed to talk to me about it, and I think Amos knew that. He is a very sensitive person, and I am so grateful that he chose me to be his wife. I know in my heart that God had already chosen us for each other before we were ever born."

I looked at Miss Emma and Hattie with tears in my eyes, and I could see they had been crying also.

"Miss Emma, she must have been a beautiful bride. Just reading these words made me feel as if I had been transported back in time to 1925. Grandma should have been a writer. She was so prolific in her description of the entire wedding. Oh, how I wish someone had taken a picture of them at the wedding. It's hard for me to imagine them young and in love; I only remember them being old. But anyone that was ever around them knew how much they loved each other. I never will forget the time my grandpa said, 'Hope, I am praying that God will send you someone to love just like I love your grandma. And I believe He will, Honey. He has a plan for all of our lives. There's some little boy out there that is being raised by two Godly parents, and he will be yours someday.'

"Oh, Miss Emma, they were so dear to me and they loved each other so much. It wasn't just physical love, it was pure devotion. I understand now why Grandma didn't live long after Grandpa died. Her heart was broken when he was taken from her, and I can better understand why she succumbed to the Alzheimer's that ravaged her beautiful mind. The greatest part of their lives as a couple was the fact that they were able to grow old together. If only everyone could be so fortunate."

"Honey, you have such a great legacy. And I have not told you this, but you are so much like your grandma. You had such loving grandparents and parents, and you have truly been blessed. Your grandfather's prayer will be heard. You just haven't met that young man yet. He's out there."

"I guess he may be, but my plans don't include a husband, especially right now. Maybe that will happen later. I've worked so hard to be where I am today, and my career is the most important thing in my life."

"I understand that, but have you thought about what God may have planned for your life?"

"To be honest, I have never really given God much consideration, especially since I became an adult. I went to church when I was little, because I had to. When I went away to college, I put all of that behind me. I had my dreams, and that was the driving force behind everything that I've done up to this point in my life."

While I was talking, I saw Miss Emma and Hattie look at each other with a look of surprise, but I felt I had to be honest with them. I wanted them to know up front what my stand on religion and faith was. The more information I collected about my family and what had happened to them, the less I wanted to hear about God. Since my grandparents and parents lived their lives devoted completely to God, I couldn't help but wonder why God allowed them to suffer so much. They never did anything to deserve what happened to them. None of it made sense to me. I decided, for the moment, to keep quiet and not elaborate on my religions views.

"Hope, someday you will understand that there is more to life than what you want. God has a plan and purpose for us all. I found that out the hard way. Just remember what I told you this morning on the way to the farm."

As Miss Emma was talking, I began to feel very uncomfortable. I had to somehow change the subject and get the conversation going in another direction. I didn't want to offend Miss Emma or Hattie, but God and religion were not for me.

Hattie spoke up and said, "Miss Hope, I been a livin' seventy-five years on 'is ol' earth, and I hate to think what my life would be like without da Lawd. W'y, chil', he be my reason for livin'. He be da reason I wake up in da mornin', and he be da reason I live every day. He wuz wid my ma and pa through hard times, and he wuz with my grandma and grandpa through 'em days of slavery. My people wuz so mistreated, but I can't let 'at stop me from lovin' da Lawd. I hear'd my grandpa tell 'bout da time da overseer on da plantation whupped my great-grandpa 'til he couldn't even walk. My grandma said 'ey left him fer dead, but da Good Lawd, he spare him. When he wuz freed, he went all over 'is country a preachin' da gospel.

"Miss Hope, 'er wuz a time when me and Samson wuz havin' a terrible hard time. We couldn't pay for a thing, 'cause we didn't have no money. Our old cow, she went dry, and our little boy, he didn't even have milk to drink. W'y, I had to make biscuit bread and co'nbread outta water. Co'nbread made wid water ain't fittin' for man ner beast to eat. We couldn't get nary a drop of milk from 'at ol' heifer. I asked da Lawd for milk for my boy, and Miss Emma, she commenced to brangin' milk to us from da store.

"Not long atter 'at, just guess what da Lawd went an' did, he sent us Miss Emma. We's been wid her ever' sense. Samson, his health it had done gone bad, and I couldn't read a lick. I didn't know how to do nuttin' but cook and clean.

"You think me and Samson do all da work 'roun 'chear, chil'? 'At jist ain't so. All I has to do is cook, and Samson he just do da easy chores outside. W'y, Miss Emma has a cleaning crew and a man 'at help Samson in da yard. Miss Emma took us in and loved us like we wuz her family. She jist love us like da Good Lawd do. God, he shore do take care of his chil'ren. It be jist like da Good Book say, 'da righteous, 'ey won't be forsaken or a beggin' fer bread.

"An' 'at purdy house she built us ou'chonder, I don't even hav'ta clean it. 'Em cleanin' people do it fer me. An' 'at ain't all. Miss Emma, she been a teachin' me how to read. I know I don't talk like I'm 'posed to, but Miss Emma never make fun of me. She is a helpin' me with what she calls grammar, but it be mighty hard to teach an old dawg news tricks. Miss Hope, she love Samson and me jist da way we is, and we love her. W'y, she's our sister.

"Now Samson, he ain't got a hankerin' to read. He says he's too old, so now I read da Bible to him. I can't do a very good job, but at least I be a readin'. So you see Miss Hope, God is so good to his chil'ren. W'y, life ain't worth livin' without da Lawd. You jist remember Hattie told you 'at. Now you best get back to yore readin', missy."

As I looked back to the journal through tear-filled eyes, I began to flip through the yellowed pages skipping over several entries. I found the date October 30, 1929.

I immediately exclaimed, "Look, Miss Emma, Grandma is talking about the crash of the stock market."

We both put our faces back in the journal, and I began to read again.

"October 30, 1929

"Amos went into Martinsville yesterday. While he was at the mercantile, Mr. Lovelace had his radio on. He is the only person in town with a radio, and all of the men in Martinsville like to gather around the store and get the latest news.

"We can't afford a radio, but we do have a Victor phonograph. We enjoy listening to all types of music on our phonograph, but we don't have many records. Mostly, Amos enjoys country music. He loves Jimmie Rodgers and the Carter Family. They are his favorites. We have the recording they did in Tennessee on August 1, 1927 for the Victor Recording Company. We also have a Victor recording by the Boston Symphony Orchestra. Amos has promised he will try to find me a record of hymns.

"When Amos returned home from the mercantile, he informed me that the stock market crashed yesterday. The radio announcer said that the market started falling on October 18, and it completely crashed on October 29. They are calling it 'Black Tuesday.' Amos said that the radio announcer reported that people were killing themselves by jumping from windows and bankers were shooting them-

selves. I don't know how this will affect Amos and me or our farm. Rutherford County is still feeling the effect of the war. Those war years were so hard between 1914 and 1918. I was just a child when the war ended, but I remember the effect it had on Ma and Papa. Ma had a baby brother, Spofford, who was killed when the United States declared war on Germany in 1917. It took awhile for Ma to get over his death. What else is this country going to have to endure?"

I looked at Miss Emma with a note of sadness, "History sure looks different through the eyes of someone who experienced the events. Grandma had no way of knowing at that time what impact the Crash of 1929 would have on the destiny of this nation and the world."

I continued to skip over entries looking for significant dates and information. I found a section she had written about two weeks before my mother's birthday. In fact, it was written on Christmas day of 1939.

"December 25, 1939

"This has been a difficult day for me. The baby is due in a few weeks and I am so huge; I am miserable. I haven't seen my feet in two months. I want to see my baby healthy and whole. Amos and I have longed for this day for fifteen years. We had lost all hope of having children when God granted us the desire of our hearts. I am beginning to get concerned, because I am so large. Sometimes I feel as big as one of Amos' bales of cotton. You would think I am going to have twins or triplets because of my size. I just hope nothing is wrong with the baby.

"We have no doctor in Martinsville since Doc Sims died, but we do have a midwife who is living in the house just down the road from us. At least that's what she said she is. She lives on the Ledbetter property. She moved there about three years ago. If Amos doesn't have time to get into Martinsville to get Miss Creola Matheney, the local midwife,

I guess we will have to use her. I worry about that, because I don't know anything about her. Her name is Prissy Walker, and she doesn't want anyone asking her questions about her past. She is an eccentric sort of character, and I'm not too sure I want her delivering my baby, but I may not have a choice. She acts very withdrawn and distant. I've tried to be a neighbor to her, but she doesn't want to associate with anyone.

"The best I can determine, the baby should be born sometime in the middle of February. I hope Amos will be able to remain close to home during that time so we won't have to call on Miss Walker. Sometimes he has to go into the mountains or down to Shelby to pick up things for the farm. Before Amos goes to Asheville to get farm supplies, he will ride one of the mules down to her place and ask her to help me if I need her. She has assured him that she will. He told her that I will ring the big cow bell on the back porch if I need her. He is planning to get everything done early so he can be with me the entire month of February.

"January 1, 1940

"Amos has gone to Ashville to get some farm supplies. I just hope he made it across the mountains. Some of the roads are treacherous and difficult to travel, and it looks like we may be getting snow. He checked with Miss Walker before he left to be sure she was around today. She assured him she would be at home.

"I had some pains this morning in my lower back, and I'm hoping it is just false labor. I just hope the real labor pains hold off until Amos returns.

"January 2, 1940

"We had a terrible snow storm last night, and I am so worried about Amos. I looked out the front window, and the pine trees in the front yard are laden with beautiful white

snow. Snowflakes are still falling, and the earth is covered in a pristine blanket of white. Amos has still not returned from his trip into Asheville. I just hope he is not stranded somewhere up on the Blue Ridge freezing to death. All I can do is pray for his safety and this new little life that apparently wants to be born today. My pains are about five minutes apart. The baby must be coming soon, because my water just broke. I'm so worried. Everything is happening too soon.

"I never knew anything could hurt so much, but I want to journal every single moment of this birth, but I guess I better ring the old cow bell out on the back porch so Ms. Walker will know to come to my rescue. Oh, I just hope she knows what she is doing."

Chapter 11

I was mesmerized by my grandma's story, so I continued to read on with anticipation.

"January 10, 1940

"Prissy Walker came when I rang the cow bell, but I don't remember much after that. I must have passed out, because I don't remember much after she arrived. I just remember the horrible pain and being in my bed crying for Amos. I do remember someone being with Miss Walker at one point. She later told Amos she had no one with her, but I knew that wasn't true. I vividly remember her talking to someone, and it sounded like a man.

"The birth pains were terrible, far worse than anything I had ever experienced. I felt as if my back would explode into a million pieces. I do remember Miss Walker giving me some kind of liquid medicine, and after that everything was a blur.

"Our little baby girl was born on January 2, 1940. Amos and I named her Amelia Ruth Martin. Because she came earlier than expected, she is very small. She is so tiny we made her a small bed in a dresser drawer. She has to be fed every hour. Since I was not able to breastfeed her, Amos tries to give her baby bottles of milk, but most of the time, he has to use a medicine dropper to feed her.

"I vaguely remember the baby coming, but I know in my heart there were two babies. I remember the pain starting up again and another baby being born. Amos said I was not conscious for days, and I must have been confused or disoriented. According to him, Miss Walker said she did not give me anything for pain. I know in my heart she did, but no one believes me. I think she must have given me some form of opium. I remember the sickening taste. I don't know where she could have gotten it, but I know she gave me something. I do know one thing for sure; I gave birth to two babies that day, and I only have one."

I looked at Miss Emma and Hattie and all three of us were speechless. *Did my mother have a twin somewhere? No wonder Grandma was depressed! Could her baby have been stolen by Prissy Walker, or did the other baby die?* I questioned myself. I simply could not speak.

Miss Emma exploded, "W'y, I never! This has got to be the secret your grandma wanted you to know. I never dreamed it was something like this. We need to read on, Hope. There's got to be more. Knowin' Prissy Walker like I did, I'm not surprised at anything she might have done. She lost her senses before she died."

I continued to flip through the journal. The next entry I found was written on January 21, 1940, and I immediately sensed the depression in my grandma's words.

"January 21, 1940

"No one believes me, not even Amos. He thinks I am having a reaction to the medication or herbs Miss Walker gave me, which, of course, still denies. At least he finally believed me when I said she had drugged me. As soon as the snow began to melt, Amos had a doctor from Shelby examine me and the baby. The doctor told him that he felt sure I had been given some type of drug or herb.

"I feel so hopeless. My only consolation has been my beautiful Amelia. Amos has already started calling her Amy. That's fine with me. We chose the name Amelia, because the first two letters in Amos and Amelia were the same. I love her so much, and I know she is a gift from God. She is absolutely perfect.

"I can't wait to take her to church. I want everyone to see her. She has the most beautiful blonde curly hair and the bluest eyes I have ever seen. But I know in my heart she has a brother or sister out there somewhere. I honestly believe that Miss Walker did something with my baby. Amos keeps trying to convince me that I only delivered one infant.

"There is one thing that is very strange though. Prissy Walker will not talk to Amos anymore about the birth. She denies that there was another baby, and she had the nerve to tell Amos that I might be going crazy. Amos, of course, knows that is not true, but I can't convince him that I delivered twins that day. Another thing is the fact that Miss Walker has quit coming around. For a few days after Amy was born, she stopped by everyday. I just don't trust her; she is a strange sort of character.

"I know Amos thinks I'm just depressed. Sometimes I know I'm depressed, and that's because I know in my heart I had two babies. I just can't get it off my mind.

I skipped over a few pages and saw that Grandpa and Grandma finally took Mama to church on April 21, 1940.

"April 21, 1940

"We finally were able to take little Amy to church. A lot of flu was going around in February and March. Because she is so small, we didn't want to expose her to anything until she gained some weight.

"I didn't do so well during preaching. Preacher Hopkins was in the middle of his sermon, and my nerves went all to pieces. I had to get up during the service and leave. I couldn't

get my other baby off my mind. I can't find peace anywhere. What in the world am I going to do? I can't seem to pull myself together. I have prayed and still can't find peace.

"I finally had to get up and leave the service. Amos brought me home and put Amy and me both to bed. He has been so patient and understanding, but he still feels that I am depressed and must have dreamed I had two babies. The doctor explained afterbirth pains to Amos and me and how they follow the delivery of the baby. Could that be what happened? I just can't believe afterbirth pains would have felt like the pains I had. One way or the other, I've got to get better for Amy and Amos' sake."

"No wonder Grandma was depressed! What a burden to bear. And she had no proof of anything. Miss Emma, we have to read on to see if Grandma ever found out anything about the other child. I know my mama never said a word about it to me. Did she ever say anything to you, Miss Emma?" I asked.

"Absolutely not! Amy always told me she would love to have a sister. She had Cletus who was two years younger than she was, but she said she always wanted a sister. When she was a little girl, she told me that there were times when she pretended to have an imaginary sister who looked just like her. But a lot of children have imaginary playmates.

"Now that I think about it, there was one time when she was about thirteen years old that she had an episode of melancholy for no apparent reason. Your grandma and grandpa had the doctor come out to the farm and check her out. The doctor gave her a tonic, but she later told me she couldn't shake the feeling that something was missing in her life."

"I do remember times when Mama would become very sad or down in the dumps for no reason. She often explained her actions as having a heavy heart, and she didn't know why," I explained.

I was devastated, and my heart was breaking for Grandma and Mama. They both died never knowing the truth. *How could a loving God allow this to happen to them?* I wondered.

Miss Emma spoke up, "Hope, let's skip over and see if we can find out anything more about this."

We flipped over to the end of the journal and I continued to read. The last day Grandma recorded was April 12, 1989.

"April 12, 1989

"I must write while I can write and think coherently. I know something is going on in my mind. Amy took me to the doctor a few weeks back. I told him that I couldn't remember anything. He said I had something called dementia. I just know I can't remember anything anymore. Today, I couldn't even remember where I keep my journal and where the secret room is. I love this little room. When I finally remembered where it was, I immediately came to it. I just hope I can remember how to get out.

"I even got confused in the outhouse the other day and couldn't figure out how to get out. I must have been in there for two hours before I remembered why I was there and how to open the door.

"I must tell Amy and Hope about this room before my mind is completely gone. Amos and I never told anyone about our secret room, not even Amy. I sure wish she knew about it.

"I'm afraid Amy is going to send me away. If she does, I can't come in this little room anymore. What will I do without this little place? This has not only been my hiding place, but it has been my prayer closet. I have prayed many a prayer in this little room. Amos used to come in here to pray, also. This was our prayer closet.

"Amos included this little room in the house plans when he built the house around his ma and pa's old log cabin. We

wanted a place to keep things that meant a lot to us. I am so thankful that I finally remembered where the room is. I just don't know what I would do without this little place.

"I hope we told Amy where the secret room is and how to get in it. But I know we didn't tell anyone, or did we? I must tell her the next time she comes to visit. Maybe I did tell her. Oh, I can't remember anything. I especially want Hope to have the things in this room. Did I tell her about the room? I think I did, or at least I hope I did. I can't remember anything anymore. My mind comes and goes so much I don't know if I did or not.

"What was I talking about? Oh, I know Amos is in heaven, and today would have been our anniversary. I am so grateful for every moment that I can think clearly. Those moments are few and far between now. Sometimes I feel like I am living in a deep, dark hole.

"I began to notice my forgetfulness about eight months before Amos died. I never told anyone, because Amos was so sick. I realized something was terribly wrong when I forgot Amos' death after he died. I kept waiting for him to come in for supper, and he never came. I cried myself to sleep, and when I awoke, I remembered his death. I have little by little gotten worse over these last four months. W'y, I even forget to take baths, and some days I forget to eat.

"Now what was I going to write about? Oh, I know, Prissy Walker. This week has not been good at all. I wandered off yesterday, and I found myself down at the old Ledbetter place where Prissy Walker used to live before she died. Her old house is about to fall down. No one has lived there since she died. I don't know why I went there. Oh, I remember, I used to think she stole one of my babies. I have never gotten over that feeling. I still have thoughts about the baby and Prissy Walker. Amos did everything he could to find out about Prissy Walker and her story, but he was never able to come up with any proof that I delivered twins. It was my

word against hers. Since I was not myself for a long time after Amy's birth, the doctor and Amos felt I was confused from whatever medicine Prissy gave me, and I probably was. As time went by, I accepted the fact that maybe I was wrong, and there was only one baby, my precious Amy.

"When I realized I was at the Ledbetter farm, I tried to look through the house for any signs that she had taken my baby, and found none. I guess I will go to my grave wondering if I have another child out there somewhere.

"Now what was I writing about? Where am I? This room is so dark. How did I get here? Oh, I remember, I'm in the secret room. I must remember to tell Amy and her little girl. Now what is her name? I can't remember anything. She was just here with Amy and Whitley. Maybe her name will come to me later.

"What was I thinking about? Yes, I remember. About three years after Amy was born Prissy Walker started acting really strange. Neighborhood folks often saw her on the front piazza of her house pretending she was rocking a baby and talking to herself. She would hold a folded blanket and mumble continuously. Nothing she said ever made sense, it was mostly gibberish. Some of the women at the church began to go check on her, and they found her dead that last time they went for a visit. She must have died a horrible, excruciating death. From her appearance, it looked like she had starved herself to death. I guess she just quit eating. No one was ever able to locate any family, so Martinsville Baptist Church took care of her funeral and the burial.

"Now who was I writing about? I guess it doesn't matter. I've got to figure out how to get out of this room. Oh, I remember her name; it is Hope, my precious grandchild.

"Hope, if you find this journal, please search for my baby, and find out what happened to her. I love you. Never forget that. Even though my mind is slipping from me, just

remember that when I am in heaven my mind will be whole again. I will see you there, my dearest Hope."

I began to sob uncontrollably, and Miss Emma tenderly wrapped her arms around me.

Hattie walked over and knelt in front of me with a look of deep concern. "It be okay, Miss Hope. I know'd 'at old Prissy Walker, and I jist hate yore grandma had to call on her to birth her baby. My pa and ma's house was jist a short piece from where she stayed. She wuz so hateful to my folks. She thought she wuz made of better mud 'an we wuz 'cause we wuz black. 'Peers to me, we all come from Adam and Eve. Lawd, forgive me fer what I'm sayin', but her mud wuz no better 'an mine. As my pa used to say, 'She wuz jist a briggity britches!'

"She wuz always a stirrin' up a stink 'bout some'um. W'y, a body know'd better 'an to cross her land; she had bear traps set ever'where. Ol' Pukey Crothers wuz a crossin' her land one day and caught his foot in a bear trap, and it took him might near two years to get well. W'y, he might near lost his foot. I'm tellin' ye, she was a bird! I don't like to be a talkin' bad 'bout da dead, but I think she was full of wickedness. And another thing, she weren't no midwife, she wuz jist a 'make-believe' granny woman.

"I wuz jist a little young'un when I know'd her, and I was scart to death of her. I wouldn't be surprised at anythang 'at wicked old woman might a done. W'y, my pa wuz even afear'd of her. He walked across her land one time, and she run him off with a shotgun. Pa said she pointed the gun at him and commence to firin'."

I looked at Hattie and said, "Hattie, you know so much about what has taken place around here. Since you are older than Miss Emma, you are going to be a great help in solving Grandma's mystery. Do you remember when Mama was born?"

"Laws-a-mercy, Miss Hope. I 'member all 'bout her. I wuz jist a young'un when she was born. I used to go over with my ma to see her. In fact, my ma helped Mr. Amos atter yore ma was born. I even helped pick cotton for yore grandpa. Mr. Amos and Miss Lillie Mae wuz da best neighbors anybody could want. Atter my pa died, they saw to it 'at my ma and us young'uns had plenty of food. Yore grandpa wuz a hunter, and iffin he kilt a rabbit, he always brung it to us to eat. Yore grandma, she didn't like rabbit, so when he kilt one, he give it to us. He wuz always a brangin' us hawg meat when it wuz hawg killin' time. Yes'um, 'em wuz two good people. Miss Hope, iffin 'ere wuz another baby, we's a gonna find it. Samson, he knows more 'bout 'ese here parts 'an I do, and I know he be glad to help, too."

I was so overwhelmed with Hattie and Miss Emma and their evident love and concern for me; I began to cry even harder. I looked at both of them through my tearstained face and said, "I feel like I truly have family now. When I left Charlotte to come here, I was so depressed and alone. You two ladies will never know how much I appreciate your kindness."

Miss Emma spoke first, "Hope, I'll be there for you anytime and so will Hattie and Samson."

Hattie chimed in quickly, "That be right, Miss Hope. You is family now."

Chapter 12

I felt as if the blood had suddenly been drained from my body. The day's events had definitely taken its toll on me emotionally and physically. I looked from Hattie to Miss Emma and took a deep breath. I couldn't seem to get the energy to speak, so I took another deep breath and leaned my head back on the sofa.

When I eventually was able to speak, I raised my head and asked, "Where do I go from here?"

Miss Emma spoke up, took my hand, and said, "Hope, it's after ten o'clock, and you have had an especially traumatic day. I say we get to bed and tackle this situation in the mornin'. We can't accomplish anything tonight, and you need to get some rest."

Looking at Hattie, Miss Emma said, "Samson has probably already turned in. I'll light up the yard and walk you home. I don't like for you to be outside after dark by yourself. Let me get a pair of slippers."

I immediately spoke up, "Please let me walk with her, Miss Emma. I don't mind at all. You both might fall. Both of you have done enough for today, and I really could use some fresh air."

"Thank you, Hope. It really is nice to have a young person around," replied Miss Emma.

"Hattie, before you leave, I want to ask one question. What in the world is a briggity britches?" I asked politely.

That brought a smile to both of their faces and Miss Emma replied, "W'y, Hope, it means someone feels like they are better than everyone else. It's a term handed down from our ancestors. A good translation might be egotistical or 'to big for their britches.'"

"I never cease to be amazed at some of the words you folks use, but I have to say, I love the way ya'll talk. Do you think I'll ever pick up on it?" I asked.

"Oh, no, Miss Hope, you gotta be reared, rared, and raised roun'chear to talk like us," Hattie laughingly replied as we left the sunroom.

After walking Hattie to her front door and giving her a big hug, I came back to the sunroom. Miss Emma locked the back door, and we made our way up the back steps to the second floor.

When we reached the top of the stairs, Miss Emma turned to me. "Now, Hope, you sleep in tomorrow as long as you need to. You need a good night's sleep after what you went through today. When you get up, we will come up with a strategy for remodeling the house and start the investigation of your grandma's other child."

"Thanks, Miss Emma, see you in the morning."

The day's events had drained my body, soul, and spirit, and I hardly remember going to bed. I must have fallen into a deep sleep as soon as my head hit the pillow, and I don't think I moved all night.

I opened my eyes to beautiful sunbeams filtering through the lovely sheer curtains in my bedroom. As I adjusted my eyes to the light, I immediately recalled what had happened the previous day. I still felt a bit tired, but I knew I needed to get up. When I finally rolled over in the bed, the alarm clock came into my line of vision. I sat straight up in the bed when I realized it was after nine o'clock. I jumped up, took a quick shower, and began applying makeup. After dressing in jeans and a tee shirt, I quickly pulled my hair up into a ponytail and hurried downstairs to the kitchen.

"Well, good mornin' sleepy head," exclaimed Miss Emma. "Since you are our only guest again today, we didn't set the dining room table. We can either eat here in the kitchen with Hattie, or go out on the sun porch.

"Let's just eat in here. I love being with Hattie. Has Samson eaten yet, Hattie?"

"W'y, honey child, he et afore da sun come up. I fried him up some ham and eggs. He loves mush so much, I fixed him some to go wid his ham and eggs."

"What in the world is mush, Hattie?"

"It sorta be like grits, but it be made with co'nmeal. Uppity folk calls it polenta, I think. Us southerners, we jist calls it mush. I still have some left if you want to try some."

"I would love to try it," I replied.

Hattie began to fill my plate with mush, eggs, and country ham. She had made homemade biscuits and had homemade orange marmalade and blackberry jelly. It was like being with my mama or grandma. I tasted the mush and was surprised how tasty it was. Of course, I had to add butter and salt.

I looked at Hattie with a smile and said, "It does taste kinda' like grits. It's great, and I really like it. Hattie, everything you cook is so good. I believe you could cook fried cardboard and make it taste good. Um-m-m, I wonder if Abraham Lincoln ate grits or mush when he was in North Carolina?"

Miss Emma replied, "Probably! He was just a little fellow when his mama, Nancy Hanks, went to Kentucky, or so the legend goes.

"I can't wait to go up to Puzzle Creek to investigate the Abe Lincoln legend, but we have more pressing matters now. Miss Emma, where do we begin with my state of affairs? I just don't know where to start. I must admit, I feel like a ton has been lifted off my back since I found Grandma's journal."

Miss Emma responded, "Hope, if you want me to, I will call a friend of mine who is a private investigator to come over tonight, and we can talk to her about finding your long lost relative. It could be an aunt or an uncle."

"That would be awesome. Thank you so much for everything. I can never repay you for all of your kindness."

"Don't even go there! You owe me absolutely nothing," she replied. "I want to help you, and it might be fun to search for this missing person. If you will allow me, I will get in touch with the building crew who renovated my house, and I'll send my crew of yard men over there to begin clearing the area around the house. Is that okay with you?"

"Sure, but how much is all of this going to cost? I inherited quite a bit of money from Mama when she died. She inherited all of Grandpa and Grandma's money, but that money is tied up at the moment in probate. I should be able to put my hands on it in a few weeks, or at least that is what my lawyer tells me."

"Oh, don't worry about that. I'll handle everything until your money is available. In the mean time, let's go back out to the farm today and see if we missed anything."

"Can we take Hattie and Samson with us? I'd like to get their take on the house and property. I would appreciate Samson's opinion on the condition of the house and out buildings," I replied.

"Great minds think alike. Those were my exact thoughts. Hattie and Samson are ready to go. Hattie has already packed a basketful of food, and Samson has filled a cooler with soft drinks, water, and ice tea. I'll go ahead and call the carpenters and the yard crew so they can make plans to get started on the renovations. Then we can be on our way."

"Miss Emma, you are amazing. I shudder to think what I would have done if Snuffy had not sent me to you."

Samson had already loaded the truck with tools, and we all loaded the food and drinks in the back of the truck while Miss Emma made the telephone calls to the builder and yard crew.

Samson and Hattie got into the truck, and Miss Emma and I got into my car. I could tell Miss Emma was not used to a small sports car. She had some trouble getting in, and to be honest I didn't know how we were going to get her out. Actually, she literally fell into the car.

As we started down Main Street, Miss Emma laughingly exclaimed, "You may have to call a crane service to come and pull me out of this little contraption. W'y, it's not much bigger than my lawn mower. We could put a blade on the bottom of it and bush hog the yard out at the farm. Laws-a-mercy, Hope, you could get killed in this tiny little excuse for an automobile. The very idea! I can't believe you came down the interstate in it. It's a wonder a tractor trailer truck didn't smash you like a bug!"

I laughed so hard at her; I thought I was going to have to pull over. "Miss Emma, don't you want me to put the top down."

"Law no! A strong nor'easter might come and blow us slam away."

I continued to laugh and watched her in amusement as she held on to the edge of her seat. One time she reached up as if she was going to hold to a grab handle at the top of the door. She didn't realize that my little convertible did not have grab handles. She turned and said, "W'y, you don't even have anything to hold on to. I'll have to hold to the door handle, but I guess that's better than nothing."

When we finally arrived at the farm, she exclaimed, "We'll bring my car next time. A body could have heart failure in this little make-believe automobile! Hope, as soon as you get your money, you need to get yourself a real car. This little thing is an accident waiting to happen. If I don't soon get out of this little contraption, I'm a gonna have a hissy fit."

"Oh, Miss Emma, this little car is safe and gets great gas mileage. It has traveled all over this state. I promise you, it's very safe."

"What good is gas mileage when you're dead? W'y, this contraption looks like a mini rocket ship that's had its tail whacked off."

We both started laughing as I began to pull her from the car. About that time Hattie walked up and said, "W'y, Miss Emma, is you a gittin' old?"

"Now you hush up, Hattie Alexander. I'm not getting old. It's not me, it's this infernalin' car. Hope needs to get herself a real car. I just told her it's not much bigger than our lawn mower," she replied with a big grin on her face.

"That be right. But we's got work to do so you best quit a quarrelin' and a mumblin'. Miss Hope, this here is my Samson. We been together for many a year. Last night he help you from da truck, and I know you don't 'member him."

I looked at Samson and reached out my hand to shake his. His large hand almost swallowed mine. He was a strong looking man and had a gentle smile on his face.

"How you be, Miss Hope?" Samson asked.

"I'm feeling much better, thank you. It's so nice to finally meet you, Samson. I apologize for you having to help me get in the house yesterday afternoon," I replied.

"Miss Hope, don't you go be a worryin' 'bout 'at. I understand you had a bad day. You wuz a lookin' mighty peaked. Hattie, she be talking 'bout chu all 'da time."

After Miss Emma regained her breath, she spoke up, "Have you ever seen such a messy yard, Samson. Hope, the yard crew will be here at one o'clock to start sprucing up the place. I told them to bring some heavy equipment to start the process."

The four of us turned to look again at my newly inherited home.

I heard Samson groaning in the background and Hattie moaning, "Um-m-m-m, I ain't ever seen nuttin' to beat 'is. I shore am glad Mr. Amos can't be a seein' all 'is mess."

"You just wait 'til you see the front piazza," I replied.

We climbed the front steps to the piazza, and I heard Hattie gasp. We made our way to the front door that entered the sitting room. As I took Samson and Hattie on a tour of the house, I explained to them that we had raked the trash out of the house the previous day, and that was the reason the piazza was piled so high with trash and rubbish.

As we toured the house, I could hear Samson moaning and groaning in the background, and Hattie was so shocked at the condition of the house she was literally dumbstruck.

When she finally regained her speech, she said, "I feels like I'm gonna commence to cryin'. "'Is house, it always wuz so clean and purdy. It might near breaks my heart to see it 'is a way."

When the four of us reached the back porch, I suggested we take a look at the backyard. I explained that Miss Emma and I had not had time to do that on the previous day. We cautiously made our way down the old wooden steps. I helped all of the others navigate the steps, because they were so rotten. Thankfully we all made it down safely, and we pushed the high weeds aside as we walked toward the old outhouse. It appeared to be beyond repair, and the barn did not look any better. I looked to my left and the old crib appeared to be in better condition than the other two buildings.

I turned to the others and said, "Let's just check out these old buildings and see if they're worth restoring."

As we approached the outhouse, I spotted some lovely yellow daffodils growing to my left. A smile crossed my face as I remembered helping Grandma plant them. Samson made a quick determination of the condition of the outhouse, and being a man of few words, he said, "Ain't worth savin', Miss Hope. It be plum' rotten."

My heart was flooded with memories as we approached the barn. I would never forget my first mule ride, or the time Grandpa let me hold the plow stock and follow the mule in his garden. It didn't take long for me to realize that plowing a mule was not my cup of tea.

We entered the barn and exited twice as fast. It looked like a war zone. Some of the rafters had dropped from the ceiling and it appeared the walls were ready to collapse anytime. The smell of rotten wood and mold engulfed us.

Samson had no problem making another quick determination. "Ain't worth savin', Miss Hope. You'uns best not be a coming' back in 'is here barn. You might git youself kilt. It be risky and it be plum' stoopid to try to fix it. 'Is barn be slap rotten."

We went into the crib and decided it too needed to be demolished.

I would have loved to save all of the out buildings, but they simply were not worth saving. The wood was so decayed and termite eaten, Samson's judgment convinced me that they were not salvageable.

I turned to Samson, "Samson, I want to demolish them in a way that will be safe for the environment, and I really don't know how to go about it. Do you or Miss Emma have any advice for me?"

Samson quickly replied, "Tain't like it be in 'da olden days, we best not burn it down or bury it. When we wuz a fixin' up Miss Emma's ol' house, we had a heap of old wood to git shed of. I reckon we could call da county and make 'rangements."

"That a great idea, Samson. Hope, we can get the yard crew to demolish the buildings and haul everything to the county landfill. The county has several ways that they recycle old wood and metal," Miss Emma remarked.

"That's wonderful. I'm real big on keeping everything environmentally safe and green."

Hattie spoke up, "Miss Hope, I don't know what green be, but I be mighty glad to hear that you be a takin' care of 'is ol' world. 'Is ol' world is a goin' to da dawgs. We need to take care of what da good Lawd has give us. I jist don't un'erstand how 'em folks at da lan'fill can take ol' wood, milk jugs, and sode cans and makes new thangs out of 'em. I thinks it be jist won'erful."

"I sure hope the house is safer and sounder than those outbuildings," I said in desperation. "But let's take a look at the smokehouse that is behind the crib before we evaluate the house."

We made our way down the hill to the old smokehouse, and it was in worse shape than the rest of the buildings. Samson quickly responded, "Miss Hope, you might as well git shed of 'is un, too."

We went back toward the house and Samson made a quick evaluation of it. "I b'lieves da house be in purdy good shape, Miss Hope. Mr. Amos he took mighty good care of da house. I b'leave he whitewashed it ever' year. W'y, 'pears 'at 'ere still be some whitewash on it. Da roof, it don't 'peer to be in bad shape a'tall, but ye might want to git it checked out."

By the time we went back to the house, it was lunch time. Samson and Hattie disappeared to the truck and came back with not only the food, but a table and folding chairs. Because of the trash from the house, we couldn't eat on the piazza. Samson retrieved a sling blade from the truck, and he cleared a space large enough for us to have our picnic beneath the majestic pine trees in the front yard.

As I watched Hattie spread a red and white checked tablecloth on the folding table and unload the picnic basket, I thought to myself, *she must have started cooking at five o'clock this morning. I've never seen so much food for four people*. She had prepared fried chicken, potato salad, home-made biscuits, and home-canned green beans, and that wasn't all. She also brought a fresh strawberry pie.

I looked at Hattie and said, "Hattie, I bet I've gained ten pounds in the last two days. You are a great cook, but I'm gonna get fat."

"Honey chil', you need some meat on 'em bones. You is too skinny. You jist commence ta eatin'. It be good fer ye."

And I did just that. I ate every bite on my plate and a large piece of the strawberry pie. We relaxed for a few minutes after the meal, and as we were clearing the table, I heard, what sounded like, several large vehicles coming down the dirt road.

As they came into view, Miss Emma exclaimed, "Wonderful, the yard crew is here. Now we can get this place shaped up."

Chapter 13

I went with Miss Emma and Samson to meet the foreman for the yard crew. Miss Emma introduced him as Sam Cook. I began to explain to him what needed to be demolished and what I wanted him to do in the yard area. I explained that I wanted to salvage all of the trees that were healthy, the flowering bushes, and especially the little area of daffodils in the backyard.

I suddenly cast my eyes toward that monstrous juniper bush. I knew deep down in my heart that smelly bush had to stay, also. It was a part of my grandparents' lives, and I would just have to learn to love it, because Grandma loved it. I asked Mr. Cook to prune the huge eyesore back and let it start growing anew. Maybe, just maybe, it would grow on me.

I listened as Mr. Cook made suggestions regarding the shrubbery that needed to be planted around the house. He explained that the house called for plants and shrubs that were commonly used in the early 1900s, yet he wanted the yard to compliment the house and the existing shrubbery. Since I knew absolutely nothing about gardening, I told him to use his own judgment when choosing the plants and shrubs for the yard. I did tell him I wanted plants that required very little maintenance, since I had never maintained a yard. I remembered that Grandma had several nandina bushes scattered around the yard, and she always used the red berries to decorate the dining room table at Christmas. I asked him to plant a few of them in the landscape.

After I was certain that he would do exactly what I wanted, Mr. Cook then turned to give his men instructions. Both of Mr. Cook's trucks had trailers attached to the back, and one of the trailers had a tractor with a large mowing machine on it. *I guess that's what a bush hog looks like,* I thought to myself. The other truck and trailer had a large piece of equipment that looked like a small bulldozer on it. The next thing I knew, the men were backing the tractor and bulldozer from the trailers.

Maybe there is hope for this place, but I still have my doubts about that smelly old juniper bush, I thought to myself.

Two gentlemen drove up in a black four-door pickup truck and parked on the dirt road in front of the house. As they approached, one of the men spoke to us and said, "Hi, Miss Emma, ya'll need to move yore vehicles. This bush hog could sling a rock and break a window. Just back your vehicles behind my truck."

Miss Emma hurriedly made her way to the two gentlemen and greeted them. She turned to me, "Hope this is Edwin Conner, the contractor who will be renovating the house." She then turned to the other gentleman with a smile and said, "And this is Dr. Michael Sanders, my pastor. We all call him Preacher Mike." She turned to introduced me, "And this is Hope Martin. She is the lady who inherited this farm. And you both know Samson and Hattie."

Samson, Hattie, and I greeted them, and I reached out to shake both their hands. I could not help noticing that Dr. Sanders seemed awfully young to be a pastor. Actually, he appeared to be close to my age.

Since I had not attended church in such a long time, I guess my idea of a pastor was a stoic elderly gray-haired gentleman. At least all of the pastors I had as a child were old, somewhat reserved, and gray-haired.

Dr. Sanders had the bluest eyes I had ever seen, and when he looked at me I felt as if the breath had been knocked out of me. *Why is this man having such an effect on me? He is no different from any other man,* I hastily told myself.

When Mr. Conner reminded us again to move our vehicles, I jumped at the chance to flee from Dr. Sanders and those sapphire-blue eyes that seemed to pierce into the depths of my soul.

Samson and I immediately went to our vehicles and moved them up the road from the house. I really didn't feel comfortable parking my car on the dirt road, but I sure didn't want it damaged by flying debris.

Samson and I rejoined the group, and Mr. Conner began to question me about the renovations. Both Mr. Conner and Dr. Sanders followed me through the house as I explained to Mr. Conner that I wanted to keep the house as close to the original structure as possible. After a quick overview of the house, we began to discuss electrical wiring and plumbing and how I wanted that carried out.

I assured him that I definitely wanted indoor plumbing. I knew I would never survive without bathroom facilities. I showed them the room where my grandparents kept their chamber pots, and he felt very sure he could install a bath-room in that area. I also instructed him to add a bathroom in the storage room on the other side of the house at the end of the hall.

As we approached the living room, I turned to face both Mr. Conner and Dr. Sanders. "I'm going to show you a room that I didn't know existed until yesterday. Evidently, my parents didn't know about it either. Miss Emma and I found it quite by accident. My grandfather included this little room when he built this portion of the house."

When we reached the secret room, I was very reluctant to open the door. I knew Mr. Conner needed to see the room to be able to correctly renovate the house. Both men seemed to be genuinely surprised when I took them into the room.

As we entered the secret room, Dr. Sanders spoke up, "I've always heard of old houses with secret rooms, but this is a first for me. I have always been interested in architecture, and I took a couple of classes while I was in college. I must tell you, the architecture in this house is remarkable. Your grandfather knew exactly what he was doing. Are you sure he wasn't an architect?"

"No, my great-grandfather designed the log portion of the house, and my grandfather designed and built the newer portion of the house. He told me time and again how he carried the rocks on a sled from the river to lay the foundation. He actually harvested the lumber that he used to build the house from the farm. Grandpa never had much formal education, but he was a very smart man. He made his living by farming this land that he loved so much. He was a cotton farmer. I hope I can find out why Grandpa felt the need to have this secret place. No one knew about the secret room until yesterday, except Grandpa and Grandma," I replied. "My mama didn't even know about it."

Looking at Mr. Conner, Dr. Sanders directed a statement to him. "Ed, just look how this door is designed to slide, and after all of these years, it still slides perfectly. I can't wait to see the beams in the attic. I am especially impressed with the way the newer part of the structure is joined to the log portion of the house."

Dr. Sanders turned to me, "Miss Martin, your grandfather should have been an architect."

"Would you like for us to get these heavy items out for you? They're gonna have to come out before we can start the renovations," Mr. Conner asked.

"That would be great. I know that desk has to be heavy and cumbersome. The trunk shouldn't be as difficult to move. It's so dark in here; you can't see your hand in front of your face. Let me go get a flashlight so you can see," I replied.

I went out of the house and retrieved a flashlight from Miss Emma's truck and returned to the secret room.

When I turned the light on, Dr. Sanders remarked, "That's more like it. Ed, let's get this trunk out of here first."

"Ed, just put the trunk and desk on the back of my truck so we can store the items at my house. Hope, we can store them in my garage until the house is finished. Is that okay with you?" asked Miss Emma.

"That would be great," I replied as I followed them to the yard.

While I was still speaking, Mr. Conner and Dr. Sanders began to move the trunk. They carried it out to the piazza and went back to move the desk. In just a few minutes, they had both items on the piazza. They loaded them on the back of Miss Emma's truck after Samson brought it closer to the house.

Mr. Connor called for me from inside of the house, "You jist might want to come back in the room with us. We found somethin' behind the desk when we moved it, Miss Martin."

We all followed them back into the house and into the secret room. There, where the desk had been, was a portrait of a beautiful young lady. It was leaning against the wall and had not been visible, because the desk blocked the view. So I could see the picture in a better light, I walked out of the secret hideaway into the living room. From the looks of it, it appeared to be very old. As I got a better look at the picture, I stopped dead in my tracks with astonishment. Had I not known better, I would have thought it was a picture of me. The woman looked just like me!

Hattie gasped, "W'y, help my time, Miss Hope, 'at be you. Why yore pic'ure be in 'is here secret room? Now how'd 'at happen?"

"Hattie, it's not me. This picture is very old, much older than I am."

I took the picture outside for closer inspection. It definitely was old. The woman in the picture was dressed in attire from the 1800s, and the surface of the picture and the frame were definitely showing signs of age. It had to be over one hundred years old.

"Hope, this has to be a relative of yours. Maybe something is written on the back of the frame or picture. We can take this picture, along with the picture of the couple you found yesterday, to the house for further investigation," Miss Emma suggested.

"I think I better go ahead and put them in the truck before they get damaged, Miss Emma. This is definitely an interesting development." I carried the pictures to the truck and decided to put them in the cab of the truck for safekeeping.

After returning to the house, I heard Hattie cry out in a loud voice, "They law me, what else is we a gonna find?"

I ran quickly into the living room and then into the secret room. When I stepped into the small room, there was yet another unexpected discovery. When Mr. Conner and Dr. Sanders moved the trunk, they did not notice a small trap door. It was after I left the room to carry the pictures to the truck that they found it. It was located where the trunk had been sitting, and due to the poor lighting no one saw it. Dr. Sander and Mr. Conner were carrying the hat boxes and clothes out when Dr. Sanders caught his foot on the edge of the trap door.

The little door appeared to be about twelve inches square. I knelt on the dirty floor in front of the area where the trunk had sat and reached out to lift the small trap door. My heart was pounding with anticipation. I simply could not understand why my grandpa had been so secretive. I began to tug on the trap door and could not get it to budge. Dr. Sanders offered to help me open it, and with his help I was able to lift the door about two inches. Mr. Conner handed me a small crowbar he had removed from his tool belt, and I proceeded to pry the door open. Suddenly, the trap door popped loose and I was able to open it.

Before me lay a metal box, and beside of the box was a stack of old documents. I lifted the documents out and began to peruse them. It was so dark in the room I couldn't make out the contents of the documents. I handed them to Hattie and tried to lift the metal box. It was so heavy I couldn't get it to budge. Dr. Sanders then reached into the hole and lifted it out for me.

I carefully raised the lid of the metal box and gasped as I beheld what was before me. I looked up at Dr. Sanders and Mr. Conner in astonishment. Miss Emma, Hattie, and Samson were looking over my shoulder with stunned expressions on their faces, also. Finally Samson was able to speak and exclaimed, "W'y, Miss Hope, you done gone and struck gold. 'At 'ere be gold and silver money. W'y, 'ey ain't no tellin' how much it be worth!"

I heard Hattie shouting, "Honey chil', you ain't 'ever a gonna hav'ta work again. You is rich. Hallelujah! Praise da Lawd!"

There were gold and silver coins in the box—a lot of them. I was flabbergasted for a few seconds and could not speak.

After examining some of the gold and silver coins, I looked up at the group surrounding me. "Well folks, there are many gold and silver coins here. Also, there are several envelopes, documents, and what looks like some old tools. This is all so strange. I wonder why Grandpa never did anything with the gold, and why in the world did he put these tools in here?"

Miss Emma knelt down beside me and put her arm around my shoulders and said, "Hope, who knows why your Grandpa did the things he did, but we can't leave this coin collection here or take it to my house. We have to put it in a safe-deposit box immediately. We need to find out where it came from and why it's here. Maybe these documents you found with the coins will explain everything."

"Miss Emma's right, Miss Logan. You need to get this to the bank as soon as possible. Why don't I take you and Miss Emma there right now to put them in safekeeping," Mr. Conner said. "First time in my life I've ever seen 'is many gold coins. It's kinda scary."

Dr. Sanders spoke up, "To be honest with you, this is the most gold I've ever seen in my life. Oh, I've seen women with gold coin rings and necklaces, but it's unusual to see this many gold coins at one time. This collection must be worth a fortune."

After Mr. Conner loaded the box containing the coin collection into the cab of the truck, they made sure the desk and trunk were secured with ropes and bungee cords.

Miss Emma looked at Hattie and Samson and gave them instructions. "Just take the truck back to the inn, and we will be along in a few minutes. Maybe these two kind gentlemen will stop back by the inn after we leave the bank and help us unload the desk and trunk."

Miss Emma turned to Mr. Conner and asked, "Hope and I will just ride with you and Preacher Mike. Is that okay?"

"That'll be fine, and we'll be glad to help you'uns get the coin collection to the bank and unload the other items. I'll have my crew out here first thing in the morning to begin the renovations," Mr. Conner replied. "I will personally do the renovations on the secret room. I'm sure you don't want ever' Tom, Dick, and Harry to know about it."

"I haven't even thought about the renovation of the secret room, but thanks for your discretion. I would love to have it wired for electricity, but other than that I would like to keep it as original as possible," I replied.

"I can do it," Mr. Conner replied. "Now let's get goin'. Hattie, you got any of yore world-famous lemon pound cake?"

"Shore do, Mr. Ed. You'uns come on in da house after you'uns unloads all 'is stuff. Me and Samson, we be a looking fer you atter while."

Chapter 14

Since Mr. Conner's truck had an extended cab, Miss Emma and I were able to ride with Mr. Conner and Dr. Sanders without a problem. Dr. Sanders helped Miss Emma climb into the front seat of the shiny black truck, which meant I would be in the back seat with Dr. Sanders.

For some unknown reason I felt slightly uncomfortable sitting so close to him. I noticed he did not have on a wedding ring and immediately thought to myself, *now why in the world does it matter to me that he has no wedding ring on? Hope, get control of yourself, you are acting like a high school teeny bopper.*

Dr. Sanders turned to me, "Miss Logan, Ed tells me you're a teacher. What do you teach?"

Turning to answer him, I could not bring myself to look into his eyes. "I-I-I teach music in the public school system in Union County, North Carolina. I-I-I teach in a-a-a high school and my students are from ninth through twelfth grades. I have two large mixed chorus classes, a ladies' ensemble, and a men's chorus."

What in the world is happening to me? I asked myself. *I sound like I'm rambling. I have never had anyone make me feel so edgy and uncomfortable, nor have I ever stuttered or stammered when I talk. Dr. Sander is going to think I have a speech impediment. Why has this man had such an effect on me? I've got to get out of this vehicle before he sees what kind of effect he's having on me. To put it bluntly, this man takes my breath away. It's those eyes. I think I'm losing it.*

So that I would not have to converse with the handsome preacher, I stared straight ahead. Being that close in the truck was very uncomfortable, and I certainly didn't want to talk to him about religion. I was not an agnostic, but I simply had no time for organized religion or so called Christians, especially preachers.

Dr. Sanders turned to me again and asked, "Where do you live?"

"I live in South Charlotte, which borders Union County."

"Isn't that a long drive for you?" he asked.

I managed to answer him that time without stammering. "No, it's not a bad drive. From where I live, I can be at school in about twenty-five minutes. Union County has always been a farming county, and the scenery along my route to school is beautiful. I enjoy every minute of the drive.

"I will only be here in Martinsville this week. I'll be going back Sunday afternoon to finish the school year. I just can't leave my students at this point in the year. It wouldn't be fair to them or the school's administration. I have already told my principal I will not be back next year; he's well aware of my situation. I'll be commuting every weekend to check on the progress of the house and farm."

"That's good. Maybe I can introduce you to some of the people in our church. I would love for you to come this Sunday with Miss Emma," he replied.

I didn't have the courage to tell him I had no intention of attending any church, so I just nodded my head without saying anything. A nagging thought went through my mind. *Everybody I've met so far is involved in some type of church related work. At some point, I'll just have to let them all know that church and God just aren't for me.*

I turned to look out the truck window and began to reminisce about past events and the painful reasons I left the church. I made a conscious decision when I went away to college to stop attending church. When I found myself on my own, I decided I would do exactly what I wanted to do. I would not be forced to do anything, by anyone, anymore. I knew in my heart that my parents were unhappy with my decision, but they never pursued the issue with me.

Thoughts began to fill my mind that I had long forgotten. The little church I grew up in was very clannish, and it seemed that there was always someone upset with someone else. I got so tired of hearing it; I decided I just didn't want to listen to church squabbling any longer. Why couldn't people just get along, especially church people?

I distinctly remembered the time Mrs. Wilma Jones, the church pianist, got mad at our minister, because he wanted to move the grand piano from one side of the church to the other. That piano was Mrs. Jones pride and joy. The pastor and deacons voted to move it, and the majority of the church members voted for the move. The only naysayers were Mrs. Jones' family and her followers.

Everyone knew the real reason she was angry. The Caubles, a wonderful family in the community, had purchased and donated a beautiful pipe organ in memory of the patriarch of their family, Mr. Harvey Cauble. Mr. Cauble had been an influential man in the church community, and the church would have been crazy not to accept it. There was no way to fit the organ in the sanctuary of the church without moving the piano. The truth of the matter was jealousy and pride. Mrs. Jones simply did not want the competition of the new organ. She was afraid it would outshine "her" piano as she often referred to it. What difference did it make? I thought church was supposed to be about worshiping God, not music instruments.

In the end, she caused the church to split. About thirty families left the church and started another little church. She took everybody in her family and all of her cronies with her, and they met in an old abandoned country store that had no piano for her to play.

To put it bluntly, I got sick and tired of the petty quarreling, gossiping, and backstabbing. I had seen my mama and daddy hurt so many times, and I simply didn't want to deal with so called Christian folks any longer. They called themselves believers, but I definitely could not see any attributes of Christ in their lives.

I was jolted back to reality when Miss Emma said, "Well, here we are. Hope, the bank is right here on the corner. Let's get it done."

Mr. Conner remained in the truck, and Dr. Sanders lifted the heavy gray metal box that contained the coins, tools, and documents from the back of the truck and followed Miss Emma and me into the bank.

The Martinsville Bank was relatively large for such a small town, and it probably was the only financial institution in town. I spoke with the teller and told her I wanted to rent a large safe-deposit box. She saw the size of the box and informed us that they may not have a box large enough. She looked at us suspiciously when she saw the pastor carrying the box, but she asked no questions.

Dr. Sanders, Miss Emma, and I followed the bank teller into the room where the safe-deposit boxes were, and she directed us to the larger ones. To everyone's amazement, the box fitted perfectly in the box she designated as mine. With a sense of relief, we went back to Mr. Conner's truck.

We again climbed into the truck, and Miss Emma began to jokingly complain as she attempted to get in the truck. "Ed, if you're gonna haul me around, you're gonna have to put some stairs in 'is vehicle! You ought to ride in that little excuse of an automobile that Hope drives. The very idea! Car makers know better than to put little tin cans with wheels on the road for people to drive. W'y, I thought I was going to meet my Maker ridin' to the farm this mornin'."

We all laughed as Mr. Conner gave Miss Emma a push from behind, and Dr. Sanders and I pulled her by her arms to get her back in the truck. When she got in, she was completely out of breath.

We could hear her mumbling under her breath, "Hope just about scared me to death in her little red death trap this morning, now Ed's trying to kill me in 'is truck. At least he has a handle over the door to hang on to, but it's not worth two cents! Ya'll still had to push and pull me in. These new fandangled vehicles just weren't made for us old folks."

We continued to laugh at her as Mr. Conner drove to Miss Emma's house. We arrived there in a couple of minutes. It was then that I realized I had left my car at the farm.

I looked at Miss Emma in desperation and exclaimed, "Oh, Miss Emma, I forgot all about my car after finding the gold and silver. We will have to go back and get it."

Mr. Conner responded quickly, "Not to worry. I can run you back out there. In fact, it's on my way home. Now let's just get this stuff unloaded, and we'll go back and fetch your car."

"Thanks, Mr. Conner, I hate to be a bother."

"Not to worry, and by the way, jist call me Ed. My daddy is Mr. Conner," he said jokingly.

Dr. Sanders spoke up and said, "And please call me Mike or Preacher Mike. Everyone at the church calls me Preacher Mike."

I dropped my head shyly and said, "Okay, Ed and Preacher Mike. I will do that, if you will call me Hope."

I immediately felt that same "fluttery" feeling in my stomach, so I changed the subject and directed the conversation to Miss Emma. "Miss Emma, I hate like everything to take up space in your storage area with my stuff."

"Now you just hush up. I don't mind at all. I am thankful to have the opportunity to help you. Don't think about apologizing anymore. Okay?"

"Okay. I won't say anymore."

Under Samson's direction and supervision, Ed and Preacher Mike unloaded everything we brought back from the farm. Ed had rolled the old map up and unloaded it. Preacher Mike and Ed took special precautions when they unloaded the two lovely portraits we discovered in the secret room. After carefully storing everything away, we entered Miss Emma's sunroom.

Miss Emma invited everyone to come into the kitchen for some good southern iced tea and Hattie's wonderful lemon pound cake. Ed and Mike had evidently tasted Hattie's famous pound cake before, because they didn't hesitate to accept the invitation.

We entered the kitchen and heard Hattie's beautiful voice singing an old gospel hymn as only Hattie could sing. She stopped singing the moment we entered the kitchen.

"W'y, Reverend, I know'd you'd come by for some of my good ol' lemon pound cake and sweet tea."

"Sure thing, Hattie, but you know you can call me Mike."

"No-o-o-o, I never call God's man anythang but Reverend. It jist be plain ol' respec', jist plain ol' respec'. I be too ol' to change now. Set you'selves down ri'chear and dig in."

Preacher Mike responded, "Hattie, you are priceless. I must tell you that you have made my short time here at Martinsville Church very special. All of those meals you have prepared for me have definitely been appreciated. You are the epitome of a true believer and Christ follower."

"Reverend, I don't rightly know what epit'me means, but I know what it means to b'lieve and follow da Lawd."

After we all were seated around the kitchen table, Miss Emma asked Preacher Mike to return thanks. After he blessed the food, everyone began to eat the delicious cake.

I looked at Hattie and intentionally redirected the conversation away from God by asking, "Hattie, what exactly do you put in this cake? I've never tasted one just like it before."

"Lan' sakes, Miss Hope, it be real easy to make. It got milk, butter, sugar, flour, lemon flav'rin, and a whole bunch more stuff. Like I say, it's easy to cook. I's learnin' to read purdy good, but I still can't write it down. I get Miss Emma to write up da recipe fer ye."

Miss Emma spoke up, "Hope, actually the recipe came from my grandmother. We try to keep several of these cakes made up if we have guests at the inn and for folks who just drop by from time to time. Hattie is known all over this county for her lemon pound cake."

"I'm not much of a cook, but I must learn how to make this. It's to die for," I replied.

"Now, Miss Hope, don't cha go be dyin' on me. Ain't nuttin in' 'is ol' world worth dyin' fer," Hattie exclaimed.

"I was just kidding, Hattie. But this cake sure is good."

"How about sharing the recipe with me, Hattie?" asked Ed.

"Shore thang, I get Miss Emma to write it up for you'uns."

"Let's talk about the coin collection and the other things we found at the farm today," I said looking at everyone.

Samson and Hattie were seated across from me and Samson replied, "Miss Hope, Rullerford County long time ago wuz a gold minin' county. I don't know iffin you know'd 'at or not."

"That's what I hear, Samson."

"Yes'um, 'at be right."

Ed spoke up at that point to expound on the mining in Rutherford County. "I b'lieve it was in the late 1700s or early

161

1800s that several gold mines were found in this county. I often heard my grandfather talk about it and how it caused a population explosion in this area. I'm not much of a historian, but I b'lieve he said that this county was the center for production of gold in the nation during that time. There were two men who opened a private mint in Rullerfordton. It was called the Bechtler Gold Coin Mint. Can you imagine this little county being a center for production of gold in the United States? Maybe you had a coin collector in your genealogy, Hope.

"Oh, and while I'm thinking about it, Hope, the coins we found today need to remain a secret among the six of us. No one needs to know about that discovery. If the public were to find out, you could possibly have a problem with break-ins."

"I hadn't thought about that. I guess I'm too trusting. At least we have it in a safe place for now. I wonder who the coins belonged to, and why were they never cashed in? I'm finding out that this little corner of the world has a diverse history and a lot of legends and secrets. Hattie told me about the legend of Abe Lincoln," I replied.

Preacher Mike spoke up, "Yea, she told me the same story, and I have found that most people around here believe that legend. It sure makes sense when you see some of the pictures of the family that he supposedly descended from."

As we finished up the afternoon snack Hattie had prepared, I commented, "These treasures and items we found today, along with the history of this county, are certainly going to make life interesting for me over the next few weeks."

"You can say that again, Hope, you can say that again!" Miss Emma responded.

Chapter 15

As the afternoon wore on, I received an education on the history and folklore of the Appalachian area. It was about four o'clock when Preacher Mike and Ed got up to leave. As they were leaving, they thanked Miss Emma and Hattie for the wonderful lemon pound cake and gave them a big hug and Samson a hearty handshake.

Preacher Mike turned to Hattie and Samson. "Samson, Hattie, I'm still looking for you both to come and visit our church."

"W'y, Reverend, ye knows we can't be gone from our little church. I done tol' you, 'em white folk at yore church might not take too kindly to black folk in 'eir congregation. Reverend, it be time you realize you is in da South. Some of 'ese white folks in da South don't be knowin' 'at da war is over. I wouldn't want to grieve 'da Holy Ghost by makin' yore white congregation upset or get 'em all in a ruckus. I know you got good folk at yore church, but it be best 'is a way.

"W'y, my pastor would think me and Samson done be backslidin' iffin we don't show up to church. We ain't missed nary a Sunday in ten years or so. And da choir, w'y, they'd be a thinkin' I done gone an' left da country. Ye know I lead da choir on da Lawd's Day, an' Samson, he unlocks da church ever Lawd's Day. We's grateful for da invite. You is mighty nice to ask us, but I promise I be a prayin' for ye."

"Hattie, you are something else. You always put the feelings of others first. You are an inspiration to everyone. I wish more people had your sweet, sweet spirit."

"Reverend Sanders, I ain't always been 'at a way, and my spirit, it ain't always been sweet. When we wuz a share cropping when I wuz jist a young'un, I wuz et up with hate in my heart toward da white folks, but den I met da Lawd, and he commence to a changin' my heart. He helps me ever'day to forget da past and how my people wuz treated. When da ol' devil commence ta makin' me recollect da past and all 'at happened to my people, I jist commence ta sangin' about my won'erful Lawd. Reverend, how 'bout talking ta our Lawd 'fore you go. I jist love ta hear you pray."

Mike responded, "Hattie, I would be honored to." He looked at each of us and said, "Let us pray."

I sighed to myself, *another one of those long theological prayers like Daddy used to pray.* As I stood there with my head bowed listening intently, Preacher Mike began his prayer. I was deeply touched by the humbleness and simplicity of his prayer. He spoke as if God was there in the room with us. His prayer was filled with praise and thanksgiving for God's blessings in his life, and the gentle way he spoke of Miss Emma, Hattie, and Samson in his prayer touched me profoundly. It was evident that he truly cherished the three of them, but when he called my name in prayer, I was taken aback and at once felt a slight bit of resentment. *Why in the world did he feel he needed to pray for me?*

But as I listened to his words, I felt an overwhelming sense of peace and a familiar tugging in my heart. When I was young, I often felt that same strange tugging when I heard my father and pastor pray. Mike asked God to be with me through the renovations of the farm, and he asked God to protect me as I traveled back and forth from Charlotte to

Martinsville. He then asked God to be my guide as I dealt with any difficult legal situations that I might encounter. I thought to myself as I stood there, *Hope, this man is real. There is something about him that is genuine.*

Then he softly said, "Father, take me, use me, and mold me into the image of your wonderful Son. Fill every area of my life with your presence and power. I want to be your servant and a true follower of your son, Jesus Christ. I ask these things in the name of you Son, Jesus Christ. Amen."

It had been a long time since I had heard such a sincere prayer, but it had been years since I had been in church. I had pushed God and anything related to him totally out of my life a very long time ago.

Growing up in a Christian home had been difficult for me at times. Our entire existence had revolved around our church and the needs of the congregation. Mama and Daddy were there every time the doors of the church were opened.

It really bothered my parents when I quit attending church, but I appreciated the fact that they never at any time harassed me about my spiritual life or church attendance. Deep in the recesses of my heart and mind, I always knew that Mama and Daddy were praying for me.

While listening to Preacher Mike's prayer, it was only natural that I asked myself, w*hy have all of these Christian people been sent into my life? Maybe God is trying to speak to me, but why has He sent such a handsome man to be the one to touch my life through prayer?*

I had always wanted to be in control of everything in my life, but I was beginning to feel like everything was totally out of my control.

When Preacher Mike finished his prayer, Ed turned to me and spoke, "Hope, come along with us, and we will take you to get your car."

"I really appreciate you doing this for me."

"Not to worry. It's on my way home, and I've got to take Preacher Mike home anyway. Thanks again, Miss Emma. We'll be seein' you soon."

"No, we should be thanking you for your help today. Did you say your men will start tomorrow?" she replied.

"Yes, ma'am. They will all be there in full force. We will start tearing out rotted wood on the inside tomorrow, and I'll have some of the building materials delivered in the mornin'. Be seein' ye."

As we were going out the back door, Preacher Mike opened the door for me and courteously assisted me as I descended the back steps. I felt a strange tingling sensation on my elbow where his hand had gently supported me. It felt as if I had been shocked with electricity, and that odd tingling continued for several minutes.

What in this world is happening to me? I asked myself. *I've never felt this way in the past when a gentleman friend has touched me.*

When we got to the truck, Preacher Mike opened the front passenger door, and he gently took my hand and helped me into the truck. Those same jittery feeling were rekindled again, and to be honest, I didn't know how to react to his touch. I certainly didn't want him to sense my reaction to him.

After Ed climbed into the driver's side and cranked the truck, Preacher Mike climbed into the back seat, and we proceeded toward the farm. While traveling back across town, Ed and I discussed my plans for the farmhouse. I again reviewed our first conversation, and I reaffirmed my desire to have as much of the original woodwork left as possible.

Out of the blue, I remembered the millwork on the piazza. The old house had beautiful Victorian millwork all across the front piazza and some of it was missing. In fact, almost all of it was missing. The style of the house definitely called for that lovely, ornate millwork.

"Ed, the lovely millwork across the front piazza and on the gables of the house, please make it look as original as possible. And do the same for the banisters that enclose the piazza. As a child, that beautiful trim work just made the house for me. It always reminded me of a gingerbread house."

"Hope, I promise I'll keep everything like you want it. Not to worry, child, everything will look just like it did when Mr. Amos lived there. I have a friend over in Marion who does Victorian millwork. I noticed that most of it had rotted and would have to be replaced. I'll get him to do that for us."

"Thank you so much for all you are doing. This means so much to me."

Suddenly, I realized that Ed was not going toward the farm. "Ed, I think you are going the wrong way."

"No, Hope, just got to take the good preacher home. It won't take but a jiffy to drop him off."

In a few minutes, we drove into the yard of a small frame house. The house was not fancy, but the yard looked well tended.

Before Preacher Mike got out of the truck, he said, "Ed, are you coming to church tonight? You know, we have that meeting involving all of the deacons after prayer meeting."

"Yea, I'll be there," he replied.

Preacher Mike got out of the truck on my side of the vehicle, and I rolled the window down as he spoke to me. "Hope, it sure was nice to meet you. I hope to see you soon."

"Preacher Mike, it was nice to meet you also. Thanks for your help today," I shyly responded as I looked into his handsome face.

He had the most beautiful deep blue eyes I had ever seen. They looked like sparkling sapphires, and they seemed to penetrate deep into the recesses of my soul. They literally took my breath away and gave me a warm fuzzy feeling I didn't quite understand.

"Oh, it was nothing. I was glad to do it. See you soon," Preacher Mike said as he turned and went toward his house.

I sighed and relaxed for the first time since I had met him. I thought to myself, *there goes one good-looking man, too handsome to be a pastor. Preachers from where I come from sure don't look like that. Hope, get hold of yourself. You're acting like a teenager.*

Chapter 16

As Ed and I made our way to the farmhouse, we discussed the renovations and plans for the house. He assured me that he would complete the construction and renovations as soon as humanly possible. I was hoping to be in the house by the end of the summer, and according to Ed that might be a possibility.

I was elated when we drove up at the farm and saw the men working on the demolition of the buildings. They had already torn the barn and outhouse down and were loading the debris in the back of two huge dump trucks. I jumped out of Ed's truck quickly when I saw what had been accomplished in my absence. I thanked Ed for the lift and waved goodbye as he drove from the yard.

I started to walk toward the barn area and decided that might not be a wise idea. I was afraid I would get in the way of the crew, and I sure didn't want to do that. I certainly didn't want to hinder them.

As I approached my car, I couldn't believe how filthy it was. The combination of the dust from the road and the demolition of the buildings had left a dusty film all over it. I got in and decided that a dirty car never hurt anyone. Furthermore, I would be glad to drive it in any condition just to get the house completed.

I made my way back to the main highway without a problem as thoughts of my grandpa and grandma began to flood my mind once again. I smiled as I thought about

Grandma holding me on her lap and singing to me and Grandpa telling me the story of our ancestors coming to America. No one could hold my interest or spin yarns like Grandpa and Grandma. *Oh, if only I could talk to them one more time and hear them tell stories of days gone by, but that's not possible now,* I lamented to myself.

I was jolted back to reality when I came to the first stoplight in Martinsville. Miss Emma had informed me earlier that the private detective would be at her house at seven o'clock that night, and I wanted to get home, relax, and get a bath before she came.

I parked my car in the small parking area next to the inn and went to the back of the house.

Samson was coming out of the garage and spoke to me. "Miss Hope, you bes' git in da house, it's a gittin' kinda airish ou'chear. You might come down wid da grippe."

"Thanks Samson, you have a good night."

As I entered the sun porch, I spied Miss Emma in the kitchen with Hattie. I knew I was illiterate when it came to their Appalachian dialect, but I had to know what Samson meant when he used the words "airish" and "grippe."

I walked toward Miss Emma and whispered to her, "Miss Emma, please don't think I'm daft, but Samson just used a couple of words, and I don't know what he meant. They were "grippe" and "airish." What do they mean?"

"W'y, Hope, "grippe" is flu or cold like symptoms, and "airish" means it is kinda cool or drafty. Child, we're going to have you talking like us before you know it," she replied jokingly. "Or at least you'll be able to understand what we are saying!"

Hattie overheard me whispering to Miss Emma, and she laughing chimed in, "Miss Hope, I know me and Samson don't talk like you, but you be a learnin' soon to un'erstand us and Miss Emma. Me and Samson, we got our ancestors' and da white folks' ancestors' ways of talking passed down to us, but we can get da point across. Miss Emma is a helpin' me wid my grammar, 'cause it ain't quite right jist yet, but she still loves me da way I am, and she ain't 'ever make fun of me and Samson. I been a talkin' 'is way all my life, and it be mighty hard to change. I get plum' wore out a tryin'."

I smiled at those two beautiful ladies and replied, "Hattie, don't you ever change! I love you just the way you are. It would be an honor to be like either one of you. I know I have a southern accent, but it is very different from yours and Miss Emma's. I love the ways you express yourselves, and I love both of you. Please don't change one thing about the way you talk! I love you, Hattie, just the way you are. My mama and daddy still used a lot of your Appalachian dialect. Oh, they lost some of it after they moved away, but they still used a lot of it. They always pronounced Rutherford County as Rullerford County."

Hattie and Miss Emma both laughed and gave me a big hug. Hattie planted a big kiss on my cheek. In just a few short days, they had come to mean so much to me.

"By the way, Miss Emma, you said the detective would be here at seven, didn't you?" I asked.

"Yes, if you want to go ahead and get dressed, dinner will be ready in about half an hour," she replied.

"I think I will," I said as I hurried up the back stairs.

As I was ascending the steps, I overheard Hattie say, "It shore is nice to have a young'un around ain't it, Miss Emma?"

I smiled to myself when I heard Miss Emma reply, "Yes, Hattie, it sure is."

I quickly got my shower and dressed casually in denim capri pants and a tee shirt. I grabbed a pair of Birkenstock sandals and hurried down the back stairs leading to the kitchen. Hattie had completed dinner and was setting the table in the kitchen.

She looked up at me and remarked, "Miss Hope, you not company no more. You's family so we'll be eatin' in da kitchen."

"Hattie, you folks have taken me in and loved me like real family. I can never thank you enough for your kindness. Now let me help you get the food on the table."

"You can start off by jist a fillin' 'em glasses with that sweet tea over yonder," she replied as she pointed to a large crystal pitcher of tea.

I proceeded to fill the glasses with delicious tea and sat them on the kitchen table. While I was helping Hattie get the meal on the table, Miss Emma and Samson came in. As we sat around the table, Miss Emma asked Samson to return thanks. We joined hands, and Samson began to pray.

That dear old gentleman began his prayer. "O Righteous God Our Heavenly Father, you's been so good to us chil'ren. You's loved us ol' sinners, and you's saved us by yore ma'velous matchless grace. Lawd, I jist wants to thank you for 'at. I jist want to thank you for 'is here food 'at is laid out afore us. O Righteous God our Heavenly Father, jist bless 'is here food to the nourishment of our bodies so we can serve you better. Lawd, be with Miss Hope an' help her find her kin. 'Is young'un, w'y, she's been through a heap in da last little bit. Precious Heavenly Father, jist give her da strength to carry on as she travels in 'is ol' worl'. I pray in da name of Jesus. Amen, an' Amen!" Samson's prayer was sincere and from his heart, and if God was real, I knew that he must have heard that beautiful, heartfelt prayer.

I looked at Samson's radiant face and said, "Samson, thank you for praying for me. It really means a lot to me."

"I's glad ta pray fer you, Miss Hope. W'y, I's prayed fer you ever' day since you come here."

We quietly ate our meal which consisted of country style steak, mashed potatoes, and lima beans. Hattie had cooked some delicious cornbread, and I loaded mine down with real butter and savored every morsel. After we finished the delicious southern meal, Hattie ran us all out of her kitchen. We retired to the sunroom to wait for the detective to arrive, and Samson went about his business in the yard.

At exactly seven o'clock, the front doorbells chimed their melodious tune of "Hymn to Joy," and Miss Emma made her way to the front door. I could hear her talking to someone as they came through the house. I heard that person speak to Hattie, and I stood as Miss Emma and the detective entered the sun porch. The petite lady with Miss Emma looked to be in her late thirties and was dressed very sensibly in navy pants and a matching jacket. She had on comfortable looking black oxfords and had her brown curly hair cut in a pixie. Miss Emma introduced her as Jan McHenry. She went on to tell me that Jan and her husband went to church with her.

Mrs. McHenry sat across from me, and I began the conversation. "Mrs. McHenry, thank you for coming, and I assume Miss Emma has filled you in on my circumstances."

"She sure has. Please call me Jan. Just start at the beginning and bring me up to speed."

Because of her northern accent, I knew as soon as I heard Jan speak that she was not from Rutherford County.

Starting with Mama's death bed request to the present moment, I quickly told her the entire story. I'm sure Jan sensed the urgency in my voice as I told her about the journal and what it would mean to me to find my relative.

"Let me ask you one question. You mentioned the midwife, Prissy Walker. She lived down the road from your grandparents, is that correct?" Jan inquired.

"Yes, that's correct."

"Is that house she lived in still standing, or are there any outbuilding remaining on the property?" she asked.

Miss Emma spoke up and said, "Parts of the old house have caved in, but some of it still remains. I haven't been in it in years. The house and property once belonged to my parents and then to me. I sold it to Homer Snyder after their death and moved here to this house. I did not grow up in that particular house, but it was on the edge of our property and my pa rented it to Prissy Walker."

"Hope, that old house is where we need to begin our search for your relative. You mentioned that your grandfather tried to find out information after Prissy died. Do you know if he searched the house thoroughly?" Jan asked.

"Jan, I can't answer that. I don't even know if he truly believed my grandma on the subject of the other baby. I honestly feel that he believed she imagined the entire thing. I have not had time to peruse all of the documents we found out at the farm. There could be something in them. We put some of the documents in a safe-deposit box at the bank, and the others are here," I replied.

"If you and Miss Emma can go with me to the Prissy Walker's house tomorrow, we will give that place a once over and start unraveling this secret you have inherited. We will then go through those other documents at a later time to look for clues," Jane replied.

"Jan, I must thank you. I actually feel like I can see a ray hope on the horizon, but we must discuss your fee. Do I need to give you a retainer fee?"

"We won't worry about that just yet. Let's wait and see if we have any luck," she replied. "This won't be like real work; it should be fun. I love solving this type of mystery. Why don't I meet you here in the morning at nine o'clock, and we'll go out to the old house. Hope, you may want to bring your grandmother's journal, and of course you will need to dress appropriately. If you have boots, wear them. We may see some snakes. Wouldn't want you to get bit!"

Miss Emma spoke up, "We'll come dressed like we're going blackberry pickin', and don't forget to use insect repellant, Jan. This county is crawling with ticks and chiggers. I'll go ahead and call Homer tonight and get permission for us to go in the house. I know he won't care. "

I smiled as I realized I hadn't heard of a chigger since Grandpa and Grandma died. I was immediately reminded of my first encounter with chiggers. Grandma and I had gone blackberry picking; that night we itched like crazy. I don't think either one of us slept all night.

Grandma explained to me that a chigger is a tiny little mite that will burrow under the skin. She covered my body with castor oil to help relieve the itching. When the castor oil did not stop the itching, she lovingly dabbed each spot with mineral spirits. I don't think I ever remembered itching or smelling like I did that night.

Those thoughts prompted me to say, "You better believe I'll cover up and use insect repellant! I personally know what a tiny chigger can do. I was their victim many times as a child."

"Well, ladies, I must be going, and I'll be seeing you around nine o'clock in the morning," Jan said as she left.

After walking her to the front door, Miss Emma called Homer Snyder and got permission for us to search the house. She then came back to the sun porch and decided we both needed a slice of Hattie's lemon pound cake. Hattie had gone home for the night, so we raided the refrigerator for some cold milk and sat down at the kitchen table to enormous slices of mouthwatering cake.

Miss Emma thought for a moment then spoke to me. "Hope, 'pears to me that we are on the way to solving this mystery. Jan is a great investigator. She was working for the New York City Police Department as a detective when the twin towers were attacked. She was not on duty at the time of the attack, due to a pregnancy. After things settled down in New York, she and her husband Al moved south. They're good people, and I know you'll enjoy being around her. Al is an attorney here in Rullerford County. Actually, they live in

Rullerfordton. I know Al will be glad to represent you if you need legal counsel."

"I could tell by her accent she was not a local Rutherford County native. I can't believe how everything has fallen into place since I arrived in Martinsville. It almost seems like someone planned just the perfect person to handle every situation I have encountered. I am absolutely amazed."

"Child, someone did plan all of this. Surely, you must realize that by now," Miss Emma implied.

"Miss Emma, I respect your strong faith, but I must admit that I don't share your beliefs. I have seen so many so-called Christians who, just to put it bluntly, were hypocrites. I watched it all through my growing up years in the little country church we attended just outside of Raleigh. Oh, I know that the faith my mama and daddy had was genuine, and so was the faith of my grandparents.

"The fact of the matter is, I watched those so-called believers hurt Mama and Daddy and my pastor and his wife so many times over the years, and I just can't forget it. To put it bluntly, they simply were not genuine Christians and were just playing church. I can't put those memories behind me and move on."

"Hope, you *must* put them behind you. You can't hold hate in your heart even if you don't believe in God and his power. It will only ruin you. Bitterness, hate, and unforgiveness never hurt anyone except the one who refuses to forgive. Don't let those feelings of the past destroy you. Don't let it make you miserable like I did for so many years."

"But Miss Emma, I've tried, and those feeling just won't go away."

"Honey, don't you understand? You can't do it by yourself. That's where God comes in. He has offered the entire human race the wonderful, free gift of His mercy and grace, and he tells us in his Word, '*Whosoever will, may come.*' And, Hope, you are a part of that whosoever, but first you must receive his free gift of salvation, redemption, and forgiveness. That's your first step on the road to forgiving others. You see, Hope, *your* sins must be forgiven by God before you can forgive others."

"Miss Emma, I heard our pastor preach God's forgiveness and redeeming love so many times as a child, but the actions of those church folks overshadowed his words. The dark cloud of their hatefulness could block out any Carolina blue sky on the brightest, sunshiny day.

"There were times when I was touched deeply and felt a strange longing in my heart for something, but I would look around me, and all I saw was dissention and strife. There's got to be more to being a believer than what I saw in the little church I grew up in. The fact of the matter is—I've been absolutely turned off to Christianity by church people.

"There was even a congregation near our church that had a problem with the pastor and his wife. I think it was more the wife than the pastor. He came in trying to change everything in the church and was very dictatorial and dogmatic. It was his way or the highway. Oh, he was a great speaker, and he could influence a congregation with his choice of words, but he had no people skills.

"His wife was a troublemaker from the beginning. She only had a few people as friends, and she continually gossiped about everyone else in the congregation. You can guess what happened. The church split and never got over it. Many of the church members came to our church, but they could never find peace because of what had happened.

"Mama and Daddy went to the funeral home the night that pastor passed away. They overheard someone tell the wife of the pastor that if anyone came in the funeral home that she didn't want to see, all she had to do was let them know and they would ask them to leave. I just can't believe how some church members act!"

"Hope, I hate that you have had such negative experiences in your life. Pastors and their wives are human, and they make mistakes just like everyone else. Surely, what you saw in your parents, your grandparents, and your pastor outweighs those hypocrites."

I looked at Miss Emma sadly and replied, "No, I guess it doesn't. I'm afraid I'm a hopeless case. Why would God even want an unforgiving bitter person like me? Unforgiveness and bitterness are certainly not the attributes of God from what I have been taught."

"No, my child, they are not, but that's the amazing thing about his mercy and grace. When God comes into your heart and life, your whole being changes, and you become a new creation. Even your thoughts, your desires, and your attitude toward others change," she replied. "Maybe these people you are talking about were not in a close fellowship with the Lord. We aren't to judge others, only God knows the condition of their hearts.

"I know one thing for sure; the bad attitudes of many Christians grieve the heart of God. Many people never come to know the Lord, because of the actions of church people. That's exactly what the old devil wants, and torment will be overpopulated because of the actions of many church members."

"I guess I've been marked for life, but I just can't seem to put all of my bitterness behind me. I know it's not right, but I guess I've not reached the point to want to change. Miss Emma, I love you dearly, but I guess I'm just not ready to take that step yet, maybe later."

"And I love you, too, Hope. I promise I won't press this issue. This is something that only you and God can fix, and I will not wear you out with my beliefs. "You go on to bed and sleep well, and we will head out in the morning to solve this mystery that surrounds your family," she replied as we left the kitchen and climbed the back steps to the second floor of the inn."

Chapter 17

After my conversation with Miss Emma, I had trouble going to sleep. I relived every word she said over and over. I had never felt so burdened before. The last time I looked at the clock it was three o'clock.

When morning came, I had to force myself out of bed. In spite of my restless night, I was up at six o'clock the next morning ready to go to the old Ledbetter house. I kept mulling over my conversation with Miss Emma as I dressed for the day. I simply had to put that conversation out of my mind.

When I arrived downstairs, I did not mention our conversation from the night before, and neither did Miss Emma. She simply gave me a big hug, and we sat down to a sumptuous breakfast with Hattie and Samson.

As Miss Emma and I approached Jan's sports utility vehicle to make our trip to the old Ledbetter farm, I laughed at her as she tried to navigate her steps. She had so many clothes on, she could barely move or breathe.

"Miss Emma, I believe we've got on too many layers of clothes," I wailed.

"Oh no, we don't. I'd put on more if I knew it would keep the chiggers and snakes from getting after me, young lady. You better hope you've got on enough insect repellant," she replied.

When we reached the car, I heard Miss Emma pretending to grumble as she tried to lift herself up into the vehicle. "Every vehicle I've ridden in this week was either so low to the ground I had to fall in it, or so high I needed a ladder to climb in it. They sure don't make these new fan-dangled vehicles for old folks like me."

Jan laughing replied, "Oh, Miss Emma, I don't want to hear that baloney. You're not old. You're just well-seasoned. Everyone knows you outwork most people in Martinsville, young and old."

I got behind Miss Emma and gave her a big push from the rear. "Here, let me help you."

"Whew, it's hard work gittin' in these new automobiles, especially with all of these clothes on. I just know as the old song goes, this old gray mare ain't what she used to be," she exclaimed.

Jan quickly replied, "Miss Emma, you ain't what you used to be, you are better. You get around better than anybody in this town."

Miss Emma quickly responded, "I don't know about that, young lady!"

Because we had slathered our bodies with so much insect repellent before we left the inn, we had to ride with the windows down in the vehicle. All of Rutherford County probably smelled us as we made our way out to the farm that day.

We arrived at the Ledbetter farm with tools, long-sleeved shirts, and more insect repellent in tow. Of course Miss Emma instructed me to tuck my jeans into my socks before we left home, and she then supplied me with a pair of high top boots which she called brogans.

As Miss Emma was getting out of the vehicle, I heard her laughingly exclaim, "Look here, Hope, this vehicle isn't so bad after all. All I have to do when I get ready to get out is just turn and *slide*."

"Me-oh-my, Miss Emma, you are a hoot!" I replied.

After unloading Jan's SUV, we started getting ready to search the house and property.

I heard Miss Emma as she approached the dilapidated old house. "I spent my growing up years on this land. The house I grew up in stood about a mile from here just over that hill. My pa rented this old house to Prissy Walker with the understanding that she would help out on the farm. When she first moved here, she helped my ma with housework. Eventually, she stopped doing that, but I never knew why. She was a strange sorta bird. As the old-timers around here say, 'She was kinda quare.' She continued to stay in this house until her death.

"I have some beautiful memories of this old farm, but I also have some that are not so beautiful. My mother sure made life miserable for my pa, and I'm sure that's what drove him to drink. Ma fussed and fumed about his drinking continually, and all the while she was the very reason he drank. W'y, I don't believe they loved each other a speck.

"Don't get me wrong, ladies, I loved her, but she was unbearable when it came to my pa. I only wish we could have found a way to help her. I honestly believe she was mentally ill. She had a horrible childhood, and I'm sure that had an affect on her actions. But that's enough about my ma and pa and this farm. Let's get this search underway."

We entered the house by way of the front door and discovered that the door was falling off its hinges, and the house reeked of decayed wood and mildew. The windows all seemed to be intact, and the floor appeared to be somewhat stable. I noticed that the walls and ceiling had the same lovely bead board that was in my grandparent's home. The house was very small and only had four rooms. We thoroughly searched each room and came up with nothing. I watched Jan as she inspected every inch of the walls and floor.

She inspected the ceiling for an opening to the attic space, and she found one in a bedroom. We pulled out the folding ladder we brought with us, and Jan used it to climb up and remove the board that covered the scuttle hole that led to the attic. Using her flashlight, Jan studied the attic area for several minutes.

Then I heard her shout, "There are several things up here, and I am going to hand them down to you, Hope."

The first thing she handed down was a wooden box that looked like an old milk crate. When I took it from her, I realized it was full of old clothes.

"I'm going to try to pull myself up into the attic to get a better look," Jan hollered down to us.

Miss Emma cautioned her saying, "You be careful, you hear me! That attic has got to be full of spiders and rats and no tellin' what else. Whatever you do, don't step on a rotten board and fall through the ceiling."

"Thanks, Miss Emma; I really needed you to remind me of creeping critters. Trust me; I'll tread softly on these old rafters. Ladies there's not much up here but a bunch of junk. It looks like someone even threw trash up here. There's an old quilt covering something over in the corner. I'm going to make my way over there and see what it is."

In a few seconds, I heard her shout with excitement, "Hope, I think I found something. There is a cradle up here and a box with some letters in it, and I believe there are some legal documents also. I'm going to hand them down to you, and we can see what we've got."

Jan came down from the attic completely covered in dust and spider webs. In fact her dark curly hair looked like she had stuck her head in a humongous spider web.

Miss Emma gave her a quick once over, dusted the spider webs out of her hair, and exclaimed, "We've got to get out of some of these clothes as soon as we can. I'm about to burn up. Let's take this cradle and box back to my place to go through the documents."

Jan spoke up quickly, "I just want to check the yard before we leave to be sure there is nothing there. I think we have searched the house sufficiently. Let's go outside and take a quick look."

We followed Jan as she went out the back door of the house. As we went into the backyard, we noticed an old outbuilding that could have been a smokehouse or crib.

Jan quickly made her way through the tall grass and bushes and surmised, "I'm surprised this building is still standing as old it is."

By the time we had entered the old building, Miss Emma informed us that the building was an old smokehouse because of the way it was constructed. It was very dark and dank inside. There were no windows in the building, and the floor had been dug out about twelve or fourteen inches below ground level. There were rotten wooden boxes all around the walls of the building and old rusty hooks attached to the rafters in the ceiling.

I jumped back toward the open door when I realized the building had curtains of spider webs hanging from the rafters. It looked like they were hung there by a gothic decorator, and the dank smell of mold and mildew took our breath away. We covered our faces with our hands to filter the air that was choking us.

Miss Emma went on to explain to us how the wooden boxes around the wall were used. "These wooden boxes would be filled with a salt mixture and the meat would be rubbed down with the salt and placed in the boxes and left there until spring of the year. The meat would then be put in white cloth sacks and hung from the hooks in the ceiling after it had cured in the salt mixture."

That information was all new to me. I had no idea that meat was preserved in that manner. I had never actually gone inside of Grandpa's old smokehouse, because he always kept it locked.

"Miss Emma, what kind of meat was cured in here?" I asked.

"They cured mostly pork, such as ham, bacon, and fat back. Sometimes they even smoked venison or bear. Pork was a staple food back in those days. All vegetables were seasoned with pork, and because of that most people died with heart trouble. Hattie still uses pork a lot, but over the years she has started using other methods to season food. But she'll tell you, in a heartbeat, that there's nothing like cooking with ham hocks and fatback."

I scanned the old smokehouse and my eyes fell on a contraption in the corner of the building. "What in the world is this?"

"Well, in this world! That's an old liquor still! Of all things! I don't know what to say!" Miss Emma exclaimed. "How can this be? Now I know where my pa got his liquor. Prissy Walker musta been makin' moonshine. And here's the rusty old car radiator she used to condense the alcohol vapor that rose up from her boiling mixture of corn mash. Hope, I bet you've never seen one of these homemade contraptions."

"No, Miss Emma, I can't say that I have."

"I always knew my pa had a hankerin' for spirits, in fact, when he died, I heard the doctor tell my ma that he suspected his death resulted from lead poisoning. It musta been all of that moonshine he got from Prissy Walker and this old still that did him in. I can't believe he drank that horrible stuff. W'y, it had to a been at least eighty percent alcohol.

"The mountains of No'th Ca'olina have always been known for bootleggin' and moonshinin'. W'y, Pa should have known that white lightning wasn't fit for man or beast to drink. Some of the mountaineers call moonshine 'skull cracker' and believe you me, it has enough kick to crack a skull. I've even heard it called 'rotgut.'

"I guess we can safely say that the smoke that came from this old smoke house wasn't coming from pork meat curing, but from this old homemade still. I have to give Prissy Walker credit for one thing; she knew just where to set up shop— down by the river side. She had to have a good supply of water to concoct her despicable old brew, and the river is not very far from here. Makes me wonder what my pa's involvement was in making this illegal 'hillbilly brew.'"

Miss Emma continued talking as if she were thinking out loud. "I guess that's the reason Prissy Walker never had to move from this house after she quit helping my ma clean house, and this contraption has got to be the culprit that killed my pa," she implied pointing to the old car radiator. "These old radiators usually had lead in 'em. Now I guess you see why I stayed at your mama's house so much, Hope. I didn't have a very happy home life, and it's a wonder I turned out as normal as I did."

"Miss Emma, I'm so sorry that your childhood was so sad, but you have nothing to be ashamed of. You have contributed so much to so many lives in this area," I quickly reassured her.

"Not to worry, my child. That's all history now, and we are *not* going to dwell on the past. It's all water under the bridge, and that's where I want it to stay. Jan, there doesn't appear to be anything else in this old building but this old still."

"No, Miss Emma, there is nothing here," she declared as she surveyed the walls and ceiling. Let's just take a look around outside and see if we see anything on the outside of this building and the house."

After checking the smokehouse and the outside of the house, we decided that there was nothing of significance there. We did find a stack of old mason jars behind the smokehouse, and we figured that Prissy had used them for her corn liquor. Before we put the cradle and box of documents in the SUV, we shed some of our clothes and sped back toward Martinsville.

When we arrived at Miss Emma's house, we unloaded the cradle and box of documents from Jan's vehicle. We then began transferring them into the sunroom, but we only made it as far as the back door.

Hattie heard us drive into the yard and met us as we ascending the back steps. "Land sakes, you ain't a brangin' 'at nasty junk in 'is clean house, is you Miss Emma?"

"I guess we better clean it up a bit before we bring it in. Hattie, if you'll get that old plastic table cloth we keep in the panty and spread it down on the floor in the sunroom, we won't make such a mess," Miss Emma replied.

"Shore looks to me like you'uns better clean you'selves up, too. W'y, you'uns got spider webs and dirt all over ye."

All three of us went back out and attempted to brush ourselves off. We cleaned up the cradle and box the documents and letters were in as best we could.

As we started back in the house, Hattie peered out the door and laughingly remarked, "Now you'uns can come in. W'y, you'd a got 'is sunroom filthy iffin you'd a come in nasty as ye wuz. Git in here! I want to see what you'uns found."

I smiled at Hattie. "I think we really found something important. Just wait 'til we show you what we found."

"Where in 'is world did you'uns find all 'is ol' nasty stuff?" Hattie asked.

"We found it in the attic of the old house on the Ledbetter farm where Prissy Walker lived," I replied. "This cradle could be the bed my mother's twin slept in. I'm so nervous and excited I can't stand myself, Hattie."

"I reckon you is, chil'. 'C'mone let's get started, I's nervous too."

Jan began inspecting the cradle. It was a simple wooden box on rockers. It appeared to be made of rough cut pine and had been sanded to make the surface smooth. It was just about ready to fall apart because of the heat it had endured in the attic of the old house over the years. In fact the wood was beginning to dry rot.

Jan turned the cradle over and on the bottom were some engraved initials. After close inspection Jan looked at me and said, "It looks like H.W.L. Does anyone know of someone with those initials?"

"I don't know how much more of this I can take today, but those were my pa's initials. His name was Henry Wentworth Ledbetter. Why in this world would my pa have made this cradle for Prissy Walker?" Miss Emma moaned.

"I don't know, Miss Emma," Jan replied. "Just don't get yourself in a panic until we have checked everything out. Just stay calm."

"'Pears to me we are finding skeletons in my closet, Hope, as well as yours. I guess there was a side of my pa I never knew about. I knew he and my ma couldn't stand each other, but this takes the cake. I sure hope he didn't have an affair with Prissy Walker," Miss Emma whispered.

Hattie heard Miss Emma's remark and replied, "To be sure not, w'y, ever'body was scart of her. I done tol' you'uns about her a shootin' at my pa. Ever'body in 'is neck of da wood wuz scart of 'at ol' woman 'cause she was so mean and quare. Yore pa wooda had'ta been mighty drunk to been a sparkin' with da likes of her."

Hattie spread the old plastic table cloth on the floor so we could empty the contents of the box. Jan and I gathered around the pile of letters on the floor and sat there "Indian style" as we went through the documents. Most of them were not of any value, in fact, the only document that could have proven be helpful was a copy of a will. Neither Miss Emma nor Hattie had ever heard of the person for whom the will had been drawn up, but everything in the will was bequeathed to Pricilla "Prissy" Walker as the only surviving relative. The will was for a Luther Walker. There was no property named in the will, only a small amount of money, twenty-five dollars, and a few pieces of inexpensive jewelry. The will was drawn up in Mecklenburg County, North Carolina.

Jan spoke up with excitement, *"Now we have a clue. We have somewhere to start searching. Let's get into these old letters."*

Most of the letters were from the Charlotte area and seemed of no importance. We finally came across a shocking letter from a man in the Charlotte area. Jan carefully opened the letter and began to read aloud.

"Miss Walker, the baby is doing well. She has adapted to our home here. She is still very small and requires a lot of attention. We will continue to keep you informed. There is a family who has shown interest in her, and they have even talked to me about adopting her. I will let you know if that takes place. Your silence is vital in this type of adoption. We will discuss the financial arrangements later."

The letter was dated April 4, 1940, and it was signed by Wilson Jones. The letter was not on any type of letterhead, but there was a return address on the envelope. It was difficult to read, but it looked like Marsh Street, Charlotte, North Carolina.

I was so keyed up I could hardly contain myself. "That's two months after my mama's birthday. We must find out more about this man and what he was up to?"

Hattie chimed in, "Sounds like he wuz up to no good to me, Miss Hope. W'y, I bet'cha he had one of 'em 'ere baby sellin' thangs a goin' on. Sounds to me like he wuz a good for nothin' scalawag."

"I do hope that dear little baby was not sold for money, and I sure hope my pa had nothing to do with it. After what we found out this morning, nothing would surprise me now," Miss Emma exclaimed.

I sat there astonished as my mind absorbed the most recent revelation and said, "I just don't know what to make of all of this information. It blows my mind that people can be so evil. To steal a little innocent baby is the most horrible thing I've ever heard of. And to think about the suffering my Grandma went through is just about more than I can bear."

"Miss Hope, 'at be what wickedness can do ta a body. No wonder she wuz a shootin' at ever'body 'at come 'round her house. We all jist figgered she was quare. Gabriel is a gonna blow his horn someday, and da Good Lawd is a gonna come back to 'is ol' sinnin' worl' and wind all 'is mess up. He done tol' us he's a comin' back some day. Yea, da Good Lawd is comin' back to 'is old worl' someday, and he's a gonna put the quiatus on all 'is wickedness. Yea, as da ol' slave song goes, it's a gonna be 'At Great Gittin' Up Mornin.'

"But da Lawd is so lovin' and kind and brings comfort to da soul. W'y, Miss Hope, he even loved 'at ol' Prissy Walker as mean as she wuz. W'y, he sent his only Son to die fer her. You'uns reckon nobody never tol' her 'bout Jesus and John 3:16?"

Miss Emma replied, "I guess not Hattie. Maybe she didn't come from a family that believed in God, and she probably just got mixed up with the wrong people. That will sure do it to a person. Bad company makes for bad business."

"Sin and wickedness shore do mess up a life. What else did you'uns find out?"

"Well, Hattie, you know as well as I do that Pa had a bad drinking problem. We found out this morning where he got his spirits. Prissy Walker was a moonshiner, and I'm afraid Pa could have been in on it."

Miss Emma reached in the pile of letters and pulled out some receipts that had Henry W. Ledbetter's name on them.

"Hattie, Look at this. My pa's name is on these receipts, Henry W. Ledbetter. I hope my die! Look at this one; it's for one-hundred dollars worth of sugar. Hattie, you know how much corn he always grew, and here are several more receipts for sugar. As sure as I'm sittin' here, my pa was in on the moonshinin' operation. Ha, it wouldn't surprise me if he made the still and was the bootlegger to boot."

"What's the difference between a bootlegger and a moonshiner? I asked. "I thought they were the same."

"Hope, the moonshiner makes the whiskey and the bootlegger or rum-runner delivers it. It's called running the moonshine. Moonshiners usually do their brewing by the moonlight so they won't get caught, and that's how it got its name. Back in colonial times bootleggers would hide their spirits in their boots, and that's how the word bootlegger originated."

Jan spoke up at that time. "Well, ladies, the plot thickens. It appears we have uncovered quite a story. Miss Emma, looks like your pa was probably a 'rum-runner.' He most likely was inspired by the prohibition era during the 1920s, and when Prissy Walker came along in 1940, your pa had the perfect set up for his illegal business.

"Let's continue to go through the rest of these letters and see if there are anymore clues. I plan to spend all of next week working on this. My plans are to go to Mecklenburg County on Monday and start researching this mystery."

Most of the letters were of no value to our investigation, but we came across one that hit us all like an atomic bomb, especially Miss Emma. The letter was from the same man in Charlotte, Wilson Jones, and it stated very incriminating evidence that Mr. Ledbetter was involved in the kidnapping. He had actually taken the child to Charlotte, North Carolina, for Prissy Walker and sold her for two-thousand dollars to Wilson Jones.

I looked at Miss Emma, and she was as pale as a ghost with a look of panic on her face. "Hattie, hurry, get a wet cloth to put on Miss Emma face! I'm afraid she's gonna pass out!"

Jan and I jumped up quickly and helped Miss Emma put her head between her legs to get her blood flowing. After Hattie brought a bowl of ice water and a cloth, I put cold compresses to her face.

Miss Emma started crying hysterically and gasped, "Ya'll just don't know how this breaks my heart! To think my pa was responsible for this atrocity, and I never knew it. I wonder if Ma had any idea what was going on. I loved him so much. I just can't believe he was so wicked. He sure had me fooled. I don't know how much more I can take. I sure hope God is not punishing me for the many years I was angry with your mama, Hope. If only I hadn't been so mean to her and Whitley."

Hattie immediately rushed to her side. "If! If! If! Don't cha say 'at no more. It's like my pa used to say, 'If *if's* and *but's* wuz candy and nuts, we'd all have a Merry Christmas.' Now, Miss Emma, you jist calm down! Am I a gonna hav'ta whup you? You know our Lawd don't do such as 'at. You ain't to be blamed for his wickedness. Even if Mr. Ledbetter did some mighty wicked things, he wuz yore pa, and I know he loved you. When a body's been a drinkin' 'ey do some mighty foolish things. It ain't yore fault, now jist remember' 'at. Oh, Lawd, we need som'body to pray right now. I's gonna go get Samson to come an' pray fer ye, Miss Emma."

In a few minutes, that dear man came in and took his hat of. He fell to his knees and began praying like I had never heard before. That wonderful saint seemed to have a special line straight to heaven. I could sense a loving presence filling the room as he prayed. He was talking to God as if he was there in the room with us.

At one point in his prayer, Samson asked the Lord to help Miss Emma with her heavy burden and "jist lift it from her heart right now."

I was amazed as he recited scripture after scripture in his prayer, because I knew he couldn't read. I had never heard anyone pray with such power and authority.

When he completed his prayer, he got up from his knees, looked at the four of us, and said, "Ain't God good? Ain't my Won'erful Lawd good?"

He turned, put his hat on, and quietly left the room with no fanfare. Miss Emma sat up and said, "That dear soul's prayers always reach heaven and take me directly into the presence of God."

I had never experienced anything like what had just taken place, and it prompted me to ask myself, *could there possibly be some genuine Christians left in the world?*

Jan and I packed up the documents and decided to put them in the garage, out of Miss Emma's sight. We carried them and the cradle out and gave them to Samson to put away.

Chapter 18

Miss Emma seemed to recover quickly, and Hattie brought us all a slice of lemon meringue pie and a glass of iced tea. We sat there with Miss Emma and made a conscious effort to veer the conversation away from Prissy Walker and Henry Ledbetter.

I began to talk about my students and some of the end-of-the-year concerts we had planned. I told them about our Christmas concert and some of the charitable things my students did at Christmas, such as performing for Hospice patients and nursing homes.

Miss Emma spoke up at one point, "Hope, your grandma would be so proud of you. She had such a love for music."

"Yes, Miss Emma, her dream was for me to carry on her legacy in music. I hope I can make a place for myself in Martinsville in the field of music. My whole life has revolved around music for so long, and I never want that to stop."

Jan responded quickly, "You will find your niche here. I have no doubt about that. You could teach in the public schools or the community college. There are a number of avenues you can pursue."

Miss Emma interrupted, "Ladies, I know you are tiptoeing around the subject of my pa. I promise I am fine now. It was such a shock to find out what a scalawag my pa was, but I know in my heart, God will give me the strength

to handle this. I've always known that I would have to live a
lifetime to make up for all of the hateful things my ma did,
but now I guess I'll have to live two lifetimes to make up
for what my pa has done. I thought Ma was bad, but I guess
Pa was worse. I'm just glad that I won't be judged for their
wickedness. I am perfectly fine now, and we need to discuss
our plans for next week. We're not going to mention Henry
and Pearly Mae Ledbetter anymore today. Let's talk about
next week."

Jan looked at Miss Emma and reiterated her previous
promise to solve the mystery. "I will take care of everything.
You and Hope just trust me to do the research, and we'll get
to the bottom of this mystery very soon."

"Since this is Thursday, I realize the weekend is
approaching, and I must go back to Charlotte on Sunday.
I've got to get lesson plans ready for school next week. Jan,
you can follow me and stay in my apartment while you are
doing your research."

"That would be great. My mother lives next door to me,
and I will get her to help with my daughter, Emily. I will
follow you, and we might be able to wind everything up in a
couple of days," she replied.

Jan got up to leave, and I followed her as she started
for the backdoor. "Hope, you take care of Miss Emma and
Hattie, and I'll see you Sunday. What time will you be going
back?"

"Probably around two o'clock. Will that be good for
you?"

"Yea, I should be able to be ready by then. I teach Sunday
School, and Al and I both sing in the choir. We usually get
out of church around noon. Yea, I can be ready by then. Two
o'clock it is."

"See you then, and thanks for everything," I replied as
she left.

After Jan left, Hattie shooed us into the kitchen for a late lunch. We sat around the kitchen table and enjoyed a satisfying lunch that consisted of a beautiful spring salad with tons of trimmings. She had also prepared homemade vegetable soup that was fit for a king.

I looked across the table to Hattie, "You are trying to fatten me up, Hattie."

"No, I ain't, but you sure could use some meat on 'em bones, little lady. You too poor lookin'. W'y, you as skinny as a pine pole, and I be'cha ye don't weigh a hundurd pounds soakin' wet."

"Oh, Hattie, I weigh more than that."

Miss Emma chimed in, "She is a tiny slip of a girl, Hattie, but so were her Ma and her Grandma. By the way, Hope, we haven't looked at those old portraits that we found in the secret room yet. Why don't we do that this afternoon? I'm feeling much better now."

"I'll go get them, and we can take the frames apart as soon as we eat if you are sure you are okay. Maybe there are some clues on the back of the pictures. Hattie, can we use that same plastic table cloth we used last night in the sunroom?" I asked politely.

"Yes'um, you shore can."

After I helped Hattie clear the table, I hurried to the garage to retrieve the portraits of the mysterious lady and the couple from the late 1800s or early 1900s. I placed them carefully on the floor in the sunroom on the plastic table cloth.

As I picked up the portrait of the lady who resembled me, I turned to Miss Emma, "This frame looks to be in pretty fair condition, but it's as heavy as lead."

The lovely oval frame appeared to be made of some type of gilded metal. The metal was ornately decorated with lovely Victorian fans and flowers forming designs on the frame. Upon closer inspection, I found that it was solid metal. It was so tarnished we had a difficult time deciding what type of metal it was. We finally decided it was probably copper or brass finished in gold plating.

I tried to reposition the gilded fame and turn it over. "This heavy thing must weigh a ton. Miss Emma, look at this domed glass; it has to be old. You just don't see that in today's framing. When I get this thing cleaned up, it will be absolutely breathtaking. Hattie, look here! Just look at this trim work! It sure has a lot of Victorian flair. I've just got to find out who this mysterious lady is! Since she looked so much like me, I wonder why Grandpa never hung it. Look, it has gilded tin on the back of the frame and is held together with screws."

"Law me, Miss Hope, 'at be the purdiest thang I ever seen. Let me get some cleaning stuff, and we'll commence to cleanin' it. I'll git it fer ye."

Miss Emma looked at Hattie and said, "Let's just use some very mild soapy water and then some clear water, and we'll need some glass cleaner for the glass. I know taking it apart may take away from the value of this beautiful piece, but maybe something is written on the back of the portrait. Hattie, hand me that small screwdriver in the kitchen, and we'll take these screws out. This is a priceless treasure, Hope."

Hattie came back in the sunroom armed with two containers of water and cleaning cloths. She also had the screwdriver and some pliers in her apron pocket. Miss Emma surprised me by getting on the floor with me to help take the frame apart.

"Miss Emma, you never cease to amaze me. You are as agile as a twenty year old. Hattie are you gonna get down here, too?"

"Law no; my autheritis is a actin' up. Iffin I got down 'ere, you'uns 'ould never git me up. My ol' bones is about slap wore out. I'll jist sit ri'chear."

I began to carefully take the frame apart by removing the tin from the back of portrait.

When I noticed an old yellowed piece of paper attached to the back side of the portrait, I slowly looked up at Miss Emma and Hattie. "I sure hope this is not more bad news. We have already found one too many skeletons in our closets today."

The piece of paper had been folded three ways and I feared it would crumble when I opened it. I gently began the process of removing the fragile piece of paper from the back of the portrait. I was afraid to look. We had discovered so much distressing information in the last few days, but I needed to know what it said. It appeared to have been written with a quill pen in very ornate script. The document was not dated but had a name on it, Rachel Minerva Jones.

"Looks like I've found another skeleton, Miss Emma. But it's in my closet not yours," I lamented with sadness.

I began to read aloud the elegant scripted letters on the brittle piece of paper. "*Rachel Minerva Jones was a twin sister to Rebecca Philomena Jones. Rebecca went with her husband, Reuben Martin, from Germantown, Pennsylvania, to the Carolinas, and they homesteaded in a place at the foothills of the great mountains of North Carolina. They followed the Great Wagon Road from Pennsylvania to the Carolinas to reach their destination. Rachel stayed behind in Pennsylvania and lived a life of ill-repute and disgrace. She had five children out of wedlock by five different men, and each child is listed in the Pennsylvania Bastardy Bonds. She died an early disgraceful death at twenty-five years of age from that shameful unclean disease "the pox." She brought dishonor to the entire Jones family and was buried far away from the family cemetery in an unmarked grave. She was queen of the dance halls in the area and sold herself for money. This picture hung in the last dance hall she danced in. After her death, this picture was sent to her twin sister, Rebecca Martin, in North Carolina."*

"No wonder Grandpa hid this picture. And what in the world is 'the pox'?" I asked.

Hattie quickly spoke up, "Child, 'at be da misery 'at bad women gets from men. I believes it be called da syphilis. I know'd a man 'at got it one time, and he went plum' crazy afore he passed. I hear it be mighty bad stuff."

"I've never heard of bastardy bonds either. What in the world are they?" I asked Hattie and Miss Emma.

"It was a document that was drawn up by the local government in those days when an illegitimate baby was born to a woman, and no father was named for the child. That was the county and state's way of absolving themselves of the responsibility of caring for the baby. The government didn't want the responsibility of providing money for the child, so they would require the mother to appear in court and give the name of the father. If she refused to name him, someone else had to post the bond. I have heard that often the mother was sent to jail if the bond was not posted. If she named the father, the officials would search for the father, serve him with a warrant, and he would be forced to post the bond. We had that same system here in Rullerford County, because I had a distant ancestor who had several illegitimate babies," replied Miss Emma.

I looked at Miss Emma dumbfounded. "This is unbelievable. I can't help but wonder what happened to those five little babies. Times sure have changed when it comes to the welfare of children. The government assumes responsibility for everyone today."

"Yea, they sure do. One of these days, the United States is gonna run out of money. Seems to me that we just make it easy for folks to live in sin, have one baby after the other, and our government just keeps right on funnelin' money and blessin's down on them," agreed Miss Emma.

"You be right, Miss Emma. W'y, I got a cousin, she done had seven babies, and she ain't married nary a man yet. She draws a check ever' month from the gov'ment and goes right on a livin' in sin. I jist don't un'erstand it. 'Is old world is shore in a heap of trouble. People's been a sinnin', a drankin', a fornicatin', and a livin' like da dawgs ever since Adam and Eve listened to 'at mean ol' serpent. It's like I always say, Gabriel's a gonna blow his horn and wind 'is mess up one of 'ese days," Hattie responded.

"You are right, Hattie. It seems that it gets worse everyday," Miss Emma replied.

With a note of sadness in her eyes, Miss Emma looked at me. "Hope, let's hope this is the last skeleton we find in either of our closets. We sure had some mighty sinful ancestors in our past, didn't we?"

"Yes, we sure did."

Hattie looked at me with a skeptical look and said, "You'uns be careful a puttin' 'at thang back together, you'uns don't want to mess 'round an' get youself cut. Might jist be some pox on at' 'ere picture!"

"Oh, no, Hattie. There's only one way to catch that disease," I replied.

"Huh, I ain't so shore 'bout 'at, Miss Hope. I ain't a gonna be touchin' it," Hattie responded as she stomped out of the sunroom.

I could hear her mumbling as she left the room. I smiled when I heard her say, "I ain't a gonna touch 'at 'ere stuff; I shore don't want da pox!"

We took the other framed picture apart and on the back of the picture was written Reuben and Rebecca Martin.

"This picture was made when Reuben and Rebecca were much older. I can still see Rebecca's resemblance to Rachel. I guess that's what I'll look like in thirty or forty years," I commented.

"Hope, just be thankful this picture didn't have another skeleton connected to it," responded Miss Emma.

Miss Emma and I finished cleaning the frames and reassembled them. I took them back out to the garage and wrapped them in a blanket for storage.

While walking back to the house, my thoughts began to ramble. *That mysterious lady presents me with quite a dilemma. What in the world am I going to do with her? I'm not so sure I want Rachel Minerva Jones' portrait hanging in my house, a brothel dance hall queen with five illegitimate children. But she was a relative of mine, and I sure do look like her.*

I certainly had a lot to think about and many decisions to make.

Chapter 19

I awoke on Friday morning to a lovely spring day, and a gentle breeze filtered through the open windows of my bedroom. Sunbeams peeped through the cracked blinds and sheer curtains like shards of glass. Birds were singing in the trees outside my bedroom windows, and several old tree frogs were croaking in the background. Also, coming from the yard was the sound of Miss Emma's wind chimes, playing their lovely melody. I could also hear piano music coming from downstairs. It had to be Miss Emma. She was playing an old familiar hymn. As I lay there, I tried to remember the name of the hymn she was playing. It finally came to me — "Great Is Thy Faithfulness."

I rolled over and looked at the clock and was surprised to see that it was nine o'clock. I couldn't believe I had slept so late. I quickly jumped out of bed, showered, and dressed in jeans and a lime green tee shirt. I bounded down the spiral staircase anxious to get out to the farm and see what the construction crew had accomplished.

Upon entering the foyer by way of the front staircase, I spied Miss Emma at the grand piano in the living room. I stood quietly for a few seconds and listened to the beautiful hymn.

"Go ahead and finish the piece, it's beautiful," I said as she stopped playing.

"Oh, I need to stop and eat breakfast. I was just practicin' for Sunday's worship service, and I thought I would wake you up to some music," she replied.

"And it was lovely. It is so beautiful outside today, and the birds are singing their own magical songs to each other. I could have stayed in bed all day and listened to them sing. You have so many birds here!"

Miss Emma smiled. "Yes, we do. Those little feathered creatures love my bird feeders and suet blocks. If you want birds, you hav'ta make sure they have somethin' to eat and plenty of water to drink."

"When I move into the farmhouse, I plan to have tons of birdfeeders in the yard, a huge birdbath, and lots of birdhouses. I would like to go out to the farm today and see what progress has been made. Would you like to go with me?" I proposed.

"I would love to. In fact, why don't we go in my car and take Samson and Hattie with us. If we have time, maybe we can ride up to Puzzle Creek and find the supposed legendary birthplace of Abraham Lincoln.

"At this point, there is really nothing you can do at the farm while construction folks are everywhere. I have already mentioned it to Hattie, and she is packing a picnic lunch, as we speak. We'll find a nice spot to have the picnic."

"Oh, Miss Emma, you have the best ideas. A week ago I would never have dreamed I would be saying this, but I'm already dreading my trip back to Charlotte. I simply do not want to leave this place, but I know I must go. I told you about my dog, and I must go check on him. I bet Leo thinks I've abandoned him. I can't wait for him to see the farm. I know he will absolutely love it. He has never been able to run free because of where I live."

"Hope, have you told Hattie about Leo?" asked Miss Emma.

"No, we've been so busy; I just haven't told her about him."

Miss Emma shouted for Hattie, "Hattie, come here. Hope has somethin' to tell you."

Hattie walked into the living room with a dish towel in her hands. She was dressed in a lovely hot pink pantsuit and a beautiful pink and white apron.

"I got breakfus' ready. What you a wantin', Miss Emma?"

Miss Emma again repeated, "Hope has somethin' to tell you."

Hattie looked at me quizzically, "Mornin', Miss Hope. You want to tell me som'um'?"

"Yes, I sure do. I have not told you about my very best friend. His name is Leo, and I just have a gut feeling you will love him."

"Ye don't say? What do he look like? Is yore young man a looker?"

"He sure is, and he has bluish-green eyes, a pink nose, and a beautiful pink tongue."

"Don't sound like no feller I ever saw? Sound plum' quare lookin' to me, Miss Hope. You sure he be normal?"

"Oh yes, Hattie, he's normal for a seventy-five pound buckskin pit bull dog."

"Well, in 'is worl'. Miss Hope, 'at be my favorite kinda dawg. Our dawg passed pirt'near a year ago, and me and Samson's we jist been lost wid'out him. Samson com'mit'nigh grievin' hisself ta death when Spike passed. When is you a gonna bring him wid ye to see us?"

"Well, until I move in the farm house, I'll have to put him in a kennel."

"You'll do no such thing!" Miss Emma chimed in. "You bring that dog with you every time you come! He will be welcome company for us all. We are dog lovers, but after Spike died, we couldn't bring ourselves to get another dog.

"As a matter of fact, Hattie, Samson, and I have come to a decision. We want you to stay here with us every weekend until the house is renovated, and when school goes out, you can go ahead and move to Martinsville and stay with us. There will be no charge, and there's plenty of room in the garage to store your things. If we run out of space, Hattie and Samson have an empty room in their house, and wouldn't mind storing some of your things. We simply want you here with us. When I talked to Hattie and Samson about this, they made it very clear that they want you here as much as I do."

"Miss Emma, that is just too much. I couldn't impose on the three of you like that. You may have people wanting to stay here at the inn, and I might be in the way."

"Don't argue with me, it's already been decided. I have already told you, we have very few folks here to spend the night, and if we have a wedding or reception, we'll just let Leo stay out at Hattie and Samson's house.

"God has sent you into our lives for a purpose, and I know that. Hattie and Samson feel the same way I feel. You may feel like you have no family, but child we want to be your family. You are so special to us, and I'm just thankful for the opportunity to do something for you mama. I think she would be happy to know that we are lookin' after you."

I was completely overwhelmed, and tears filled my eyes as Hattie spoke up. "Miss Hope, Samson an' me has only know'd you 'bout a week, and we already is a feelin' like we got ourselves another young'un. Our boy is a busy doctor an' we don't git to see him much. Please let us be yore kin. We ain't got da same blood, and we shore ain't got da same color, but we love you, chil'."

"I'm overwhelmed. Letting me stay with you is one thing, but Leo? He's a dog, and I'm afraid he would get in the way, even though he is a good dog."

"Trust me, Hope. When Samson hears that Leo is coming, he'll be thrilled. He truly has not been himself since Spike died," Miss Emma replied.

"That's right, Miss Hope. He shore miss 'at dawg. W'y, he's been a grievin' like he did when his pa and ma died. We'd be beholden to you iffin you'd bring Leo wid you nex' time ye come."

"But you will have to let me pay you something. We just can't come in like squatters and take up residence."

"Now you just hush up! It's all settled, and we aren't going to talk about it anymore. We've got a picnic to go on and breakfast to eat. What do you say we go to the kitchen and eat breakfast?" Miss Emma exclaimed.

"Yes'um, I got flapjacks and some good ol' maple syrup with some mighty fine homemade sausages my nephew brung me yesterday. Let's eat right quick like so we can be a goin'. I's mighty hongry." replied Hattie.

Miss Emma turned to me with an impish look. "Hope, I hope you don't mind, but I was talking to Preacher Mike early this morning. I had to phone him about the music for Sunday's service, and I invited him to go with us on the picnic. I hope that's okay with you. He has no family here, and we try to include him in some of our outings."

I detected a mischievous grin on Hattie and Miss Emma's faces. "You ladies wouldn't be trying to play cupid would you?"

"W'y, Miss Hope, you know us better 'an 'at. We's jist a bein' neighborly," Hattie responded with a wicked grin on her face.

"No, I don't mind, but I still think you two have something up your sleeves. I don't know what I'm going to do with the two of you."

Chapter 20

We rolled the windows down in the car, and the ride out to the farm was breathtaking. It was a lovely spring morning, and the breeze that filtered through the car windows smelled of country air and sunshine. Miss Emma drove her car, and Hattie and I put Samson in the front seat. I noticed that Samson seemed to be moving slowly, and I asked Hattie if he was okay. She said that his arthritis was bothering him.

Miss Emma's car was definitely not what I expected. I guess I expected a luxury vehicle with all the amenities that could be offered in a car, but that was not the case. I had never really paid any attention to her car when we were in her garage; I just knew it was white. Much to my surprise, she drove a simple 1988 white, four-door Chevrolet sedan. It didn't even have electric windows or locks. It was just a basic car and confirmed to me that Miss Emma was not a wasteful pretentious person, even though she could afford to be. Her home did reflect extravagance, but I was sure that was because it was used as a business.

Samson had packed our picnic lunch in the trunk of the car along with soft drinks, bottled water, and iced tea. Hattie and Samson could not quit talking about my dog and his expected arrival. They wanted to know everything about him. I explained to them that his buckskin color gave his beautiful coat the color of a palomino horse. I heard Samson talk more that day than anytime I had been around him. He seemed thrilled that Leo was coming with me the next weekend.

I couldn't believe Miss Emma had invited Preacher Mike to go with us on our outing. Spending the entire day with him was all I could think about. Abe Lincoln definitely took second place in my thoughts that morning as we left the inn. All I could think about was that handsome young preacher and those mesmerizing sapphire-blue eyes that captivated me. No, maybe it was his warm, gentle smile that drew me to him. Everything about him fascinated me!

When we reached the farm, I was shocked. The land-scapers had accomplished so much in four days. The old outbuildings were gone, the dead trees had been pushed up, and they had leveled the grounds around the house. I was so excited I started screaming with delight. With Miss Emma, Hattie, and Samson close behind me, I jumped from the car to see what had been done inside the house.

Ed's construction crew was busy replacing rotten wood on the inside and electricians were rewiring the entire house. A plumber was surveying the area where the bathrooms were to be.

So we would not be in the way of the construction workers, we hurriedly inspected the work that had been done and subsequently decided to be on our way.

As we were walking across the yard on our way to Miss Emma's car, Preacher Mike pulled up in a gray SUV. Those beautiful eyes came into my line of vision, and my heart skipped a beat. I had never seen such a handsome man.

I thought to myself, *how in this world will I make it through this day? I can't take my eyes off this man! I can't even breathe normally. What's wrong with me?*

With a smile that seemed to make the sun glow brighter, Preacher Mike approached us dressed in faded jeans, cowboy boots, and a white polo shirt. He certainly didn't look like any pastor I had ever seen. He hugged Hattie and Miss Emma and gave Samson a hearty pat on the back.

He approached me, and I timidly dropped my head as he spoke softly, "Hope, it's so good to see you again."

I thought I would pass out when he reached out and gently touched my arm. I guess he felt he didn't know me well enough to give me a hug. If he had put his arms around me, I probably would have fainted. I knew then that I was going to be a nervous wreck before the day was over.

Miss Emma began giving us riding instructions. "I think we can all get in my car. Preacher Mike, you just park your car on the roadside. It should be okay there. Just be sure to get it far enough from the house so that flying debris will not hit it. There's hardly any traffic on this road."

Hattie, Preacher Mike, and I crowded into the back seat of Miss Emma's car, and of course, Hattie made sure I sat next to Preacher Mike. Because we were so crowded, Preacher Mike put his arm around me to make more room for the three of us. I immediately felt as if someone had shocked me with an electrical current across my shoulders where he placed his arm. Dr. Mike Sanders unnerved me like nothing I had ever experienced in my life, and he smelled so good.

Sitting so close to him, I was intoxicated with the soft woodsy smell of his aftershave and the smell of peppermint on his breath. Strangely enough, after a few minutes, I began to relax and felt an overwhelming sense of peace and security.

While pulling away from the farmhouse, Miss Emma spoke, "Let's head toward Bostic."

She looked at me in the rearview mirror and said, "You know, Hope, the subject of Abe Lincoln's birth up on Puzzle Creek has been kinda taboo for many years everywhere, except here in Rullerford County. Several books have been written on the subject. Lincoln himself stated that he was born February 12, 1809, in Kentucky. That statement is only based on tradition. W'y, a lot of folks don't even think that date was correct. Lincoln himself probably didn't know what day he was born. W'y, he probably didn't even know how old he really was. People here in Rullerford County will always believe he was the son of a No'th Ca'olina farmer. If he was, there is still the question of where Nancy Hanks, Abe's mother, was living at the time of his birth. Also, if the Rullerford County man was his father, he truly was illegitimate."

"Is there any way DNA can be checked?" I inquired.

"I have heard that some of the historians involved in the research have been working on that," Miss Emma replied. "If this Rullerford County legend is true, there has been a major cover-up over the years. The dispute over the paternity of Lincoln has been told and retold for almost two centuries. However, there has never been a dispute over his maternity. I think everyone agrees that Nancy Hanks was his mother, yet there is no denying that the pictures of Abe Lincoln definitely resemble the supposed relatives that have lived here in Rullerford County over the years."

Samson spoke up, "Miss Hope, I's a ol' man, and I recollect a hearin' 'bout folks 'at even saw da baby. W'y, some of 'em old women even got to hold 'Little Abraham' on 'ey laps. I b'lieve it wid all my heart. Yes'um, I b'lieve it. 'Ey can do all 'em DNA's 'ey want to, but I b'lieve Abraham Lincoln wuz born ri'chear in 'is county, and I always will."

"Yes'um, and I do too," Hattie replied. "My grandma, she know'd a woman who said she rocked "Little Abe" to sleep for Nancy Hanks one time. 'Course she wuz pirt'near one hundred years old when she tol' my grandma 'at. "Miss Emma you best be a turnin' ri'chear. It's jist a piece down 'is here road. I b'lieve it be at da crossroads of Bostic-Sunshine Highway and Walker Mill Road."

Samson leaned forward in his seat. "Ri'chear, Miss Emma. Ri'chear. 'Ere it is!"

Miss Emma began to slow down and pulled her car to the shoulder of the road. After exiting the car, we approached a large granite monument that was located in an open field. After reading the inscription on the monument, we surmised that the "Abe Lincoln Legend" was in fact believed by the people in Rutherford County.

The Rutherford County Historical Society had even gone to the trouble of erecting that stately monument in 2001. The bronze plaque on the monument stated "Traditional Birthplace of Abraham Lincoln the 16th President of the United States." There was a directional arrow pointing to the east and it stated "1 Mile East." *So this isn't the actual birthplace,* I thought to myself.

"We are gonna have to go east one mile to see the actual birthplace. There's not much else to see here, just this open field," Miss Emma commented.

We got back into the car and headed east, and after traveling about a mile, we came upon what is believed to be the actual birthplace. But there wasn't much there, just a marker. And it was actually very near Puzzle Creek.

All of us stood there in silence, and I thought about the impact that one small baby had on America. And to think, he and his mother may have actually lived in that spot. I felt cold chills going up and down my spine as I thought about the influence he had on the Civil War and slavery. Truly, Abraham Lincoln had been a great leader, no matter where he was born. I felt sure that Rutherford County old-timers would keep the legend alive for many years to come, no matter what DNA evidence proved or disproved. I knew in my heart that the children and grandchildren of Rutherford County natives would be told about the tall, lanky gentleman with the distinct, rugged face and long arms, who was born up on Puzzle Creek. They would also be told how he changed the course of history in the United States, and became one of the greatest presidents who ever lived.

Preacher Mike spoke up. "You know if this legend is true, Rutherford County produced one of the greatest statesman that has ever lived."

With that being said, we quietly returned to the car and rode for a few minutes without saying a word.

I turned to Hattie and broke the silence. "There is something special about that little spot we just visited. I have to agree that our sixteenth president was very likely born here in this county, but it's so sad that the nation doesn't know about this legend."

I looked at Miss Emma. "Thank you so much for bringing me up here."

"And me too," responded Preacher Mike. "I've heard about this place for so long, and now, I can say I've been there."

As we continued on our journey, Preacher Mike commented, "Rutherford County is absolutely one of the loveliest places I have ever seen. It's not too hot and not too cold. The land around here is so fertile, and there are so many majestic trees. This county was truly blessed by God when he created the earth."

Miss Emma explained that Rutherford County had always had a very unique climate and had been known for years as the Isothermal Belt. She further explained that the Isothermal Belt means—constant temperature—and the temperature in Rutherford County always remained constant and was mild and generally pleasant in comparison to surrounding counties.

Hattie spoke up and said, "Miss Emma, where is we a gonna eat? I'm a gittin' hungry!"

We all laughed as Samson responded, "W'y, Hattie Girl, you is always hongry!"

"It won't take long to ride up to Lake Lure. Hattie, I thought we would stop along the road somewhere in the mountains around Lake Lure or Chimney Rock and eat, if that's okay with everybody."

Hattie responded, "I reckon I can wait 'at long, but I'm 'bout to perish."

We all agreed that we would love to go up into the edge of the mountains for our picnic. Sure enough, it didn't take but a few minutes, and we were winding up the mountain road that led to Lake Lure.

We found a picturesque spot along the roadside to spread our lunch, and as Hattie and Miss Emma were spreading out the food and drinks on a large wooden picnic table, Samson, Preacher Mike, and I walked down to the mountain stream that flowed near the picnic area.

Samson spoke, "I shore wisht I had my fishin' pole wid me, Reverend. I'd catch us a mess of fish for supper."

"Samson, I haven't fished since I was a boy. We'll have to go fishing sometime," Preacher Mike replied. "Have you ever been frog gigging?"

"Yes sir-ree, I shore have, Reverend. We'll git Hattie to cook us up a mess of fish and frog legs. 'At's some mighty fine eatin'," Samson responded as he turned to walk back toward the picnic area.

After Samson retreated to the picnic area, Preacher Mike and I stood alone on the edge of the mountain stream and quietly listening to the rushing water as it made its way over the rocks and boulders in its path. There was a wonderful floral fragrance filling the air, and the view was breathtaking. A soft mountain breeze swept my blonde hair away from my face as we stood there.

Preacher Mike turned to me and looked into my eyes. Those sapphire-blue eyes seemed to penetrate the very core of my being. He slowly leaned toward me, as if he were going to kiss me. He drew back when we heard Hattie call us to eat. He cleared his throat and placed his hand on my back and led me back to the picnic area.

As we approached the picnic table, I caught Hattie and Miss Emma whispering and giggling. I knew right away that they felt their efforts to "fix me up" with the handsome preacher had worked.

After a hearty lunch of ham sandwiches and potato salad, we loaded up the car and headed back toward Martinsville.

I regretfully told Preacher Mike goodbye when we arrived at the farm. He seemed a bit sad to part company with us, and he waved goodbye as he got into his vehicle.

That night over dinner we recapped the events of the day. Listening to Samson, Hattie, and Miss Emma discuss the Abe Lincoln legend had been like a mini course in North Carolina history. They were so knowledgeable about North Carolina history, especially the Civil War period. Being third generation descendants of slaves, Hattie and Samson could tell the stories with so much knowledge and passion. Before retiring for the night, we continued to discuss the history of Rutherford County and the Civil War over coffee and dessert.

It amazed me that neither Hattie nor Samson seemed to have any bitterness toward anyone because of the way they or their people had been treated over the years. Hattie again reaffirmed what I already knew, only because of God had she been able to forgive and forget. She and Samson laughed about the funny stories from slavery days and their growing up years. They even shared with me their courting days and their wedding.

I smiled as I listened to Samson talk about the time he first met Hattie. He knew right away that she was the woman he wanted to share his life with.

With sparkling eyes and a radiant smile, he said, "W'y, Hattie was the purdiest little thang I'd ever saw, and Miss Hope, 'pears to me Reverend Sanders got his eyes on you. I b'lieve he's a pinin' for ye."

Hattie had to put her two cents worth in. "Shore lookin' like he be crazy 'bout chu, Miss Hope."

"Oh no, he's just a friend," I replied.

"I shore ain't never seen no man look at a friend like he be lookin' at chu. W'y, he got courtin' on his mind, Miss Hope. "W'y, 'at be da same look Samson had when he commence to courtin' me. Yes'um, I knows 'at look."

I grinned shyly and dropped my head. It was quite obvious that Hattie and Samson had a love that was genuine and unpretentious. My desire had always been to have a love like that in my life.

I began to consider what Hattie and Samson had revealed to me, all the while, wondering if that kind of love would ever happen to me. *Is it possible that Dr. Mike Sanders could be the love of my life?* I hesitantly asked myself. *That can't be, we are polar opposites. I don't even go to church.*

Chapter 21

Saturday arrived with a glorious sunrise and a fresh mountain breeze blowing through the trees. Miss Emma, Hattie, Samson, and I enjoyed coffee and breakfast on the flagstone patio in the backyard. I couldn't believe that only a week ago my three special friends had been total strangers to me. In such a short time, they had become my family. I felt a love for them that I did not completely understand.

While enjoying Hattie's scrumptious breakfast, we discussed the possibility of finding my lost relative and the effect it would have on all of our lives. I got the feeling that the three of them enjoyed helping me with my unusual situation. A thought suddenly occurred to me, *could the search for my long lost relative have brought unexpected excitement to these three lonely senior citizens?*

I had such a heavy heart because of everything that had taken place in my life. My coming to Martinsville had unearthed so many secrets, and dear sweet Miss Emma's lifelong trust in her father had been shattered. I could not help but wonder if we would ever bring resolution to the secrets of the past?

I decided to go ahead and pack my belongings on Saturday so I would be ready to leave on Sunday. So that I would be able to leave without any hustle and bustle on Sunday, I gathered everything from the garage and loaded my car. I wanted to finish reading through the rest of the journal and all of the documents we found in the secret room.

Over dinner that night, Miss Emma asked me to go to church with her the next day. I had only brought jeans and tee shirts with me to Martinsville, and when I told her, she seemed a bit disappointed. However, she did not let it affect her mood. She was such a remarkable woman and had been so kind to me. Frankly, I felt guilty that I had to decline her invitation. Thoughts of Dr. Mike Sanders almost tempted me to go out and buy an outfit so that I could go with her to church. I had been open and honest with Miss Emma. She was aware of my feelings about attending church; therefore, she did not press the issue.

Frankly, I was dreading the trip back to Charlotte. I had grown to love Martinsville and the people I had met there, but I knew I had to finish the school year and close out my affairs in Charlotte. I would have to get a release from the lease on my apartment or pay out the amount of the lease. I needed to pack all of my furniture and clothes for the move to Martinsville. Also, I had to pack up my classroom supplies at school.

Sunday morning arrived with an early morning rain shower. Because there had been no rainfall since I had arrived in Martinsville, it was refreshing to smell the fragrant rain as it soaked the trees and flowers in Miss Emma's yard.

I had so many memories of rain showers on the farm. Grandma, Grandpa, and I used to sit on the piazza and watch the rain as it fell on the beautiful white pines in the front yard. I could still recall that smell of fresh rain on the pine trees and the old juniper bush.

I wanted the rain to stop before I had to leave. I did not like to travel on the interstate, but I liked it even less when it was raining.

Miss Emma arrived home from church about twelve-thirty and informed me that Hattie and Samson would probably not be there until about one o'clock. I felt my heart skip a beat when she told me that Preacher Mike had asked about me. Dr. Mike Sanders had completely overwhelmed me with his blue eyes and good looks. It was probably evident to everyone that I was completely besotted with him.

Before I realized what I was doing, I excitedly asked, "What did he say?"

"Oh, he just wanted to know when you would be leavin' and when you'd return," she replied. "He also commented on your lovely personality. It appears to me he is head over heels in love with you, little one."

"Don't go there, Miss Emma. He is a minister, and I don't even attend church. You're imagination is running wild. He would never have feelings for the likes of me. He's so dedicated to his calling."

"He's dedicated alright, but he's still a good lookin' man, chil', and his blood is still a flowin'! Just remember Preacher Mike was a man before he became a preacher!" she replied with a smile on her face.

I was so embarrassed; I didn't know how to respond to Miss Emma's observation.

I simply dropped the subject after I heard the doorbell. I quickly scooted out of the sunroom to answer the door. Jan had arrived and was ready to leave for Charlotte. She was very understanding when I explained to her that I wanted to stay until Hattie and Samson came from church.

Upon arrival from church, Hattie threw her arms around me. I thought I detected tears in Samson's eyes as I put my arms around him. I couldn't believe how I had grown to love that dear couple. As a result of getting to know my new friends in Martinsville, my life would never be the same.

After eating a quick lunch, I said my goodbyes. Jan and I set out for Charlotte, she in her SUV and me in my little red sports car. With a great deal of sadness, I watched Martinsville fade from view in my rearview mirror. I felt I was leaving a huge chunk of my heart behind in that little town nestled in the foothills of the mountains of North Carolina. That little corner of the world had become home to me, and I had not even realized it was happening. I couldn't believe what had transpired in my life in the last seven days.

The sun came out from behind the clouds, and the sky was crystal clear after we traveled about twenty miles. As the sun peeped through the clouds, millions of sparkling raindrops glistened on the trees and flowers along the roadside.

We traveled for about forty-five minutes and pulled into a fast food restaurant off the interstate to go to the restroom and get something to drink. While we were at the restaurant, I decided to put the top down on my convertible.

Riding with the top down, I was intoxicated with the smell of fresh rain and sunshine. With my blonde hair blowing in the wind, large tractor trailer trucks were whizzing by me at breakneck speed. Even though I didn't like to drive on interstate highways, I managed to enjoy the ride back to Charlotte. I was so thankful when I spotted the beautiful skyline of the "Queen City." That beautiful city had been my home for such a long time.

The skyscrapers that draped the horizon of the Charlotte skyline had always been a favorite view of mine, especially the lovely Wachovia building and the towering Bank of America building. That day they glistened in the sunlight like fine crystal. The radio shape of the Wachovia Building was by far my favorite. Every time I looked at it, I was reminded of an old radio that my grandparents had when I was a child. Tears filled my eyes as I recalled them sitting by that old radio every Saturday night listening to the Grand Old Opry.

When we arrived at my apartment in South Charlotte, I helped Jan unload her luggage and laptop. I retrieved my luggage from my car, and decided to go ahead and put the top up on my car. The beautiful Carolina blue sky was threatening rain again. Clouds were forming in the south, and I needed to pick up Leo before the rain started again.

After getting Jan settled in the spare bedroom, I asked her if she would like to ride with me to pick up Leo. I explained to her that a friend had been keeping him for me, and I really needed to relieve her of her duty. She agreed to ride with me, and we made our way to Mollie's apartment to get Leo.

As I pulled my car into a parking space at Mollie's place, I could hear Leo barking. He always recognized the sound of my car, and he never failed to greet me at the door. I turned to Jan, "Now, don't be afraid of him, he's a big dog. I think you already know he is a pit bull, but a very gentle one."

"Oh, don't worry, we have a boxer whose name is Socks, and he weighs about eighty pounds. I'm used to big dogs," Jan replied.

Mollie opened the door, and Leo bounded into my arms. He was overjoyed to see me and immediately lay down on Mollie's doorstep so I could rub his stomach.

I turned to Mollie, "Mollie, this is Jan McHenry. She's the private detective I told you about. Jan, this is my best friend, Molly Ferguson. We teach together."

At that point, I introduced Leo to Jan. I felt a surge of pride, very close to parental pride, as Leo reached his paw toward Jan to shake her hand. I knew right away that Jan had a special rapport with dogs when I saw her give Leo a treat.

I was shocked and asked her, "Where in the world did you get that treat?"

"Oh, I always keep treats in the car for Socks. He meets me every time I arrive home, and I always have something for him. Sometimes I even have a bone for him. I retrieved this treats out of my car before we left your place."

We entered Mollie's apartment, and being a true southern hostess, she graciously asked us if we would like something to eat or drink. We informed her that we would not be staying long and graciously declined her offer.

Mollie anxiously inquired, "Hope, you've got to tell me what you found out about that relative you are looking for. When you called on Thursday, you filled me in on finding the journal, the visit to Prissy Walker's house, and your findings there. Have you found out anything else? I have been so worried about you!"

"Not to worry, Mollie, that is why Jan is here. She is going to try to locate documents here in Mecklenburg County tomorrow that will give more information regarding this mystery. We believe the baby was brought here to Charlotte and sold into a "black-market" adoption ring. The baby was put in an orphanage or some type of home, and from there we don't know where the baby was placed."

Mollie's big brown eyes were as large as saucers, and her short spiked blond hair made her look as if she had been electrified.

"Wow, this is unbelievable," she exclaimed after hearing my story. "Girl, your life has certainly changed over the last few weeks. Who would have thought a year ago that your life would go in such a direction? Are you really sure you want to move to Martinsville? We are going to miss you so much at school!"

"Yes, Mollie, when I first went to Martinsville, I had no intention of remaining there. But after spending time there, I know, beyond a shadow of a doubt, that I can never leave that little town.

"We need to get out of here and let you get some peace. Has Leo been good for you?"

"Leo's been great! He is so used to me; he and Tag have had a ball together. Tag's going to be lost without him," Mollie replied.

I stepped across the room to pet Tag, who was a beautiful brown boxer with a very docile personality. As I stroked his fur, I knew he would miss Leo for a day or two, but he probably would be glad to get some peace and quiet after a while and Mollie's undivided attention.

I thanked Mollie for watching Leo and offered to pay her, but she wouldn't hear of it.

"Hope, how could I take money from you? You have kept Tag so many times for me. Besides that's what friends are for."

"Mollie, you are such a true friend, and I will miss you so much when I move. You'll have to come and visit real often."

"I plan to do that just as soon as you get moved. In fact, I plan to help you move," she replied. "Oh, by the way, you know I had Tag bred with another boxer, and the puppies are ready to be taken from their mama. Do you know anyone that would like to have a boxer? Their bloodline is flawless, and they would be ideal pets for anyone."

My mind started turning like the wheels of a speeding bicycle. "Mollie, I just might know someone. Just let me check on it and get back with you," I replied.

Jan and I said goodbye to Mollie and loaded Leo between us in my little car.

On the ride back to my apartment, Jan spoke up, "Hope, have you thought about what it will be like when you meet your aunt or uncle for the first time?"

"I have thought of nothing else. I'm really frightened about meeting this person. I just hope we find him or her soon. I can't stand the suspense much longer. I just want to get this school year over with, get back to Martinsville, and begin my new life there. I feel like I'm in limbo. I just want some stability in my life," I replied.

"Hope, I promise I will do my best to get this mystery solved as soon as possible. We will find your relative, and life will return to normal for you." Jan declared.

Chapter 22

After getting everyone settled for the night, I fell into bed. I tossed and turned for hours. My mind was spinning like a March whirlwind with so many unanswered questions. My biggest dilemma was the handsome preacher with the sapphire-blue eyes. He was always in my thoughts. Dr. Mike Sanders had come into my life like a soft gentle breeze, but had created a windstorm of emotions in my heart. After tossing and turning for hours, I think I finally fell asleep about two o'clock.

I awoke in a fog when the alarm sounded at six o'clock the next morning. I felt as if I had wrestled with a bear the entire night and was totally exhausted from lack of sleep. Knowing I had to go back to work that morning exhausted me even more. However, I managed to drag myself from my comfortable bed and get ready for school.

Jan and Leo awoke about seven o'clock, and after letting Leo outside for a few minutes, I got him settled for the day. Jan assured me that she would begin her investigation and would call me if she found any information of importance.

My first day back at school was a disaster. I was so tired I could not concentrate on anything. My mind was still reeling from the events of the previous week. My students were getting restless and ready for school to be out, but I managed to make it through the day without collapsing. I must have looked as terrible as I felt, because when I spoke with Principal Benson during lunch, he suggested I take the remainder of the week off from teaching. Dr. Benson was so understanding, and he realized the gravity of my situation. When I informed him of my recent discovery and how close I was to solving the mystery that surrounded my family, he again insisted that I take care of my situation and then return to school the next week.

I really hated for my students to have another few days with a substitute teacher, but for me to bring closure to the mystery surrounding my family, I knew I had to find my relative as soon as possible. My substitute teacher was a retired music teacher, and she was as capable of teaching my students as I was. Even though I felt guilty about being away from school, my need to find my relative outweighed all of the guilt I felt.

By the end of the day, I was a nervous wreck. I had not received a call from Jan, so I assumed she had not discovered the whereabouts of my missing relative. By two o'clock that afternoon, I was getting antsy for my cell phone to ring with some sort of information.

I was preparing to leave my classroom when my cell phone rang. When I realized that it was Jan, my heart started pounding like a race horse that had just run the Kentucky Derby. She could not contain herself. She was talking so fast I couldn't understand her.

I interrupted her, "Whoa, whoa, slow down, Jan. I can't understand a word you're saying."

"Hope, I think I'm on to something! In fact, I know I am. How long will it take you to get to Charlotte from where you are now?"

I stood speechless at the door of my classroom for a few seconds.

"I can be there in thirty minutes, but what did you find out? I have to know!" I stammered breathlessly.

She excitedly responded, "I didn't go to the Register of Deeds but decided to see if the house still existed on Marsh Street. After doing a search on my computer, I actually found Marsh Street and went there. It's in the historic district of Charlotte, and all of the houses have been restored or are being restored. There weren't but seven houses on that particular street, and I went to all of them.

"A lovely young couple live there, and when I told them I was looking for a house on Marsh Street that could possibly have been an orphanage or center for black-market adoptions, they were flabbergasted. The husband invited me in and went on to explain that he found a box in the attic of the house when they started renovations. In the box was concrete evidence that suggested the house had been, not an orphanage, but a center for buying and selling babies.

"Hope, they haven't gone through the entire contents of the box. I told them why we were looking into this, and they are anxious to help us. If you can, they want you to come over and go through the box today. Can you meet me at the house? I want you with me when we open the box!"

"I'm on my way! Tell me how to get there," I replied with excitement.

Jan quickly gave me directions to the house, and I knew exactly where it was. I literally ran like a speeding gazelle to my car. It was a miracle I didn't get a speeding ticket, because I looked like a NASCAR driver at Lowe's Motor Speedway as I sped toward Charlotte.

When I turned onto Marsh Street, I spied Jan's vehicle parked on the side of the road at the end of the street. As soon as she saw me, she jumped from her car and met me in the front yard of the house.

The house was located among so many huge oak trees you could barely see it, and the enormous trees looked to be at least one hundred years old. *What a perfect place to commit a crime! It's secluded among trees and can hardly be seen from the road,* I thought to myself.

As we drew closer to the front door, I recognized immediately that it was an old style American Foursquare house that was so popular back in the 1920s and 1930s. It was a two story box shape with a hipped roof and one large dormer in the center of the house. The red brick it was constructed from had aged to a deep shade of red. The paint was peeling, but appeared to have been white at one time. Jan and I went to the front door and were greeted by a young couple who were probably in their late thirties or early forties.

Jan turned to the couple and made introductions, "Sarah and Jack Babcock, this is Hope Logan, the lady I spoke with you about earlier. Sarah and Jack have just moved here from Colorado and are painstakingly remodeling this house. Let's just hope we can find some clues in the metal box you found in your attic."

Sarah invited us into the living room, and it was evident that the room was being renovated. There in the middle of the room sat the metal box that would, in all probability, change my entire life. I began to shake like a leaf in a windstorm, and I was so nervous I could not contain myself.

Seeing how anxious I was, Jan gently patted me on the back and said, "Hope, just calm down. If this is not what we need, we will look elsewhere."

Sarah turned to Jan and me with a welcoming look.

"Can I get you ladies something to eat or drink?" she asked.

"No, but thank you, Sarah. I'm too nervous to eat or drink anything," I replied.

Jan declined, also, as we gathered around the rusty old box. Sarah left the room and came back with face masks and rubber gloves. "When Jack and I first opened the box, we were engulfed with the smell of mold and mildew. Jack went to Home Depot after you left this morning, Jan, and got us some gear for us to put on before we open this old relic again. Jack, why don't we take the box outside to open it so we won't get mold spores in the house?" Sarah suggested.

"Sounds like a great idea!" he replied.

We followed Jack through the house to the backyard and watched him as he placed the relic on a large wooden picnic table. We donned the masks and gloves, and as Jack opened the old metal box, a tainted smell of mold and mildew engulfed us penetrating our masks. For some strange reason, I felt as if we were disturbing a grave.

As Jack was opening the box, he turned to me. "When I first found this box in our attic, I didn't know what to think. It was tucked in a small alcove beside the dormer and was completely out of sight. Whoever put it there certainly didn't want it found easily."

He began to lift the contents from the box and carefully placed them on the picnic table. In the bottom of the box was an old ledger book that was so decayed and molded, I was afraid it would disintegrate when we touched it. I hesitantly reached for the book and began to turn the yellowed pages.

Before me was page after page of entries confirming that a black-market baby-selling ring had operated from the Babcock's house. I could not believe what I was seeing!

As Jan went through the other documents, I continued to flip through the pages of the ledger book. "Look here, ya'll, it appears there was more going on than we thought. They not only were baby-peddlers, they supplemented that income with bootlegging. And I bet I can tell you where they got their moonshine. They were selling corn liquor from Prissy Walker's still, because here is her name and Henry Ledbetter's, also. They were both scoundrels."

The Babcock's had only been told about the kidnapping of my relative, so I proceeded to fill them in on the rest of the story involving the moonshining and the bootlegging.

"This really makes this house more interesting to us. What did you say were the names of the people involved in the baby-selling and bootlegging?" Jack asked.

"There were only three that we know of, and they were Henry Wentworth Ledbetter, Prissy Walker, and the man who owned your house, Wilson Jones," I replied.

"This is unbelievable," Jack exclaimed. "We had no idea any of this history existed when we bought this house. Sarah and I have always wanted an old house to remodel with a flamboyant history. Wow, did we ever get one, but the history may end up not being so charming after all."

A lot of the contents in the box seemed to be of no value, but we continued to search. When we came across documents pertaining to illegal adoptions, we pulled those out.

The biggest surprise of all was the fact that Wilson Jones was an attorney in Mecklenburg County in the 1930s and 1940s. That revelation explained how the adoptions were done. He had all of the inroads to the court system, which made his crimes easier to carry out. It seemed to me that he would have needed an accomplice to carry out his illegal business.

While doing the investigation into the contents of the box, we found the address for Wilson Jones' law office in downtown Charlotte. He evidently was viewed by the law community as a reputable attorney. We even found an award he received for being an outstanding attorney in Mecklenburg County. That man had the whole Charlotte area hoodwinked, and my poor grandma and no telling how many other victims suffered untold years of misery because of him.

Sarah looked up with an odd expression on her face. She was holding an old newspaper article.

"Look at this piece of information. It's Wilson Jones' obituary, and there is a wife listed. Listen to this, *Mr. Wilson Jones, Attorney at Law, died Wednesday, May 26, 1948. He is survived by his wife, Flora Higgins Jones. Mr. Jones was an asset to the Charlotte area and a highly respected citizen. The viewing will be held at Richards Funeral Home on Thursday, May 27, 1948, at 3:00 P.M. and the funeral service will be held Friday, May 28, 1948, at the funeral home chapel at 3:00 P.M. Interment will follow at the Jones Family Cemetery in Cabarrus County.*"

"Now we have something," Jan exclaimed with enthusiasm. "All I have to do is find out what happened to Flora Higgins Jones. She's either still alive, which I doubt, or buried beside of him. Yea, now we're getting somewhere. Evidently, Mrs. Jones continued to live in this house, and their bootlegging and "baby peddling" business was never discovered. I just wonder if she kept the business going."

As we continued to search, Jack unearthed a small Bible, and the name in it was Flora Jones. Inside of the Bible was a handwritten entry which evidently had been written by Mrs. Jones.

Jack began to read. *"I am so glad to be out from under this horrible yoke of bondage that Wilson had me caught up in. For so long, my conscience has been so burdened with guilt and despair. What can I do to undo the atrocities that were committed by Wilson and his cohorts?*

"All of those innocent little babies snatched from their mothers and sold like puppies to the highest bidder. I was forced to care for them until they were sold to the adoptive parents. I didn't mind caring for them, in fact, I loved them. My heart would break every time another baby would arrive at our house. How he continued to get away with it is beyond me. I have to give him credit for one thing, he was smart. He put up a good front for everyone and had the entire world fooled, except me.

Will I ever be able to find peace with this knowledge? When I found out about the bootlegging, he threatened to kill me if I ever revealed anything about his illegal activities. I found out about the illegal whiskey not long after we were married, and the baby-snatching started about five years after that. I dared not reveal that to anyone, because I knew it would be the end of me.

What was I to do? There was so much evil in Wilson's heart. It was like he was under the control of a force that was stronger than he was.

My heart is so heavy with the sin; I don't know which way to turn. I simply can't tell anyone. I have no family left and no children. Since Wilson was in the baby-peddling business, I always found it ironic that he did not want children of his own.

He really had me fooled. I had just finished college, and he was an outstanding lawyer when I met him. I was overwhelmed by his charm and good looks. He was a tall handsome man with dark brown hair and beautiful green eyes. He won my heart very quickly, and we were married within a year.

The abuse started about a week after we were married. Wilson was such an immoral man. Each time he abused me, I could see an evil gleam in his eyes. I managed to endure the verbal and mental abuse, but the beatings were more than I could stand.

When I found out he had cancer, I have to admit a part of me was happy. God forgive me, but I knew my suffering would be over soon and it was. Wilson did not live but two months after he found out he had cancer. I took care of him as best I could. After he was confined to his sick bed, he continued to verbally abuse me and ordered me to continue his black-market business.

For the first time in my life, I stood up to him and told him I absolutely would not continue to sell little babies and children. I told him I would not have a part in the selling of illegal whiskey, also. Even on his deathbed, he tried to reach out and grab me. He was so weak he couldn't lift himself from the bed. I will never forget that evil look in his eyes when I stood up to him. I know he would have killed me if he could have gotten his hands on me.

As I watched his body being lowered into the ground today, I knew in my heart that my suffering on this earth was over. Could God ever forgive me for not going to the police? I just read in my Bible that if I confess my sins and believe in my heart, God will reach down and save me and forgive my sins, and I believe that with all my heart. God have mercy on my soul."

We were all speechless and stared at each other with stunned expressions. The only noise in the backyard of the Babcock's home that afternoon was the sound of birds in the majestic tree and traffic in the distance.

Jack finally broke the silence. "This is unbelievable, ladies."

"Yes, it is," I replied. "What we have found here today definitely changes everything. What a wicked man he was, and what a victim she was!"

"We need to finish going through the rest of these items. We just might find something else," Jan responded.

With only a few items remaining to peruse, we dug back into the documents. I continued to flip the yellowed pages of the old ledger book. When I got to the last five pages of the ledger book, I suddenly felt faint and could not believe what I was seeing. There before me was a list of every baby that had been sold and the names of the families they had been placed with.

I finally managed to regain enough composure to speak. "Oh-h-h-h, me, oh, my, lo-o-ok at t-t-this." I wailed.

I handed the decaying ledger book to Jan, and when she saw what was before her eyes, her mouth flew open in disbelief.

In a few seconds she, too, regained her composure. "Hope, this is it! This is what we need. Look here at this entry. It states that a baby girl was brought to this home on

January 4, 1940. It also states that the baby was one of Prissy Walker's. And look at this. The baby girl was sold to a Mr. and Mrs. Franklin Farr from Charlotte, North Carolina, for two-thousand dollars on April 26, 1940."

That last bit of information did me in. "Two-thousand dollars!" I shouted. "That was a fortune in 1940. Mr. and Mrs. Farr must have wanted a child desperately."

I stood speechless for a few moments. My thoughts were drawn back to the time when my mother's twin had been abducted and brought to this house as an innocent little baby. *What makes people do the things they do? Why did this atrocity have to happen? Why did no one believe my grandma when she tried to tell everyone that she had another baby? What a horrible life poor Flora Wilson endured. Could she still be alive?*

I watched Jack as he carefully transferred the documents and ledger book back into the box.

He turned to me, "Hope, looks like I missed something. There's a large envelope that is stuck to the side of the box. Let's see what it is."

I watched him as he carefully removed the envelope from the box and emptied the contents onto the picnic table. There before us lay a picture of a bride and groom on their wedding day.

He turned it over and exclaimed, "Bingo, this is a picture of Wilson and Flora. Now we know what they looked like."

Flora was dressed in a beautiful gown with a long flowing train, and Wilson looked dapper in his dark three-piece suit. He was a handsome man, and I could now understand how he swept Flora off her feet. He had a devious looking smile and piercing eyes. Flora was a lovely bride and looked so happy and in love. From the expression on her face, it appeared she had no idea what a scoundrel she was marrying.

Jack and Sarah graciously offered me the contents of the box, but I felt it was only fitting for them to keep it with the house. I had gotten what I needed, and I knew they were trying to preserve the history of the house.

Jack spoke up, "Hope, I have a copy machine and a scanner. I will make you copies of everything in this box."

"Thanks Jack, I really appreciate that. I will reimburse you for the costs."

"I wouldn't think of charging you anything," he replied.

Jan turned to me, "Hope, don't you think we need to do something with this information? Someone in the local government needs to know about it."

"Our minds are running along the same track. I was just thinking the same thing," I replied.

Jack interrupted us, "I will be glad to take it to the authorities for you. I agree with you; we can't keep this quiet. It affects too many lives, and the people involved need to have access to this information. I'm sure many of them are deceased."

I was relieved to hear how he felt about the documents. "Jack, you and Sarah have been so kind to let us intrude into your busy lives. I can never thank you enough for your help."

"We were happy to do it, and all of this information just gives the house more character," he replied. "I will get the information to the police department tomorrow morning and get back in touch with you."

After giving Jack my telephone number, we said our goodbyes and left. As I was getting into my car, a troubling thought came to my mind. *I wonder what else happened in the Babcock house. Kidnapping, black market adoptions, bootlegging, and spousal abuse were certainly enough! Maybe, just maybe, Jack and Sarah will find something else.*

Chapter 23

Early the next morning, I awoke to the sound of the telephone ringing. After fumbling around in the bed and trying to reach the phone, I finally was able to pick up the receiver.

Sarah Babcock was on the line. "Hope, I know I'm calling early, but I just had to let you know something. Late last night, Jack and I went back into the attic area, and you'll never believe what we found. We found additional pictures. Where can we meet with you and Jan? Most of the pictures are of babies, and I know you will want to see them before Jack goes to the authorities."

I awoke immediately when I heard the latest revelation. "We can meet you anywhere today. You just name the place and time," I exclaimed breathlessly.

"Jack suggested we meet at the Arboretum at the intersection of Providence Road and Highway 51 at McDonalds about eight o'clock. Can you be there?"

"Absolutely, we will be there!"

"I thought we could eat breakfast together while we're there. Jack likes a huge breakfast and lots of coffee."

"We'll be there at eight o'clock sharp. See you then."

I heard Jan and Leo stirring as I went into the living room. My little apartment was small, and the walls were paper thin.

Jan puttered into the kitchen stretching and yawning and rubbing her eyes.

"Who was that calling so early? It's only six o'clock," Jan asked between yawns and stretches.

"Sarah," I replied. "You will never believe this, but she and Jack have found some baby pictures, and they want us to see them before they turn them over to the authorities. We are to meet them at eight o'clock for breakfast."

Jan looked at me with a look of astonishment. "How much better can this get? God is definitely on our side. Hope, I don't know how you feel about the power of God, but I hope you can see his hand in everything that is happening to you. Everything we have touched has fallen into place. It's been like a jigsaw puzzle, and we have watched every piece come together perfectly. All that has happened over the last few days has not been an accident. God's an awesome Heavenly Father, and we just need to thank him. Do you mind if we have a quick prayer of thanksgiving?"

"Of course not," I replied, somewhat taken by surprise.

Jan took my hands, and we stood there in the middle of my kitchen in our pajamas as she prayed. To say the least, I was somewhat shocked that she offered to stop where we were and pray. It was a simple prayer of praise and thanksgiving with no large theological words, just heartfelt thanks and gratitude to a God I realized I did not know. I had heard about him my entire life, but I was beginning to realize I never knew who he really was. But I knew one thing for sure, a force larger than me was controlling my life, and I would eventually have to reckon with it.

Leo must have suspected we were in a hurry to leave, because he stood back and watched us buzz around like two honeybees in a clover field on a mission. We managed to get ready and were out the door by seven-thirty.

I spied Sarah and Jack the moment we entered McDonalds. They were waiting for us to order our food, but I wanted to see the pictures first. We found a booth out of the way, and Jack handed me a manila envelope. I slowly opened it, and there before me were more pictures of Flora and Wilson and many pictures of infants. On each of the baby pictures, Flora held an infant in her arms with a genuine look of love for the child.

Jack cleared his throat and spoke emphatically, "Hope, you need to look on the back of each picture."

I turned the pictures over. Recorded on the back of the pictures were the birth dates, length, weight, and gender of each baby. Also, listed were the names of the families who had adopted the infants and the source from which the babies came. I began to shuffle through the pictures and soon found one that was dated January 4, 1940.

"Jan, this has got to be Mama's sibling. My mother had very few pictures taken when she was young, but this baby does look like the ones I have of Mama. As a matter of fact, this baby not only looks like Mama's baby pictures, but she looks like mine, too."

I began to weep uncontrollably when I saw Prissy Walker and Henry Ledbetter's names as the source. "I just don't understand all of this. This has all come together so quickly. I'm at a loss for words. I can't help being sad for my poor grandma and mama. They never had the opportunity to know this little baby. Why has it fallen my lot to be the one to find this person? And poor Miss Emma, she's going to be so upset when she hears this."

Jack looked at me with a look of gentleness and concern, "Can I tell you something, Hope? Sarah and I are believers, and we prayed long before we bought the Jones house that God would lead us to a home where we could be a blessing to people. It's been only one week since we signed the contract on the house, and God has already sent you into our lives."

"And I am so grateful to you, but why has all of this happened to me the way it has? I'm so confused." I responded in desperation.

"Have you ever thought that God may be trying to speak to you through your circumstances? God uses circumstances to speak to people many times. He used my tour of duty in the Middle East during Desert Storm to bring me to himself. Through an experience in that war torn area of the world, I met God. Up until that point in my life, I had absolutely no time for God. It was there in Kuwait that I realized my life was completely out of my control. I watched as my best friend was shot to death before my eyes.

"I was raised in a Godly home, but I decided I didn't want God in my life. Deep down in my heart, I know that God used my circumstances to speak to me. What's he saying to you now, Hope?"

I dropped my head as tears began to flow from my eyes. I felt a familiar longing in my heart for something, and I knew right away what it was. It was not a something but a person. It was God. I had felt that same feeling many times as a child in church but had never surrendered to it. I raised my head and saw Sarah, Jan, and Jack looking at me through tear-filled eyes.

"I don't know what he's trying to say to me. What do I need to do, Jack. What does God want from me?" I cried in desperation.

"Hope, you have a space in your heart and soul that's empty and longs to be filled, and it can only be filled with the presence of God. Nothing else will fit there. Oh, you can try to crowd other things into that space, but only God himself through the person of his Son and his Spirit will fit there. Nothing else will work.

"Hope, it's difficult to put a jigsaw puzzle together, but when you do, you will discover that the last piece is the most important piece in the puzzle. Why? Because the picture will never be complete without that last little piece. Hope, your life will never be complete until you receive that last piece of the puzzle, and that is Christ, himself. He wants to fit into that special little place in your heart if you will let him. It's your decision, Hope. It's totally up to you."

I looked into Jack's eyes and whispered, "I can't believe I'm saying this, but I do want him in my life."

"Hope, do you believe that Jesus Christ died for your sins, and because of his death on the cross, he opened the *only* way for you to know God and have eternal life?"

"Yes, I do." I whispered.

Jack continued to question me. "Do you now accept this last piece of the puzzle?"

"Yes," I whispered between sobs.

"Do you want to tell him that now and ask for his forgiveness? Will you do that?"

I bowed my head, totally oblivious to my surroundings, and really prayed for the first time in my life. "Lord, please forgive me of my sins. I now understand that I need a Savior. Come into my heart, and take away this emptiness that I feel. I feel like I'm drowning. I need you, Lord. I do believe." I paused a moment and then continued. "Fill me with your presence and make me whole, Lord."

I raised my head, and everyone around the table was in tears, but I had a glorious smile on my tearstained face and felt a joy I had never felt before.

I looked at Jack, and when I managed to speak, I whispered, "What do I have to do now?"

They all started laughing, and Jan finally answered me. "Hope, Jesus did it all on the cross. All he wants from you is for you to believe in him and trust him. And when you confessed your sins and your need for him, he forgave your sins and your heart is perfectly clean before him."

Sarah took my hand and whispered to me, "Just obey him, trust him, and he will lead you in everything you do or say. You've found the last piece of the puzzle, and that's what makes all the difference."

Chapter 24

I don't know what I expected after my encounter with God, but I immediately felt a sense of peace and joy I had never felt before. God had brought me to the precise place of his choosing to bring me to himself. I smiled as I realized I had just had an encounter with the living God of the universe in McDonalds, of all places. I was overwhelmed and very humbled to realize that he had chosen me for his very own, and he waited patiently as he tenderly drew me to himself. God didn't force himself on me, but he let me choose him.

After we completed breakfast, Jack and Sarah said their goodbyes and headed toward the police station to turn in the information that was uncovered at their home.

I excused myself and went to the restroom. I just needed some time alone to absorb what had just taken place. The events that had just transpired in my life were so new to me, and I needed to get a grasp on my new found faith.

I guess I thought I would look different when I gazed into the mirror over the sink, but not so. There was no visible difference in my physical appearance; however, I felt a joy and an overpowering sense of peace. I recalled a Bible verse my parents had made me memorize as a child, and for the first time, I actually understood it. *For man looketh on the outward appearance, but the Lord looketh on the heart.*

Standing there looking at myself, I realized that only my heart and soul had been changed and not my physical body.

I recalled another scripture verse that I had memorized as a little girl. *Know ye not that ye are the temple of God, and that the Spirit of God dwelleth in you?* For the first time in my life, I understood what that verse meant. The Spirit of God was living in my heart, and the Great Creator had come to live within my soul. That empty space was no longer empty in the deep recesses of my heart, because it had been filled with God's wonderful presence. I knew at that moment, my life would never be the same.

I bowed my head, standing there alone in the restroom, and thanked God for not giving up on me. I thanked him for what he had done in my heart and life, and I asked him to be my guide. I remembered hearing my daddy talk about a peace that would pass all understanding. When I finished my prayer in the restroom that day, I can honestly say I understood what he was talking about.

Jan was waiting for me at our table, and as I approached her, she spoke. "Hope, you have made the most important decision of your life. God will be with you forever. You belong to him now, and he lives within you by the power of the Holy Spirit."

"Oh, Jan, I am so grateful. I just have to tell someone what has happened. I must call Miss Emma, Samson, and Hattie. I've just got to tell them. They are my family now."

"Do it now. You have your cell phone. After you call them, we can be on our way."

I proceeded to call Miss Emma's telephone number and was somewhat troubled when I didn't get an answer.

With a worried expression on my face, I looked at Jan. "I'm not getting an answer. I wonder if something's wrong?"

"Surely not, they are probably outside. You can try again in a few minutes," she replied.

After leaving McDonalds, we decided to look for the cemetery where Wilson Jones was buried. We went back by my apartment to do a search on the computer to find the location of the cemetery. While we were at the apartment, I again rang Miss Emma's phone.

On the third ring, Hattie picked up. "Hello, Ledbetter res'dence."

"Hattie, how are you and Samson? Miss Emma, how is she? I called a few minutes ago and didn't get an answer. I got kinda worried."

"Lan' sakes, Miss Hope, we wuz jist a talkin' 'bout chu. We jist fine. We wuz outside with Samson a helpin' him. His autheritis is a actin' up, and we wuz helpin' him unload some plants and bushes from the truck. Miss Emma, she's a gonna make another flower bed. How you a doin'?"

"Hattie, I'm doing great, and I have something to tell you. Is Miss Emma or Samson close by?"

"Miss Emma's ri'chear wid me. Samson, he's jist ou'chonder in the backyard."

"Go get Samson, and tell them to stand close to the phone. I have something very important to tell ya'll. I'll hang on while you get Samson. I want all three of you to hear what I have to say."

I anxiously waited until Samson came into the house.

Miss Emma took the phone. "Hope, we are here. I've got the speaker phone on. What's happened?"

I could picture the three of them standing near the phone anxiously waiting to hear what I had to say. "Miss Emma, Hattie, Samson, something wonderful happened to me this morning. I know ya'll have been praying for me. Well, your prayers have been answered. I met God this morning, and he is now living in my heart."

I could hear all three of them rejoicing on the other end of the phone line. Hattie was the first to speak, "Praise da Lawd! We shore has been a prayin'. You truly is in our family now."

Miss Emma finally spoke, "Hope, I can't tell you how happy we are to hear this news. We have been praying everyday since we met you that God would speak to you. How in this world did this happen? Tell us all about it."

I proceeded to detail the events that had taken place. When I told them it took place in McDonalds, I could hear Samson in the background. "Well, in 'is worl'. What a place to be. I know'd 'em 'ere hamburger joints wuz good for some'um 'sides eatin'. Jist goes to show ye, God can get yore attention anywhere. Chil', I's so proud of you!"

"You three will never know how much you've influenced my life, and I am so grateful. Hattie, I'll never forget our conversation about how God helped you forgive white folks that had abused your people. I have now felt that same forgiveness toward hypocritical church people, and I know God will continue to help me forgive those who have hurt me and my parents over the years."

Hattie responded quickly, "Ain't it amazin' what our Won'erful Lawd can do in yore heart?"

"It sure is, Hattie. I never knew what forgiveness was until now. It feels so wonderful to have those feelings lifted and to know God has forgiven me. I just had to call ya'll before I continued the rest of the day.

"The thing that amazes me is that God accepted me just as I was. I only had to ask for his forgiveness, believe in him, and trust him to save me. I don't know what I expected, but I am a new person now. Oh, I look the same, but my heart is changed! I'm going in a different direction and I'm not going to look back. Is that what repentance means?"

Miss Emma replied, "Absolutely. Hope, that's the great thing about God's love and mercy. It reaches down at just the right time, right where we are, and rescues us."

"I think I can face anything now with God's help, and I know he will help me solve this mystery that surrounds my family," I replied.

"Jan and I are going to a cemetery where we think the leader of the baby-selling ring is buried. Continue to pray that we will find some answers today. And I love ya'll so much."

"Miss Emma, Hattie, and me'll shore be a prayin'. In fac', we is a gonna stop right now and talk to da Lawd jist as soon as we quit a talkin' to ye," Samson said.

After saying goodbye, I turned to Jan. "They were over-joyed with my news. I'm so glad I was able to get in touch with them. Now we can be on our way if you have located the road the cemetery is on.

"I sure have. It is very close to the Cabarrus-Mecklenburg County line, and it appears to be just across the county line in Cabarrus County. Let's be on our way."

Chapter 25

After perusing the directions Jan had printed from the computer, we decided that we could locate the cemetery without any difficulty.

The countryside along the way to Cabarrus County was absolutely breathtaking. We passed an old farmhouse that reminded me of my farm in Rutherford County. Cows were grazing in the pasture and two fine-looking mules were standing among them as they enjoyed the succulent green grass. The scene before me looked like a masterpiece from the collection of a great landscape artist.

It suddenly dawned on me that the scene before me had been painted by the finger of the Master Artist himself. A mere mortal could never paint anything as lovely as what my eyes were seeing. God's creation was inexpressible, and for the first time I realized he created it for mankind to enjoy. Somehow, the world appeared lovelier than it had ever been before. The sky seemed bluer and the grass had never looked greener. God had not only changed my heart, he had also changed the way I viewed his creation.

Jan suddenly turned on a narrow gravel road just over the Cabarrus County line, and as she made the turn, she said, "Hope, I believe the cemetery is just down this road a little way. The information I found on the internet said it is located on Butler Road, and this is Butler Road. Keep your eyes open for it. Since it's an old family cemetery, it may be overgrown."

I scanned the countryside as Jan slowly steered the car down the overgrown dirt road. After riding approximately one mile, I spotted what looked like an overgrown fenced-in area. Jan parked the car on the side of the road, and we made our way through tall weeds and prickly briars to a black wrought iron fence. When we arrived at the fence, our pants legs were covered in cockleburs and beggar lice. I smiled as I recalled the many times Grandma had picked those prickly cockleburs and beggar lice from my clothes as a child. Grandpa and I got them on us every time we went down to the river.

The fence appeared to be very old and had definitely not been maintained. It was so pitted and covered in rust that portions of the fence had actually collapsed, making it easier for Jan and me to enter the cemetery.

We could see several granite monuments throughout the fenced in area. They were all shapes and sizes.

I looked in Jan's direction. "This has got to be it. Let's see what we can find among these old tombstones and tall weeds."

We located several small grave markers that had no names or dates on them. They were simple slabs of blue slate rock. There were several children's graves mixed among the larger grave markers. Most of them were simple granite headstones with just the names of the children with their birth and death dates. Several of them had doves carved on them, and one actually had a carved lamb sitting on top of the grave marker.

As we pushed back the weeds, we located some graves dating back to the early 1800s. Many of them were difficult to read, but the more recent graves were much easier to decipher. Age and weather conditions had not been kind to the grave markers. The engraving on most of the older tombstones was impossible to read, because they were so pitted from wind and rain.

We saw several different types of headstones. There were two box-tombs and several tall obelisks that towered above the other markers. They looked like tall columns or miniature replicas of the Washington Monument. One of the pedestal grave markers was topped with an urn. My curiosity was aroused when I noticed one of the gravestones had an inverted torch carved in the granite.

I turned to Jan and questioned her. "Jan, I wonder what that inverted torch means?"

"I have researched old graveyards in the past and noticed that same type of carving. I did research on the internet and found that it is a symbolic figure of life being snuffed out by death," she replied.

I noticed a large oak tree growing at the back of the cemetery. The majestic tree dominated the burial ground and offered shade to the graves surrounding it. As I approached it, I noticed it was growing at the base of a tombstone. It was the strangest thing I had ever seen. The tree had evidently started the growth process after the monument was put in place. Over the years, the growth of the tree had pushed the monument to a forty-five degree angle. It actually appeared as if the grave marker was growing out of the base of the tree trunk.

This tree's roots have likely penetrated the coffin and its contents. This is really ghoulish. The little squirrel that planted that acorn had no idea he was storing his food so near a grave, I thought to myself.

As I slowly drew closer to that strange looking tree and monument, I stumbled on something. I tried to break the fall, but everything was happening so fast. I fell forward face first against the granite grave marker. When I came to, Jan was standing over me with a horrified look on her face talking on her cell phone.

I looked up, and Jan's face came into view. Everything was unclear and fuzzy. The world around me was spinning, and I felt as if I had a severe case of vertigo. I felt something on my face and reached my hand to my forehead. It was then that I realized I had more than just a scratch. I was bleeding profusely. Jan ran back to the car and found a towel to put on my head to apply pressure.

"Please, Hope, don't try to move or get up. You are going to need to see a doctor. You have a bad gash on you head and a lump the size of a baseball," she spoke as she applied pressure to my forehead.

I could tell Jan was frightened and had been crying. I tried to focus but could feel myself slipping into unconsciousness.

Jan frantically began to talk to me. "Don't you dare pass out on me again, Hope Logan! You've got to stay awake. Do you hear me?"

I slowly opened my eyes and looked at her. "Jan, I'm getting sick to my stomach, and my head's hurting."

"You need to go to the nearest hospital. From the way you are bleeding you must have a deep cut," Jan exclaimed. "I've called 911, and they are on the way. Just relax if you can."

"I'll be okay. You shouldn't have called anyone. I'll be alright in a few minutes," I whispered as I attempted to get up.

"No, no, no, you're not okay. Now lie still! Do you hear me! You took a pretty bad blow to you head," Jan responded as she pushed me back to the ground.

My vision began clearing somewhat, and I slowly turned my head to look at the tombstone I had fallen against.

"Jan, look, at that headstone," I exclaimed weakly, as I pointed to the marker I had fallen against. "I can't believe my eyes. Am I hallucinating?"

Jan knelt down beside of the simple marker and began to read the inscription to me. "Wilson Jones, Attorney, Born May 1, 1899, Death May 26, 1948. Hope, Flora is dead also. She was born August 8, 1902 and died June 4, 1956. This is exactly what we're looking for. I guess that answers our question about Flora. I guess that wicked old Wilson Jones had to crack your skull to get your attention."

While Jan continued to put pressure on my forehead, I attempted to get up on my knees to get a better view.

Jan gently pushed me back to the ground. "Hope, I don't want to upset you, but you've got to lie down and be still! I'm telling you; you've had a severe head injury. You were knocked out cold for a while. I thought you were dead at first. When I called 911, they told me to keep you perfectly still, and that's exactly what you're going to do, young lady! Do you understand?"

"Okay," I responded weakly. "Jan, I feel so sick. I hate to throw up."

Continuing to apply pressure to my head, she responded, "Just relax, but you can't go to sleep! My mother always said to keep someone awake after a head injury. Now don't you go to sleep, young lady!"

Jan began talking to me about everything she could think of, but all I wanted to do was go to sleep. I finally begged her to just let me go to sleep, but she kept rattling on as fast as she could. Every time I tried doze off, she would immediately wake me up. I remembered thinking to myself, *Jan, just be quite. You're driving me crazy. Just let me sleep.*

In my foggy state of mind, I heard Jan say, "You know it's kinda ironic that a tree's growing out of this grave. I imagine the roots of the tree have penetrated the actual grave itself. I probably shouldn't say this, but old Wilson Jones has ended up being just plain old fertilizer for a big oak tree. I think it's only fitting that this beautiful oak picked this particular gravesite to grow and flourish."

Chapter 26

I heard a siren as it approached the cemetery. Upon arrival, the paramedics went into action. They put me on a flat board and stabilized my head. I immediately got nauseous again, and my head began to pound like a jackhammer pounding on a concrete sidewalk. The next thing I remember was vomiting. Everything was spinning around and the waves of nausea would not go away.

One of the paramedics began to talk to me. "I believe something more than just a minor lick on the head is going on here. We're gonna need to transport you to the nearest hospital, and that's in Concord."

"Okay." I gasped between waves of nausea and vomiting.

I remember thinking to myself as they were placing me in the ambulance, *Wilson Jones wasn't content to ruin my grandma and aunt's life; now, he's reaching out from the grave to ruin mine.*

As the paramedics were getting ready to close the door of the ambulance, I heard Jan say, "Hope, I'll follow the ambulance to the hospital. You just hang in there, and I'm praying for you."

I must have passed out on the way to the hospital. When I awoke, I was utterly discombobulated and didn't know where I was. Because of the nausea and dizziness, I kept my eyes closed. I soon realized I was in the emergency room at a hospital.

A doctor came in to examine me and immediately sent me to have a CT scan. The scan revealed that I definitely had a severe concussion. After I was given an injection for pain and nausea, I fell into a drug induced sleep.

When I awoke I thought I heard familiar voices. I raised my head from the pillow and spotted Preacher Mike at the foot of my bed.

I saw a smile cross his face. "Well, young lady, what have you managed to get yourself into?"

I started to speak, but instantly succumbed to waves of nausea and pain. As I repositioned my head on the pillow, Hattie and Miss Emma came into view. When I turned my head, I saw my dear friend, Samson. *I must be dying,* I thought. *They have all come to say their goodbyes.*

I managed to speak, "Why are ya'll here? What happened to me?"

Miss Emma took my hand, "Hope, don't you remember anything? You have had an accident. You had a nasty fall while looking for Wilson Jones' gravesite. Jan called us immediately after she got you to the hospital, and you have been here two days. Tell us what you can remember about your accident."

My mind was foggy, and my thought would not come together. I felt totally confused.

When I realized I could not remember anything, I began to cry. "I can't remember anything."

I must have dozed off again, because when I awoke I realized that Preacher Mike was praying. I listened quietly to his beautiful prayer. I was deeply touched and very thankful that he was there with Hattie, Miss Emma, and Samson. His prayer was so simple, yet direct. He asked God to give me peace and rest and restore me to good health. Just before he closed his prayer, he sounded tearful as he begged God to let me remember what had happened in my life. I was so humbled that he cared that much for me. After the prayer, I felt that same comforting presence enfolding me that I had felt the morning of the accident. It was then that I realized I was beginning to remember what had happened.

When Preacher Mike finished his prayer, I saw those beautiful blue eyes swimming in tears. I was so overwhelmed that his tears were in my behalf, and I knew I had to speak up and let him know I was awake and remembered everything.

"Preacher Mike, I do remember falling face first on Wilson Jones tombstone. C-C-C-Can you believe that? But more important than that, I remember inviting Christ into my life," I whispered as I struggled to speak.

I saw relief wash over his face as he gently took my hand and said, "Oh, Hope, I'm so grateful you're awake and have you memory back. You had us all scared to death."

"Oh, Miss Hope, you cou'da got yoreself kilt. Law me, you got a big ol' gash on yore head. What is we a gonna do wid ye, young'un," cried Hattie.

I placed my hand on my forehead and felt a huge bandage. "Wow, I guess I do. But why are you here Preacher Mike?"

"Hope, when Miss Emma called to ask me to pray for you, I volunteered to bring her, Hattie, and Samson to Concord. We got hotel rooms very near the hospital, because we had no idea how long you would be unconscious. Jan and Miss Emma stayed with you last night."

"Law me, Miss Hope, I's watched mo' television 'an any man oughta watch today. Me and Hattie, we ain't got no television an' it be a good thang we don't. 'Ey shore is some powerful wicked stuff on 'at thang. I jist glad you is a feelin' better. You still lookin' a might peaked."

"I'm sorry to be so much trouble. It was such a foolish accident. I was walking along, minding my own business, and the next thing I knew I had cracked my head on Wilson and Flora Jones' tombstone. If I didn't know better, I would have thought the old rascal reached out from his grave and tripped me, but I'm certain I tripped on a rock or something."

Preacher Mike gripped my hand in his and said, "Jan told us everything that happened at the cemetery. She said you must have tripped on a vine growing over the grave. She also said you were conscious for a few minutes after the accident, but you kept trying to go to sleep on her. I'm just grateful you were not there by yourself. I could have lost you."

His words ignited those same jittery feelings, and my heart melted as I looked into his beautiful blue eyes. "W-w-where is Jan now?" I stammered.

"She'll be here in a few minutes. She continued with the investigation this morning, and I think she has some information for you," he replied with a gleam in his eyes.

"Do you know what she's discovered?" I asked him as I tried to contain my excitement.

"I don't know all the details, so I'm gonna let her tell you what she found out," he replied.

I looked from Preacher Mike to Miss Emma, Hattie, and Samson. I felt sure they knew exactly what Jan had discovered, but they weren't about to tell me.

"Ah, come on, tell me what you know. I'm dying from curiosity, and it's not fair to keep me in suspense as sick as I am," I whined pitifully.

"Okay, Hope," Miss Emma replied. "We are certain that she knows where your relative is. She will tell you all about it when she gets here."

"This is unbelievable. I'm so excited. I have to get out of here! I've got to get up!" I exclaimed as I tried to sit on the side of the bed.

While gently pushing me back on the bed, Miss Emma emphatically responded, "Wo-o-o, young lady, hold your horses, you'll do such a thing! You have had a serious concussion, and the doctor will have to see you before you can think about getting up or leaving."

The room began to spin around; I knew right away that my quick movement had been a mistake. I lay very still with my eyes closed trying to ward off more nausea and pain.

We heard a soft knock, and Jan peeked through the crack in the door of the hospital room. "How's my partner in crime doing?"

"Come in, come in," I heard someone say. The room continued to spin around as I tried to focus on Jan. Even though I was desperately trying to remain awake, I felt myself losing consciousness again.

When I opened my eyes, Preacher Mike was sitting beside my bed. "How long have I been asleep?" I asked. "My head hurts so-o-o-o much. Please get me something for pain. I feel like I'm going to be sick again. Every time I open my eyes I get sick. I hate to complain."

Miss Emma appeared at the other side of my bed and took my hand. "I'll call for the nurse, and she should be here shortly. You just keep your eyes closed and try to relax until she gets here, Hope."

The nurse arrived in a few minutes and put some medication in my IV. I had not even realized I had an IV until that moment. I slowly opened my eyes and looked at Preacher Mike. His face was shrouded with concern and compassion. Miss Emma and Hattie stood by my bedside with that same concerned look. I turned my head slightly and spied Samson sitting at the foot of the bed with his head bowed as if he were praying. *I must really be sick or dying,* I told myself.

I allowed myself to succumb to the medication and closed my eyes for a few moments. When I awoke, I heard whispering. I tried to raise my head and look around the room, but I was consumed with vertigo again. I thought I could hear my mama talking in the background. I again tried to raise my head, and at that moment, I saw her. I was totally confused and did not understand what was happening to me. *Maybe it's the drugs the nurse put in my IV.* I quickly told myself. *This can't be happening. Mama's dead. I must be hallucinating.*

I began to sob uncontrollably. When I was finally able to speak, I reached for the apparition before me.

"Mama, Mama, it's you," I cried softly. "Am I dreaming?"

Hattie and Samson ran to my bedside and began consoling me.

"Miss Hope, you's gonna make you'self start throwin' up again. Jist calm down. Honey, 'is ain't yore mama, 'is is your aunt. Jan found her fer you while you wuz a sleepin'," Hattie whispered in my ear.

Jan stepped forward and took my hand. "I'm afraid we should have waited until you were better, but I knew you would throttle me if I didn't bring her here to meet you."

Standing there before me was a beautiful lady who looked exactly like Mama. She had the same lovely smile that my mama always had.

She gently reached out and took my hand. "Hope, I don't want to tire you, but I just had to see you."

I tried to speak, but the words would not come. She took a tissue and wiped my tears and whispered to me, "Don't try to talk; we have plenty of time for that. I just want to sit by your bedside for a while and look at you. You just go back to sleep and rest, and we will all be here for you until you're better."

I felt her wipe my tears a second time, and once more I succumbed to the effect of the drugs the nurse had given me and dozed off to sleep.

Chapter 27

When I awoke I realized it was getting dark outside, and beautiful moonbeams were filtering through the window of my hospital room. I turned my head and saw Preacher Mike sitting in a chair by my bed. There was no one else in the room, and he had fallen asleep in his chair and looked as if his neck would break.

"Preacher Mike, where is everybody?" I asked weakly.

He awoke quickly and came to my bedside without delay. "Hey there, they all went to get something to eat. You just lie still so you won't get sick again."

Preacher Mike was gazing at me with an unusual look. It was a look that I had not seen in his eyes before. It seemed to be deep concern and something else I couldn't quite put my finger on.

Standing very close to my bedside, he looked down at me and spoke softly. "Hope Logan, you just about scared me to death. When I left Martinsville to come to Charlotte, I was afraid I might lose you before we could talk. I've just got to talk to you about something, but we can do that later. I don't want to upset or excite you in any way."

"G-G-Go ahead, I feel much better now," I stammered curiously. "Please tell me what you want to talk to me about."

I held my breath as he began to speak. "I don't know where to begin, but I guess the best thing to do is start at the beginning. This has all been so unexpected, and I just don't know how to say this."

He hesitated for a moment and then continued. "You have touched me in a way that I've never been touched before. When I first heard about your accident, my heart was crushed. You have been on my mind night and day since I first met you, and the thought of losing you was more than I could stand. Please don't think me forward for saying all of this. These feelings are so new to me. I have deliberately not allowed myself to become involved with anyone romantically because of my ministry and God's calling on my life. But, Hope, you have swept me off of my feet, and I don't know what to do about you. W'y, I'm even having trouble preparing my sermons. Lady, I just can't get you out of my mind. You're driving me crazy!"

Preacher Mike gently took my hand in his and lifted it to his lips. He tenderly kissed my hand and looked into my eyes. At that instant I felt faint, and my heart started pounding like a jackhammer. I asked myself, *can a person pass out lying flat on their back, and how can this be happening to me? This wonderful man is actually attracted to me and takes my breath away.*

"Hope, you are the most beautiful woman I have ever met, and I want to get to know you better. I want to know how you think, what you enjoy doing, all about your child-hood, and I want to be your best friend. But most of all, and I can't believe I'm saying this; Hope Logan, I've fallen madly in love with you. When you came into my life, you turned everything upside down, and you have, without a doubt, stolen my heart! When I heard you had become a believer, well, that was the icing on the cake.

"But there is one thing we have to rectify first and that's my name. Everybody in Martinsville calls me Preacher

Mike, but you are not to call me that anymore. From now on, I'm just plain Mike to you."

Hearing Mike's declaration of love for me had left me totally speechless. As I attempted to speak, I looked into his beautiful blue eyes and unexpectedly realized his face was closer than it had been before. He reached his hand to my battered forehead and gently touched my face. Before I realized what was taking place, he had lovingly kissed me on the cheek.

At that moment, my heart literally melted. My eyes were drawn to his like a magnet, and I could no longer deny my feelings for him. I timidly raised my hand and gently traced the outline of his strong jaw.

"Mike, I too must be honest with you. I was drawn to you from the first moment you walked into my life. You affected me in a way that I have never been affected before, as well. The first time I met you, I couldn't even make a sensible sentence. I was afraid you'd think I had a speech impediment. The day of the picnic, I was in heaven just being with you. Honestly, Dr. Sanders, you take my breath away."

His face lit up with the most amazing smile I had ever seen. He took both of my hands in his and gently touched his lips to mine. As he was pulling away from me, he whispered, "We will talk about this more later, but for now, we've got to get you well."

Mike sat on the side of the bed and was gently patting my hand when we realized we had an audience.

"They law me, what's a goin' on in here," Miss Emma exclaimed with a big grin on her face.

We were suddenly jolted back to reality, and neither one of us could utter a sound. When we regained our composure, Mike stood and faced the group that had entered my hospital room. I saw smiles on all of their faces, including my aunt.

"Don't be embar'sed. We know'd you'uns had eyes for each other from da start. W'y, me and Samson and Miss

Emma, we's been a prayin' that you two chil'ren would see what wuz right in front of ye eyes," Hattie exclaimed with a wicked little grin. "We know'd all along that you'uns 'ould git together. Didn't we, Samson?"

"Shore thang. I could feel it in my bones. Reverend Sanders jist had 'at courtin' look in his eyes. I know'd it da minute I seen you'uns together," Samson replied with a radiant grin on his face. "W'y, it made me recollect my courtin' days wid you, Hattie."

My aunt stepped forward and came to the side of the bed. "Hope, I'm so glad Jan found me today. I have always felt that there was a missing link in my life, and now I know what it is. I never had the opportunity to know Amelia, but I'm so grateful you have been sent into my life."

She leaned over and kissed my cheek. "Hope, my name is Elizabeth Rose James. My adoptive parents, Franklin and Martha Farr, named me after both of my adoptive grand-mothers. Everyone calls me Elizabeth. Only God could have brought us together.

"I must tell you that I have had a wonderful life. I never knew I was the victim of a kidnapping or an illegal adoption, and I don't think my parents realized it either. God blessed me with two amazing parents who raised me in a Christian home. I never lacked for anything, and I married a great man who was a pastor, just like your friend here. He went home to be with the Lord two years ago. I live alone, because we never had children. That's one of the reasons I am so excited to find you. When Jan told me the entire story about the birth and the kidnapping, I was completely speechless. Everything seemed so unbelievable. You are a Godsend, and I look forward to getting to know you. My Heavenly Father has sent me a treasured gift, a child, my sister's child."

Tears began to flow from my eyes in what seemed like a never ending stream. Mike tenderly patted my hand and reminded me to remain calm.

"I want to call you Aunt Elizabeth if that's okay. You deserve a special title, and I think it is only fitting that I call you Aunt Elizabeth. You look so much like Mama. In fact, you look exactly like her. Your hair is the same lovely gray that hers was. Believe it or not, she styled her hair very similar to yours. You're the very same size she was, and I bet you wear a size eight dress. Your eyes are the same lovely blue that hers were, and your voice even sounds like hers. Your expressions and movements are just like hers. This just blows me away. I can't believe everything has taken place so quickly. A little over a week ago, I didn't even know you existed. Now here you are standing before me. We sure have a lot to catch up on."

Aunt Elizabeth again kissed my cheek and said, "I would be honored to be called Aunt Elizabeth, Auntie, or whatever you want to call me. I'm just so thankful that we have found each other. But for now, you need to rest. When you recover, we can talk more. My dear niece, I plan to spend a lot of time with you."

We heard a faint knock at the door, and Dr. Benjamin Singleton and his nurse came into the room. After speaking to the group surrounding my bed, he turned to me. "Miss Logan, you seem to have stabilized for now. Let's see if you're ready to go home."

He turned to "my family" and asked them to step out for a few minutes. He proceeded to check my vital signs and put me through a neurological examination with the help of the nurse.

After finishing the examination, he changed the dressing on my forehead and declared, "Ms. Logan, it appears you are ready to be released, but you need to remember one thing. You didn't just get a little ding on your head; you had quite a blow, and if that wasn't enough, you reacted to one of the medications we gave you. That's why you slept for so long.

You had a severe concussion, and that's not something to take lightly.

"I will agree to let you leave the hospital if you will promise to have no activity for a few days, and I mean *no activity*. You can't risk another lick on the head. That could be very dangerous. If your headaches increase or if you start vomiting again, you will need to come back to the emergency room immediately. Also, you need to watch for signs of drowsiness, dizziness, or confusion. If any of these symptoms occur, go to the nearest emergency room right away. Your symptoms should subside in about two weeks. If symptoms continue after that time, you need to let me know immediately, and I would like to see you in my office in about ten days to remove the stitches. I don't think you will need any plastic surgery since the scar is in your hairline."

"That's good to know, and I promise I will rest if you'll just let me go home. I'm a teacher; when will I be able to return to school, Dr. Singleton?" I asked.

"Well, if all goes well, you should be able to go back around the first of May. If you are still having any problems, it probably would not be a good idea to go back then. I'll make a decision about your return to work when I see you in my office," he replied.

Dr. Singleton opened the door to let "my family" back into the room. "Folks, I am letting Miss Logan return home if she promises to do nothing for two weeks, and I mean nothing. It's very important for her to rest and allow her body time to heal. She has had severe trauma to her head and needs complete rest for a few days."

Miss Emma spoke up immediately, "She lives alone in Charlotte. Can we take her to Martinsville to recuperate? It is about a two hour drive from here depending on the traffic."

"I think that will be okay. She's going to need someone to be with her for a while."

Hattie stepped up and boldly addressed the doctor, "We's her family, and I promise she be in good hands. I's a gonna watch her like a hawk. She ain't gonna do nary a thang she ain't s'posed to do."

"Then I'll go ahead and sign your discharge papers, and you can call my office to set up an appointment for your recheck visit," Dr. Singleton replied.

After he and the nurse left the room, I looked at "my family" gathered around my bed and said, "Let's get out of here. I've always hated hospitals. We do need to go by my apartment and get a few things and also get Leo. Has someone checked on him?"

"Law me, Hope, Mollie has been taking care of Leo and he's just fine," replied Miss Emma. "And your Aunt Elizabeth is going to Martinsville with us. She will be staying at the inn with us for a while. She wants to be there for you."

"Ya'll have taken care of everything," I said.

"We sure have," Miss Emma replied. "And Preacher Mike is going to take you in his car, and Hattie and Samson will ride with Jan. I'm gonna ride with Elizabeth to be sure she doesn't get lost. We planned all of this while we were eating supper. Leo can ride with Jan. Oh, by the way, your friend Molly called, and she will be coming to Martinsville this weekend to see you, also.

"Before I forget it, your principal, Dr. Benson, came by to visit you while you were sedated. I couldn't believe he drove all the way from Union County to Concord to check on you. He seems to be such a fine man. We all met him, and he seemed genuinely concerned about you.

"He wants you back to finish the school year, but he is more concerned about your recovery. He understands your situation, and he wanted me to tell you that everyone misses you. He told me you have been an asset to his school, and you will truly be missed. Your substitute is on standby to finish the year for you, if necessary."

"That's a relief. He is such an understanding person and was so kind during Mama's illness and death. He even drove all the way to Raleigh for her funeral. Principals like that are few and far between. Every school should have an administrator like him. He's a believer, and it's very evident by his conduct. He knows each student by name and is genuinely concerned about each one of them. He runs a tight ship, and that's why our school has done so well. Some of the teachers and students think he has eyes in the back of his head. He's a feisty little fellow and doesn't miss anything that happens in his school. Most importantly, he's fair. I shudder to think what will happen when he retires, and he can do that in two years. I can rest much easier knowing he understands my situation," I replied weakly.

Mike got the discharge papers from the nurse and went to get his vehicle to bring it closer to the door of the hospital. The rest of "my family" followed me as the nurse pushed me in a wheelchair to the discharge area of the hospital.

After getting me settled in the front seat of Mike's SUV, we met the others in the parking lot and headed toward my apartment.

Chapter 28

Mike was very nervous driving from the hospital to my apartment. He was afraid he would cause me to bump my head again. I assured him I was fine, but he was so afraid he might hit a bump in the road or slam on brakes suddenly. I didn't have to worry about getting sick to my stomach, because the nausea medication I had received earlier was still working.

I looked over at him and said, "Mike Sanders, where is your faith? Don't you trust God to protect us? By the way, we haven't had a chance to really talk about what happened in my life the morning of the accident. Some things may still be a bit foggy, but nothing, absolute nothing, can take away what happened the morning of my accident."

Mike's face broke into a glorious smile. "Hope, Miss Emma called me as soon as she hung up from talking with you, and you'll never know how thrilled I was. Your encounter with God was a definite answer to prayer. I have been praying for you everyday since you walked into my life."

"Mike, I'm so grateful that God never gave up on me. I pushed him away for so many years, but he patiently brought me to himself in his own gentle way. I am so thankful for his unrelenting love for me. I let other people rob me of many years I could have spent with him. I feel like God has given me a second chance, and I certainly don't want to flub it up. I almost did when I cracked my head on old Wilson Jones' tombstone."

"Hope, just remember this. Just because you're a believer now doesn't mean you won't have problems and trials. You now have someone to lead and guide you during those times of trial. God was right there beside you when you fell, and I know that nothing happens to one of his children that he doesn't allow. He uses our trials to make us more like him."

"I know you're right, and I'm so happy that we now share a common faith. I now know what it means to experience the very essence of God's Spirit in my heart and life."

"Hope, I knew the moment I met you that you were a special person. I intend for us to cultivate a relationship and see where it leads," Mike said as he reached across the car and took my hand.

Before I realized what was happening, Mike had pulled up in front of my apartment. Sprawled across the front window was a banner saying *Welcome Home, Hope*. The banner had Leo's paw prints in blue scattered all over it.

"Oh my, who did that?" I exclaimed.

Mollie burst out of the front door followed by Leo who was yelping and jumping up and down. Sarah and Jack Babcock were close behind. Mollie calmed Leo and held him back so I could get out of the car. After gently helping me from the car, Mike led me into the apartment. I was overwhelmed by the concern of everyone, and I felt like a celebrity being bombarded by the paparazzi.

I leaned down and affectionately wrapped my arms around Leo. He must have sensed that something was not right, because he leaned his head against me and started whining and crying. I thought to myself, *what a faithful friend you are, Leo. You've always been there for me. What would I ever do without you?*

I looked into Leo's big eyes and whispered, "Buddy, don't be sad. I'm okay."

Mollie looked at me with tears in her eyes, "Girl, you just about scared us all to death. You need to lie down and rest before you head to Martinsville."

Mike directed his eyes to me and then to Mollie. "I think Hope needs to spend the night here, and we can leave for Martinsville in the morning. I'm afraid she's going to overdo. If we leave now, it will be at least ten o'clock before we can get to Martinsville."

Jack spoke up, "I agree with Mike. You don't need to travel until tomorrow. You certainly don't want to push yourself. You've probably had enough activity for today."

I nodded silently, agreed with them, and curled up on the sofa as soon as we got inside my apartment. Leo quickly found his place beside me on the floor. Mike covered me with my favorite blue throw that I kept on the back of the sofa. Mama had crocheted it for me not long before she got sick. As I was wrapping myself in the soft afghan, I felt as if Mama had tenderly wrapped her arms around me.

Mollie retrieved a pillow from the bedroom and tried to make me as comfortable as possible. She reminded me of a mother hen as she gently tucked me in.

Sarah knelt beside me and took my hand. "Hope, Jack and I feel such a special bond with you. When Jan called us the night of your accident to tell us what had happened, we were so distraught and worried.

"We have no family in the area, and because of your accident, we have met all of your friends. Jan gave Mollie our telephone number, and she asked us to come over tonight to see you. We knew absolutely no one in Charlotte until we met you and Jan. Then we met Mollie and the rest of your friends at the hospital your first night there, and we feel like you are our family now."

I looked into Sarah's eyes and saw tears forming like pools of water. "Sarah, we are family, God's family. I'm so thankful you met my friends. I didn't know ya'll were at the hospital. I was kinda out of it for a day or two. I know you and Jack must have made the sign out front. It was a welcomed surprise."

"Yea, we did, with a little help from Mollie and Leo. Leo was so funny. He had to be in the middle of everything we were doing. I think he must have realized we were making the sign for you. I guess you noticed his paw prints. We used washable blue ink, and I wish you could have seen him as he carefully put his prints on the banner. He even let us wash his feet without a fuss. Of course, we were outside when we were making the banner."

"Thank you, my friends. This has been an unforgettable welcome home celebration!" I replied.

I was beginning to feel sleepy from the nausea medicine, and it was all I could do to stay awake. Leo remained curled up beside the sofa next to me, and it was evident my loyal buddy did not intend to leave my side. Because of his keen perception, he sensed that something was wrong. Every few minutes he cried out and looked up at me with the saddest look I had ever seen on his face. He finally rested his face next to mine on the sofa. I'm sure the bandage on my head had him confused.

Mike leaned down just before I dozed off and kissed my cheek. "Hope, you probably need to go on to bed. We don't want to disturb you. Let me get some of the ladies to help you to bed?"

"Yea," I whispered. "I can hardly stay awake. I'm so tired I don't think I can move."

Before I knew what was happening, Mike tenderly lifted me up into his arms and carried me to the bedroom. He called for the ladies to help me get to bed. Hattie had already turned the covers back, and Mollie had some pajamas ready for me to put on. Mike again kissed my cheek and left the room.

After getting me settled in bed, I heard Sarah comment to Mollie, "That handsome preacher sure seems to be besotted by our Hope, doesn't he?"

"He sure does. But she has never mentioned him to me. Wonder when all of this happened?" Mollie questioned.

"I'll tell you when it happened. It happened the day they laid eyes on each other in Martinsville. I knew immediately he was smitten with her," replied Miss Emma. "Hattie, Samson, and I knew all along that they were drawn to each other, and when Preacher Mike found out about her accident, I thought the boy was going to have a stroke."

I smiled to myself when I heard Hattie say, "W'y, 'em two loves each other. I jist feel it in my ol' bones. I betcha when we get back home, he'll be a hangin' 'round our house like General Grant hung 'round Richmond durin' da Civil War."

I dozed off when I heard the ladies leaving the room giggling about me and my handsome preacher.

When I awoke the next morning, Leo was standing beside my bed with his head propped on the mattress and his face next to mine. My faithful friend had not left my side all night.

I heard someone talking in the kitchen and realized there must be several people there. The smell of coffee permeated the air in my apartment. I pulled myself up in the bed to get my bearings and threw my legs over the side of the bed very carefully. I was still dizzy, and my head was pounding. Just as I was getting ready to stand up, someone knocked on the door.

"Come in," I responded.

Mike stuck his head through the crack in the door and gave me a huge smile. "How's my girl this morning?"

"Better, I feel much better. I must be improving. I think I can eat something."

"That's great news. Hattie has prepared a huge breakfast for everyone. Let me help you to the table."

As I stood beside my bed, I caught a glimpse of myself in the mirror on my dresser. The word "shock" doesn't begin to describe how I felt when I saw myself for the first time since the accident.

"Oh, no, Mike, I look horrible! I can't go in there looking like this. Just look at my face! I can't believe I'm letting you see me this way. My eyes are black and blue and my hair looks horrible, what little bit of hair you can see. This bandage is wrapped all the way around my head. I look like a mummy. I can't let anyone see me like this," I cried as I tried to cover my face.

Mike looked at me with a twinkle in his eyes, "Honey, they all saw you last night, and they all love you just the way you are. Let's get your robe on and go in the kitchen. Besides, you look beautiful to me."

I smiled shyly, since I was not accustomed to compliments from a man. With Mike's help, I put my bathrobe on and slowly made my way into the dining area with Mike on one side and my faithful dog on the other. Miss Emma and Hattie were chatting away over a cup of coffee.

Miss Emma spied me as I entered the dining area. "Now that's the prettiest sight I've ever seen. Hope, sit down with us. Hattie has fixed a wonderful breakfast. I must say you look stronger today."

"I do feel much stronger today, and I'm a little bit hungry. That's got to be a good sign, but I'm definitely not a pretty site."

"Oh, yes, you is, my chil', you look mighty purdy to me," Hattie responded as she placed a plate filled with grits, ham, and eggs in front of me. The moment I got a whiff of the food, I started getting nauseous.

"Hattie, I think I'll just have some ginger ale and crushed ice, maybe a piece of dry toast. I'm feeling a little nauseous."

"Miss Hope, you's a movin' around too much, too fast. I don't b'lieve you is ready to go to Martinsville yet."

I looked from Hattie to Miss Emma and then to Mike and said, "Oh, yes I am, Hattie. I'm ready to go home with my new family."

While I was sipping on the ginger ale and nibbling on the toast, I heard voices in the living area. "Who else is here?"

Mike grinned at me and replied, "Your entire new family. Hope, your Aunt Elizabeth was here at daybreak. In fact, she got here right after I got here with Hattie and Samson. Miss Emma spent the night here, as did Mollie. Mollie called Jack and Sarah, and they are on their way over to say goodbye to you."

"Ya'll are making too much fuss over me. I just got a little lick on my noggin."

"Now, Miss Hope, you jist hesh up. You know you got more 'an a little lick on yore noggin. W'y, from what yore doctor tol' us at da horspitil, da bones in yore head is a pushin' in on yore brain, and 'at ain't good. You's gonna hafta be mighty careful for da nex' while. And I's gonna see to it 'at you do."

I turned my eyes toward Hattie, "Hattie, do you know how much I love you? You are wonderful. You treat me like I'm your very own child."

"Hits 'cause you is, chil'."

Miss Emma was seated across from me drinking a steaming cup of coffee.

She looked at me very seriously and asked, "Hope, are you sure you're able to go to Martinsville today? We don't want you to push yourself."

"Yes, Miss Emma, I can recline the seat in Mike's car and sleep most of the way there. I just want to go home."

"Okay, that settles it. As soon as we can get you ready, we'll be on our way," she replied.

After finishing the ginger ale and toast, Miss Emma went with me to get ready for the trip.

After entering the bedroom, I looked at Miss Emma in desperation and cried, "Miss Emma, I'm a mess. I need to soak in a tub of hot water. I promise I won't get my bandage wet. I've probably still got dirt on me from the cemetery. I've absolutely got to take a bath. I know I had a sponge bath at the hospital, but I need more than that."

"The only way I'll let you do that is for me to be close by in case you pass out."

"Okay, I'll pull the shower curtain closed while I'm in the bathtub."

After running me a tub of warm water, Miss Emma helped me into the bathtub. Never in my life had a bath felt so good, and I must have soaked for fifteen minutes. When I emerged from the water smelling of lavender, I felt like a new person. After my bath, Miss Emma helped me into a pair of jeans.

"Miss Emma, see if you can find me a pretty blouse or tee shirt to put on. I want to look my best for Mike. He must think I look awful."

"No, my chil', I don't think so. I think the good preacher has been smitten by you, he doesn't even notice what you look like," she replied as she went into my walk-in closet and came out with one of my favorite blouses.

It was a lovely lilac smock type blouse with a floral embroidered yoke in the same lovely color. I always felt beautiful when I wore that blouse.

"Do you think we can help my looks with a little bit of makeup?" I asked.

"We can do that, but you look fine to me," Miss Emma replied.

We painstakingly applied some light makeup, and I did look some better.

Miss Emma lightly combed my hair into place, what she could comb, and said, "Hope, you look beautiful to me, but you must know that Preacher Mike doesn't care what you look like. You should have seen him when you were unconscious at the hospital. I thought the boy would grieve himself to death. He was so afraid you weren't going to make it. Hope, that man really does love you."

"Miss Emma, I have to admit I care deeply for him, too."

"You don't have to tell me that. Hattie and I knew it all along."

"How could you tell?" I asked.

"W'y, they law me; a body would have to be blind not to notice. The way you two look at each other was a dead giveaway. It was as plain as the nose on ye face. Even Samson picked up on it."

"Well, I'm just thankful God finally brought us together," I replied as we stepped out of the bedroom.

Mike met us at the door of the kitchen with a surprised look on his face. "Hope, if you didn't have that bandage on your head, no one would know anything was wrong. You look beautiful," he said as he put his arms around me. "Of course, I thought you were beautiful before you fixed yourself up."

"Mike Sanders, I believe you're either blind or daft," I replied jokingly. "But I'm ready to hit the road to Martinsville. Has everyone had breakfast?"

"Yes, Jack and Sarah finally arrived, and we have all eaten. Hattie has cleaned the kitchen and Samson has walked Leo. Jack, Sarah, and Molly are waiting to tell you goodbye."

When I stepped into the living room, everyone stood to their feet as if I was an important dignitary, and I tearfully starting speaking. "I want to thank each of you for all you have done for me. I don't know what I have done to deserve friends like ya'll. Molly, I'm going to miss you so much."

I turned to Jack and Sarah, "Jack, Sarah, there are no words adequate to tell you how much I appreciate you and all you have done for me. You not only helped me find my Aunt Elizabeth, but you allowed God to use you to open my eyes to his love and forgiveness. And for that I will always be grateful. Thank you, my dear, dear friends."

Molly spoke up, "This is not goodbye. Miss Emma has invited us to Martinsville next weekend—all of us. And guess what, they want to get the boxer puppy I told you about. So we will be bringing him, also. Hattie and Samson are so excited they can't stand it.

"I spoke with Dr. Benson, our principal, yesterday before I left, and he is very concerned about you. I told him that your return to school was still uncertain, and he is fine with that. You know, Hope, he is such a fine man. He has your best interest at heart. Your substitute has agreed to be there until the end of the year if you can't return."

Mollie handed me a card to open. "All of your students signed this card and wanted me to tell you how much they miss their favorite teacher. When I left school yesterday, I told the faculty that I would be with you today and they send you their love. Today is a teacher workday, and that allowed me to be here with you."

Tears filled my eyes as I gazed at the beautiful card from my students. Inside the card were group pictures of all of my classes and a group picture of the faculty. I knew I would miss each one of my students and colleagues, but my life had taken a new direction. My hopes and dreams changed when God changed my heart and life.

Aunt Elizabeth walked over to me and lovingly wrapped her arms around me. "Hope, are you sure you're able to make this trip? I can stay here with you until you're able to travel, if you don't think you're ready."

"Aunt Elizabeth, I feel so much better this morning. Knowing you will be there with me for awhile means the world to me, but I am ready to go home."

Goodbyes were never easy for me, but knowing Mollie, Sarah, and Jack were coming the next weekend made it easier for me to bid them farewell. Molly packed my clothes, and Mike put them in the back seat of his SUV. I climbed into the front seat with Mike's help and made myself comfortable with a large fluffy pillow and my blue afghan.

We waved our goodbyes to my Charlotte friends and headed toward my new home in the foothills of the Blue Ridge Mountains.

Chapter 29

Due to the fact that I slept the entire trip, the ride to Martinsville was uneventful for me. We arrived in Martinsville at eleven o'clock on Friday morning, and between Aunt Elizabeth, Miss Emma, and Hattie, I knew I would be inundated with love and attention.

Mike carried my belongings up to my room while Miss Emma got me settled in the sunroom in her plush chaise lounge. She opened some of the windows to allow fresh mountain air to filter through the room. The soft mountain breeze that filtered through the windows renewed my faith and hope that all would be well with me very soon.

Leo found a spot beside of the chaise lounge and lay there as if he were guarding me from the evils of the world. He had not left my side since I returned from the hospital, and it was evident that he had no intention of letting me out of his sight.

Leo seemed to have developed a fondness for Mike. Mike knew how much I loved my dog, and I guess because he loved me, he automatically loved Leo. I think Mike knew in his heart that Leo and I were a package deal. I also sensed that because of his keen perception, Leo knew exactly how I felt about the handsome preacher.

I closed my eyes and listened intently as the little birds harmonized together in song. I faintly heard an old crow cawing in the background, and the aroma filtering through the windows from the flower garden was utterly breathtaking.

When I opened my eyes, Mike was standing over me with a gentle, loving look on his handsome face. He reached down to pet Leo and gave him a treat as he sat down beside me on the edge of the chaise lounge. Everyone else was in the kitchen preparing lunch, and I realized we were all alone, except for my faithful friend, Leo.

My heart began to race like it always did when Mike was near, and before I knew what was happening, he had gently touched his lips to mine. I faintly heard Leo whining as if to say, *now what in the world is going on here?*

After kissing my lips, he tenderly cupped my face in his hands and kissed the tip of my nose. "Hope, promise me you will take care of yourself. I don't think I could stand it if something else happened to you. I never knew that I could care so deeply about someone. I'm going to leave for a while, because I have a meeting at church tonight with the youth committee, but I will come by afterwards to check on you."

"Mike, you need to go home and get some rest. From what I hear, you didn't get any rest while I was in the hospital. I promise I'll take it easy. My plans are to completely rest and get to know Aunt Elizabeth. That's all that's on my agenda for the next few days. She and I have so much to catch up on, and when I'm feeling stronger, I need to go through the rest of the journal and the documents we found out at the farm," I replied. "And as soon as I'm able, I need to get the coins, tools, and documents out of the safe-deposit box."

"We've got plenty of time for that. Just promise you won't overdo!"

"I promise," I said as he kissed me goodbye.

When Mike left the sunroom, I felt as if a part of me was missing. No one had ever affected me the way Dr. Mike Sanders had. He had come into my life like a soft gentle breeze, but every time I was around him, he caused a whirl-wind of emotions in my heart. I closed me eyes and began to whisper a prayer of thanksgiving for him and my new found faith. I gently drifted off to sleep, dreaming of my handsome young preacher with the beautiful blue eyes.

During the days following my return to Martinsville, I was never alone for a moment. I was coddled and pampered by Aunt Elizabeth, Miss Emma, and Hattie. My dear friend, Samson, brought me fresh flowers every day from his well-tended flower garden. But the best part of my days were the visits from my handsome young preacher. He was in and out of the inn everyday, and some days he was there two or three times throughout the day.

Leo had finally adjusted to his new surroundings and was beginning to follow Samson around in the yard. Samson, Hattie, and Miss Emma had already made Leo a certified family member of the Martinsville Inn. They treated him as if he were "King of Rutherford County." They had him spoiled rotten.

During those days of recovery, Mike and I shared our hearts with each other. I came to know him not just as a preacher but as a man. I discovered that he loved baseball and had played in college. His favorite football team was the Dallas Cowboys, and he was an avid fan of the Atlanta Braves. I also found that he was a meat and potatoes kind of guy, loved sweetened iced tea, and homemade apple pies. He also loved history and collecting antiques, and he liked researching his genealogy and was eager to help me with mine.

Mike talked to me about his growing up years on his father's farm in Tennessee. His parents died while he was in the seminary, and he was an only child. His family had strug-gled financially; therefore, he had to work during his college years at Wake Forest to pay his tuition. He also worked his way through his years of seminary training at Southeastern Baptist Theological Seminary.

Mike was always open and willing to share his faith and beliefs with me. I listened intently as he explained scripture to me during our Bible studies. He never made me feel inferior because of my lack of spiritual knowledge. He prayed with me every day and stressed to me the importance of talking to God on a daily basis.

Those days of recovery were filled with times of spiritual growth and renewal. I developed a personal Bible study plan and began to view life from a spiritual perspective. The changes in my life had been sudden and unexpected. It amazed me that not only had my outlook on life changed, but my hopes and dreams had changed also. Everyday brought renewed physical and spiritual strength.

While talking one day, I expressed to Mike that I wanted to join his church. His face lit up like a full moon at my revelation, and a beautiful smile appeared on his handsome face.

As he took me in his arms, he said, "That is absolutely wonderful. You know that the church was named after one of your ancestors. When the church was first organized it was named Martinsville Baptist Church, but later the name was changed to First Baptist Church of Martinsville. In fact, two of your ancestors' pictures are hanging in the church. Lady, you come from mighty fine stock."

"That's what everyone tells me, and I do want to see the picture of my grandfather and great-grandfather. Mike, I have one question. Will I need to be baptized?"

"Yes, you will, and it would be an honor to baptize you, my lady. As soon as you're able, we will talk about the baptism and joining our church."

Chapter 30

The times I spent with Aunt Elizabeth were priceless moments. We shared our life stories, and she especially wanted to know everything about Grandpa, Grandma, and Mama. We wept together as she read the journal to me. I had not been able to read the entire journal before going back to Charlotte, so we delved into it. We discovered many things about Grandma that even I didn't know. There was one thing that was certain; Grandma never really accepted the fact that she only had one baby when my mother was born. She always believed in her heart that she had another child somewhere out in the world.

Aunt Elizabeth had so much fun going through all of the documents and paperwork we had discovered. A lot of it was of no significance, and much of it dealt with the day to day operation of Grandpa's farm. He saved receipts for everything he purchased for the farm. He even saved paperwork and receipts for every bale of cotton he sold and every bag of fertilizer he bought. His ledger books had been kept in perfect order.

I had so many memories of Grandpa and Grandma to share with Aunt Elizabeth, and I did just that. I educated her on the Appalachian dialect that was used by most of the old-timers in Rutherford County. We laughed together as I told her that Grandpa's word for fertilizer was guanner, and his pronunciation for tomatoes was damaters.

I explained to her that because Grandpa's father died when he was young, he had to drop out of school when he was fourteen years old to keep up the farm. That did not stop his education. He was a self-educated man. He was an avid reader and was more educated that most people in Martinsville. He just didn't have the diploma. I went on to explain to her that even though Grandpa and Grandma spoke with the Appalachian brogue and colloquialisms, their writing was prolific with no grammatical errors.

One afternoon Aunt Elizabeth and I were perusing some of Grandpa's documents when we came across an envelope that had not been opened. It had been among the stack of paperwork that was found in one of the desk drawers.

"Hope, look at this. This envelope has not been opened, and it's addressed to your mother. On the back of it is written, 'To be opened upon my death by my loving daughter, Amy.'"

She handed the envelope to me, and I immediately recognized the writing.

"Go ahead, Aunt Elizabeth, open it. You are his daughter as much as Mama was," I exclaimed, handing the envelope back to her."

"No, Hope, I would feel better if you opened it, since your mother's name is on it," she replied.

"Okay, I will open it, but I insist that you read it."

Aunt Elizabeth handed the envelope back to me, and I began the process of opening the document. After opening the envelope, I handed the beautifully scripted document back to her and she began to read.

"My Dearest Amy,

"I feel so blessed to have been given the opportunity to be your father. You have been a wonderful daughter and

have blessed my life in so many ways. You have brought so much joy to our home. Then you gave us Hope, and for her I will always be grateful. I am so proud of you and your little family.

"I have some things to tell you that you need to know, and that is the purpose of this letter.

"Your first ancestor in America brought several German coins with him when he came to America. He added to his German collection many American coins. As the years went by, each one of your ancestors kept up his hobby. I am the only Martin in our long line of ancestors who has not been involved in coin collecting. The collection was large at one time, but I took many of the coins and cashed them in during our lean years.

"I left some of the rarest coins for you and Cletus. There is still a fine collection of gold and silver left. I received over four million dollars from the coins I sold, and that will be you and your brother's inheritance in addition to the remaining coins. I was wise enough to have kept the collection until the depression was over. If I had cashed it in and put the money in the bank, we would have probably lost everything.

"I've tried to invest the money wisely over the years and that nest egg has grown to a sizable fortune. When your ma and I are gone, everything will be for you and your brother. I just ask that you see that the grandchildren are well taken of. I especially want them to get a good education.

"Your ancestor, Reuben, got involved in gold mining in the early 1800s here in Rutherford County. Much gold was mined during that time here, and the first private mint in America was located in Rutherfordton. I left all of the gold coins in the collection that were minted by the Bechtler Mint for you. They have been in our family for many years. I know they are valuable. Reuben Martin passed them to his son, David. David then passed them to his son, Henry. Henry then

passed them on to your grandpa, William, who was my pa. The collection was then passed on to me at my pa's death.

"I saved the map of a gold mine that Reuben worked in. He never had much luck mining, but he sure did like to collect coins. The gold mine indicated on the map was up close to Rutherfordton and has been closed for many years. Reuben mined for gold in every mine in Rutherford County, or so the story goes. The story of Reuben's obsession with gold mining has been the talk of the family for years. He kept his coin collection a secret, because he was afraid he would be robbed. He had many Confederate coins and a lot of paper money, but he foresaw the fall of the Confederacy and cashed them in just in time. Reuben was a genius when it came to money, but he hoarded his fortune until his death. We can all thank him for his stash of money.

"Amy, the coins are yours and Cletus' now. Ya'll can cash them in, or do whatever you want with them. Just make sure Cletus profits from the collection. You will find the coins in the secret room in a hiding place under your grandma's hope chest. I have not even told you about the secret room yet, and I must do that soon. The map is in there, also.

"Your grandma and I have told no one about the collection. I have no idea how much it is worth, but it is yours and Cletus' to do with as you please.

"The hand tools in the box with the coins are some old tools my pa had, and I just put them away for safekeeping. There are some old buggy wrenches, an old plane, and a hammer. They aren't worth much, but I wanted to save them for you and Cletus. They are a part of your heritage.

"I must tell you something else that breaks my heart. When you were born, I was not around for your birth. There was a terrible snow storm the night before you were born. I had gone to get some supplies for the farm and felt sure your ma would be fine. It wasn't time for you to be born, so I felt it would be safe for me to leave your ma. Because of the storm,

I couldn't get back to the farm that night, and I will always regret that I wasn't there for her.

"Your ma went into labor while I was gone. She had a rough time after you were born, and I regret I could not help her more. She had to call on a neighbor, Prissy Walker, to deliver you. I will regret that until the day I die. The neighbor told us she was a midwife and I believed her. When I returned home, there you were. You were the most beautiful baby girl I had ever seen.

"Your ma was in an awful state of mind. She insisted that she had delivered two babies. I tried to convince her that she was confused. Nothing I did or said would console her. Prissy Walker assured me that there was only one baby, but your ma was absolutely convinced she had delivered two.

"Amy, I thought your ma was having mental problems at the time, but as time went by, I realized that she was not confused or disoriented. She eventually recovered and seemed to accept the fact that she didn't have but one baby, but I became more and more convinced that she may have been right all along.

"I started watching Prissy Walker, the midwife, especially at night. I began to notice that she had a lot of visitors during all hours of the night, and I could see Henry Ledbetter's truck at her house at least three or four times a week. I grew more and more suspicious and decided to check the situation out one night.

"That night I waited until your mama was sound asleep, and I made my way through the woods down to the river. I didn't want to take a chance on being seen, so I didn't go over the bridge to get to the old Ledbetter farm. I used my small boat that I kept tied up down at the edge of the river and crossed over to the other side.

"It was a cloudy night and a new moon. It was pitch dark as I made my way through the woods to the old Ledbetter house. I was scared to death I would step on a bear trap

or get shot. It was common knowledge that Prissy Walker had traps set all over her property, and she would shoot at anything that moved.

"As I approached the house and outbuildings, I detected some activity in the smokehouse. I spied Henry Ledbetter's old truck, so I dropped to my knees and crawled toward the old smokehouse through the high weeds. The weeds had grown head high around her house, but they were a blessing that night. Prissy Walker might have been able to hear me, but there was no way she could have seen me.

"I could hear a man and woman talking as I crawled toward the smokehouse. When I finally got close enough to hear them, I recognized Prissy Walker and Henry Ledbetter's voices.

"I listened carefully as they carried on their conversation. I heard them mention a Wilson Jones and a baby-selling operation. Prissy seemed upset, because Mr. Jones was pressuring her to deliver another baby to him. That was all it took for me. I rose to my feet, stepped out of the shadows, and walked around to the front of the smokehouse. Believe you me; surprise doesn't even begin to describe the looks on Prissy Walker and Henry Ledbetter's faces.

"Prissy immediately pulled out her shotgun and started shouting and screaming cuss words. I had never heard such filth coming from anyone's mouth in my life. I didn't just stand there and take her cussing. I stepped up and confronted her, but not before I noticed an old liquor still in the corner of the smokehouse. There were jars all around the walls filled with moonshine.

"Ignoring the shotgun, I stepped toward them and confronted them about our baby. She, of course, denied again that there were two babies when you were born. Right away, I told her I was going straight to the sheriff and tell him about the still if she didn't tell me the truth. She then cocked the gun and aimed it at my chest. She was fixing to

pull the trigger when Henry Ledbetter stepped between us. He snatched the gun from Prissy and looked her square in the eyes.

"Henry started trying to reason with her by telling her that they definitely didn't need a murder on their hands. Amy, my child, she looked at me with a wicked gleam in her eyes, and I felt surrounded by evil.

"Then she commenced to spitting out these hateful words, 'Amos Martin, so what if I took your other baby girl. She's gone now, and you'll never know what happened to her. If you open your mouth about what you've seen here tonight or what happened when your twin girls were born, I will have Lilly Mae and Amy killed and hunt the other baby down and have her killed, also. You can't mess with me old man and get away with it. You just better keep your big mouth shut tight. I can have all of you killed and nobody would ever know what happened.

"'And another thing, Amos Martin, you best not think about finding your other child. If you do, you better believe I will tie you up and have Lilly Mae tortured right in front of your eyes. Trust me, I know the right people to get the job done. Now you get away from here. Do you understand me?'

"Amy, I turned and walked away. I knew I was dealing with pure evil. I was just plain scared to death, not for me, but for my family.

"As I made my way back down to the river, then back through the woods to the house, I felt as if my whole world had collapsed. I was caught between a rock and a hard place. I knew she was mean enough to carry out her threat, and I had to protect my family at all cost.

"I couldn't live without your mama, and I certainly didn't want Prissy Walker to harm you or your sister. I knew then that your ma had been right all along. My guilt has been more than I can bear, but I couldn't afford to say anything.

"I never told your ma what I discovered. I felt she had suffered enough, and I knew she would want to find her other child even if it meant her death. I just wanted to protect everybody. God forgive me if I was wrong. When Prissy Walker and Henry Ledbetter died, I guess their secrets died with them. I have no idea where your sister is.

"So you see, Amy, I let you and your twin sister down. I should have tried to do something about Prissy Walker. I always will believe Henry Ledbetter had something to do with the kidnapping of your sister.

"I have no idea where she took her, but I did hear her mention a Mr. Jones and his boss. Amy, she had connections with organized crime. I found that out after she died. I went in the house to see if I could find anything that might lead me to your sister. I found paperwork indicating that she worked for a Mr. Jones, and he was involved in organized crime. The fact that illegal whiskey was being made and baby-selling going on, she couldn't have been operating alone. Prissy Walker just wasn't that smart. I found several letters about her bootlegging operation, and I also found a letter about the baby-selling ring. None of the paperwork had addresses, just a man's name, Wilson Jones. I had no idea where to look for your sister. Please forgive me.

"Prissy Walker went absolutely crazy after Henry Ledbetter died, and I was really afraid of what she might do to Lilly Mae. She would walk up and down the road talking and mumbling to herself, always carrying an umbrella. No matter what the weather conditions were, she wore an old raincoat and had a rain bonnet on. She would yell cuss words to everyone she saw and could be seen on her piazza rocking what looked like a baby.

"Several people from the church went to check on her one day, because no one had seen hide nor hair of her in about a week. What they found was horrible. She had evidently died

from starvation, and she was nothing but a hank of hair and a stack of bones. They found her in bed with a baby doll.

"After her death, I never told your ma about our other child. She had finally reconciled herself to the fact that you and Cletus were her only children. I have never forgiven myself for what happened. All those years I knew I had robbed you and your ma, but most of all, I had robbed your twin sister of a life with her real family. If you ever find your sister, please tell her that her ma and pa loved her even though we never knew her. Love, Pa"

Aunt Elizabeth and I were weeping uncontrollably as we held each other. Neither one of us could speak for several minutes.

Finally, Aunt Elizabeth looked into my eyes and spoke. "Hope, now I understand everything. We have to go forward from here and be a family for each other. They did love me, and they did the best they knew how. Oh, how I wish I could have known them, but at least I have you. When I think how close I came to losing you, I literally get sick."

Aunt Elizabeth put her hands on each side of my face and whispered between sobs, "Hope, I can never replace Amy, and I would never try, but please allow me to be your special aunt. I love you so much. Only God could have brought us together. After my husband died, I began to feel worthless and my life seemed to have no meaning. I found myself as a pastor's wife with no pastor. I had no one. A few days before Jan found me, I asked God to help me find hope and joy in my life and he sent you, Hope. You are truly an answered prayer and a gift of hope from my Heavenly Father."

We were both weeping, and I looked into Aunt Elizabeth face and replied, "Aunt Elizabeth, I have been so blessed in the last few weeks, and I know now that everything that has taken place has been orchestrated by God. As soon as I am able, I will have a lawyer redo the estate. Jan's husband, Al, is an attorney, and I will see him very soon to see that you get your rightful portion of Grandpa and Grandma's estate. Grandpa wanted me to have the house, but I will gladly give it to you or you can live with me. I just want you to know that everything will be split in half."

"No, Hope, you don't have to do that. My adoptive parents left me very well off, and I think you need to keep the house, but I will build one near you if that's okay."

"Okay?" I shouted. "That's more than okay, it's more than wonderful. Aunt Elizabeth, the Martins have truly come home, and it will be like having my mama next door."

Chapter 31

Since my return to Martinsville, I had seen the hand of God in every aspect of my life. He not only had spared my life and given me amazing people to love, but He had instilled a renewed hope within my heart and breathed new life into my soul.

I was looking forward to the arrival of my Charlotte friends with eagerness. When the weekend finally arrived, I was beside myself with joy and excitement. My new friends were a blessing from my Heavenly Father, not just my friends in Martinsville but, also, my Charlotte friends.

When my Charlotte friends arrived, Mollie presented the beautiful boxer puppy to Miss Emma, Hattie, and Samson. Prior to their arrival, I had arranged the purchase of the dog with Mollie, and the cost of the dog was worth every penny I spent to see the excited looks on the faces of Miss Emma, Hattie, and Samson.

Samson's face lit up like a light bulb, and Hattie started crying. Miss Emma took the little boxer puppy from Mollie and held him in her lap for several minutes. She looked up at Samson and Hattie and said, "W'y, he's the sweetest little thing I've ever seen. He's the color of a Snickers candy bar. I say we call him Snickers."

"Oh, Miss Emma, 'At be da purdiest name I ever hear'd. Snickers it'll be!" replied Hattie.

The three of them were hilarious as they argued over whose turn it was to hold him. Snickers attached himself to Samson right away and would run to him anytime Samson spoke. It was quite evident that the two of them would be friends for life.

That weekend was an amazing time for me. Since I continued to have headaches and had not gotten out of the house since the accident, my Charlotte friends chose to remain there at the inn with me until Saturday afternoon.

Mike had come over to have lunch with us on Saturday, and when he told Jack and Sarah how close they were to the Blue Ridge Mountains, they decided to take a scenic tour and asked everyone to go with them. Mike also told them the story of the Abe Lincoln birthplace, and they, of course, wanted to see it.

Miss Emma volunteered to go with them to see the monument in Bostic and then take them up near Chimney Rock and Lake Lure for a short trip. Since they could not all get in one car, they had to take two vehicles for their trip.

Realizing we were totally alone for the first time that day, Mike looked at me and breathed a sigh of relief. "Finally, I get to be alone with you!"

We sat on the sofa in the sunroom, and Mike talked to me about his past life and his decision to become a pastor. As he shared his heart with me, I wept when I realized what he had sacrificed to follow God's plan for His life. He shared how he had felt God's calling at the tender age of twelve, and he had lived his entire life since then by faith and trust in his Heavenly Father.

He talked to me about his parents and their deaths and the lives they lived on their little farm. My heart was stirred as he told me about the menial jobs he performed during his college and seminary years.

Mike had grown up in an entirely different world from mine. His Christmases and birthdays were nothing like mine.

He never owned a shiny new bicycle; he put his first bicycle together out of scraps from a junk yard.

It was after hearing Mike's past that I realized what a fine man he was. God had truly blessed my life when my path crossed with Dr. Mike Sanders.

My life had been a piece of cake compared to his. Therefore, I did not elaborate on a lot of things in my past. Actually, I was ashamed that I had never known what it meant to sacrifice financially. But I did share with him what my dreams had been in the past and why I chose teaching music as a career.

Mike was fascinated as I talked to him about my love for music and young people. He seemed touched when I told him that I wanted to find God's will for my life in the field of music in Martinsville.

He looked deep into my eyes with those dreamy blue eyes of his and asked, "Hope, can we talk about our hopes and dreams for the future?"

"Yes, I would like that, Mike. I hope to get to know you better and make my life here in Martinsville meaningful. I want somehow to impact this little town in a positive way. I guess I can sum it up like this, when I am gone from this life, I want the people in my little corner of the world to be able to look out and say, 'Hope Logan passed this way.'

"My ancestors have left their mark in every corner of the world they have lived in, and I want to continue their great legacy. I don't want recognition for anything I might accomplish. I just want to serve God and others through music. I just don't know how I will fulfill that dream."

"That's great! I know that God will give you the wisdom to know exactly what he wants you to do. Now, I have something for you to consider."

My first thought was, *he is going to offer me a position in the music department at the church.* I knew the choir director was getting ready to retire. When Mike slowly eased himself down on the floor in front of me and clasped both of my hands in his, I knew he definitely didn't have church or a music position on his mind.

"Hope, I have really prayed for God's wisdom in every decision I have made in my life, and what I am going to talk to you about now is no exception.

"You want God to use your life to impact this community, and I can think of no better way than to become a minister's wife. Hope Logan, will you marry me? I don't have a lot to offer you except my love and devotion, but I promise I will love you until the day I die. I didn't realize I could love another human being as much as I love you. I want to know everything about you. I want to grow old with you, and I want to have children with you!"

I was absolute blown away by Mike's question and was totally speechless for several moments. Tears began to puddle in my eyes as I watched Mike reach into his pants pocket and remove a small black velvet box. I gasped when he placed the tiny box in my hands.

He continued to look into my eyes as if he were trying to interpret my thoughts. I lowered my eyes to see what was in the lovely little box. Tears began to flow from my eyes like a river as I open the box and saw the most exquisite diamond ring I had ever seen. The emerald-cut stone was set in a gorgeous platinum setting, and on each side of the large diamond were clusters of smaller diamond baguettes.

Mike slowly removed the beautiful ring from the small velvet box and placed it on my left ring finger. I was totally speechless. Everything was happening so fast.

"Hope, I know we have only known each other for a short while, but I feel in my heart that this is right. Please say you will be my wife! Being a pastor's wife will not be easy, but we can do this together. I can't begin to tell you how much I love you," Mike whispered as he gathered me in his arms and kissed me.

His passionate kiss left me breathless. I could not believe what was happening to me.

Between sobs and tears, I looked into those dreamy blue eyes and finally spoke. "Dr. Michael Sanders, I would be honored to be your wife. I love you more than life itself. I can't believe this is happening to me. I have never done anything to deserve someone like you. You are wonderful."

"Don't say that. You are a treasured gift from God to me, and I want to build a home with you more than anything in the world. I promise I will cherish you forever, and I sure hope we don't have to wait long for the wedding!"

"You sound as if you're desperate to marry me," I laughingly replied.

"You better believe I am. You have no-o-o-o idea what you have done to me. I can't concentrate on anything. I'm even having trouble preparing my sermons. I can't sleep, and I can't get you out of my mind! Woman, you're driving me crazy!"

I looked pleadingly into his eyes. "Mike, I would love to be married at the farm in the shadow of my lovely pine trees. I want a wedding just like my grandma and grandpa had, but most of all, I want a marriage like they had."

"Anything you want is fine with me. I will light a big fire under Ed and his men to get the house finished very quickly, and we will do everything to make your dreams come true."

"Mike Sanders, I love you, and you will never know how much."

Chapter 32

Mike and I spent the afternoon making our plans for the future and talking about the wedding. We were busy making plans when we heard our friends return from their excursion in the mountains. Hattie and Miss Emma burst into the sunroom like a whirlwind, and Sarah and Jack were filled with excitement after the trip to the mountains, as was Mollie. They all gathered around Mike and me babbling about their outing in the Blue Ridge.

Suddenly, Miss Emma held her hand up to hush the conversation, and I realized she had seen the ring on my left hand.

"They law me, looks like Preacher Mike has been a mighty busy fellow since we left!"

Mike and I both broke into smiles as Hattie looked at us. "What's a goin' on?"

Mike stood to his feet and walked over to Aunt Elizabeth and placed his hands on both of her arms. "Aunt Elizabeth, you are now Hope's next of kin, and it's only fitting that I handle this situation properly. I would like permission to marry your lovely niece."

"Oh, my, Oh, my, what a surprise!" she replied as she took him in her arms. "Of course, Preacher Mike. I knew it was coming but didn't expect it this soon. I would consider it an honor to welcome you to the Martin family."

Everyone started clapping and Hattie started shouting, "Praise da Lawd! Samson, da Reverend and Miss Hope is finally gonna jump da broom!"

Hattie's remark caused an uproar of laughter, and everyone gathered around me to see my exquisite ring.

Hattie continued talking. "Reverend, 'at be the purdiest ring I ever did see. You done mighty good, but I betcha it cost a purdy penny."

"Hattie, Hope is worth every penny it cost. She means more to me than any amount of money; as a matter of fact, she is a priceless treasure. I know God has given her to me.

"Now you bunch of ladies have got to plan a wedding real soon, because I refuse to wait very long. Since I'm the minister around here, the only problem I foresee is finding someone to marry us."

Jack spoke up rather shyly, "That shouldn't be a problem. I haven't told you all this, but I'm an ordained minister. I have never been the senior pastor of a church, but I was ordained as a youth pastor in this state a few years ago when we lived in Elizabeth City, and I have performed several wedding ceremonies."

"Oh, Jack, that would be wonderful," I exclaimed. "You not only led me to a personal relationship with God, but now you can join me to this wonderful man that has come into my life. I can't believe how God is moving in my life and how everything has fallen into place so perfectly. I feel like my heart is going to burst with joy!"

"Then it's settled," Mike replied. "Hope wants our wedding to be at the farm, in the front yard, much like her grandparents' wedding. I say we plan for an early autumn wedding. At the rate Ed is moving with the construction, everything should be finished at the farm by the first of October."

After the excitement began to fade somewhat, we all gathered around the kitchen table as Hattie served everyone a helping of her delicious lemon pound cake and a glass of sweet tea. Their faces lit up when I informed them that I wanted each of them to participate in the wedding.

Samson had not said very much, but I knew he was thrilled because of the radiant smile on his face. I reached across and took his weather beaten hand in mine and asked him if he would say a prayer at the wedding.

"Oh, Miss Hope, you is like my chil'. I be glad to do it."

Mike spoke up at that moment. "Samson, I would be honored if you would be my best man, also. I don't have a father or a brother, and I can't think of another person that I had rather have than you to serve as my best man."

Samson looked at Mike through rheumy eyes and replied, "Laws-a-mercy, Reverend, I be so proud to do it. I jist want to thank ye for askin' me. I feel like I's gonna cry."

"Samson, don't cry. Just know that we both love you, and this is what we want. Aunt Elizabeth, I want you to give me away, and Hattie I want you to sing," I said.

Aunt Elizabeth replied, "Hope, I will be honored to do that. I already feel like you are my child."

Hattie was so excited she was beside herself, and she grabbed me and exclaimed, "W'y, Miss Hope, I'd do 'bout anythang you want me to do. I ain't never sung at a white weddin' afore, but I'll do my best."

"Miss Emma, I want you to be my maid of honor. You are so special to me."

"Oh, Hope," Miss Emma whispered between tears. "You are like the child I never had, and you have brought so much hope and joy to my life. I would be honored to be your maid of honor, but don't you think I'm too old?"

"Heavens no! What difference does that make?" I exclaimed. "It's my wedding, and that's what I want. Mollie and Sarah, you are to be my bridesmaids along with Jan. I would like to have each of you dressed in 1920s vintage attire.

And if I can get in it, I will wear Grandma's antique wedding dress and hat. That old cedar chest preserved it quite well."

"Sounds like we've got our work cut out for us. Preacher Mike, do you really think the house and yard will be ready in six months?" asked Miss Emma.

"Absolutely, if I have to work night and day to see that it's finished! I know Ed will get it done when I tell him about the wedding," Mike replied as he stood to his feet and looked down at me. "Hope, I think you have had enough excitement for one day. I think it's about time for me to leave so you folks can go to bed. I think with all of the excitement about the wedding, we have forgotten that you are not completely healed from your accident."

I was a bit tired and had a headache, but I couldn't bear the thought of being away from Mike for one second.

When he unashamedly reached down to kiss me in front of everyone, I heard Hattie whisper, "Now ain't 'at sweet, and ain't 'ey a gonna have purdy young'uns."

Everyone got a chuckle out of that remark. Hattie always had a unique way of summing up every conversation.

That night after retiring to my room, I got the Bible down that Miss Emma had given me earlier in the week and began reading. She had also given me a devotional guide, and my reading that night was from Romans 8. I prayed prior to opening the Bible and asked God to speak to me through his Word. As I was reading, my eyes focused on the twenty-eighth verse which said, *And we know that all things work together for good to them that love God, to them who are called according to his purpose.*

Wow! I thought to myself. *God really does speak through his Word. This verse is speaking directly to me.*

Coming from a music background, I immediately thought of my chorus students and the many hours I had spent perfecting a piece of music with them. I recalled the many times I worked tirelessly teaching them to blend their voices as if they were one voice, and at that moment something clicked in my heart and mind. *That's exactly what God is doing in my life. He has called me to himself and is meticulously orchestrating and harmonizing every facet of my being to fulfill his purpose in my life.*

Tears began to flow from my eyes as I dropped to my knees beside of the bed. The prayer that fell from my lips was not a beautiful fancy prayer, just a few simple words of praise and thanksgiving to a God who loved me and pursued me, and most importantly, never gave up on me. I crawled into bed with a renewed sense of peace and joy, knowing that my life was being directed by the Master Director. I could sense him harmonizing every area of my life to fulfill his will and purpose.

Chapter 33

Mike took me for my recheck visit with Dr. Singleton in Concord the next week. After a thorough examination, he removed the stitches from my head and released me to a doctor closer to Martinsville. Because of the severity of the concussion I had suffered at the hands of "Old Wilson Jones" gravestone, and the fact that I was continuing to have headaches, he felt it unwise for me to return to school.

It was difficult for me to call Dr. Benson, my principal. I felt so guilty for letting my students down. Because Dr. Benson had been so kind during the ordeal of my mother's death and the events that had transpired after her death, I certainly didn't want to disappoint him. After I explained my health situation to him, he assured me that he totally understood and was not disappointed in me. He assured me that he would explain the circumstances to my students, and he invited me back for a visit, if I felt up to it, before the end of the school year. After speaking with him, I felt relief and freedom to begin my plans for the wedding and my new life.

I finally was able to attend church with Mike and Miss Emma. The church building was so beautiful. It was a traditional Baptist church with the customary steeple and columns on the large front portico. The sanctuary was decorated in shades of blue and the furniture was made of dark mahogany.

The choir was unbelievable. It was such a joy to hear the old hymns of the church blended with praise songs.

Everyone at the church had heard the news of my accident and showered me with attention. When I saw Mike enter the majestic pulpit for the first time, my heart began to swell with unexplainable pride. As I listened to him preach from the Bible, I saw an entirely different side of the man I was going to marry. I realized at that moment that he would never be totally mine. I would always have to share him with God's calling on his life, and his parishioners. It became very clear to me, while listening to Mike's sermon, that I would be a very important part of his ministry. I became a member of Mike's church that first Sunday and was baptized the next.

What an honor it was to be baptized by the man I was going to marry. I had witnessed many baptisms during my growing up years at the little church in Raleigh, but they all seemed so insignificant and miniscule in comparison to my baptism. I was overcome with emotions as I descended into the baptismal pool and saw Mike standing there in his white baptismal robe. For the very first time, I think I realized what a wonderful man of God he was.

He gently took my hand, and looked into my eyes with a look of reverence and adoration I had not seen before. I will never forget the words he spoke just before he immersed me into the baptismal waters. They were indelibly etched in my mind and will remain there throughout eternity. As I looked up into his eyes, I didn't see him as my future husband, but I saw him as my pastor and mentor. I listened intently as he began to speak.

He took both of my hands in his and prayerfully proclaimed, while continuing to gaze into my eyes, "Hope Logan, in obedience to the command of our Lord and Savior Jesus Christ, and upon your profession of faith in him, I baptize you, my sister, in the name of the Father, the Son, and the Holy Spirit. Amen."

After the proclamation and just before he lowered me into the water, he whispered softly in my ear, "Hope Logan, I love you. You're my treasured gift from God. You will not only be me wife, but we will be one in him."

I had never been involved in such a moving experience. Not only was my pastor baptizing me, but also my future husband. I ascended from the water with tears streaming down my face, and as I made my way out of the baptismal pool, I thanked God for giving me new life and hope.

Hattie and Samson had surprised me by attending the service. I felt so honored that they had attended. I knew how much their church meant to them, and yet they sacrificed their desires to attend my baptism.

After church that day, Mike and I went back to the inn for a delicious meal of fried chicken, creamed potatoes, green beans, and lemon pound cake. Hattie had gone all out in preparing the meal. She and Samson were so proud of me and kept telling me over and over how much they loved me. Hattie kept telling Mike what a good preacher he was, and he accepted the compliments with humility and grace.

While sitting around the kitchen table, I decided it was time to share my heart with my new family.

"Miss Emma, Hattie, Samson, I feel like I will burst if I don't tell you something. Because of you three amazing people, my entire life has changed. By your exemplary lives, you have introduced me to what it means to have a relationship with God. Most importantly, your lives are true examples of how that relationship with God should be lived out. I have witnessed faith and love in action by watching each of you. As long as I live, I will never forget what you've done for me. You've introduced me to this outstanding man I'm going to marry, and mere words are not sufficient to describe how I feel about you. Most importantly, you've taught me the meaning of forgiveness."

I noticed Miss Emma's eyes began to fill with tears. "Now, Miss Emma, don't you start crying! I see those tears. I just love ya'll so much and just had to tell you."

Miss Emma finally spoke. "Hope, we love you, but I'm thinking about the time when you and Leo will leave us to move to your new home. We are gonna to be lost without you. You have become an important part of this family."

Mike spoke up. "I promise I'll see to it that she comes by often for a visit, and you now have that beautiful boxer puppy to keep you company. Samson, you and I can now become fishing partners, and you can pretend I'm your son-in-law."

"Law me, Reverend, you will be our son-in-law and 'at 'ere pup is some'um else. W'y, he follows me ever'where I go. We'll jist have'ta take him fishin', too," Samson replied.

Hattie always had that innate ability to make anyone laugh, and she got a roar of laughter from us all as she proclaimed, "Miss Hope, you is jist like our very own young'un, and, Reverend, you is gonna be a part of 'is family as soon as you'uns jump da broom! An' 'at ain't far off!"

Chapter 34

The next few weeks and months were filled with visits to the farm, working on wedding plans, and spending a great deal of time with my future husband. Mike took me to Union County before the school year ended for a visit with my students and the faculty. I was extremely proud of my former students as they sang several selections for Mike and me. Both the students and faculty were excited about my upcoming wedding.

The girls in my classes seemed to be smitten with my handsome future husband, and I even heard one of them whisper, "I can't believe he's a preacher. My preacher sure doesn't look like that. If he did, I'd be there every Sunday."

Mike, with the help of several of my former students, gathered my personal items from my classroom and loaded them into the back of his car. A feeling of sadness overwhelmed me as I said goodbye to everyone, but I left the school with a great sense of pride and joy, knowing that I would be able to bring closure to that phase of my life without regrets.

Those weeks of rest and recuperation gave me the opportunity to get to know folks in our church and many of the local people in Martinsville. The members of the church visited me regularly. Mike and I became regulars at the Red Bird Cafe, and dear sweet Snuffy became a very close friend.

We spent a great deal of time listening to him spin yarns and tales from days gone by. Snuffy had a unique knack for telling a story, he always made his audience feel like they were actually there when the event took place.

Listening to him over lunch one day at the Red Bird, the thought came to me, *it's too bad he can't write his stories and yarns down for future generations.*

Since Snuffy attended our church, we got the lowdown on everything, good, bad, and ugly that had happened over the last fifty years. Some of his stories made us laugh and some made us cry.

He shared a tale about the choir director who left town with one of the women in the church. He was comical as he described the affair and how they thought they had everyone fooled. I laughed at him as he described how the woman would flirt with the choir director and all of the men in Martinsville.

He looked us square in the eyes and said, "W'y, law me! She weren't nuttin' but an ol' Jezebel, and 'at music man, he wuz jist plum' et up wid wickedness. 'At 'ere wicked woman, w'y, she'd sashay 'round town wid her short skirt on jist a makin' eyes at all da men. She even tried to court wid me, but I took off like a scalded dawg. When she commenced to makin' eyes at me, I didn't want nary a thang to do wid her. She wuz bad, she wuz very, very bad."

I asked Snuffy if they ever came back to town, and his reply was, "Not to my recollection. 'Ey took 'emselves and left town atter da preacher caught 'em a kissin' in da church. It wuz plum' shameful, plum' shameful! It took might near two year for our church to get over da shock. Yea, it wuz plum' shameful!"

One afternoon Mike and I decided to eat lunch at the Red Bird Cafe, and we found Snuffy sitting in his customary spot just outside the front door. When he saw us coming down the street toward him, he stood up and leaned on his walking stick. "W'y, Reverend, how in 'is worl' is ye today, and Miss Hope, how is ye?"

"Snuffy, we're great. How about you, my friend?" Mike answered with a question.

"Ah, my ol' autheritis is a killin' me, but I ain't 'bout to let it git me down. I tell ye, 'is mountain air shore is a stinkin' 'is mornin'. It stinks worse 'an kyarn. I reckon some of 'em ol' mountain polecats has come down from da Blue Ridge 'is mornin'."

"Yea, those skunks sure do leave a distinct trail," Mike replied with a grin on his face.

"Is you'uns a gonna eat here today?" Snuffy asked.

"Yea, what's the special today, Snuffy," I inquired.

"W'y, Lucy cooked up a mess of chicken-n-dumplin's 'is mornin'. 'Em dumplin's is mighty good. She fried me up a cornpone to go with mine. You'uns needs to try one of 'em cornpones. 'Ey's mighty tasty and good fer ye, too boot. 'At's iffin ye eat it wid buttermilk. You'uns might should git on in 'ere 'fore 'em dumplin's git et up."

"Won't you come and sit with us while we eat, Snuffy?" Mike asked.

"I be in directly. I wuz a watchin' for Charlie Beaty. He said he might could come by an' brang me some molasses. He's a tryin' to get shed of what he has afore he cooks up 'is year's crop of sugar cane."

Before we entered the cafe, I leaned over and whispered in Mike's ear. "What in the world is kyarn?"

Mike roared with laughter and turned around and asked Snuffy, "Snuffy, this city girl don't know what kyarn is. Would you tell her?"

"Little girl, w'y, kyarn ain't nuttin' but rotten road kill. W'y, it could be an old dead 'possum or an' old dead rabbit. Don't make no difference. Any of 'em ol' rotten dead critters. I can't believe ye never heard of kyarn. Preacher, ye better teach 'is woman how us folks 'round here talk afore you'uns get hitched," he replied.

Mike and I were both laughing as we entered the cafe where Lucy and Sissy were busy as bees waiting on the customers. Everyone seemed to be enjoying lunch.

Upon entering the cafe, Mike leaned down and whispered, "Hope, kyarn is the Appalachian pronunciation for carrion, which means flesh that is dead and putrefied. Just think about the word carrion and put an Appalachian flair to it, and you come up with k-y-a-r-n. Not a very good subject to discuss prior to eating."

I looked at Mike and commented, "Don't worry about that, because I love this little place. I love the way these people talk and, especially, the way they express themselves. They are real! I know no other way to say it except, they are real!

"I feel like I have stepped back to a simpler, less complicated time. I've learned to love small town living and small town people. A few months ago I would never have dreamed I could love this lifestyle. Good clean air, and good old salt of the earth country folks, that's what I love about this little town. They are so genuine and unpretentious. Like dear Snuffy, he is a fine example of a genuine person."

"That's exactly what attracted me to this place. I love it here. These folks are wonderful," Mike replied.

About that time several old-timers from the church spotted us. Henry Conover yelled at us from across the room. "Preacher, Miss Hope, mornin'. You'uns gotta try some of 'ese dumplin's."

After speaking with everyone, we found a booth near the back of the restaurant and enjoyed a mouth-watering southern meal of chicken-n-dumplings, green beans, and creamed potatoes with white milk gravy. We were enjoying a cup of coffee and a huge slice of apple pie when Snuffy came in with his arms full of mason jars. Mike ran to help him with his load and placed the jars on the table.

"Preacher, I ain't never et no molasses as good as what Charlie Beaty cooks up. I got you and Miss Hope a jar a piece."

Mike thanked Snuffy for the molasses and offered to pay him. "I ain't a takin' no money, Preacher. W'y, Charlie give 'em to me."

As I took the jar of thick amber colored liquid, I turned to Snuffy. "Thank you, Snuffy. My grandpa used to make molasses every fall when I was a little girl, and I haven't had molasses since then. I know Hattie and Samson will love this with some of her hot biscuits. Grandma used to mash up butter with a fork in my molasses, and I would dip one of her hot biscuits in the syrup."

"'At's da bes' way to eat 'em, Miss Hope. I jist love soppin' a good hot biscuit in smashed up butter and molasses. W'y, I even like 'em wid one of Lucy's cakes of cornbread."

"Preacher, I jist had an idear. I want to help ye git ready fer da big weddin'. I know you'uns are a gonna git married in da front yard at da farm, and I want to help git ready fer it. Jist let me know what I might could do."

Several others around us heard Snuffy's offer and jumped in the conversation. Before we left the restaurant, we had an army of volunteers to help set up for the wedding.

As we left the cafe that day, a thought occurred to me, *these dear people truly know what it means to be salt and light in the world.* I remembered a Bible verse from my childhood, *"Jesus went about doing good." These dear people truly know what it means to be like Jesus.*

Chapter 35

We watched the farmhouse slowly take shape, and by the end of September, the entire project was complete. I couldn't believe my eyes when I saw the finished product. Mike and I went out to the farm after Ed called to let us know that everything was ready for final inspection.

I had a surprise waiting for Mike when we arrived at the house, but I wanted to wait until just the right moment to show him. I had instructed Ed to tell no one about the surprise, and I would not let Mike go out to the farm the entire month of September.

A breathtaking view awaited us when we arrived at the farm that day. Soft green grass had begun to grow, and shrubs dotted the landscape as if an artist had painted them there. I knew autumn would soon to be upon us, and the leaves would begin their death process by slowly changing from green to lovely shades of amber, gold, and crimson. The wedding was planned for the second Saturday afternoon in October, and I was hoping for a picturesque autumn landscape.

When I opened the front door of the sitting room of the farm house, I was ecstatic. The interior of the house radiated a charm of days gone by and a future yet to come. I had no idea the bead board walls would come together so beautifully, and the pine floors radiated a soft satiny glow with character marks from many years of traffic. I requested that

Ed leave as many of the character marks on the floors as possible, and their creaking only added to their beauty and charm.

The light fixtures were made of antique brass, which complemented the lovely antique bead board walls. The sitting room and dining room were painted a soft almond color, as was the kitchen. Grandpa and Grandma's bedroom had been painted a lovely sky blue. The small room next to their bedroom had been transformed into a beautiful bathroom done in blues and browns.

The hallway dividing the house was painted a soft buttery yellow and was adorned with family pictures. I had the entire hallway lined with pictures from both my family and Mike's. I wanted to maintain a sense of family history in every nook and cranny of the old house. I decided to go ahead and hang the picture of the "bad seed" in the family. Even though Rachel Minerva Jones had lived the life of a brothel queen in Pennsylvania, her five illegitimate children's descendents were as much a part of the family tree as I was. Along with her picture was the painting of Reuben and Rebecca Martin. I also hung many of the documents that were found in the secret room, such as the maps and the letter Grandpa had written to Mama.

The living room was painted a softer shade of yellow than the hallway, and was to be furnished later with lovely antique furniture in soft shades of rose and sea foam green. I knew my spinet piano would fit perfectly where Grandma's old upright piano once sat.

The back bedroom and bathroom were painted a soft pale shade of brown. I was shocked when I saw how Ed had been able to transform the old storage room at the end of the hallway into a lovely vintage bathroom with an updated modern flair. I had never seen such a charming master bath.

When I saw the fixtures in the beautiful vintage bathroom, I began to cry as I turned to Mike and whispered, "I feel so guilty. Grandma and Grandpa never had anything this nice. Look at this lovely bathtub. I can't believe it is ours."

I knelt down to inspect the vintage claw-foot tub and the antique looking commode. The commode even had a pull chain for flushing. Both the tub and commode added vintage character to the bathroom, but the huge glass enclosed shower stall was definitely modern and not at all reminiscent of the early twentieth century.

I turned to Mike and declared, "We definitely will not call this a bathroom. We will call it our "water closet." This will be our bedroom and "water closet." The other bedroom will be the guest bedroom."

After Mike came into my life, I knew the house would need an office. I instructed Ed to do redo the secret room, and put an entrance into the hallway. My instructions were to transform the little area into an office fitting for a minister. It was the perfect size for a small study.

When Mike saw my surprise, he was so shocked he could not speak. Bookshelves had been installed all along the wall where the back of the fireplace was, and the little niche beside of the closet was perfect for two filing cabinets.

Mike turned and drew me into his warm embrace. I could tell he was fighting back tears.

While holding me in his arms, he finally spoke. "Hope Logan, I love you. I know how much this secret room meant to you, but you chose to make it into a study for me. Why did you do that?"

I looked lovingly into his eyes and whispered, "Mike, I love you more than words can say. You are my life, and the past is the past. I think Grandpa and Grandma would have wanted it this way. No more secrets, no hidden agendas, nothing to hide—that's just what I want from our marriage. There have been far too many secrets and mysteries in this house, and I want then to stop as of right now."

"Hope, you are something else, but we better not stay in this little room too long, Ed might wonder what's going on. We sure don't want one of my deacons catching us making out in the pastor's study like two teenagers," Mike whispered with a sly grin.

As we retreated to the back of the house toward the kitchen, Mike noticed the vintage glass doorknobs that were installed on every interior door in the house.

"Where in the world did Ed find these beautiful glass doorknobs?"

"That's another surprise I had for you. These were salvaged from the old Ledbetter house where Miss Emma grew up. When it was demolished, she kept them for sentimental reasons, but she wanted us to have them for our new home. They are a priceless gift from a true friend."

"We can never repay her for all she has done for us. She is a true friend, Hope, and such a blessing to everyone," Mike replied.

I couldn't believe my eyes when we entered the kitchen. Ed had spared nothing in modernizing that area. Every appliance had a vintage touch, but they were also state-of-the-art. Storage cabinets surrounded the walls, and the sink was positioned under the kitchen window. I could see where the barn and the old outhouse had been, and I knew right away that we would have to build another barn soon.

Ed had to have a new well dug in the backyard, because the old one on the back porch was not serviceable any longer due to contamination. He had the old well closed up, but had the well house refurbished just for appearance sake. He was even able to salvage Grandpa's old dented water bucket, the old pulley, and the windlass and crank that were used to hoist the water from the well.

I looked at the lovely old well and remembered the many times I heard Grandma say, "Hope, you be careful 'round that well. You might fall in." She had me scared to go anywhere near it.

Being completely satisfied with the completion of the house, we went back to Martinsville bubbling with excitement.

October arrived with a brisk breeze and plenty of sunshine. I decided not to move into the house until Mike and I were wed. I wanted us to begin our life together as a couple in the old farmhouse. I decided to remain with Miss Emma, and that gave us the opportunity to plan the wedding.

Everything was in place for the wedding to take place the second Saturday in October. Aunt Elizabeth's new house was under construction directly across the road from the farmhouse, and I couldn't wait to have her for a neighbor. It was such a joy to have her around, and the town's people sure got a shock when they met her and heard about her kidnapping. They welcomed her with open arms and accepted her as part of the church and community. She was so thrilled to have family. She was not just my long lost relative, but she quickly became my friend, as well. She looked so much like Mama that I often forgot that she was not my mama.

A week before the wedding, Mike and I took a walk down to the edge of the river. The scene at the riverbank that day was spectacular with vibrant colors. I could smell autumn in the air, and my mind began to wander as I looked at the beauty that surrounded me.

While I was gazing up at the trees, it suddenly dawned on me, *within a few weeks the little birds singing in these magnificent trees will find themselves surrounded by no leaves at all. Some of the little creatures will fly south to warmer weather, but many will remain behind to brave the cold mountain air. Only God could have planted that instinct within them.*

Thoughts continued to flood my soul as I beheld the beauty surrounding us that day. *God's creation is awe-*

inspiring. Truly, nature and the seasons are wondrous works of God. Spring has always brought rebirth and life, and summer has always ushered in the beauty of life at its fullest. Even though autumn is the most beautiful season of the year to me, I know it's the beginning of a death ritual in nature.

These trees, both great and small, seem to know that a long hard winter of death is approaching for their beautiful foliage. Nothing can be done to stop the approaching winter, and when "Old Man Winter" finally arrives, these majestic trees will no longer be adorned with vibrant autumn colors, but will lose their splendor for only a season, because spring is just around the corner, promising renewed life and beauty.

As I stood there with Mike, it suddenly dawned on me, *the seasons have never failed to come and go. Even though each season of my life has been different, each has come and gone with consistency. Surely, that has been orchestrated by my Heavenly Father, and this season has brought a hope and joy I have never known before.*

Chapter 36

With the help of Snuffy and his friends, Mike and I spent the last two weeks before the wedding moving furniture into the farmhouse. Mike, Snuffy, and Samson made a trip to Charlotte with a rental truck to clear out my apartment.

We enjoyed every minute of the decorating. We purchased quite a bit of new furniture and several antiques from Waxhaw, a little town in Union County. My favorite antique purchase was a Victorian print of the Guardian Angel that Grandma had hanging in the sitting room when I was a child. Of course, I hung it in the very same spot where hers once hung. The beautiful antique china cabinet and dining room table we found in Waxhaw complimented the vintage dining room perfectly.

Miss Emma, Aunt Elizabeth, and Hattie were with Mike and me for every purchase we made. I think they enjoyed the shopping as much as we did.

I found a lady in Rutherfordton to make draperies for the entire house. When we finished the decorating, it looked like a picture from a *Southern Living* magazine.

Several days before the wedding, Mike and I took Aunt Elizabeth, Hattie, Samson, and Miss Emma to the Red Bird Cafe for lunch. We worked that morning getting the house in shape and were in need of nourishment for our tired bodies.

I noticed as we left the farm that day, Mike seemed unusually quite and withdrawn. That continued throughout the meal at the cafe. I wondered if he was coming down with a flu bug or if he was upset about something. I knew something was wrong, and I had to find out what it was.

As we completed the meal, I turned to Mike and asked, "Are you okay? You seem bothered about something. Have I done something?"

"No, Honey, it's nothing you can help me with. I'm just concerned about a friend that I met when I was in the seminary. He called me this morning before I left home. He pastors a rural church in a small community in Kentucky. His fourteen year old child was attacked by some boys from her high school. As a result, she is now twelve week pregnant. I just can't seem to get the family off my mind. They are such good people and are at their wit's end as to what to do. Of course, abortion is not an option. The child is devastated and doesn't know which way to turn. Because of the injuries she sustained, she has been in and out of the hospital since the attack. They just found out about the pregnancy yesterday.

"She is an honor student at her school and a strong believer, but this has taken its toll on her physically, mentally, and spiritually. Apparently, this gang of boys has done this to several girls in the town they live in.

Tears began to form in Mike eyes as he explained the situation. "Cindy was coming out of the town's library when they attacked her and dragged her into a car. She had been doing some type of research for school and didn't realize how late it was. When she arrived at the parking lot, they jumped her. She evidently put up quite a fight. The gang of boys beat her up pretty bad and left her unconscious in the library parking lot. One of the library workers found her and called the police. She was in a coma for several days, and when she regained consciousness, she told the police the entire story. Actually, the boys tried to kill her and left her for dead. Thankfully, she did not die. The boys were taken into custody and are awaiting trial. Of course, it came out in the papers. Since that time, eight other girls have come forward and admitted to the authorities that those same boys attacked them. They were not injured to the extent that Cindy was, but they were afraid no one would believe them. It took Cindy almost being killed for them to have the courage to come forward. Cindy was just a little girl when we were in the seminary together."

I was distressed to hear about his friend's daughter, and it broke my heart to see him so distraught. I took Mike's hand in mine and placed a kiss on it, and Hattie took his other hand.

Hattie whispered as she held his hand, "Reverend, we serve a mighty powerful Lawd, and all we might be able to do is pray for 'em. It be mighty hard to see good folks a sufferin'. We can't hardly understand ever' thing' 'at happens on 'is ol' sinnin' earth, but da Good Book says 'at da Lawd won't burden a body wid more 'an a body can bear."

My heart was breaking as I watched Mike's heart being ripped apart. I did not know what to say to him.

I looked into his tear-filled eyes and whispered, "Mike, we really need to pray about this. I know there has to be a solution to this problem. It breaks my heart to see you hurting like this."

Miss Emma spoke up quickly. "I believe we need to have a prayer meeting, an old-timey one. The kind Hattie and Samson talk about from days gone by."

"I agree," Aunt Elizabeth responded.

"I say we go back to the inn and do just that," Miss Emma said.

After saying our goodbyes to Snuffy, Lucy, and Sissy, we loaded up and went back to the inn. We all gathered around Miss Emma's kitchen table, and I watched her as she retrieved her tattered old Bible from the end table in the sunroom. She opened it to the eighth chapter of Romans and started reading. My ears perked up immediately when she reached the twenty-eighth verse, and I remembered the night God spoke to me from that very same verse.

A flood of tears streamed down my face as I listened to Miss Emma read from the Word. *"And we know that all things work together for good to them that love God, to them who are called according to his purpose."*

Miss Emma continued to read to the end of the chapter, and I knew in my heart that the Holy Spirit was definitely in our presence.

When she completed the reading, Miss Emma looked at Samson and said, "Samson, will you lead us to God's throne of grace in prayer?"

That humble giant of a Christian fell to his knees, and we all followed suit. I had never in my life witnessed anything like the event that took place that afternoon. I had never seen people pray with such power and conviction before. I knew in my heart that my life would never be the same after that day. We rose to our feet knowing that Cindy and her family were in God's hands. We also knew that everything would work together for their good, because they truly loved the Lord and had been called according to his purpose.

Nothing was the same for any of us after that day of prayer. There was a common bond between the six of us that was held together by the love and power of Almighty God. We had shared a moment in time that was priceless and holy, and we knew in our hearts that God would bring good from Cindy's situation.

Mike spoke with his friend later that week and found out that Cindy was still having major physical problems from the beating she had endured, but her spirits had remained strong and her faith had not wavered. She had been placed back in the hospital because of continuing health problems from the head injuries and chest injuries she sustained. We continued as a group to meet daily and sometime twice a day just to pray for Cindy and her family.

The morning of the wedding rehearsal, Mike came over for breakfast. I met him at the front door, and as he took me in his arms and held me, I knew immediately that something was wrong.

He looked into my eyes and said, "Hope, Cindy lost the baby last night. She is doing fair, but her condition is still very fragile."

"Oh, Mike, we just have to remember that God is in control of this situation, and there has to be something good to come from this."

"I know, Honey, but what could it possibly be? I'm not going to mention this until we have finished breakfast. I want to enjoy a good meal with my family," he replied as he reached down to kiss me. "Tomorrow is our wedding and I don't want anything to spoil it. And you and I have a big announcement to make, also."

"We sure do. Everyone will be so surprised," I replied.

We all gathered around the kitchen table for another one of Hattie's delicious southern meals. She had outdone herself with a spread of homemade biscuits, grits, country ham, and eggs. She also had some homemade apple butter and the molasses Snuffy had given us.

Samson spoke up after saying the blessing and looked at Hattie with a sparkle in his eyes, "Hattie Girl, da older ye be getting' da better yore cookin' be. Um-um-um."

We all laughed at that dear man's sign of affection for his wife. Their love was so genuine and unpretentious, and I knew that was exactly what I wanted in my marriage. They not only had been in love for years, but they were best friends, also.

After the meal, Miss Emma informed Mike and me that the four of them had come to a decision and wanted to make an announcement.

Mike spoke up and said, "Before you begin, I want to give you an update on Cindy. Also, Hope and I have an announcement to make."

Everyone looked at us curiously, as if to say, what in the world do they have to announce?

Mike began, "Cindy lost her baby last night. She had so many injuries from her attack; her frail little body could not carry the child. She's just a tiny slip of a girl."

I heard Hattie whisper, "Oh, me, oh, my, 'at poor young'un. What else is a gonna happen to her."

Miss Emma spoke up at that point and said, "You know, Preacher Mike, when we prayed as a group, we asked God to bring good from Cindy's situation. After hearing about her situation, God led me to a decision that involves Elizabeth, Hattie, and Samson. Because of Elizabeth's past and my father's involvement in her kidnapping, we have come to a decision. We have prayed about this, and with God's help we are going to start a home here at the inn for little unwanted babies and orphans. We can be there for them until they are adopted. I know there will be a lot of legalities to work out, but we can do it. God has assured me of that. It's time for this inn to be used for something worthwhile. Hope has been the only person staying with us for several weeks, and we haven't had a reception or party here in months. It's time for me to give this place to God and let him use it for his glory."

Mike and I sat there totally speechless as Miss Emma continued. "I know this is a shock, but God is totally in charge of this decision. I have more money than I will ever need, and this is precisely what we want to do with it. Elizabeth and I both, along with Hattie and Samson, are so excited about this decision. We feel that God has called us to do this.

"And because none of this would have ever happened had you, Hope, not come into our lives, we are going to name this place *House of Hope*. Child, you were handed a destiny in life that seemed unfair in the beginning. You have always said you want to leave your mark on this little town and carry on the Martin legacy. I can't think of a better way than to bring hope to little helpless babies."

"Oh, I can't believe this," I exclaimed between sobs. "I don't know what to say. I'm overwhelmed."

Aunt Elizabeth took my hand in hers and spoke, "Hope, I was snatched away from my family and taken to a house that had no love and was sold like a puppy from a puppy mill. I, too, want to leave my mark on this earth, and this is a golden opportunity for me."

"Miss Hope, me and Hattie Girl is a lookin' forward to da day when 'ese littluns get here. We's a gonna love 'em and teach 'em about our Won'erful Lawd."

Mike finally was finally able to speak as he unashamedly wept, "What a testimony of God's amazing grace and power. This just proves Romans 8:28 is true, *And we know that all things work together for good to them that love God, to them who are called according to his purpose.*"

"I must tell ya'll that the eighth chapter of Romans has become an anchor for me. I have seen the hand of God in so many ways, and I now know He does work everything for our good," I whispered between sobs. "And I have to tell ya'll something else. This is really going to be a shock for all of you. I only found this out yesterday afternoon.

"Mike and I went to the bank to look at the old coin collection yesterday afternoon, and he recognized a 1913 Liberty nickel which he thought might be a rare coin. Mike knows a coin dealer who is a member of American Numismatic Association, and we took the collection to him yesterday for appraisal. Mike and I were totally flabbergasted when he told us that that one nickel is valued in excess of one million dollars, and the entire collection is worth over six million dollars."

I heard a unified gasp and then silence. It appeared I had rendered the entire group speechless. They all sat there with their mouths hanging open as if in shock.

Finally, Miss Emma regained enough composure to speak. "Hope, I don't know what to say. I knew your grandparents left a large inheritance, but had no idea it came from a coin collection. This is absolutely wonderful."

"Of course, Aunt Elizabeth, half of it is yours. It's as much yours as it is mine."

"Oh, no, Hope. I've told you before, my parents were wealthy and they left their fortune to me. I don't want you to think I'm bragging about their wealth, but I want you to keep that money. It's only right that you keep it, because I will never have to worry about finances. Everything I have will be yours someday anyway. I have already had my lawyer in Charlotte draw up a new will for me and it's already in effect. I just haven't had the opportunity to tell you about it."

It was my turn to be shocked. "Aunt Elizabeth, I don't know what to say! You didn't have to do that."

"I know that," she replied. "You are my only living relative, and I feel like you are my own child. This is exactly what I want to do. I hope you realize how much I love you, Hope."

I looked into my dear aunt's lovely blue eyes and replied, "Oh, Aunt Elizabeth, I do. I do. You mean the world to me."

"Well, my dear friends, looks like we have some millionaires in our little prayer group," Mike commented. "Looks like I'm marrying an heiress. Hope, are you sure you want to marry just an ordinary run-of-the-mill preacher?"

"Mike Sanders, hush you mouth. You are not a run-of-the-mill preacher, and you will never be rid of me. This money is ours, and I don't want to hear another word about it. My greatest inheritance and treasure is not this money, but my relationship with my Heavenly Father and then my relationship with you. Money can't buy eternal life, happiness, or the love of a good man.

"I have thought about this long and hard. I prayed last night and this morning that God would open a door for me to prudently invest my fortune. It looks like House of Hope is the answer to my prayers. It's going to be quite a financial endeavor, and I definitely want to be a part of getting this project on its feet," I said with great conviction.

"With God's help the six of us can make a difference in many lives," Aunt Emma replied.

"Miss Hope, jist remember 'at verse in Romans and don't cha forget it. 'And we know that all things work together for good to 'em that loves da Lawd, to them who is called accordin' to his purpose,'" Hattie reminded me.

Samson took my hand and prayerfully said, "My, oh, my! God shore does move in mysterious ways. Yes 'um, he shore does! Our Won'erful Lawd shore did plan all 'is out mighty fine. Miss Hope, I know ye didn't understand in da beginnin' why ever'thang wuz a goin' wrong fer ye, but God had a plan. Yes, he did! And child, he done brung you through da valley, and now you is on da mountain. Praise da Lawd!"

Chapter 37

S arah, Jack, and Mollie arrived from Charlotte on Friday afternoon just in time to have a short wedding rehearsal. It was a delight to see my friends again. They had become a very important part of my life.

On Saturday, the day of my wedding, I arose at eight o'clock to prepare for the day. I could not have ordered a more glorious day for my wedding. The beautiful Carolina blue sky had never been lovelier. Sunbeams filtered through the trees in Miss Emma's yard like shards of glass, and a gentle breeze caressed the earth.

After finishing breakfast with the family, Miss Emma and Hattie helped me load my car with my suitcase and wedding dress. I had previously told them I wanted some time alone at the farm before anyone else arrived. They graciously allowed me that precious time.

The ceremony was to take place at three o'clock in the afternoon, but I arrived at the farmhouse at one o'clock that afternoon to make sure everything was in place and progressing on schedule.

As I stepped from my car, I was overwhelmed with emotions. The aroma of the new shrubbery and exquisite autumn flowers engulfed my senses. I could hear the river roaring in the background, and heard its beckoning call.

I followed the narrow little path that led to my favorite little spot on the farm. As I drew near the riverbank, I felt the slight spray of water on my face as I watched the stream making its way over the rocks in its path.

The woodsy smell of autumn and pine trees drifted down toward the river from the yard, and I could faintly hear a chorus of birds singing in the trees. The entire farm and woods were ablaze with vibrant warm autumn colors of red, gold, and orange.

I stood there feasting on the splendor surrounding me, realizing that God had blessed me in so many ways since I had come to know him in a personal way. The world even seemed lovelier to me.

As my mind absorbed the wonders of nature, I felt a need to pray. My heart was bursting with thanksgiving and praise, and I felt I must talk to the Master Artist himself.

Kneeling on the riverbank that morning, I prayed a simple short prayer. "Again, Lord, I want to thank you for all you've given me. You've given me a new life, Christian friends, and an amazing husband. Life as I knew it was hopeless, and I didn't even realize it until I met you. Through the sacrifice of your son, I now have a new life and a new hope. May I never lose sight of what you have done for me. Give me the wisdom to be a wise steward of the financial blessings you have given me. Help me, Lord, to be a good wife to Mike. Fill our home with your presence. Lord, I love you and praise you. In Jesus' name, Amen."

After the prayer, I slowly made my way back up the hill to the farm. I surveyed the area where the reception was to be held. It was to be relaxed and casual with outdoor games for adults and children. I just wanted an old fashioned wedding and reception that was reminiscent of the 1920s.

Areas in the backyard had been set up for croquet games and jump rope. Snuffy and some of his friends had hung two charming tire swings in two of the large oak trees in the backyard. Since all of the out-buildings had been demolished, the backyard was large enough for at least two hundred people. If it rained, I was prepared. I had ordered a large white tent to be put up where the barn had once been.

Since there was no rain, the reception tables were being set up under the tent. The tables were decorated with pretty white tablecloths overlaid with smaller sheer peach colored cloths for contrast. The centerpiece was a captivating basket of lovely cut flowers consisting of peach roses and white daisies. Pumpkins and autumn leaves had been carefully placed on the tables where the guests would be seated.

Snuffy commented to Mike and me one day at the Red Bird Cafe that our reception just wouldn't be fun without a friendly game of horseshoes. Therefore, he and Mike set up an area on the lower side of the yard for horseshoe pitching.

Since the reception was to be open and informal, we asked the guests to dress casual. We knew Snuffy and some of the other old-timers from the Red Bird Cafe would be in their overalls, and we wanted everyone to feel welcome.

Everything in the backyard was absolutely breathtaking. I had been surprised by the kindness of the church members who graciously volunteered to help us prepare for the event. Samson, Hattie, Miss Emma, and Aunt Elizabeth had been busy as bees helping in any way they could.

I made my way to the front yard where the wedding was to take place and felt as if I had walked into a lovely English garden. The sun was filtering through the boughs of my beautiful white pines, and a soft fragrant wind was showering the earth with lovely autumn leaves. The new green grass had been manicured to perfection, and the colorful leaves that blanketed the yard had created the look of a vintage crazy quilt from days gone by.

Our dear friend, Snuffy, had done an excellent job supervising the set up of the wedding in the front yard. Several men brought folding chairs from the church and arranged them, creating a walkway for a center aisle. One of Snuffy's friends built a white pergola for the altar area and placed it near the majestic pines in the front yard. Beneath the pergola, a white kneeling bench had been placed.

The floral designers had worked their magic with lovely arrangements of fresh autumn flowers that flanked each side of the altar area. The arrangements looked like colorful clouds of white and yellow daisies, white chrysanthemums, flame red sedum, and deep purple asters. Beautiful peach roses had also been added to the arrangements. Potted white and fuchsia chrysanthemums and ornamental grasses filled the altar area, only leaving room for the wedding party. Ivy mingled with Stephanotis was cascading from the pergola, and small nosegays of those same lovely flowers in the altar area were attached to the end of each row of chairs.

The floral designers decorated the piazza with ornamental grasses. Beautiful arrangements of potted gold chrysanthemums and lovely white potted daisies interwoven with dried grapevines and fall leaves were strategically placed on the ends of each step. Everything was absolutely perfect.

I stood in awe on my beautiful piazza, mesmerized by the beauty that lay before me. I couldn't believe my special day had finally arrived. While looking at those majestic pine trees in the front yard, I suddenly realized something. They no longer seemed to be weeping with sadness. Those old trees had witnessed more than their share of sadness over the last century, but they had also witnessed much joy. They could not verbally speak to me, but I felt them whispering in my spirit, *Hope, this is your day. God has brought you here to this place and time, now "rejoice and be glad in it."*

Beholding the beauty surrounding me, a thought occurred to me. *How can anyone deny that God created this magnificent world? This beauty surrounding me today definitely portrays the finest work of the Master Artist, God himself. Only God could create such beauty. Many artists have tried to capture the beauty of God's majestic creation on canvas, but in all of their trying, their efforts have failed.*

My eyes were drawn to the pergola where Mike and I would stand before Jack and exchange our vows. As I thought about what God had done in my life in just a few short months, tears of joy began to spill down my cheeks like a never ending stream. God not only had given me new life and a new beginning, but He had also given me a wonderful man to share it with.

I bowed my head and said another very simple prayer, "Lord, God, thank you. Thank you for bringing hope and joy to my life!"

Chapter 38

W hen I entered the house to begin getting ready for the ceremony, I did a final inspection to be sure nothing was out of place. I checked every nook and cranny and then proceeded to the back porch to make sure nothing was out of place there.

Our little back porch was one of my favorite spots. The old well had been plugged, but the old well house looked as good as new. Grandpa's old dented water bucket, the old pulley, and wooden windlass and crank were all in place and were surrounded by an array of pumpkins and gold chrysanthemums. The white porch swing beside the well house was gently swaying in the breeze just waiting to be sat upon.

As I reentered the house by way of the kitchen and dining room area, I heard Hattie, Miss Emma, and Aunt Elizabeth coming in the front door. Together we went to the master bedroom. I sat down on our lovely Victorian bed and began to weep.

"Honey chil', what be da matter?" Hattie cried.

"I'm just so happy; I can't do anything but cry."

Aunt Elizabeth sat down beside me and put her arms around me. The next thing I knew, Miss Emma was praying. As she prayed for me, I thanked God in my spirit for the three beautiful mothers God had given me. He had taken my earthly mother to be with him, but he had given me the precious gift of three lovely ladies to fill that empty place in my life. I felt so blessed.

After the prayer, Hattie whispered, "Miss Hope, you's got to get started. I jist saw da Reverend come in with da rest of da men folks to get ready. 'Ey is on da other side of da house a gittin' 'ere glad rags on. You'uns is gonna look so purdy and have such purdy babies."

Jan, Mollie, and Sarah arrived a few minutes later already dressed for the wedding in their 1920s attire. Miss Emma and the bridesmaids looked stunning in the lovely peach colored dresses I had chosen for them. Aunt Elizabeth wore a dress made from a darker peach colored fabric. All of the dresses were tea length and had simple lines with handkerchief hemlines and were accessorized with simple faux pearl earrings and strands of faux pearl necklaces. They looked exactly like they had stepped out of a 1920s fashion magazine or a silent film.

I didn't ask them to wear a headpiece. I wanted everyone to see their lovely "Roaring 20s" hairstyles. A hairstylist in Forest City had managed to craft finger waves in their hair to create the vintage look. You would have thought Clare Bow had come back to life by looking at their lovely finger waves.

I requested that Hattie wear her white satin choir robe adorned with a silver colored stole. She looked like an angel standing before me. The hairdresser had also styled her radiant silver hair in a 1920s hairstyle.

Prior to the wedding, Mike and I inspected my grandparents' wedding attire and came to the conclusion that they were too fragile to be worn. Therefore, I had a dress designer in Rutherfordton replicate Grandma's dress. It was made of flowing ecru silk and was definitely reminiscent of the 1920s era. The tea length gown had very simple lines with the same dropped waistline and handkerchief hemline as Grandma's dress. I was able to locate and order a vintage cloche hat very similar to Grandma's from a boutique in Atlanta. The hair-stylist from Forest City had outdone herself as she designed my shoulder length blonde hair in beautiful finger waves. Grandma's strand of faux pearls was the perfect finishing touch to my vintage bridal attire.

Aunt Elizabeth and Miss Emma helped me get into my wedding dress, and Mollie placed my hat gently on my head. Before I knew it, it was time for the ceremony to begin.

"Hope, your time has arrived. Just listen to that lovely string quarter playing those beautiful classical pieces you have chosen," Aunt Elizabeth gently whispered in my ear as she handed me my lovely bridal bouquet of peach roses and stephanotis.

"I want to thank you for allowing me to give you away today. It is such an honor to stand in for your mother and father, but most of all I want to thank you for finding me and bringing hope and joy into my life. Your mother named you correctly when she named you Hope. Hope has returned to all of us since you stepped into our lives with your gentle sweet spirit. You are an answer to my prayers.

"Now, let's get this show on the road, young lady. I hear the 'Bridal Chorus' beginning."

After the wedding party was in place around the pergola, Aunt Elizabeth and I stepped out of the hallway onto the piazza and everyone stood to their feet. The air was filled with the sounds of the stringed quartet as they played Wagner's "Bridal Chorus." I could even hear the birds in the trees singing with them. What a glorious sound it was.

There had to be at least two hundred people in our front yard, and it was a great idea of Snuffy's to have a shuttle service for the guests. I could not believe my eyes. People were everywhere. My beautiful bridesmaids and Miss Emma were in place, as were the groomsmen Mike had chosen to be in the wedding. He did not choose anyone from the church, just old seminary buddies.

I scanned the entire crowd until my eyes fell on my betrothed. His face was beaming like sunshine after a spring rain, and his infectious smile radiated his happiness and joy.

I held Aunt Elizabeth's hand as we descended the steps, and I never took my eyes off of my wonderful husband to be. When we reached the altar area, Mike stepped to my side never removing his eyes from mine. Samson and Miss Emma took their places beside of us, and I handed her my bridal bouquet of peach roses and stephanotis. Samson, in his gray pinstriped suit and black tie, and Miss Emma, in her vintage peach colored dress, were striking as they stood up for us.

Jack looked at Mike and me with a glowing smile and began the ceremony. When he asked, "Who gives this woman to be wed to this man," a loud roar of laughter was heard as Aunt Elizabeth replied in her sweet southern drawl, "Her mama and daddy and I, Miss Emma, Hattie, Samson, and Leo." She then kissed my cheek and placed my hand in Mike's strong hand.

We had decided earlier to have Leo attend the ceremony, and he obediently found his place at Samson's feet. Being the well behaved dog that he was, he sat quietly throughout the entire ceremony.

I looked into Mike's eyes and vividly recalled some powerful words from my grandma's journal. *God definitely knew that it was not good for man to live alone.* What a wise lady she had been.

Since returning to Martinsville, my entire world had been turned upside down. It suddenly dawned on me, *for the first time in my life I know what true happiness is. Here before me stands this amazing man, dressed in his gray three-piece suit and black tie.*

It was then that I realized, as I dropped my eyes to the ground, Mike had on Grandpa's old gray spats. *Today, Mike and I will become two lives joined together as one by God in love. How much more could a girl ask for?*

At that moment I heard Jack reading from the Bible the words Grandma had written in her journal the day after her wedding to Grandpa. *"And the Lord God caused a deep sleep to fall upon Adam, and he slept: and he took one of his ribs, and closed up the flesh instead thereof; And the rib, which the Lord God had taken from man, made he woman, and brought her unto the man. And Adam said, 'this is now bone of my bones, and flesh of my flesh: she shall be called Woman, because she was taken out of Man. Therefore shall a man leave his father and his mother, and shall cleave unto his wife: and they shall be one flesh.'"*

After the scripture reading, Jack challenged us to love each other faithfully and reminded us that God should forever be the center of our home. He then nodded to Hattie to sing the first hymn.

With no accompaniment, Hattie lifted her lovely voice toward heaven and sang that great old hymn of the church that was sung at Grandma and Grandpa's wedding "O Love That Wilt Not Let Me Go." As she beautifully sang those old familiar lyrics, I wondered if God was allowing my parents and grandparents to peek through the clouds to witness my special day. I began to weep and felt a deep sense of loss because of their absence. Then I felt as if God lovingly enfolded me in his arms. He gently reminded me that both my parents and grandparents were with him, and I would see them again someday.

I was jolted back to reality when I heard Jack charging us. "Hope and Mike, today you shall become one in him, and I know you realize that through God's infinite wisdom and knowledge, he chose you for each other before the foundation of the world. Now go forth from here, and fulfill his plan for your life together as man and wife."

After his pastoral charge to us, Jack nodded for Hattie to begin her next solo. In her lovely contralto voice, she began singing our favorite hymn, "Great is thy Faithfulness," as only Hattie could sing. The sun had gone behind a cloud just as she started that great old hymn of the church, but when she reached the chorus, the sun burst forth through the clouds and the heavens seemed to open as she belted out those unforgettable words.

I knew I had experienced the presence of Almighty God many times in the last few months, but at that moment, God's presence became so real I felt as if I could reach out and touch him.

After exchanging the traditional wedding vows and wedding rings, Jack began the declaration of marriage. "Because Hope Logan and Mike Sanders have consented together and declared their love for each other before God, their family, and friends, I pronounce that they are husband and wife, in the name of the Father, the Son, and the Holy Spirit. What God has joined together, let no man put asunder!"

Jack then turned to our dear friend, Samson, who was standing beside of Mike as his best man and said, "Brother Samson Alexander will now pronounce the benediction."

I heard Samson clear his throat and I detected a slight trembling in his voice as he began to pray. "Oh, Righteous God our Heavenly Father, you's brought us here together to join 'is man and 'is woman in marriage. But Lawd, 'is ain't jist a weddin'. It be a time to praise yore Holy Name. I been a watchin' Miss Hope and Reverend Sanders learn to love each other and learn to love you Lawd more and more, and I thanks and praise you fer it all. W'y, I watched 'em as you brung 'em together. I know'd all da time 'ey wuz a gonna get together. I know, Lawd, you got yore hand on 'is couple. Miss Hope, Lawd, she be jist like my own chil'. Me and Hattie, we feel like you's sent her to brang new hope into 'is ol' couple's last days on 'is ol' earth. She's like a gift from you, Lawd. Now you watch over 'em and take care of 'em like only you can do. 'Ey's a gonna have some hard times but some mighty good times, too, in 'is life, but I know 'ey can weather the storms of life when you is a walkin' wid 'em. God, you is so good to us old sinful creatures. We ain't done nary a thang to deserve yore love and kindness. We let you down ever' day, but you is always 'ere to lift us up. I ask you, Lawd, to wrap yore big arms 'round 'em and hold 'em close to yore bosom. Lead 'em through 'is life and when 'ey is done on 'is ol' earth, lead 'em into yore glorious presence. In da name of yore son, Jesus, I ask all 'ese thangs…Amen, Amen, and Amen.

Everyone in the altar was weeping as Samson finished his prayer. No one could pray like Samson Alexander, and I knew it was because he stayed in constant contact with his Heavenly Father. I reached over and kissed him on the cheek, and Mike took his work worn hand in his and hugged him. We then hugged Jack and Miss Emma.

Through his tears, Jack looked to the guests and announced ecstatically, "Ladies and gentlemen, I now present to you Dr. and Mrs. Michael Sanders. Mike you may kiss your bride."

And what a kiss it was. The clapping and congratulations from the guests drowned out the string quartet as they played Martin Luther's powerful hymn, "A Mighty Fortress is Our God."

I actually felt numb when it suddenly dawned on me; *I'm a married lady, and a pastor's wife.* I knew in my heart that God had brought me to that moment, and Samson's heartfelt prayer confirmed it.

After picture making and the cake cutting, we spoke with all of our guests. I was pleasantly surprised when I realized my former principal, Dr. Benson, and his wife had driven all the way to Martinsville to attend the wedding. They also brought two of my teacher friends with them. It was such a joy to hear news from my old stomping grounds. They were so happy for me and presented us with a lovely engraved silver tray as a wedding gift from the school.

The stringed quartet continued to play throughout the reception. Some of their selections were songs from the 1920s mingled with many contemporary songs. My ears perked up as I heard them playing "Rhapsody in Blue" and "It Had to Be You." They also played some Appalachian bluegrass selections and "Carolina Moon Keep Shining."

Everyone had a great time playing the games we had set up, especially the horseshoe pitching. Our dear friend Snuffy was supervising that event. The children were swinging, and many were playing croquet with the wooden mallets and balls. Leo enjoyed himself playing "fetch the ball" with Samson and Hattie, and they watched over him as if he were a little child. I knew he would be spoiled rotten when we returned from our honeymoon.

As Mike and I turned to leave the event to prepare for our honeymoon in the mountains of North Carolina and Tennessee, we stood on the back porch and surveyed the ocean of friends standing before us. We waved goodbye to everyone and turned to go inside the house. Mike gently lifted me into his arms and carried me over the threshold of the back door. Hearing the screened door slam behind us, he stood me on my feet and wrapped me in his embrace.

"Mrs. Sanders, welcome home," Mike said as he tenderly kissed me standing in my grandma's old dining room.

"Dr. Sanders, I love you with my whole heart. You have fulfilled every hope and dream I have ever had."

Mike continued to hold me in his embrace and whispered softly in my ear, "Hope, you are a treasured gift from God. You have brought so much joy into my life during the short time I have known you, and my prayer to our Heavenly Father is that we can serve him for years to come in this little corner of the world. I just want to grow old with you nestled here in the foothills of the Blue Ridge Mountains."

We quickly changed our clothes and prepared for our departure. To our surprise, when went out on the piazza, there before us sat a vintage horse-drawn carriage driven by none other than Snuffy himself. Our dear friend had done so much to make our wedding day perfect.

All of our guests gathered around us and wished us well. They flooded us with a deluge of bird seed that had been distributed by Jan's daughter, Emily, during the reception.

As we approached the carriage, Snuffy looked at us, "Well, what you'uns a waitin' on. I got cha car parked at Lum's house jist up da road. I tol' 'em to lock it up in da barn so nobody would gom it up with shoe polish or shavin' cream. I ain't a havin' my preacher ride out of town with his automobile all gommed up. Didn't want nobody to pull no tricks on Miss Preacher neither. Now hop aboard you two."

Everyone burst into laughter. As Snuffy sat there in his overalls and straw hat waiting for us to climb aboard, I hugged Aunt Elizabeth, Miss Emma, Samson, and Hattie. I stooped down to give Leo a hug and thought I detected tears in his eyes, but I knew Samson would take good care of him while we were away. After waving farewell to the crowd, Mike's helped me climb aboard the lovely carriage.

I felt like a princess with my prince charming as Snuffy yelled, "Gid-e-up, Nellie." I heard him snap the reins, and it was at that moment I realized that our horse was a mule. The sounds of laughter and joy followed us as we drove from the yard that day. The noise of the tin cans tied to the back of the carriage replaced the sound coming from the crowd, as we drove away from the farm.

We turned to wave to our friends one last time. I knew in my heart as we left the farm that day that the lovely fall leaves would be gone when we returned from our honeymoon, but I was comforted knowing that those beautiful North Carolina pines would be there waiting for us. They would always be a constant reminder of days gone by.

With anticipation, I was already looking forward to the first snow of the winter season, but my heart longed for springtime in our new home. I recalled the previous spring when I arrived in Martinsville. I came there alone and sad with no hope for the future. Miraculously, that spring season brought a hope and joy I had never experienced before.

As we rode away from the farm that day in our mule-drawn carriage, a breathtaking sunset was forming over the Appalachian Mountains, and the Carolina blue sky was fading to shades of crimson, rose, amber, and gold.

Mike looked into my eyes and whispered, "Hope, just look at that sunset. God, the Master Artist, has painted it just for us. The Psalmist said, '*The heavens declare the glory of God; and the firmament sheweth his handiwork.*' Hope, we serve an awesome God! He has blessed us in so many ways, but the greatest blessing of all is the hope we have in his Son, Jesus Christ!"

"Yes, Mike. I feel like my life has finally come full circle. When I first arrived here in Martinsville, I was totally alone and had no hope. My heart was filled with bitterness, hostility, and unforgiveness. Because of God's powerful love and mercy, I now have hope, joy, and forgiveness. You know, Mike, I can say with full assurance that hope has returned to this little corner of the world."

Printed in the United States
154585LV00001B/2/P

9 781606 470695